THE PRIDE
OF
RIVERSTONE

THE PRIDE OF RIVERSTONE

Daughters of Riverstone - Book 2

MANDY SCHIMELPFENIG

To my children, who had to deal with their own problems while Mom
was working on her book.

ROYAL FAMILY

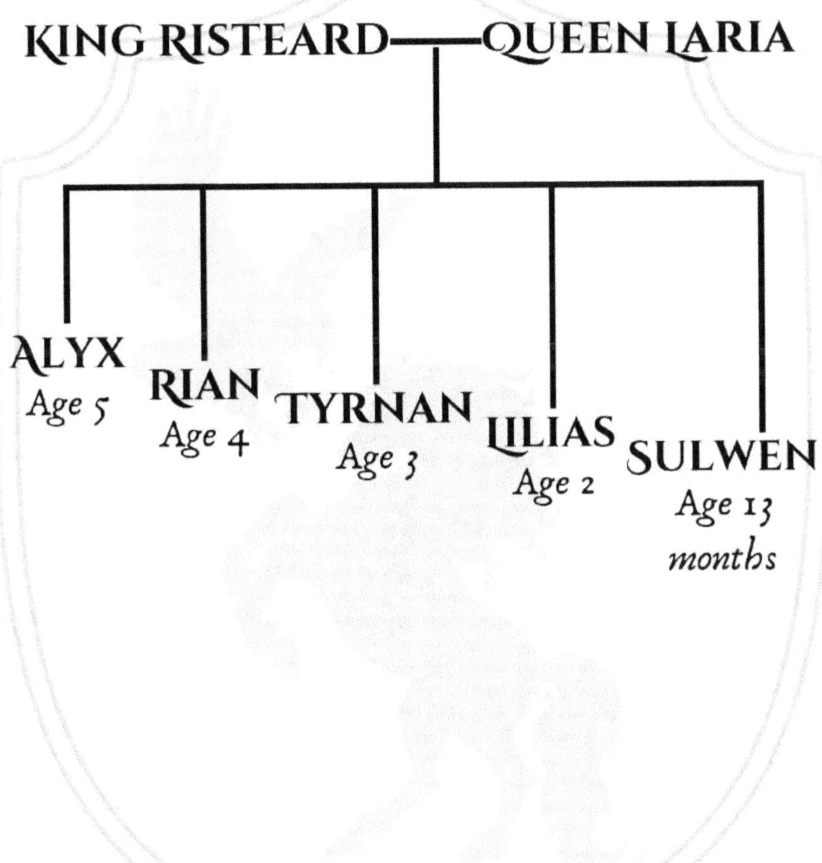

Chapter 1

A scrap of cloth covered my eyes, the fabric roughened with age, enveloping me in darkness, the only sounds distant, muffled laughter. I reached toward the sound, swinging my arms wildly, hoping to grasp something solid. Air slipped through my fingers. The swish, scraping of my toes shuffling along the ground in search of obstacles shuddered up my legs as I tried not to trip. A deep laugh resonated in my ear, only to be cut short. I was becoming dizzy from turning in circles, and I hoped there would soon be an end to this game.

Something soft brushed against my calf, but I wasn't fast enough to grab it. Footsteps hurried away, and I chased them, knowing my freedom depended on it. A high-pitched noise from behind distracted me into a pause and the footsteps vanished. I groaned in frustration and stuck out my arms, searching for deliverance. A rustle of leaves made me freeze, and I held my breath to listen. The crackle of shifting branches came from high overhead, followed by a stifled laugh. I stepped forward, arms outstretched, until my palms rasped against a rough surface. My fingers inched upwards, groping in the darkness. Leaves shook and branches rattled, pelting my face with debris. A startled gasp, and my hand closed around something warm.

"Gotcha!" I cried and removed the blindfold.

The disappointed face of my four-year-old nephew, Rian, peered through the branches of a rather prickly tree. His lower lip trembled and his green eyes flashed in irritation.

"Haven't I told you not to climb so high? Come down before you fall."

He made a great show of climbing down, grumbling and scuffing his boots across the rough bark. Ignoring him, I brushed splinters off my palms and picked dirt from under my nails. His little feet hit the ground, and I ruffled his dark hair.

"I know you're good at climbing, but if your mother saw, she'd punish you until the end of time. Who would blame all the messes on Tyrnan if that happened, hm?"

A glimmer of unabashed mischief twinkled in his eyes. Rian was always ready for adventure but just as ready for a joke. Tyrnan, being a year younger, bore the brunt of his teasing. Alerted to the possibility that something was being blamed unfairly on him, the aforementioned brother toddled up.

"Did Aun' Ula win?" three-year-old Tyrnan asked, his enormous blue eyes gazing inquisitively up at me.

"Aun-*t*, Tyrnan. Don't forget the 'T' at the end. Just like in your name, remember?"

He nodded shyly and repeated the word, correctly this time. Though often the target of pranks, Tyrnan nonetheless idolized his elder brother. He was a sensitive, sweet prince, with eyes the color of the deepest ocean, his hair waves of raw umber.

If you asked me eight years ago how I pictured my life at twenty-one, I would have guessed *I'd* be the one married with five children. Not my independent older sister, Laria. At thirteen years, I was accomplished, demure, and already emulating my mother's beauty, so it was only a matter of time before offers of alliances flooded in torrents rivaling the Rhyvor in spring. I watched Laria rebel against suitors, but I'd overcome my shyness and do what was necessary for my family, for Riverstone. Though the thought made my palms sweaty and stomach clench.

Then the siege happened, and everything changed.

Ripped from our beds into a night on fire, the Audrey's turned from nobility to servants quicker than a spark ignites dry grass. Overcome with fear, I remained silent as Ilano soldiers bound our hands and led us from Riverstone without allowing us to dress or put on shoes. Even the news of my father's death couldn't elicit a sound from my tightened throat. Laria stayed close, but once we reached Praed Castle, I was led away, separated from my sister and Mother and condemned to life as a seamstress. Even at thirteen, I understood how helpless our situation was, no matter how hard I tried to believe Mother would find a way out of it.

For three years, I saw the sunlight in tiny glimpses through narrow slits in stone. Never did I feel its warmth. The only comfort I had were the fleeting moments Laria snatched to visit me. If you asked me then if I believed her capable of what she was plotting, I'd have fallen over laughing. I dearly love my sister, but patience and organization are traits she sorely lacks.

While I mended, washed, and sewed, Laria was mounting a rebellion. What was more shocking was who she was conspiring with.

Our enemy.

Risteard had been at King Conall's side when he invaded Praed. A terrifying knight clad in black, I never would have guessed Laria would trust him enough to free her people.

Or marry him.

After three years of living in a nightmare, Laria and Risteard liberated Praed, and our country became allied with Ilano. An ancient law crowned them king and queen, but hard work made them truly beloved rulers. Five years after the liberation, I couldn't imagine a life more perfect than being my sister's lady-in-waiting.

I took my nephews' tiny hands and led them back to the rest of our party. We'd taken advantage of the warm spring day to picnic in the lush field at the base of the White Mountain. Rolling hills of long, green grass undulated in the cool breeze coming off the mountain. Tyrnan shivered and brushed a hand across the locks tickling the base of his neck. The wind shifted, bringing with it warmth from the valley and the scent of wildflowers speckling the grass in shades of pink, purple, and yellow.

We stopped short when Alyx leaped triumphantly from behind a boulder, chest puffed out and fists resting on his hips. The five year old towered over his younger siblings in both height and authority, a true heir to the throne of Praed and Ilano. His black hair and striking blue eyes matched his father's, but the young boy was outgoing where King Risteard was reserved.

When my initial fear of him waned, I asked Laria why her husband kept an invisible barrier between him and everyone else. She said he found people touching him uncomfortable, almost painful, unless he and the person were very close. I'd kept a respectable distance from him thereafter.

"You didn't find me!" the first-born son of my sister, Queen Laria, declared boldly.

I bowed. "Well done, my lord prince."

He laughed and launched himself into my arms, knocking me off balance. A pair of strong hands steadied me so I wouldn't fall.

"Careful, Your Highness," a male voice warned. "You're getting stronger by the day. Soon, your aunt won't be able to lift you and you'll have to carry *her*!"

Alyx laughed with exaggerated exuberance, doubling over and slapping his knee.

"You're funny, Sir Olim! But that'll never happen."

King Risteard assigned Olim as my personal guard when I assumed my role in the castle five years ago. I accepted the arrangement without question, but Laria wasn't content to allow it without a discussion.

"Is she in danger?" Laria had asked her husband. "Should I be worried?"

"It's just a precaution," Risteard said.

"I'm not sure I approve of having a young knight tossed in her path. Not after what happened to me." She smiled suggestively, and I turned away in embarrassment. If he understood her meaning, he gave no indication.

"I don't believe your sister has any intention of mounting a rebellion against you. Unless you feel there's reason to fear such a consequence?"

My eyes widened, and I blurted out, "I'm not doing anything of the sort, I promise!" They both looked at me in surprise, as if they forgot I was there. Laria laughed and assured me they were only teasing.

"If you feel Ula should have her own personal bodyguard, then of course I'll respect your decision," she said to Risteard. "I trust you to choose a trustworthy and honorable man."

Olim had become my constant shadow, watching over me as I navigated life as lady-in-waiting. His smooth cheeks and blonde curls made him appear younger than his twenty-five years, but he wore the strain of knighthood at the corners of his light blue eyes. Ever ready, Olim always wore chainmail, even when I teased him about excessive perspiration. Over the armor he proudly wore a surcoat distinguishing him as a knight of importance in Praed Castle: light blue with a rearing horse on one side and red with a diving black eagle on the other.

At times he acted the overbearing older brother, and though his concern was endearing, I found his tendency to overstep annoying. But, I reasoned, it was his duty to protect me, so I brushed aside my ire and chose to regard his overprotectiveness as a sign of his devotion. We'd grown from protector and protected to close friends in the last few years, and I'd be lost without him.

Alyx, Rian, and Tyrnan played around my feet, rolling around in the dirt like puppies. Sitting in the shade of a tree with two nurses was the lovely Lilias, the two-year-old much anticipated first-born princess. The boys were absolute terrors at her age, but Lilias was the epitome of a prim and proper lady whose only frustration was a slight lisp that sometimes made it difficult to understand her. Despite assurances that she may grow out of it, she regarded her lisp as an embarrassing flaw, an impediment. I thought it was adorable.

Her face and arms were still baby round, but she focused better than a child beyond her years. Her lips puckered in concentration as she threaded wildflowers into crowns. The flowers were sorted by color a foot away from her. Lilias rarely lost her temper, but if a stray piece of dirt marred her pristine cream colored dress, her day would be ruined. I'd never met a tidier child. Not even the wind billowing around her could dislodge the pins in her tightly coiffed golden brown hair.

A squeal pierced the air, and the youngest of the royal brood came running unsteadily toward me. The tiny creature was Laria's copy: ginger hair, green eyes, and full of fire. Sulwen wasn't content to sit with her sister and play princess. Rather, she wanted to climb trees and play in the dirt with the boys. She'd just learned to walk, but Sulwen longed to run.

I scooped the feisty girl into my arms, hugged her tightly, then gave the poor nurse panting after her a pitying look.

"Did you draw the short straw today, Agnus?"

The older lady nodded, her round face red and covered with sweat. Wisps of hair escaped from her kerchief, framing her face in gray frizz. She was approaching fifty and didn't have the stamina to keep up with a mischievous toddler.

Sulwen smiled innocently up at me, showing all her nubby white teeth. I wasn't fooled.

"Are you being troublesome for Agnus?"

"No!" she said emphatically. To be fair, it was one of the only words she could say clearly.

Olim chuckled beside me. "Sounds convincing."

The three boys bounded across the valley, their dark heads bobbing in the long grass as they pretended to be knights on a mission. Sulwen squirmed from my grasp and made a valiant effort to follow, but her tiny legs were no match for the speed of her older brothers, and she ended up collapsing, kicking up dirt and dust in a fit of frustration.

"You're never going to catch them if you sit here crying," I said. I lifted Sulwen in the air like a bird and ran after the boys. She giggled and screeched with laughter, bearing her fingers like claws and growling when we gained on her brothers. The boys gaped in surprise and dove into the thick underbrush, sending plumes of petals and insects into the air. My skirts swished and dragged across greenery, no doubt staining my hem. Like Lilias, I once would've been mortified to tarnish my clothes. But after living in threadbare linens while working beneath the castle for three years, I learned there are more important concerns than soiled skirts. There was no sense stressing over such little matters.

Recalling memories from the past prompted me to glance up at Praed Castle, the white turrets just visible atop the mountain. When I was a little girl, the bright stones shone like a beacon signaling impending excitement. Since my father was King Llewlyn's favorite knight, the royal family greeted us on the front steps with open arms. Laria dreaded family trips to Praed Castle and the inevitable swarms of people vying for Mother and Father's attention. I wasn't thrilled about crowds either, but I loved the gowns, the swirls of color, the dancing, and the music. Laria preferred hiding in the library. I couldn't blame her. Mother made it clear my sister's purpose in life was to parade herself in finery to find a husband, a life goal Laria didn't share. I smiled, remembering Mother's reaction when Laria showed up covered head to toe in dirt after spending all day watching knights train for the joust.

"That gown was packed especially for the Reaping Ball," Mother had said, pinching the bridge of her nose. "It's practically ruined now."

Laria snorted. "Better the gown be ruined than me. Haven't you heard the rumors about how many babies are born nine months after the Reaping Ball?"

Laria wobbled for three days following that comment.

Now my impossibly wild sister was queen and currently conducting a council meeting to discuss the logistics of the king's plans to travel to Ilano, the homeland of his people. Laria informed me days prior about the king's decision, and I'd been in a state of anxious worry ever since. I'd never left Praed before, nor did I ever feel the desire to travel. Praed was my home, and though I'd experienced terror and hardships beyond imagining, for the last five years it was safe. Who knows what evils may lurk beyond our borders? But as the queen's lady-in-waiting, I had no choice but do what my sister wished without argument.

After I became breathless with exertion, I handed Sulwen to Olim and informed him it was his turn to torment the boys with her. He held her awkwardly, like he wasn't quite sure how even after years of watching me. I hid a smile behind my hand, and we walked, carefully, while he held Sulwen as if a slight breeze would shatter her like glass. At least she still found the game amusing, even at the slower pace.

The summer sun warmed my face, and I closed my eyes and inhaled the sweet perfume of the wildflowers. After living in the bowels of the castle under the rule of the former King Conall, I would forever appreciate these moments of freedom. Being forced into servitude narrowed my world into a small corner of the workroom where women toiled to clothe those living elegantly above us. It was dark, confining, and stifling, filled with the scent of unwashed bodies and starched linen. When Laria set us free, I vowed to go outside every day, even if only for a minute.

Sulwen's impatient urging of Olim to 'go fat-ter' drew me out of my reverie. He was from Ilano, but hadn't returned since arriving long ago, before the uprising.

"What do you think of the king's proposal of visiting Ilano?" I asked. "Do you miss it?"

"I miss my family," he said. He tightened his grip on Sulwen and tiptoed around a log. "My parents, particularly. But I was nothing there. My home is here."

"Everyone misses the place they were born. Praed Castle has become my home these last five years, but I'll always love Riverstone."

"Your life there was very different from the one I led in Ilano."

I knew very little about Olim's former life, and it wasn't for lack of asking. He only told me his father worked in an orchard and his mother was a skilled weaver. From his description of them, I guessed they didn't own the land they worked, and though he didn't seem ashamed of this, he wasn't quick to speak of them in public. For his entire life, he and his family had to work hard to succeed, and I feared he resented the wealthier class.

He swooped Sulwen down toward Rian. The children howled with laughter, and the little boy dashed into the shelter of the orinberry bushes. The orange fruit was juicy and ripe this time of year and scarce after being harvested by hungry growing boys.

"I admit I'm uneasy about leaving Praed. I've never been anywhere else."

"You'll be fine. The people are good, honest folks in the farm country. The central city seems larger, but I think that's because everyone isn't spread out. People don't have great estates like they do here because most of the land is devoted to growing crops."

"Like apples!"

"Yes." He smiled, condescendingly I thought, but it could have been the angle of the light. "But much more than that. Apples are the staple crop, certainly, but we grow ice grapes, plums, and sweet squash. Sheep are very important for the weavers."

"I heard the Ilano weavers can make a thread so thin that when they weave it into cloth, it's so soft it's like wearing a cloud!"

"I'm sure the queen will buy you a new wardrobe so you can feel for yourself."

"I know you don't like talking about it. I appreciate your indulgence."

He handed Sulwen back to me, her eyes drooping with the struggle to stay awake.

"It's natural to be curious about a place you've never been. I hope Ilano lives up to your expectations."

"Are you certain I haven't offended you?"

"Nothing you could do would be offensive to me." His voice held a strange undertone. I tilted my head and raised an eyebrow questioningly, but he said no more. His attention was fixed on the mountain. I followed his gaze. My sister and brother-in-law were galloping toward us, leaving a cloud of dust in their wake. I waved and rushed to meet them, careful not to disturb the sleepy toddler.

Olim bowed at King Risteard and Queen Laria while they dismounted and tossed their reins to their escort. Laria's face was brilliantly framed in sunshine, her smile as radiant as her ginger hair. She opened her arms to her boys amid cries of "Mother! Mother! Mother!" Risteard patted their heads, but he had eyes only for the tiny bundle in my arms. We carefully shuffled the princess between us and he cradled her against his chest. Her eyes fluttered at the disturbance, then she saw his face and smiled.

"Fa-fa," Sulwen said in her sweet, tired voice. She sighed and snuggled into his black doublet.

Black. The color of his doublet, the color of his close-cropped hair, his beard, his breeches. Only the crown glinting atop of his head lent vibrancy to the king's wardrobe. Initially, I shrank from his piercing cerulean eyes, his stare intense with authority and hidden menace. Laria assured me I had nothing to fear from my brother-in-law, but I couldn't forget images of flames reflecting off a black helmet the night our stables burned. My fear dimmed over the last five years, but sometimes when I glimpsed the scars running down his face, one on the left extending from his forehead to just below the eye and one on the right cheek, a tremor would shake loose memories of an evil regime. Then he'd hold one of his children like a priceless treasure or surreptitiously hold Laria's hand under the table and my trepidation would vanish. Risteard's gruff exterior belied the gentle husband and father beneath.

Laria watched silently as the children climbed into a wagon for the journey up the mountain, the corners of her mouth tugging upward. A wisp of ginger hair tickled her cheek, and she casually brushed it aside, leaving behind a smudge of dust.

"How did it go?" I reached out to wipe the dirt away with a handkerchief.

She waved me away and said, "Well. We should be prepared for travel within the week."

I twisted my fingers in the fabric of my gown. "So soon?"

She turned to me with a knowing smile.

"Don't be afraid, Ula." She interlaced her arm with mine. "It will be an adventure."

"Does Mother know?"

Laria's eyes narrowed. "Ula, we are grown women. We no longer require Mother's permission for everything."

"I know! But shouldn't she be informed in case she needs us?"

"Mother has never 'needed' us." Laria clenched her jaw, grinding her teeth so hard I felt the vibration in *my* ears.

"That may be true, but she's still our mother, and she's trying to be better. She's so devoted to the children."

She breathed slowly and deeply from her nose.

"Very well. Send a message to Riverstone."

She stalked away, and I couldn't help grinning. Laria could be stubborn and hold a grudge for dear life, but with the proper application of pressure, she could easily be swayed. I was intelligent enough to use this leverage sparingly and only for noble purposes.

I hurried over to the tree and grabbed my sketchbook and pencils. Though I barely had a moment to draw or paint, I brought it with me wherever we went just in case. I flipped through the pages of half drawn flowers, animals, and portraits of the children while I walked to the wagon. Laria encouraged me to spend time painting, but I was content to wait and devote myself entirely to my family.

The sway of the wagon rambling up the mountain lulled Sulwen into a gentle slumber. She'd been resistant to being relinquished by her father for the journey to the castle, but it didn't take long for the motion to ease her troubled brow and pouting lips. Below us, Market Town was bustling with traders and customers, a mingling of peoples from Praed and Ilano. It was a particular point of pride for Laria that her diligence to unite the people was successful, and that Praed enjoyed the peace it so richly deserved. Five years prior, these people wouldn't have looked twice at one another let alone exchange pleasantries and engage in business. We visited Market Town once a week, and the people loved seeing the royal family conversing with the vendors. Laria always noted anyone new, and later would consult her map and glow at the possibility of extended trade routes. Ilano had a history of border trade with the eastern continent, but Praed historically kept to itself. The former kings were wary of outsiders, always suspicious of eyes on their crown. In the end, closed borders didn't save King Llewlyn, Praed's beloved king who'd been overthrown by Conall eight years ago.

I glanced across the wagon at Duveesa, one of the children's nurses, holding sweet Lilias in her arms. Like Olim, she was from Ilano and decided to remain in Praed after Laria and Risteard seized the throne. At twenty-two, she was a stunning beauty with cinnamon-colored eyes, dusky brown skin, full lips, and a perfect heart-shaped face.

As a young woman, she unfortunately attracted the attention of an older man accustomed to getting his way. When she rejected his request for her hand, he retaliated by ruining her father's business, calling in debts, and spreading rumors alleging her 'loose morals.' His status as a wealthy landowner lent credence to the tales, and her family escaped to Praed after the war to start a new life. Despite her low chances of securing an honorable marriage, Duveesa remained compassionate and friendly. She loved children and leapt at the opportunity to serve the queen to care for the royal brood. We'd grown close in the ensuing years, and though she was only a year older than me, I considered her wisdom to extend beyond my own.

The boys' moods were starting to deteriorate, signaling their need for naps. Alyx insisted five was too old for naps, but his drooping eyes and thunderous expression suggested otherwise.

"Stay on your side, Rian!" Alyx shoved his brother toward the other side of the seat.

"I can't help it!" Rian argued, pushing back. "Tyrnan is on my side!"

"Boys," I said in my best warning tone. "Enough fighting. We'll be back in the castle soon and there will be enough space for all of you."

"Ow!" Rian whined when Alyx pinched his arm.

"That's quite enough of that!" Agnus, the older nurse exclaimed with a sweep of her broad arm. The boys froze, mouths agape, and she continued. "Keep squabbling and your father will hear of it." She glared, and I hid a smile, knowing full well Risteard never punished the children nor was he likely to. The threat effectively silenced them for the rest of the trip up the mountain.

When the wagon stopped at the steps of Praed Castle, I carefully handed Sulwen to Risteard. He shifted the child to one arm and assisted me to the ground, then without a word left me standing alone. His abrupt manners were difficult to understand when I first knew him, and I was equally offended and guilt stricken whenever he acted aloof. I gradually learned he meant no insult, and every move he made was fraught with purpose. Right now, his priority was for Sulwen, and if he delayed in placing her in her cradle, she might awaken and then we'd all be in trouble.

Laria took Lilias from Duveesa, and my friend and I in turn extended our arms to Rian and Tyrnan, their eyes heavy and arms hanging limply at their sides. Tyrnan snuggled against my chest, his body warm and smelling of sunshine. I peered over his shoulder so I wouldn't trip and froze the second my foot touched the smooth stone of the front steps. My heart pounded and I clutched Tyrnan tighter in my trembling hands. *Calm down*, I repeated to myself while breathing in deep, cleansing chestfuls of air. The fear brought on by distant memories subsided over the last five years, but sometimes flashes of a time before invaded my thoughts like a conquering army, reducing me to a panic-stricken mess.

"It's over, Ula. Breathe. Relax. It's over."

Laria's voice enveloped me, soothing like a blanket in a storm. I opened my eyes and met her determined stare. No pity, no sympathy in the depths of her verdant eyes. Just a simple truth: it was over.

I nodded, and the three of us walked into the castle holding our precious burdens. Behind us Alyx clutched Agnus' hand, the tired little boy no longer resistant to the idea of a nap.

In my own room, I removed the pins from my hair and allowed the thick black locks to tumble down my shoulders. Unlike the gentle waves of Laria's hair, mine was straight like Mother's. I contemplated my reflection as I absentmindedly brushed out the few tangles. A slight pink hue shaded my cheeks from the day's exertions, a stark contrast to the rest of my pale skin. Even at twenty-one, it was flawless, which Mother contended came from her side of the family. She placed great stock in appearances, which was one of the reasons she never warmed to Laria. Where I always felt the dusting of freckles across her face suited her, Mother regarded them as a personal affront. Beauty, she believed, was the key to connections and advantageous marriages, and her eldest daughter was horribly flawed. I wondered if she still felt that way, but I didn't have the courage to ask.

***

There was barely room to turn around in Laria's bedchamber. Between the trunks covering every inch of floor space and the maids filling them with clothing, I was becoming overly warm and anxious. I opened the shutters and inhaled the refreshing early evening air. The sun hung low in the sky, casting eerie shadows in the corners of Laria's room. It was a moderate space by royal standards, certainly not large enough to host dignitaries. But Laria preferred the comforts of a small room, one just large enough for a vanity, bathing tub, dresser, and an enormous bed draped in lush blue and purple. A little door next to the bed led to the king's dressing room, but everyone knew he spent his nights with her.

Laria was busily organizing the packing for our impending departure, chewing at her lower lip and tugging a strand of hair while she consulted her list.

"Are you at all nervous about leaving?" I asked.

"Not at all," she said without looking up. Ensuring the comfort of several people on a long journey was daunting, but Laria tackled the task with relentless determination. And lists. Many, many lists.

"Where's His Majesty?" I asked. "Shouldn't he be helping us, especially since it's also his clothes we're packing?"

"You know you don't have to call him that when we're alone."

I glanced around the room at the other ladies. "But we're not alone."

"We're in *private*," she clarified. "Yes, I believe that will be quite enough gowns for Princess Lilias," she informed one of the maids. "But Princess Sulwen will require at least double. You know how she is." The two ladies shared a knowing chuckle, and the order was carried out.

I fidgeted with the bell of my sleeve. "I know he's the king, but shouldn't Risteard be helping?"

"Organizing the packing of clothes isn't exactly his forte." Her eyes twinkled with unrestrained mirth. "Besides, I told him if he tried to 'help' as I expected he would, it would only burden me more."

"How could that be?"

"Too many hands in the pot, so to speak. He would only get in the way and probably do a poor job of folding my gowns." The ladies in the room tittered and my eyes darted from them to Laria. She shot them a withering look, and their smiles vanished.

Laria took my hand and gave it a reassuring squeeze. "I know you're uneasy about traveling, but Risteard assures me there will be no danger on the roads. Even if there was, we will be well protected."

"It's not just that." I sat on a cushioned settee at the foot of her bed. "I don't know how to act in a new place. Praed is familiar. I can be myself. But what if I say something wrong in Ilano and not even know it?"

Laria tsked. "It's not so different from Praed that you have to make yourself upset over an imagined blunder. Act as you normally would and they will see what a lovely and intelligent young woman you are."

My cheeks warmed at the praise, and I busily resumed packing to distract myself. "I understand we'll be staying with the Lord Protector?"

"We'll be housed in the capitol building," Laria said. "That's where the Lord Protector lives while in office. It's not exactly a castle, but it's large enough for all of us to stay. They make laws there and hold trials and assemblies."

"Have you met the Lord Protector?"

Laria smiled wistfully. "Yes. A long time ago."

"What sort of man is he?"

"Efram Ekhane is a kind and generous man. I owe him a great deal."

I waited expectantly, but she offered no further explanation, so I continued folding gowns.

"I've been reading about Ilano," I said. "Did you know they have something called a 'Harvest Blessing'? Apparently, people go to farms and wave crystals around so the crops are plentiful."

Laria snorted. "Nonsense. Reminds me of the ridiculous things that went on in Queen Shaeli's rooms."

She stilled, her gaze distant. I'd only seen the former queen a few times, but I'll never forget her unsettling milky gray eyes. Laria once told me the queen claimed her blindness allowed her to see visions from beyond the veil, visions predicting the rise and fall of kings.

"Well," I said quietly. "The Ilani certainly embrace their mystical beliefs. Will we have to participate in some rituals?"

Laria's shoulders slumped and she released a heavy sigh. "If I want to present myself as an endearing queen, I suppose we'll be forced to."

"They're *your* people, too, now." I squeezed her arm. "They've been so accepting of you."

"I know, and I honestly don't mind. I'm just being contrary."

After hours of preparation, Risteard made an appearance, and the ladies and I were dismissed. I was invited to the kitchens for a morsel before enjoying some music and dance in the Living Room, formerly the Trophy Room. When Laria became queen, she effectively destroyed all evidence such a place existed. She replaced the ancient armor, stained furniture, and taxidermy with comfortable furniture and a new piano and decreed it would be open to all residents of the castle. The household staff dubbed it the "Living Room" thereafter. I declined to join the other ladies there, opting instead to retreat to the library.

The favorite room of both myself and Laria also underwent a dramatic change. Defiled in the days of the oppressive King Conall, the shelves remained empty of everything besides dust and memories. Laria made the library a welcoming place once again, filling the shelves with volumes of books on all subjects, including several from Ilano. The massive fireplace was the focal point of the room and was surrounded by comfortable chairs and side tables. I selected a red leather-bound novel with gold accents. The title on the cover was *Unruly Seas*, but when you opened to the title page, it read *Tangled Sheets*. I'd been indulging in it secretly, knowing if Laria knew she would tease me relentlessly. It was filled with chance encounters, charming men, and blatantly unrealistic romantic situations. Another young lady introduced it to me, and I couldn't resist. The book in hand, I tucked myself into one of the well cushioned chairs, found my place, and eagerly read.

The ship rocked in the rolling waves, but the tumult inside of Arella was more violent than the tossing of the vessel as she gazed into the dark eyes of its captain. He smiled roguishly, knowing full well the effects his charm had on her delicate femininity. She clutched the side rail to steady herself, both from the motion of the ship and to keep from fainting.

"Captain," Arella said unsteadily. "You mustn't look at me that way. For when we embark at port, it will be to deliver me to my intended husband."

"Tell me you love this man, and I will bother you no more."

Arella turned away, knowing she could not, for this meeting would be their first.

I lay back against the chair, the book open in my lap. The poor heroine of my story had the misfortune of loving one man but was destined to marry another. Would her betrothed turn out to be a scoundrel or the true love of her life? Only time would tell. The door opened and closed behind me, and I guiltily hid the book under a cushion before Olim sat in the chair opposite me.

"Are you unwell?" he asked. "Your cheeks are red."

"I'm fine," I said, the last word spoken much too loudly and off-pitched.

His eyebrows disappeared under the curls fringing his forehead, but he didn't pry.

"I want to apologize for my behavior earlier," he said. "You have a right to ask questions, and my being from Ilano makes me a reasonable source of information."

"Are you sure? I could ask someone else."

"Not necessary." He held out his hands to calm me as one would an edgy mare. "I will answer any question you ask without being obstinate about it."

I shifted closer and lowered his hands. "Our friendship matters more. I really can ask someone else if talking about Ilano makes you uncomfortable. Or I could read more of these books," I said, gesturing around me.

"No, I insist. You won't offend me, I promise."

"Very well." I took a deep breath. "What made you want to leave Ilano?"

He flinched and looked away.

"I wanted to be more than what my parents became. They're good people, but they're content to work the land at home. I wanted more. I admired the knights who carried the big eagles and protected the country." His color deepened and he smiled sheepishly, running a hand through his blond curls. "I grew up listening to stories of the heroism of Alyx Elejick, and later his son, Risteard. As a young man, he achieved more than knights twice his age. I came here to learn from him."

"Was it what you hoped for?"

The corner of his mouth curved upward. "Everything and more."

Chapter 2

Laria insisted on riding horseback for most of the journey to Ilano and invited me to join her. I was happy to ride through Praed, but after a few days, I opted for the safety of the carriage. Despite her reassurances to the contrary, I was still worried about the possibility of bandits.

Rocky prairie gave way to vast green valleys with tracts of trees perfectly arranged in neat rows. People worked among the orchards watering, pruning, and inspecting the crops that sustained their economy. The air was cool and heavy with moisture, and though there was no shortage of greenery, there was not a pasture crowded with horses in sight. Laria rode beside Risteard on a magnificent gray mare, smiling up at him affectionately. At least someone delighted in such a change.

After several days of travel, the novelty of the journey wore thin, and the children's patience was in tatters. Tyrnan tossed in my lap trying to find a comfortable position to nap while Rian perused a picture book and occasionally glanced out the window at his older brother riding with his father on the last day of the journey.

Rian threw himself against the seat. "Why does he get to do everything?"

"He's older than you," I said.

The closer we traveled to Ilano, the more Duveesa cast surreptitious glances out the window, fidgeted, and lost track of conversations.

"Don't worry," I said. "Everything happened so long ago. I'm sure it's all forgotten."

"Certain things are never forgotten."

"You're in a respectable position now. Surely no one can look down on you when you serve the queen?"

"Perhaps not in public, but behind closed doors, there will always be whispers."

"The queen will take care of you."

Duveesa's mouth twitched into a poor imitation of a smile before she returned her attention to the princesses.

"Look!" Rian called, pointing out the window.

Lush farmland and orchards had given way to sturdily built wooden houses, and from those dwellings emerged the working class of Ilano, shielding their eyes from the sun's glare. They dressed in a style I recognized, the men in tunics and plain breeches and the ladies in long dresses and aprons. But where the working class of Praed wore sedate shades of brown, gray, and faded blue, the farmers of Ilano stood out from the landscape in bright yellows, greens, and reds. The bold colors filled the senses and tugged bursts of laughter from our mouths.

"They're all out to see you," I told the eager little boy. I smoothed my gown and tucked a stray lock of hair behind my ear. "I hope I look presentable enough after such a long journey."

Duveesa held Sulwen up to watch the waving and cheering crowd.

"You're perfect," she said.

The knights drew in closer, but the people were still afforded a view of their king and queen. Laria waved enthusiastically at everyone as if *she* was returning home after a long absence, Risteard roding stoically beside her. Alyx took on the task of addressing the people for his father, waving and accepting accolades in the form of blossoms and well wishes.

Tyrnan lifted his sleepy head and rubbed his eyes. I opened the window so he could see better. "Wave to the people. They're excited to meet you." He looked toward his brother for guidance, and my heart melted when Rian smiled and took his brother's hand in his. Together they waved their entwined fingers out the window, eliciting coos and admiring gazes. Sulwen stuck her chubby hands out the open window and clapped excitedly while the perfectly poised Lilias extended the crowd a perfect regal salute. Our arrival in Ilano was in stark contrast to the previous king's march into Praed, and I squeezed my eyes tight to banish memories of torn feet leaving bloody footprints on dusty roads.

We passed under a curved archway entwined with vines blooming with pink flowers, and the road transformed from dirt to expertly laid cobbles. The capital city lay before us, the stone buildings leading toward the center like a classic study in perspective. Ahead of us loomed a large sand colored stone building covered on one side with climbing vines and replete with windows. It was three stories high, and from the roof rose a peaked glass conservatory. Sunshine reflected off the deep green glass, temporarily blinding me. By the time spots stopped dancing in my vision, we were at the front of the Capitol Building. People pressed tightly together trying to catch a glimpse of the royal family, and Rian drew back, uncertain. I ruffled his hair reassuringly, then leaned out to admire the pristine facade and formally dressed nobles and knights.

At the top of three rough stone steps, six people stood apart from the throngs of onlookers. We stopped at the bottom of the steps, and I emerged from the carriage as Laria rushed toward an elderly gentleman, throwing her arms wide and wrapping him in an emotional embrace. He had a noble bearing, his gray hair combed back and oiled to a brilliant shine. He wore a tawny doublet and breeches draped with a billowing light blue sash. He had to be Efram Ekhane, the Lord Protector. The crowd erupted into cheers, approving the warmth and affection between them.

Rian gripped my hand, and behind me Tyrnan gasped, his giant blue eyes taking in the waving crowds, glittering windows, and colorfully dressed ladies waiting to be introduced. Lilias clung shyly to Duveesa's hem while Sulwen squirmed in her arms and reached out to Risteard as he presented his eldest son to the Lord Protector.

"His Highness, Prince Alyx." Risteard introduced the boy with evident pride in his baritone voice, a smile creasing the scars around his eyes.

"Thank you for opening your home to us. We are honored to be here," Alyx said in a sweetly self-important voice.

Efram bowed and smiled warmly. "The honor is mine, Your Highness. I look forward to meeting your brothers and sisters."

"Why?" Alyx asked, his lip curled in confusion. The adults laughed and Risteard clamped a hand on Alyx's shoulder to cease any further inquiries.

"Your Majesty, you know my children of course." Efram beckoned the five people standing behind him forward, and they all bowed respectfully.

"It's been a long time," Risteard said.

Lord Protector Ekhane indicated a taller man with thinning blonde hair, thin lips, and rigid posture. "My eldest son, Fynn, and his wife, Eve. Fynn is a great help to me in the capital, and I hope to see him distinguish himself in office."

Fynn raised his chin proudly, his narrow chest not quite filling out his muted yellow doublet. The color certainly wasn't flattering to his pallid complexion. His wife stood mutely with an arm casually draped through his. Her perfectly tailored light blue gown accentuated her narrow waist and snowy white skin, high cheekbones, and straight nose. She studied us intently, her dark eyes darting to each person with calculating precision.

"Naturally," Laria said with a half-smile.

"My daughter, Fidelma Patel and her husband, Oskar, who holds one of the largest tracts of orchards in Ilano." A woman with the same shade of hair and poise as her brother stepped forward. Her deep burgundy gown brought out the golden undertones of her skin and flush, rounded cheeks. She smiled, flashing brilliant white teeth. The man on her arm was gray at the temples but no less handsome. He wore a doublet to match his wife and his cream colored breeches were spotless.

Laria appeared duly impressed.

"And here, my youngest son, Finton." He waved a young man with deep chestnut brown hair forward. He bowed, his hazel eyes shining behind a pair of spectacles. He combed slender, sun-bathed fingers through the messy strands falling over his forehead.

"Finton," the Lord Protector continued, "studies medicine. Spends most of the day with his nose in a book." He smiled good naturedly as the subject of his teasing shuffled and adjusted his glasses.

"It's a pleasure to meet you all," Laria said.

"You must be worn out from your journey. Please, come in." Fynn gestured for us to enter the capitol building. "We can resume introductions once you're properly settled." His movements were stiff and his speech bland, likening him to a wooden puppet.

Risteard extended his elbow to Laria, and she buried her face in his shoulder. She tried not to laugh and expertly covered her amusement by feigning fatigue. The nurses and I proceeded with the children, followed by Lord Protector Ekhane and his family. Laria surreptitiously glanced at me over her shoulder and made a silly face. I snorted before I could contain myself, which made her nearly lose her composure. She clamped a hand over her mouth and muffled a laugh into Risteard's arm. He glared at me, and the blood drained from my face. Instinctively, I pointed at Laria, indicating that she was to blame for this nonsense. He looked down at his wife, and she fixed him with an innocent stare and pointed back at me.

"I can't take you anywhere." He shook his head, a reluctant grin twitching at his mouth.

While the younger children were tucked in for naps and Alyx was given a snack to prevent a nasty temper, Efram took us on a tour. On the lower floor, indoor mews housed the eagles and falcons of the residing families, and large doors opened onto an expansive training yard. The Master Falconer showed us the hatchery where we observed the progress of an eaglet emerging from an egg bigger than my fist.

"Once the shell cracks," the Master Falconer said, "it takes about two days for the eaglet to fully hatch. This one should be out this time tomorrow."

He moved on, gesturing for us to follow, but Risteard hung back to watch the tiny beak peck through a small hole. We waited for him to catch up, then the Master Falconer indicated a large, weathered door with bars over the windows.

"This is the fledgling yard, Your Majesty," he said to Laria.

Her eyes darted to Risteard. "Where the boys meet their eagles?"

"Exactly. Perhaps, when they're ready, the young princes will enter the yard to find *their* soulmates just like the king when he was a boy." The Master Falconer grinned proudly, but Risteard didn't answer his enthusiasm. The man's smile faltered. He cleared his throat and ushered us along.

Again, Risteard stayed behind to peer through the bars into the yard. The Master Falconer and Lord Protector's voices faded down the corridor, and I glanced over my shoulder to see if Laria was behind me. She'd remained with Risteard. He gripped the bars of the door and stared longingly at the eagles. Laria wrapped her arms around him and propped her chin on his shoulder.

"Can you go inside?" she asked.

He shook his head and drew in a shuddering breath.

"You're not allowed a second chance?"

"If I wanted to, I could. But I don't." The sense of loss was heartbreaking. During the fight for our freedom, Risteard faced King Conall's son, Prince Brannon, in single combat. Risteard's eagle, Aquila, flew to his aide and was tragically killed. Laria told me losing an eagle to an Ilano was like a Praedan losing their horse—like a piece of your soul is ripped away.

Laria hugged him tighter. "I miss her, too."

I hurried after the Master Falconer and Lord Protector and found them waiting in the main housing. The king and queen joined us shortly thereafter, and Risteard was composed once again.

Aside from the spacious rooms draped in bright fabrics, the second floor contained a brightly lit Great Hall with long tables flanked by pillars carved to look like trees. The council chamber where laws were made and criminals were tried featured tiered seating so no one would miss a word. The library also served as a school of higher learning, and under the glass ceiling on the third floor was an expanse of greenery the Lord Protector explained contained the first strains of apples that created the economy of Ilano. It was quite impressive to have so many facets of Ilano life crammed into one building.

After the tour, Fynn stood before the king like a soldier at attention. "I know you've only just arrived, but there is much to discuss, and we are quite eager to begin. If it would please Your Majesty, let us withdraw to the council chambers. I have outlined several topics that I feel require your attention."

"If you wish."

I was continually amazed at Risteard's ability to keep a placid expression when faced with situations that would reduce a lesser man to hysterics. We'd only shared a few words with Fynn Ekhane, and already I could define him as a dull, ridiculous, and vacant man. He extended his hand allowing the king to precede him, but when Laria joined him, the confused man blocked her path.

"Forgive me, Your Majesty," he said, his tone condescending—apparently the only emotion he was capable of projecting. "My invitation was for the king only. I apologize if I misled you into believing your presence was required at council."

My eyes widened at the man's stupidity and Laria flushed red, her green eyes burning with anger. Risteard moved to her defense, but she raised a hand to stop him. She wanted to deal with this upstart herself.

"Are you planning a surprise for me?"

Fynn cocked his head in confusion.

"That's the only reason I can think of why you would exclude your queen from council," she said. "Since my birthday has already passed, I assume we may proceed."

"Your Majesty, I—"

"If there are matters within my kingdom requiring discussion, the only person who will be excluded from such meetings will be yourself if you ever dare treat me so disrespectfully again."

Fynn flinched as if slapped and stepped back in surprise. He looked to the Lord Protector for support, but the older man looked as disappointed in his son as the rest of us.

"I'm sure you can appreciate that I'm a queen who involves herself in the affairs of her kingdom," Laria continued, giving the poor man a condescending smile of her own. "Now, if you will kindly step aside so we may be underway?"

Fynn was smart enough to heed her warning and bowed low. She extended a hand to Risteard, and the pair led the group into the council chambers. Laria told me numerous times I was more than welcome to attend council meetings with her, but I had little interest in politics. The exit of the queen and gentlemen left me in the company of Eve and Fidelma with Olim standing at a respectable distance.

Summoning my courage, I smiled at Fynn Ekhane's tall, thin wife.

"Eve, wasn't it?" I asked.

She nodded mutely.

"I'm Ula, the queen's lady-in-waiting. I'm also her sister."

"How charming," Eve said, her voice dripping with sarcasm. She stared down her perfectly straight nose at me, and I twisted my fingers in the bells of my sleeves.

Fidelma sidled up to me, her full red lips curved in a sly smile. "You must have a million stories to tell about the queen. I do enjoy a good tale."

"You shouldn't gossip with the girl, Fidelma," Eve said. "You're too old for such nonsense."

I studied her silky blonde hair swept into intricate braids atop her head, the smoothness of her lightly sunkissed skin, and thin waist.

"You don't look very old," I said.

She tittered. "You're sweet." She tapped me on the nose with the tip of her finger. "But with three children and a husband, I'm positively ancient!"

I rubbed my nose and tried not to scowl. I turned to Eve and asked, "Do you have any children?"

"A son." She spoke without the note of tender warmth I expected from a mother. "And yourself?"

"Oh, no children. I'm not even married." A blush crept across my cheeks, and I cursed my awkwardness.

"Why-ever not?" Fidelma asked with wide-eyed shock. She leaned forward in anticipation, her soft brown eyes roving over me as if searching for a source of scandal.

"No inclination." When I offered no further explanation, the ladies quickly grew bored and asked if I wanted to join them in the drawing room for cards.

"No, thank you," I said. "I'd like to explore some more."

"Try not to get lost." Eve gave an exaggerated head toss. "We don't want to have to send a search party."

I laughed, but quickly realized she wasn't joking.

"I won't." I blushed further and hurried away, the shadow of a knight trailing after me.

Olim caught up to me. "That was awkward."

"Do any of these people have personalities?" I whispered.

"Living in the capitol building drains it out of them."

"Have you visited here before?"

"A long time ago. Why?"

"I don't want to get lost. I would hate for Eve Ekhane to come after me."

We turned down a long hallway and I stopped to inspect the paintings. There were portraits of past Lord Protectors and other dignitaries, landscapes, and sketches of the city.

"Can you show me which one's His Majesty's grandfather?" I asked.

Olim led me to a large portrait of a gray-haired man with a kind eye and pointed to a placard inscribed with the name 'Davian Elejick.' Below it hung two portraits, one of which I recognized as the oppressive King Conall. I shuddered and looked away before the memories of his reign invaded my thoughts. The other was a handsome, dark-haired, strong-jawed man with a half-smile. I read the plate on the edge of the frame and discovered this was a portrait of Risteard's father, Alyx Elejick.

"The king looks so like him," I said, admiring the face. "I can see little Alyx in him, too."

"Yes." Olim sighed and traced the name reverently.

Painting was a hobby I enjoyed immensely, but being lady-in-waiting to a busy queen with five children hardly allowed time for the accomplishment. A flash of red snagged my attention, and I stopped to admire a landscape with rows of bright green plants leading up a hill to an estate with crimson peaked roofs. The houses were tucked cozily among heavily leafed trees, the deep greens and teals a stark contrast to the white-washed walls. I leaned closer to study the brushstrokes. Beside me Olim tensed and placed a hand on the hilt of his sword. I jumped away from the wall and worriedly stepped behind him, believing myself to be in danger. Standing a few feet away was the youngest Ekhane son, Finton.

"Hello," he said. He stood with his hands in his pockets, smiling brightly. "I noticed you trying to climb into the picture and wanted to offer you a tour of the orchards. The weather is very fine."

"Thank you." I took a deep breath to settle my nerves and laid a hand on Olim's sleeve. He relaxed, recognizing the man was not a threat. "However, I don't think I should leave the capitol building without the queen."

He looked Olim up and down. "You're in her entourage?"

"Her lady-in-waiting…and her sister."

"A personage of great importance." He smiled wider, crinkling the corners of his eyes.

"I was wondering." I tried to sound dignified despite my shyness. "These don't look like apples."

Finton came forward and Olim tensed again. I rolled my eyes and lightly shoved him aside. Hesitantly, Finton stepped beside me, fixing his eyes warily on Olim before inspecting the painting.

"Ah. That's the vineyard at Fionchar. It was the former estate of…" He paled and gave me an apologetic look.

"Of King Conall's family?" I offered.

He nudged the bridge of his spectacles. "Yes. It was of course confiscated and given to a respectable family."

"I'm curious about the dowager queen, Mwiryn," I said. "She was so young, and Her Majesty said she was kind. I haven't the nerve to ask what became of her." Mwiryn became queen when King Conall died and his son, Prince Brannon, assumed the throne.

"I believe she returned home. I could ask Father if you'd like?"

I shook my head. "I don't wish to inconvenience him with such a trifle."

We walked down the hall silently while I studied the paintings. With each passing frame, I longed more and more for the opportunity to paint myself. A particularly colorful scene of an apple harvest caught my eye, and I sighed in admiration of the bright oranges, yellows, and reds.

"It's lovely, isn't it? Harvest is my favorite time of year. The leaves are changing, the weather becomes colder, and everyone comes out together to pick apples. When Father wasn't looking, I would sneak one and take bites until Fynn would catch me and rat me out." Finton laughed, and I enjoyed the humor of the memory with him. I caught a glimpse of Olim rolling his eyes skyward and drumming his fingers on his hips. I couldn't account for his attitude and hoped Finton didn't notice.

"I understand the festivals are particularly...festive...that time of year." I cringed inwardly at myself for not speaking as eloquently as Laria. He probably thought I was a blundering idiot.

He stifled a smile. "Yes. People come from many miles to enjoy the cider and delicious treats from recipes passed down through generations."

"Do you know who the artist is?" I asked, hoping to distract him from my stupidity.

"I must disappoint you again, I'm afraid. But I can find out if you wish."

"Not necessary." I hurried away.

"Wait!" he called. "I'm afraid I was remiss in introducing myself. I have a horrible habit of forgetting basic manners."

"Oh, well, I'm the queen's lady-in-waiting."

He laughed, and I wanted to bury my face in a pillow and scream.

"Yes," he said, "you told me that already. Might I have the honor of your name?"

My attention drifted over his shoulder to Olim sighing in exaggerated annoyance.

"It's Ula," I said. A little too loudly.

"I'm Finton."

"I know. I mean, you were introduced outside when we got here. I heard your name then."

"Perfect. Now we're properly acquainted."

I pointed behind him. "That's Olim. He's been assigned by the king to protect me."

Olim's eyes widened, and I shrugged awkwardly.

Finton grinned crookedly at the flustered knight. "Duly noted. I will consider myself warned."

"That's not what I meant!"

"I'm not offended. A truly vigilant king will always ensure the safety of his family. King Risteard is a wise man."

"Did you know him? I mean, before he was king?"

"Only by sight. He's older than me, closer to Fynn's age, but even so they weren't exactly friendly. My father was very loyal to Sir Alyx, so naturally he supported His Majesty in his endeavors."

"The queen owes him a debt of gratitude, I believe, though she won't say what it is."

"I could find out if you'd like?"

"I don't wish to pry--" I stopped short when I noticed the wry grin on his face. "You're teasing me."

"Apologies, miss. I couldn't resist."

I coughed to cover the audible groan coming from Olim and shot an angry glare in his direction.

"Well, sir, I don't wish to keep you." I curtseyed. "If you will excuse me."

I fixed Olim with my most intimidating stare when I walked away from Finton's bow. The knight followed me dutifully, and the moment we were out of earshot, I whirled on him.

"What were you doing?"

"Please." He waved his hand as if batting away a pesky insect. "That man was so false he might as well have been in one of those paintings. You should be thanking me."

"False or not, he is the son of the Lord Protector, and your rudeness was inexcusable!"

"He didn't even notice."

"I noticed! I was embarrassed for you! We're here to represent my sister and you're making faces behind his back."

Olim had the decency to appear abashed. "I'm sorry. I just can't stand that pretense of kindness."

"How do you know it was a pretense? We don't even know him!"

"These well-bred men are all the same. They simper and compliment and endear themselves to you while hiding their true intentions."

"And what was his true intention, Olim? To deceive me into thinking he really ate apples surreptitiously at harvest?"

"You can't always trust the cute stories they tell."

"I'm sorry if you have resentment toward people of his social standing, but you cannot allow it to cloud your judgment nor carry it over into every situation. It isn't fair, Olim."

He wouldn't look at me, and I worried that I'd hurt him. Over the past few years, Olim had not only become my valiant protector but a companion, a friend I relied on. I reached a hand toward him, then pulled it back.

"That was cruel of me," I whispered.

"No. You're right. I do have a grudge against people who are handed everything and never have to work a day in their lives. I shouldn't allow my personal feelings to affect my duty. I'm sorry if I embarrassed you."

"Let's put this behind us." I patted him on the shoulder. "I'm determined to use this trip as an opportunity to overcome my shyness and I'll need your help. No more making faces or strange noises behind people's backs."

"What about afterwards?"

"In private you may laugh about them as much as you wish as long as it's warranted, especially in regard to Fynn and Eve Ekhane."

"Understood."

"Now, can you please escort me to my room? I'd like to rest before the queen requires me again."

He bowed and extended his elbow, which I accepted with the reluctance I had moments ago expressed a wish to conquer.

Alone in my room, I wrapped myself in a blanket and burrowed into an overstuffed chair with the contraband book. The journey left me drained of energy, but I knew I would never be able to sleep in a strange place long enough for it to make a difference, so I chose this stolen opportunity to read my secret novel.

Arella gripped the railing and began climbing, her feet cold and slick on the smooth surface. She held fast to the ship and peered cautiously over the side to the dark water below. In a few days, the ship would make port, but she was determined not to be aboard. Whomever this man was she was supposed to marry did not hold her heart, and without it, she would be doomed to live in misery. She closed her eyes and saw the face of her beloved captain, the man she could never have. Clutching her hand around her mother's locket, she relinquished her grip on the railing and welcomed the comforting hands of death.

Lost in the fantasy of the story, it was endearing to consider a forbidden love transcending even the darkest of hours. My eyelids fluttered closed as I pictured myself in dire peril, perhaps torn between the affections of two men. The absurdity of the scenario made me giggle, for the most ridiculous notion of all was the possibility of not one but two men falling in love with me. Before I could resist, I drifted into a blissful sleep, replete with dreams of damsels in distress and heroic knights rescuing them from terrible fates.

Chapter 3

A gentle shake roused me from my pleasant nap, and I opened my eyes to Laria's gentle smile.

"I hate to wake you, but it's nearly dinner."

"Oh!" I sat up quickly, my book tumbling to the floor. Laria snatched it before I could stop her, and I jumped from the chair, fully awake.

"Please," I said, extending a hand toward the book. "Give the book back so I can put it away." Too late. Laria was already reading an open page aloud.

"Arella was completely at the mercy of the captain's penetrating dark eyes, and she knew it wouldn't be long before she could resist him no more. She stood outside his cabin, hand poised to knock, bosom heaving with trepidation, and her heart completely made up that she would not leave this ship without knowing him in all his entirety."

Laria's eyes shot up and met mine, then she wiggled an eyebrow and one side of her mouth curved upward.

"I didn't want you to know I was reading this." I grabbed the book from her hands, my face hot with embarrassment, tossed it into my trunk, and slammed the lid shut.

Her smile was ridiculously wide. "There's no reason to be ashamed."

"Isn't there?"

"Of course not. It's perfectly natural to be curious. Where did you get it?"

"One of the ladies at court. She said it was amusing."

"It certainly is!" Laria stifled a snort and sat on the edge of the bed. "Perfectly scandalous." She tried valiantly to suppress her amusement, but if there's one thing Laria couldn't resist it was a good laugh.

"Don't tease me," I pleaded. "I knew you would. That's why I didn't show you."

"I'm sorry! You know I don't mean anything malicious by it. And I won't begrudge you a little fantasy and intrigue."

The corners of my mouth twitched, and her expression turned serious.

"Ula," she continued. "If you do have questions, please don't feel uneasy about asking. I would hate for you to think this is how real people interact with each other."

I sagged onto the bed, leaned my head on my sister's shoulder, and released the tension from my body in a slow, even breath.

"I wonder sometimes if I will ever fall in love. I've never worried about it before, but I see how happy you are and…"

"You wish for such happiness for yourself?"

I swallowed past the tightness of my throat. "Yes."

"Be patient. Love will find you when you're least expecting it. In my experience anyway."

"How did you know? That you loved Risteard, I mean."

She sighed and fell back on the bed. I stretched out beside her and propped my head in my hand, eagerly awaiting her story.

"I'd seen and experienced so many horrific things in the castle under King Conall's rule, some so terrible I will never speak of them again."

Her mournful tone made my chest ache, and I almost stopped her. Instead, I took her hand and squeezed lightly, hoping my presence was both encouraging and comforting.

"Risteard kept trying to tell me not everything in the world was ugly, that there was beauty in it, but how could I believe that if I'd never experienced it? One day, I had a brilliant idea. Risteard had been my trusted friend for years at this point. So, I asked him to kiss me, to give me one experience untainted by misery or hate. When his lips touched mine for the first time, everything changed."

"You knew you loved him right away?" I whispered so I wouldn't break the magic.

"At first, I didn't understand what I felt besides confusion. Looking back, I know I was gradually falling in love with him, but it wasn't until we kissed that I became consciously aware of it."

"One kiss."

"A kiss is a very powerful connection. It's not just the touching of warm, sensitive skin. It's the mingling of breaths and the joining of souls."

"Does it still feel like that? Even after being married for so long?"

"Ha! We haven't even been married for six years! But to answer your question, yes. Every kiss with Risteard fills me with the same thrill as the first. More even."

"Have you ever felt your 'bosom heave with trepidation'?" I giggled, and Laria burst into a fit of laughter so potent she could hardly breathe.

"Well." She brushed away a tear and took several deep breaths. "I can't say it's ever been with trepidation, but my bosom has certainly heaved."

We collapsed into uncontrollable laughter until the door burst open and Risteard barged in looking particularly annoyed. I buried my face in a pillow to recover my composure and hide by burning cheeks. Laria raised herself on her elbows and blinked at him innocently.

"Yes?"

He tapped his fingers on the doorframe. "Were you planning on joining us?"

"Of course, my love. I only need a moment to regain control of my heaving bosoms."

At Laria's words, I choked on my disbelief and snuck a peek at my brother-in-law. His expression was characteristically blank as we cackled like idiots.

"Well, as soon as you're done with that, please come down to dinner," he said dryly.

"You're not going to offer me assistance? What kind of a noble king are you?"

I pushed Laria over and gave her my best shocked 'please shut up now' look.

A glint of mischief flickered in his eye. "One who waits for permission."

Laria's lips curved knowingly and she winked.

I died of embarrassment.

"We'll be down soon," Laria told him. He nodded and left without another word.

"That was disgusting," I said. "Try not to flirt with your husband in front of me again."

"No promises," she said, her eyes still trained dreamily on the closed door.

***

Dinner wasn't the private affair I'd hoped it would be. Much to my dismay, the entirety of the Ilano elite were assembled in the large dining hall of the capitol building. Though not the grand, arched-ceilinged work of architectural splendor of Praed Castle, the Great Hall was nevertheless spacious, with clean lines in light colored stone. The waning light of sunset accompanied by chandeliers crafted to resemble tree branches bathed the room in a warm orange glow. Rows of tables were packed with elegantly dressed ladies and gentlemen, and at the end of the room was a table designated for the distinguished guests elaborately decorated with sprigs of apple blossoms. It was comforting to see other children. The princes and princesses wouldn't find themselves bored once the food stopped coming. Laughter echoed off the bare walls, rippling the banners bearing crests of elite families hanging from the ceiling. Regardless, the room full of strangers was disconcerting, and my stomach roiled with anxiety.

Risteard and Laria sat in the middle of the table, Efram Ekhane and his dull son, Fynn, on the king's right. Fynn talked incessantly in a monotone voice, testing Risteard's patience more than a squabble between the children. Laria was doomed to sit next to Eve and Fidelma, and throughout dinner she disappeared behind her hands to hide her rolling eyes. Along with Laria's children, the Lord Protector's grandchildren were placed across the wide table, their nurses interspersed among them. I sat with the children so I wouldn't be stuck next to a stranger, which irked Laria since she was counting on me to rescue her.

Laria told stories of the lavish feasts at Praed Castle under King Conall's rule, and it appeared this was an Ilano tradition. There were several dishes of greasy meats and cheeses, fruit pies, and colorful squashes. I'd never been allowed rich meals when I languished as a seamstress in the workroom of the castle, and as lady-in-waiting under Laria's rule, the food was the traditional lighter fare of Praed. I took a few bites of the juicy, tender meat Duveesa explained came from the belly of the short, fat, square nosed creatures called 'hogs.' The taste was unusual, a mix of salty and sweet, and brought an involuntary smile to my face. But after several bites, the oily meat started giving me indigestion. I rearranged the food on my plate in neat piles while my stomach settled, hoping nobody noticed.

"Is the food not to your liking?" a voice asked from across the table. "Should I ask for something else to be made?"

My knife froze and I slowly lifted my gaze across the table at Finton Ekhane. His head tilted quizzically, regarding me and my barely touched meal.

"Not necessary," I said, shaking my head before shifting my focus back to my plate.

"We can't risk displeasing the lady-in-waiting and sister to the queen. What would Her Majesty think if we allowed you to starve?"

"I'm not displeased!" I dropped the knife, and the loud clang drew the attention of the few people around me. Tyrnan expressed concern that I'd broken something. Duveesa stifled a grin and assured him I wasn't in trouble.

"Apologies," Finton said, suppressing a grin of his own. "I forget you're not familiar with my humor and it can appear I'm being serious when I'm merely jesting."

"It's a very odd way to speak to people." I glared when Tyrnan called down the table asking if I needed him to cut my food for me and Finton could no longer contain his amusement.

"I'm sorry," he said. "I'll ensure we become better acquainted so I don't risk inadvertently insulting you."

Despite Olim's assertions that a pleasing temperament may bely nefarious intentions, I couldn't help the smile playing at my lips. I glanced down the table at Laria engaging in conversations with the distinguished ladies of Ilano regardless of her personal feelings towards them. Taking my cue from her behavior, I took a deep breath and addressed Finton.

"I understand from the Lord Protector that you hope to become a surgeon. How does one achieve such a career?"

He grinned. "Years of diligent study. I started studying the three sciences when I was seventeen and graduated to medicine at twenty. I apprenticed under a surgeon the last year of medical school, and now I'm working to complete a rigorous course of study before I'll be permitted to become a registered surgeon myself."

"What made you want to pursue such a profession?" Mother taught me how to engage in proper topics of conversation—the weather, music, the latest fashions. How dismayed would she be if she knew I encouraged such an unladylike topic?

"I suppose the proper response would be to say I enjoy helping people, but if I'm being honest, I would say my choice stems from my desire to understand the science of the inner workings of the body. I find it very fascinating. We are often referred to as a vessel of the soul, but that doesn't give the flesh the credit it's due." His tone was serious though his eyes glittered, the flecks of gold among the dark brown and subtle green shining in the candlelight.

"An interesting perspective."

"There's so much we don't understand about how the body functions. I am a strong proponent of the idea that the more we learn, the greater our ability to cure ailments and treat injuries."

Fynn's exasperated groan interrupted Finton's passionate speech. "There you go again talking about subjects which are not appropriate for the dining table. How many times must I tell you not to speak about your 'work' when people are eating. Especially in front of ladies?"

Finton's smile tightened as he turned toward his brother. "Apologies if you find my profession abhorrent. I hope I haven't soured your stomach."

Fynn shook his head and addressed the Lord Protector. "Honestly, Father, I don't know why you indulged him when he came to you declaring he wanted to cut into people."

Finton's hand curled in a fist and he flushed from neck to hairline. "That's not an accurate portrayal of the conversation."

"Really, gentleman," the Lord Protector said. "Try to mind your manners and refrain from quarreling in front of the king and queen."

At their father's admonishment, the men retreated into themselves, shoulders hunched and cheeks red. I almost laughed at how childlike they appeared, like my nephews after a scolding.

When the tension faded, Finton leaned toward me and said, "I didn't mean to express myself so graphically. Sometimes I get carried away when talking about my work."

I offered my most encouraging smile. "I wasn't offended. It sounds quite fascinating."

"I won't delude myself that you're truly interested in hearing more, but on the off chance you are, would you like to resume this conversation later? Tomorrow perhaps? I teach a class in the morning and should be finished before the lunch hour."

"I am interested, but I don't know if or when I might be available. As you know, I'm at the mercy of Her Majesty's schedule."

"Ah, yes. Your time is not your own. Well, I'll be spending most of the day in the library doing research. Should you find a moment for yourself, I would be honored if you joined me."

"I'll try." I looked away to hide the color rising in my cheeks. I'd never been invited to do anything with a gentleman before besides dancing, and I was determined not to allow my reserved nature prevent me from becoming more sociable.

Apparently Laria shared the same goal. After dinner when everyone retired to the music room, she immediately volunteered me to display my talents on the piano. I paled and stuttered that surely it was Her Majesty the people would want to hear, but she declared her abilities so poor they would scramble over themselves to escape. Those nearest enough to hear begged me to oblige, and I begrudgingly shuffled over to the beautiful instrument and played a simple, yet uplifting melody. The piece drew very little attention, and after it was over, I rose from the bench.

"What do you think you're doing?" Laria asked, hands on her hips like a perturbed mother.

"Giving the other ladies a chance to exhibit?"

"You've hardly displayed what you're capable of, Ula, and I would like to show off my very accomplished sister."

Feeling as if everyone in the room was staring, I tensed and frantically scanned the room.

"In front of all these people? I can't." I'd played for my family dozens of times, but strangers made me nervous. What if they hated my playing? What if it wasn't good enough? I tugged at my sleeves and shook my head.

"Yes, you can. It's good for you. Continue to argue with me further and I'll make you sing." She was smiling, but I knew she wasn't joking.

"One more. Promise me."

"As long as it's an appropriate example of your abilities."

I resumed my seat in a huff and glared at Laria's back. Feeling impossibly irritated, I placed my fingers on the polished keys and played a melancholy tune that took me years to learn. Slowly, conversations quieted, until music was the only sound filling the room. If I glanced up, I'd lose my nerve, so I focused on the keys and my dancing fingers. The notes emerged confidently, one moment bright and the next low and mournful. When the melody faded, no one spoke. Hesitantly, I raised my head to gauge the people's reactions. There was shock, appreciation, and awe intermixed with a few envious and resentful glares. Laria was smiling with sisterly pride, and I took this to mean my performance was acceptable. Using the instrument to steady myself, I rose, curtseyed, and escaped to the corner of the room.

"Show off," Olim teased when I hid behind him.

"It's the queen's fault," I said. "She insisted I make a proper display of my talents."

"I would say you succeeded. No one will want to follow your performance."

I groaned and buried my face in my hands.

"This is what you wanted, though, isn't it? To overcome your shyness?"

"Not on such a grand scale. I only wanted to be able to talk to someone without stumbling over myself. Perhaps make a new friend or two."

"Well, think of this as an introduction. You've shown people who you are, and now you just have to wait for them to come to you. Brilliant idea, actually."

I lowered my hands and quirked an eyebrow, unconvinced. "Do you think so?"

"Would it cheer you up?"

"Possibly."

"Then, yes. We both know approaching strangers is your biggest hurdle anyway."

As if to prove his point, several people complimented me on the performance, and I received invitations from a few ladies for afternoon tea, to which I answered in vague terms of acceptance depending on the queen's consent. Even Eve Ekhane had kind words for me, albeit in her expressionless tones.

"You must play for us again. Your performance was quite correct," she said.

I promised I wouldn't allow her compliments to go to my head.

One by one, the children fell asleep wherever they could find a spot to curl up. Sulwen was comfortably drooling on her father's shoulder while Tyrnan rocked in Laria's arms. The nurses started gathering them up for bedtime, but Alyx and Rian were nowhere to be found. Olim and I joined in the search, peering under furniture and looking behind curtains, but the boys weren't in the music room.

I confided the situation to Duveesa, asked her not to tell the queen, and ducked out of the room with Olim to look for the wayward princes.

"I'm sure they got lost exploring," Olim said. He tried to sound reassuring, but his voice cracked on the last word.

I tried to tell myself he was right, but I couldn't ignore the sinking feeling in my stomach. We ran down the hallway, poking our heads into every room and calling out their names. Any moment Laria would sense something was wrong and enquire after us, and if she found out we couldn't find her first born sons, the entire country would be locked down.

I opened the door to the library and yelled for Alyx and Rian, but there was no answer. My shoulders slumped and I breathed heavily from the exertion of running mad through the capitol building. Olim searched around corners and behind shelves, but he found no sign of them. He turned toward me and froze, his hand automatically resting on the hilt of his sword.

"What?" I asked breathlessly before spinning around. Finton was standing there, his face etched with concern.

"What's going on?" he asked.

"I'd ask you the same question," Olim said in an accusatory tone. I gawked at him incredulously, but he wouldn't relent. "How is it you came to be here?"

Finton didn't flinch. "I was looking for the lady."

"Why is that?" Olim shouted, and if I could have reached a book to throw at him, I would have.

"To compliment her on such an exquisite performance. But when I found she was no longer accompanying the queen, I quit the music room. I heard yelling, and I recognized her voice. I worried something was wrong."

Before Olim could say more, I stepped between them. "Something's wrong. We cannot find Prince Alyx and Prince Rian. We've searched the entire floor."

"Everywhere? You're certain?" Finton asked.

"Yes," Olim said firmly.

"Have you checked the mews? Maybe they wanted to see the birds."

"That's a good idea. Can you take us there?" I asked.

"I know where it is!" Olim said, but Finton already beckoned us to follow and was heading out the door.

I moved to chase after him, but Olim grabbed my arm. "I don't trust him. It was very convenient for him to show up just now. He could be leading you into a trap."

"All the more reason for you to come with me." I shrugged out of his grasp and asked if he was coming. He sighed, nodded, and we both dashed out of the room.

When I caught up to Finton, I said, "We need to hurry. If the queen notices we're missing and can't find her sons, she'll tear down the capital looking for them."

"Understood."

We hurried down the stairs, and I slipped in my haste and nearly fell. Both men reached out to steady me, but I awkwardly waved them away.

The expansive mews were lit with only a few sconces, but darkness aside, our senses were assaulted by a loud cacophony of flapping wings, screeches, shrieks, and crying from the cages. Something about the crying struck me as odd. I spread my arms to halt the men and listened. The pitch and wails sounded very human.

"Alyx! Rian!" I called.

"Aunt Ula!" Alyx yelled back.

We raced down the row of cages amid the boys' shouts and tiny hands banging against the wall. Olim unlatched one of the doors and threw it open, and both boys fell sobbing into my arms.

"Alyx," I said. "What happened? How did you two get locked in there?"

"There were two big boys," he said between sniffles. "They asked if we wanted to play a game of hide-and-seek. When we hid in there," he pointed at the empty cage, "they closed the door, and we couldn't get out. We could hear them laughing."

Finton crouched next to us. "What were their names?"

"Don't know," Alyx said. "One boy said he lives here."

"What did he look like?" Based on Finton's tone, I guessed he had an idea of the boy's identity.

Alyx bit the tip of his finger and furrowed his brow. "Tall…"

"Dark hair or light?"

"Light."

"Skinny?"

Alyx nodded, rubbing his eyes.

"He said if we told we'd get in trouble," Rian said.

"Because his father is going to be Lord Protector," Alyx added.

My eyes narrowed. A boy whose father aspired to be Lord Protector? It had to be the son of Fynn Ekhane.

"I see." Finton stood, and I looked up at him, wondering if my suspicions were correct. "Don't worry about them." He patted Alyx's little head. "They won't bother you again. And I'm sure your aunt will make you feel better in no time."

"Come now," I told them, but neither boy was willing to walk of his own volition. I picked up Rian and turned to Olim with pleading eyes, knowing how uncomfortable it made him to hold the children. His eyes darted nervously from me to Alyx clinging to my dress.

"May I help?" Finton said.

"Not necessary," Olim said before scooping up Alyx and stalking down the aisle.

"Have I done something to offend your protective knight?" Finton asked while we followed Olim up the stairs.

"That's just his way with people he doesn't know very well," I said. "Please don't take offense. He's nice once you get to know him."

"Has he been with you long?"

"Oh, yes. Many years. He came to Praed when…the other king was there."

"You're fortunate to have such a loyal knight to watch out for you."

"He does make me feel safer. Especially in a strange place. And we've become friends since he was assigned to look after me, so that's been nice. I don't have many friends."

"Really? I find that surprising."

"I haven't much occasion to make friends," I said, willing myself not to blush. "Besides, I find it difficult to talk to people I don't know."

He chuckled. "Which makes my compulsive forwardness even more distressing, I'm sure. I find I must apologize to you once again if I've made you uncomfortable in any way."

I shook my head. "No need. I'm trying to overcome my social ineptness and talk to people more. Her Majesty says it's good for me."

Up ahead, Olim was waiting outside the music room. I handed Rian to Finton and instructed the men to wait for me there.

"And be nice," I mouthed to Olim before slipping inside to find Duveesa.

Duveesa rushed over, pale faced, and frantically glancing toward the queen. "Well?"

"Found them," I said. "They're in the hall waiting to be put to bed."

"The queen asked about them and I told her they were already in bed. She was disappointed not to be able to say goodnight."

"If she asks where I was, I'll tell her I was helping put them to bed."

Duveesa nodded and without another word left the room. The lies would have to satisfy Laria for the evening, though I knew she wouldn't believe me. She said it was because I had an honest face, but I knew it was simply because I couldn't stop myself from blushing. Predictably, Laria cornered me the second she saw me and asked where I'd been. When I told her I was helping with the children, she narrowed her eyes suspiciously.

"The entire time?" she asked.

I sighed. "Let's talk about it in the morning."

One eyebrow raised, and she smiled wickedly.

"Did your absence involve heaving bosoms?"

Well, yes, but not the way she was implying.

I rolled my eyes. "No."

"Tomorrow then," she said. "I'm ready for bed myself." To prove her point, she yawned loudly.

"As you wish, my queen," I said with a flourishing link of our arms.

Chapter 4

Finton did indeed know the culprit who accosted the princes. The ten-year-old son of Fynn and Eve Ekhane, Gerrid, was the ringleader, and his cousin was quickly given up as his accomplice when Gerrid was questioned. The lads were scolded fiercely by their parents, who promised the queen profusely this would never happen again. Laria was not pleased when she learned the true reason I was absent for the latter part of the evening, though she bore the information with poised grace. She smiled and adopted a 'boys will be boys' stance on the matter, but she made it clear her generous bestowal of mercy would not be repeated. Whether the boys truly felt guilt over the situation I wasn't certain, but based on the fear crossing their features, they would not risk displeasing the king and queen. Gerrid gulped audibly when he glanced up at Risteard's imposing form, and his cousin went white when he encountered Laria's dark stare. I personally would have liked to have seen a strap across their backs, but I knew Laria hated corporal punishment for children and was satisfied with the threat of bodily harm as opposed to inflicting any. Regardless, I kept a close eye on young Gerrid Ekhane from that moment on.

***

Our first venture to an Ilano orchard was planned for the afternoon, and the anticipation of picking apples lifted the princes' spirits. The Lord Protector explained we would be visiting one of the largest orchards in Ilano, spanning several hundred acres and containing many varieties of apples, ice grapes, and a new crop called "pears." The air was warm and dry, and the sun was high overhead when we traveled along the tree-lined road through the countryside, waving to farmers we passed. Women approached the queen with gifts of bouquets and handmade jewelry and the children were handed sweet treats, which were enthusiastically gobbled up as fast as they were placed in their excited hands. I was in awe of how much green spread out to the horizon. Praed's rolling hills of muted grass, wildflowers, and miles of hayfields contrasted sharply with the lush verdant carpets and rows of trees swollen with fruit. Before the apples formed, I was told, blossoms of white and pink filled the trees and fell in delicate petals, signaling the onset of the growing season. I breathed in the fragrance of ripening fruit and earth, closing my eyes to enjoy the sensation fully with the warm sun on my face and the pleasing sound of the children giggling.

At the crest of a sweeping vale was a large manor house made from sand colored stone. Waiting outside was the Lord and Lady of the estate, a couple with two children, and a very familiar face. I gasped quietly when I saw the tall, graceful figure of Mwiryn Derville, her golden hair luminous in the rays of sunshine spilling through the trees. She smiled at our approach and bowed low when the king and queen greeted her family.

"Your Grace," Lord Derville intoned with a bow to Risteard. "You honor us with your visit."

Risteard nodded perfunctorily, leaving Laria to thank the Lord and Lady for their hospitality. They were introduced to Lord Derville's son and his family before Laria addressed Mwiryn.

"Your Ladyship," Laria said with a respectful curtsey. Though the lovely former queen of Praed no longer held her title, she was still afforded the respect of a dowager in Laria's estimation. After all, it was she who abdicated and placed her own crown on Laria's head, and for this my sister would always bestow upon her the homage she deserved.

"Your Majesties." Mwiryn dropped a low curtsey. "I trust you had a pleasant journey?"

"I've found Ilano to possess astonishing natural beauty," Laria said. "And the people have been incredibly hospitable and kind."

"We look forward to giving Your Majesty a tour of our orchards. They are a true testament to the pride of the hard-working people of our country," Lord Derville said.

Laria smiled. "I have no doubt. Please, lead on."

His Lordship bowed and extended his hand toward the back of the manor, and he and his family walked down the hill with Risteard, Laria, and the Lord Protector beside them. He began to narrate the history of the estate in excessive detail, his voice fading as the distance grew between us. I could tell by the children's fidgeting and wide eyes that they were anxious to explore, but we held fast to their hands.

"It's perfectly all right if the children wish to play."

I blinked at Mwiryn in surprise. I expected her to walk with the distinguished guests and her parents.

"Father won't mind. And they won't hurt anything."

"Can we please?" Alyx pleaded, his blue eyes melting my resolve.

"Very well," I said. "Don't go too far, though. Keep us in sight."

The boys cheered and ran off into the trees. Sulwen tried to follow, but as usual her tiny legs were no match for their speed. Lilias took her sister's hand and helped her walk among the orchard to retrieve fallen fruit with Duveesa trailing behind.

"They're absolutely adorable children," Mwiryn said while we walked together down the rows of trees.

"They are." I beamed, my shyness overcome by the pride I felt toward my nieces and nephews. "And not lacking in exuberance."

Mwiryn's laugh was like crystal glasses tapping together in a gentle cheer. "I would expect not at such young ages."

"Forgive me for saying so, My Lady, but I did not expect to see you back at your father's house. Were you not given an estate of your own?"

"Please, there is no need to address me so formally. I prefer to be called by my name." When I nodded, she continued. "I was bequeathed a living after my...husband's...death, but I chose not to accept."

Mwiryn's deceased husband was Prince Brannon, the man who crowned himself king shortly after the mysterious death of his father, King Conall. I couldn't imagine what it must have been like to be married to such a monster. Laria spoke very little on the subject, I suspect to save me from knowing the horrible truth. We were silent for several seconds while I desperately tried to think of another topic.

"It must be very comforting to be united with your sister, to be her lady-in-waiting, and to watch your nieces and nephews grow," Mwiryn said.

"Yes. I couldn't want anything more."

"Oh? I wonder." She glanced at me sideways. "Do you ever desire a family for yourself?"

"Not really." I lowered my gaze to my intertwined fingers. "I mean, I suppose every woman dreams of romance now and then, but I don't strive for it. Do you?"

The lightness emanating from her faded. "I don't believe I shall ever marry again."

"I hope your first marriage hasn't tainted your views. It's not fair for you to have to spend the rest of your days alone if you've always wished for companionship."

A slow, mournful smile creased her delicate features, and if she hadn't averted her gaze, I could have sworn tears formed in her eyes.

"I do not wish to marry against my nature ever again, therefore I shall end my days in my own company."

I didn't understand what she meant, but I didn't pry into a seemingly painful subject.

"We should find some romance for *you* while you're here," she said in a brighter tone.

I blushed and shook my head furiously.

She giggled as if we were young girls and took my arm. "There are plenty of fine gentlemen in Ilano. If nothing else, it will be a pleasant distraction from your duties."

When we caught up with the group, Lord Derville was explaining how to determine when an apple is at its peak of ripeness. The echo of the children's voices traveled along the orchard, and Laria turned to me with a raised brow. I indicated the direction they ran off to with a nod and reassuring smile, and satisfied her brood weren't about to disappear into a well, Laria returned her attention to our host.

Lord Derville offered Laria a shining red apple, which she took with a grateful bow of her head. She sank her teeth into the fruit with unrestrained zeal, the juices running down her chin. She closed her eyes while she chewed, reveling in the sweet taste.

"One of my favorite foods are the berries I picked from the bushes around my home as a child," Laria said once she finished her mouthful. "I never thought anything should rival their flavor. Until today."

Lord Derville accepted the compliment with evident pride, bowing low and thanking her profusely for the honor. Laria certainly knew how to flatter with sincerity.

She turned to the king and offered him the fruit, and I bit the inside of my cheek to keep from laughing at his dubious expression. He clearly didn't think it necessary to partake, probably because he grew up here and was familiar with the taste. Laria narrowed her eyes and shoved the fruit at him insistently. His shoulders slumped in resignation. He grabbed the apple, took a large, enthusiastic bite, and placed it back in her hands. Flesh side down. By the look on Laria's face, he was going to pay for that later.

"Please feel free to explore the orchard and vineyard at your leisure, Your Majesties. You are my guests," Lord Derville said.

Laria turned to me with pursed lips, the apple perched in her cupped hands.

"May I offer you a bite?" she asked.

Calmly, I took the fruit from her and wiped her moist hands with a handkerchief. She gave her husband a sideways glance and grasped his arm before he could escape.

"Come, my dear," Laria said through gritted teeth. "Let's go see what sort of trouble our children are getting into."

"I'm sure there's no trouble," Mwiryn said, her face etched with worry. "They're such lovely children, Your Majesty. My compliments to you."

Laria grinned at Mwiryn and said, "You are graciousness itself, Your Ladyship. But you mustn't worry yourself over my manner of speaking. I know it is quite foreign to you."

"Yes, indeed."

"Shall we?" Laria asked Risteard without the previous hostility. After the barest acknowledgement of our presence, my brother-in-law led my sister into the trees in the direction of the children's voices. She pulled him close to whisper in his ear, her grip tight on his arm. The dark look he pierced her with was nothing short of primal.

She shook her head slowly, deliberately mouthing no over and over. They stepped behind a tree before I could work out the odd exchange.

"It's true I've heard the queen speak very little, especially in the past, but I believe I've heard the king speak even less. Does he ever talk at all?"

"He speaks," I said, my lips twitching with restrained mirth. "Though he is a man of few words. The queen says he is quite verbose in private. Much to her dismay as she sometimes jests."

"They have an interesting relationship then?"

"It was difficult to get used to at first. My mother and father didn't speak in the same manner, but then they rarely conversed at all. The king and queen can be in a heated discussion one moment, teasing each other the next, and incredibly loving all at the same time. I confess watching them together is the only time I long for marriage myself."

We wandered through the rows of trees, sunlight trickling between branches to warm our faces. I wished I'd brought my sketchbook, but I could easily rely on my memories. Fresh earth, vibrant greens, and the shining, red—

"Would you like to try an apple?" Mwiryn asked, pointing up a tree.

Above my head among lush green leaves were hundreds of ripe apples begging to be picked. There was a particularly deep red one beckoning to me, and my mouth watered imagining how juicy it would be.

"I would like that one," I said. It was too high for Mwiryn to reach, so she said she would have to find one of the workers to help.

"No need," I said and started climbing.

"You shouldn't. What if you were to fall?"

"I've been climbing trees my entire life. Perhaps not as often as the queen, but enough to be confident I won't slip."

Mwiryn chewed at her bottom lip as she watched me ascend the tree, the rough bark scraping my gown. I stretched toward the apple, but it was just out of reach of my fingertips. I shuffled along the branch I was perched on and tried to grasp the elusive fruit.

Snap! I pitched forward but caught myself. Before I could slide back toward the trunk, the branch broke completely, and I fell headfirst. Mwiryn screamed. My legs tangled in the branches, and I scrambled to stop from hurtling to the ground. My fingers closed over a clump of foliage, but it wasn't enough to hold my weight. Leaves ripped free and I squeezed my eyes shut, bracing myself for the inevitable impact. Strangely, it wasn't as painful as I expected. I landed abruptly, enveloped in arms. Hesitantly, I opened one eye, and Olim's reddened, concerned face was staring back at me.

"What?" He inhaled deeply, his chest heaving with exertion. "What are you doing?"

He'd caught me just before I hit the dirt and laid sprawled on the ground beneath me. He spoke again, but his voice was hazy, as if he were in another room. Slowly, I turned toward the sound, and his face was blurred and unnaturally bright.

"You…you…" A wave of dizziness overtook me, and I closed my eyes. I raised a hand toward my temple, but I lacked the strength, and it flopped uselessly in my lap.

Running footsteps barreled toward us, and I heard my sister's voice above the roar of blood in my ears.

"What happened?" Laria called.

There was a whirl of activity around me, and I clung tighter to Olim's tunic.

"She fell," Mwiryn said. "I'm so sorry, Your Majesty. I should have prevented it."

"Are you injured?" Laria asked, her face inches from mine.

I shook my head vaguely, unsure.

"You can instill her in one of our rooms," Lord Derville offered.

Risteard's firm voice echoed above the din. "No. We'll take her back to the capitol building. Olim."

Risteard's use of the knight's name was a clear order, and I was carried to our carriage. The children bounced around me asking questions, but the nurses held them back. Laria climbed into the carriage ahead of me and held out her arms to Olim. He lowered me into her waiting embrace with the same stiff reserve he exhibited with the children, as if he feared I'd shatter. I raised a shaky hand toward him, but my fingers brushed against the silken fabric of the shut door. The rush of fear ebbed, and joy flooded into my veins. In a true display of courage, Olim saved my life. I tried to sit up to catch one more glimpse of him, but my head was too heavy to lift.

I lay in Laria's lap, and she smoothed my hair and whispered comforting words. A dull ache pulsed in my leg, growing until sweat broke out on my brow. I curled into a ball and whimpered. Laria's fingers stilled, and she asked where it hurt. My mouth moved, but no sound emerged, The sway of the carriage and the trauma of the fall drained my energy, and before long I drifted into an empty sleep.

* * *

When I awoke, I wasn't sure which sensation to attend to first: the sound of Laria's pacing or the feel of something touching my leg. I jerked away violently when I realized it wasn't some*thing*. It was some*one*.

Laria placed her hands on my shoulders. "Lie back and relax."

I looked down the bed. Finton's hands were raised, a surgical tool in one and a threaded needle in the other. Panic rose in my chest and tightened my throat.

"What's going on?"

"Your little excursion left you injured," she said. She nodded at Finton to continue, but he looked at me for confirmation.

I glanced down at my leg and saw a jagged wound running from mid-calf to ankle. A wave of nausea crept up my throat at the sight of my own blood, and I settled back into the pillows to recover my composure.

"Go on," I managed to squeak out.

The moment he touched my leg, a wave of pain burned up my leg. I cried out, tears slipping from my closed eyes. Laria squeezed my hand and dabbed my forehead with a damp cloth, whispering words of encouragement I was certain would become a lecture once the pain receded. Finton rustled through the black bag at the foot of the bed.

"Here," he said. He cupped the back of my head and brought a glass vial to my mouth. "It will dull the pain."

I sipped the clear, thick liquid. Warmth spread through my body like a blanket in a snowstorm. Laying back on the bed felt like falling against a cloud. I sighed, my lips curling into a contented smile. When Finton resumed tending my wound, there was no pain.

"What were you doing in the tree?" Laria asked quietly.

"Getting an apple." My words were slow and slurred.

"You could have asked for help."

"I wanted to do it myself. You would have."

"Perhaps. But you're not an expert climber like I am."

"Maybe I wanted to prove I am."

"You have no need to prove such things."

I peered at Laria through heavily lidded eyes, blurring her face at the edges. "Don't you think it was awfully lucky that Olim saved me?"

"Very lucky. We owe him a great debt. He's certainly proven himself valuable."

"It was very brave, don't you think?"

Laria grinned crookedly and agreed it was indeed brave. A heavy fog settled in my brain, and I could barely lift my eyelids.

I sighed. "I don't know how I shall thank such a noble deed."

"I'm sure he will not require your thanks."

"He'll think I'm ungrateful if I don't." The words dripped lazily from my lips, oozing from my mouth like honey from a spoon.

"Whatever you feel is best, my dear one."

I drowsily opened one eye and peered at Finton. "How much longer?"

"Oh, no you don't!" Laria said. "You're staying in this bed until you're healed."

"Is that really necessary?"

Finton's attention darted to Laria then back at me. "It's perhaps not necessary to stay in bed until you're completely healed, but you shouldn't strain yourself for at least a few days. And thereafter you will require the aid of a walking stick until the stitches can be removed."

I squinted. "Which will be when?"

"Two weeks," he muttered before going back to work.

"Uhhhhh! How unfair."

"Enough of that," Laria said. She bit her lip to keep from laughing, and I crossed my arms petulantly. "You're beginning to sound like me."

"A tragedy in itself."

Laria chuckled and rose to leave, but I grasped her arm.

"Could you send Olim in please?"

"I will," she said. She shifted her attention to Finton. "Thank you for attending to my sister. Your skills are appreciated."

While waiting for Olim, I stared up at the ceiling and fidgeted while mentally composing a speech that would properly convey how important his actions meant to me and my family. Finton meticulously stitched my leg, occasionally trying to engage me in conversation. I ignored him and he gave up when I didn't answer.

A rapid knock echoed from the door, and with as much volume I could muster called out, "Come in!"

My pulse quickened and my already warmed cheeks pulsed with heat when Olim stepped inside. He paused briefly when he saw Finton before striding forward.

"I'm glad to see you're on the mend," Olim said.

"I'm so thankful for what you've done for me, Olim." I stretched a hand toward him.

He took it and sat beside me. His palm was sweaty, and his cheeks were pink. He must have been training with the other soldiers.

"It was my duty. I was happy to help," he said.

"Duty? It was more than that, surely?"

His color deepened and he glanced at Finton before leaning closer.

"Of course," he whispered. "When I heard Lady Derville scream your name, I was afraid for your safety."

I squeezed his hand, and my cheeks hurt from smiling. "I'm so lucky to have such a devoted friend."

Olim smiled awkwardly and shifted in his seat.

Something sharp pinched my leg, and I hissed in pain.

"Finished," Finton said. "Apologies for my roughness. I didn't want the knot to unravel." He busied himself with packing his supplies back into his bag while I inspected the neat sutures. I probed the area, but the pain was minimal, and soon Finton was covering the wound with a clean bandage.

"Will it scar?" Olim asked.

"It will, but faintly," Finton said. His movements were sure, and his tone was terse. He looked up at me, and his hard expression softened. "Rest yourself. Too much activity may cause the sutures to strain the tissues and possibly break."

Olim sneered. "Could you perhaps be a little less graphic and more tactful?"

"Apologies, again. I will tend to your sensitivity when we next speak." He placed a vial on the nightstand. "For any further pain you may experience. Take only a sip at a time and no more than once every four hours." Finton left, the slamming door vibrating throughout the room.

"He seems cross," I said.

"Don't pay him mind. People like that run hot and cold and you can't predict it."

I rubbed the crease between my eyebrows and peered at Olim from underneath my hand. "I should have thanked him,"

"Don't bother. His rudeness negated any thanks he might have deserved."

I dropped my hand and squinted at him, confusion mixing with the haze of the pain elixir. It wasn't like Olim to express such harsh opinions. Could his general dislike of people living in the capital be the cause or was his cynicism more personal?

"Let's not speak of him any longer," he said, waving away my concerns. "Let's talk about how we're going to keep you from going mad from lying in bed for the next several days."

Lying in bed was more difficult than expected. By the next day I was anxious and bored. I tried to rest, but I wasn't very tired once I regained my strength. I completed an embroidery project within a few hours and was halfway through a new book. I'd drawn pictures of every bauble and piece of furniture in the room and sketched rough drafts of family portraits. How many hours *were* in a day?

The children were permitted to visit if they stayed off the bed, and I was delighted to hear their voices and laughter as they talked over each other and inundated me with questions.

Alyx bounced up and down on the edge of the bed and pointed. "Can we see it? Can we see it?"

I lifted the bed covers to reveal the bandaged leg.

"Don't touch," Laria said. "It hurts Aunt Ula."

"That why you told me not to climb trees?" Rian asked.

"Yes," I said. "I should have listened to your mother."

Laria read to me for several hours on the second day, which I insisted wasn't necessary since she was sure to have other important matters needing her attention.

"You're my sister," she said matter-of-factly. "What could be more important?"

"Continue then." I snuggled into the warm blankets and closed my eyes to listen.

Laria read: "Arella boldly stepped into the captain's quarters at his beckoning gesture. The sound of the lock engaging sent a signal straight to her heart, quickening her pulse as she realized this would be the last time she could look herself in the mirror and see a maid." Laria paused for a drink of water and I took the opportunity to do the same.

"'What service do you require of me, my lady?' the captain asked. Arella worried that if she spoke, she would lose her resolve or stumble over her words, so instead she loosened the tie of her robe and allowed the thin satin fabric to fall to the floor, exposing her alabaster skin in all its glory to the captain's admiring gaze." Laria paused, her cheeks rosy, and she glanced away from the book and smiled secretively.

"What is it?" I asked.

She shook her head as if to clear her thoughts. "Nothing. Just remembering something. I think we're about to get to the salacious bits."

I took a deep breath. "I'm ready."

"Are you sure? You look like you're preparing to have a tooth pulled."

I released the strong grip I had on the comforter and my lips quirked.

"I'm fine," I said. "Continue."

"The captain's eyes darkened. Arella's chest heaved, and her heart pounded. Her breaths came out in shuddering gasps as the captain approached, his steps confident. He unbuttoned his shirt and discarded it carelessly. He hovered over Arella. 'Do you know what you're doing?' he asked. Still not trusting her voice, she nodded and placed a trembling hand against his well-muscled physique. His skin was hot and moist, as was the juncture between her legs."

Laria had to take a moment to collect herself after that line.

"Her hands moved up his chest, reveling in the smooth skin. The captain placed his hands over hers and directed her movements downwards, along his chest and tight abdomen, to the edge of his breeches. He loosened his belt and allowed the garment to slide down his strong thighs, introducing Arella to her first view of an unclothed man."

Abruptly, Laria shut the book and set it aside.

"Now what?" I asked.

"That's all for now," she said. "We'll resume from there tomorrow."

She bustled out of the room in a swirl of skirts before I could protest. I fell against the pillows in a huff and stared at the door as if I could will her to return with the force of my thoughts. She claimed no duties were more important than me, but her flushed cheeks and hasty departure suggested otherwise. Laria may be a mother of five, but as a young woman of only twenty-four, her desire for her husband was a duty she'd no sooner forgo than food.

Sunshine streamed in my room and across my bed, warming my body and making me wish I could be enjoying the outside. I reached into the light and danced my fingers as if they were trailing through the waters of the Rhyvor. Were we at home, I could be sitting on the banks now, watching the children splash in the shallows trying to catch dragonflies. Laria would be sitting on a blanket with Lilias weaving flowers in her braid, and Risteard would be watching over Sulwen throwing rocks and clapping with joy at the resulting splash that tickled her face. I dropped my arm on the bed with a sigh, frustrated that the fantasy could not completely assuage my ennui.

Someone knocked, and I called out excitedly for them to come in. After a week of being bedridden, I was so desperate for company Eve Ekhane could be behind the door and I would gladly welcome her presence.

Finton entered the room with his black bag and an annoyingly large smile.

"Good afternoon," he said.

"What's so good about it?" I grumbled.

He peered at me over his glasses. "Growing weary of your confinement?"

"Now I understand why the queen always insisted on forgoing a similar imprisonment during the end of her pregnancies."

"Ha! I'm not surprised." He indicated my leg. "May I?"

"Please do." I lifted the bedcovers along with the bottom hem of my nightdress. "And tell me good news!"

"I'll do my best." He carefully removed the bandage. I hissed when he pulled off the last layer sticking to my skin, and he froze, wincing with me.

"I'm sorry." He cleansed the area and inspecting it closely.

"Tell me honestly." I took a deep breath. "Will I keep the leg?"

"This time." He straightened and began replacing instruments into his bag. "I think it's safe for you to walk. Slowly. With the aid of a stick."

"Thank you! I could hug you for that."

"Yes, well." His face flushed and he cleared his throat. I quirked my head at him as he struggled to compose himself. "Er…by the way. We don't just go chopping off body parts anymore. Medical science has made some incredible advances in the last several years."

"Oh?"

"We never had a chance to continue our discussion. If you're still interested, you can find me most of the time in the library when I'm not tending to patients. We might find something to capture your attention, especially since your activities will be limited for the next few weeks. If you wish to, that is."

"I will listen to whatever you have to say as long as I don't have to do it from this bed."

"At your convenience then." He bowed and hastily left the room.

Chapter 5

Cautiously, I moved down the corridor acting nonchalantly whenever anyone passed. Freedom was close at hand, and I could practically taste the outside world. Excitedly, I stepped forward to pass into the vestibule, and I nearly collided with a large figure blocking my path.

"What do you think you're doing?"

"Olim! I was just—"

"You were just walking around on your bad leg." He wrapped an arm across my shoulders to support my body weight. My cheeks grew hot at his proximity, and I mumbled that I was allowed to be out of bed now.

"On whose authority?" he demanded.

"Finton said—"

"Oh, *Finton* said! He told you your leg was healed enough for you to run around outside?"

"Not exactly. But he did say I could start walking around with aid."

"Of which you have none. Come, I'll take you back to your room until the queen decides you're well enough to venture out."

My disappointment was acute, and I spent the rest of the afternoon pouting. It was comforting to know so many people cared for my welfare, but I found the contradictory orders frustrating.

The next morning, Laria appeared within an hour of being summoned looking every bit the concerned sister.

"What is the matter, dear one?" She clutched my hand. "Is your leg giving you pain?"

I took a cleansing breath. "Yesterday, Dr. Ekhane said I could walk with the aid of a stick. Olim said I required your approval beforehand. May I please have it? I'm going mad."

She laughed. "Of course! I'll have one brought up right away and you'll be out of this bed in no time. I don't think I'll need to remind you not to push yourself, do I?"

I shook my head vigorously.

"If you're feeling well enough, Efram has arranged a ceremony in a few days. Apparently, some robe-wearing dignitary is going to bestow the blessings of ancestors on the children or some such nonsense."

"Spoken like a true queen accepting the ways of her people."

She narrowed her eyes, but a flush of shame colored her cheeks. I crossed my arms and raised an eyebrow in a perfect imitation of Mother. She looked away with a resigned sigh.

"You're right, of course," she said. "It's an Ilano tradition and I shouldn't make light of it. That's why I need you there. To make sure I behave."

"Isn't that what your husband is for?"

"He has more to worry about than making sure his wife doesn't embarrass him."

I grinned. "It is an all-consuming task."

Olim appeared shortly thereafter proudly presenting me with a oak walking stick intricately carved to resemble flowering branches topped with a round, ripe apple. We made our way slowly along the hallway, my weight supported on the cane while he kept his arms outstretched in case I faltered. We garnered a few stares, which was embarrassing, but a few kind residents offered words of encouragement that brightened my mood. We stepped into the afternoon sunshine, warm and heavy with the scent of greenery. The gardens at the back of the capitol building bordered the exercising yard, and several men were out weathering their magnificent birds. Black wings were stretched out to absorb the sun's rays. I was never brave enough to approach one closely enough to touch it, but Laria said their feathers were quite soft. My feet sank into the lush grass as we strolled, the pain in my leg inconsequential compared to the elation I felt at being outdoors.

"Is the pain very great?" Olim asked.

"Not at all. Thank you again for doing this, Olim. It's good to feel the sun on my face again."

"I can't imagine what it must be like to be so confined."

"Unbearable. I can only embroider so many handkerchiefs before becoming horribly bored."

"I'm sure you'll be dancing again in no time! There's a grand Capital Ball being held in a few weeks signaling the beginning of harvest. It would be a shame for you to miss it."

"I do love to dance. It seems like forever since I enjoyed the pleasure."

"And you will, even if I have to carry you around the dance floor."

"That would certainly make it awkward for whomever I'm dancing with!"

"If he's a true gentleman, he'll be more concerned with your comfort than his. If that proves too much for the men of the Ilano court, then I suppose you'll have to spend the entire night dancing only with me."

The thought of spending an evening in Olim's arms left a strange feeling in my stomach I couldn't account for. I leaned against a tree when a wave of dizziness flooded me, and my chest tightened.

"Ula? Are you all right?"

I swallowed the tension in my throat. "I'm fine."

Olim wasn't convinced. "Perhaps you've walked too far today."

"No! I'm all right, I promise. I would like to continue."

"You shouldn't push yourself." He directed me back toward the building. "You need to rest now."

"Olim, please!"

But he was insistent, and I couldn't resist him even at my strongest. Resignedly, I allowed him to lead me back to my room, but I didn't make it very easy for him. I dragged my feet the whole way, and he practically had to carry me. By the time we got to my room, he all but pushed me into bed and propped my cane against the door.

"Rest now," he said. "Tomorrow we'll go out again for a few minutes longer if you're feeling up to it."

"You can't make me stay here!"

His shoulders slumped, and his expression softened. "No, but I hope you'll listen. I care about your comfort."

I focused on my fingers as I fidgeted with the bedsheets. "I know."

"I promise we'll go out again tomorrow." He smiled. "I would hate for you to overexert yourself and harm the wound."

"I understand."

I watched him leave and waited for his steps to recede down the hallway, but I didn't hear them. Of course, he *would* stand guard outside my room to make sure I complied. I crossed my arms and waited impatiently for my leg to heal.

Olim's consideration was pleasing, but I didn't like being coddled. I yearned for more freedom, and I wouldn't be granted such a request from my ever-vigilant knight.

It was very late in the evening, and I hoped he wouldn't be standing guard outside my room. I shuffled silently over to the door and opened it just enough to see into the hallway. Much to my relief, he was gone. The soft clicking of the cane and my shallow breaths echoed down the empty hallway as I slowly made my way to the library.

Laria and I shared a great love of reading, and gazing in awe at the rows of books filled me with a sense of ease. Within these walls, I could find relief from boredom amid the pages of these vast tomes. Beyond the bookcases, dark wooden tables and chairs were placed before a raised dais where professors lectured students on subjects from composition to botany. I ran my fingers along well-polished spines, reading the titles of works I'd never heard of. The room was cloaked in near darkness, the barest of light emanating from a few sconces along the wall. The soft tap of the cane and my reverent footsteps were the only sounds as I traversed the large space, reading a page here and there while I tried to decide which book to take back to my room. Idly, I pulled an elaborately filigreed tome from a shelf and started reading the first page.

When I neared the back of the vast space, a rustle of paper broke the silence. I stilled, listening intently, but heard nothing more. Carefully, I edged around the bookcase and looked toward the tables. A candle flickered over several open books, casting shadows over a hunched figure. I gritted my teeth and shuffled backward to avoid detection, reaching to replace the book back on the shelf. Before I could catch it, the book slipped from my trembling hand and hit the floor with a loud *thud.*

A chair scraped across the floor and a voice called, "Is someone there?"

Sheepishly, I peered around the corner. Finton stood at full alert before me, his appearance decidedly untidy. His hair was in disarray, and there were dark circles under his eyes. He'd shed his jacket and the sleeves of his undershirt were rolled up to his elbows, the laces at his neck loosened.

He relaxed when he recognized me and said, "Oh, it's you, Ula. You startled me."

"Sorry." I eased forward. "I didn't think anyone else would be here at this hour. I don't wish to disturb you."

"Not at all. Please." He indicated a chair.

I took a seat beside him, propping the cane against my hip, then gazed around at the books opened on the table. He moved some aside, explaining he had been studying. I slapped my palm down on one to stop him from closing it.

A disturbing drawing of a person without skin was covered two pages of text, the scarlet flesh raw and open. I gulped. "Is that what a person looks like on the inside?"

"Yes." He scooted closer to me. "The red parts covering bones are muscles."

"There's so many!"

"Every move you make, from lifting your arm to wiggling your toes, requires the contraction and relaxation of muscles."

"How many are there?"

"Hundreds. And everyone has the same. Whether man or woman, we all look similar underneath our skin."

"And this?" I pointed to another drawing. "Are those all bones?"

"The complete skeleton, yes."

"Do men and women have the same number of those?"

"They do, but there are subtle differences distinguishing both sexes. There have been fascinating studies on the subject."

His eyes glittered with enthusiasm, and I couldn't help but smile back. My eyes traveled around the open pages with drawings and texts detailing the inner workings of the human body.

"You've read a great deal, but I'm sure you've seen many interesting things in person."

"Some."

I detected a trace of irritation in his voice, and I frowned.

"It can be difficult studying to be a surgeon in Ilano. There is only so much to learn from pictures and firsthand accounts."

"I don't understand."

"To be a really accomplished surgeon, a man needs to experience and see things for himself. To study real specimens. There are a few to be had here, but Ilano in general does not allow dissection of human corpses."

The blood drained from my face, and I swayed. "W-what?"

Finton placed a steadying hand on my shoulder. "I'm so sorry! That was tactless of me." He squeezed my shoulder, and I offered a weak smile. "Allow me to explain. Umm...when you learn to ride, someone explains the dynamics and demonstrates for you, correct?"

"Yes," I said in a tremulous voice.

"What if that was all you were allowed? Would you expect to become an expert rider?"

"Not without being able to ride myself."

"Exactly! You practice, perhaps on a gentle mount, before tackling a wilder animal. Therein lies my frustration. I'm not allowed to study real human bodies and am expected to be an expert merely by reading lines in a book. It's an important foundation, but without experience, I can never truly be a good surgeon."

"But you're a doctor. Surely you've garnered some experience?"

"Yes, but not enough. I want to be able to see organs and vessels in situ in order to better understand their function and how to repair them. Such things are not permitted here because it's considered disrespectful. A soul cannot pass beyond the veil if the body is dissected. At the great medical institution in Hrgun, however..." His voice trailed away, and he became lost in his own thoughts, his features a mixture of melancholy and longing.

"I've heard Hrgun boasts many institutions of higher learning as well as universities for artists and musicians."

He shook his head sharply. "Yes. Hrgun developed an incredible city where people of all professions and areas of study can gather to hone their crafts and perfect their skills."

"Have you ever been there?"

"No, never. I wish to someday, but Fynn says Father can't afford for me to leave Ilano."

"I'm sure he would miss you." I laid a hand on his arm. It was warm, and the coarse hairs tickled my fingers.

His eyes locked on my hand where it touched his skin. Trepidation tingled up my body, and I snatched my hand away. Awkwardly, I shifted away from him and hoped he would forget my forwardness.

"And I would miss *him*," he said. "But I suspect my brother is using Father's feelings as an excuse to keep me here under this thumb."

"Why would he do that? Doesn't he want you to pursue your dream of becoming a surgeon?"

"Fynn has never approved of my choices. He would prefer I stay at home and tend the family estate."

"Well, that's not so terrible. Your family estate is important, and he probably wishes for the family to take care of it together."

He grinned. "A pretty thought, but his true motive is he wants me to stay home so he doesn't have to. He aspires to one day become Lord Protector and cannot be bothered with such small matters as sowing and harvesting."

"If he has his own hopes for the future, surely he cannot fault you for having your own?"

"Not all siblings are supportive of one another. Fynn has always placed his own needs above everyone else's."

"I'm sorry."

"No, I must apologize. I shouldn't have talked about my brother like that. Our family quarrels aren't something you should worry about."

Finton regarded the open books with a resigned expression. He had ambitions that may never be realized, and I sympathized with his plight. He was an intelligent man, and it was a shame his talents would be wasted in the orchards. Laria had been protective of me since we were children and was always loving, kind, and supportive. It was a new and interesting perspective to meet siblings who were not dedicated to one another as we were.

"Can you speak to your father directly? Perhaps if he supports your aspirations, he can speak to Fynn on your behalf."

"Father has enough to occupy him at present. I do not wish to trouble him with our petty squabbles."

"It isn't petty!" I insisted a little too loudly. I blushed furiously and he blinked several times in stunned silence. I continued in a quieter tone, "I mean, your decisions regarding your future are not something that should be considered so lightly."

He smiled warmly. "If my brother defended me as passionately as you, I would be in Hrgun already. But alas, I must bide my time and wait until my brother tires of watching me mope."

If I were in his position, I don't think I'd bear the disappointment gracefully. I yawned audibly, and I covered my mouth in embarrassment.

"I've kept you talking quite late," he said. "Do you need assistance getting back to your room?"

I shook my head, but when I placed the slightest amount of weight on my injured leg, I winced, squeezing my eyes tightly.

He stood, his arms hovering toward me in case I needed support, and asked if I was sure.

I nodded emphatically with a tight-lipped smile and hobbled out of the room. Finton watched me lean heavily on the cane. I avoided his gaze, not wanting him to see how painful my movements were. When I stumbled, I caught myself and leaned against the wall. Finton took a step toward me, but I didn't ask for help. With my leg throbbing, I made the arduous journey back to my room, and though I knew I would pay for it in the morning, I was satisfied to have accomplished the distance on my own.

The exertion and liquid medication on my nightstand kept me in bed until well past breakfast. Not even the maid who attended to my morning ablutions could rouse me. When I finally rolled over and stretched my aching muscles, the sun was high and streaming rays of warmth into the room. Someone knocked, and I sat up in surprise, clutching the bedcovers to my chest.

"Yes?" I called out. "Who is it?"

"It's Laria. May I come in?"

"Of course!"

"I heard you were still asleep." Worry etched her features. "Are you unwell?"

"No, just tired."

"When you're dressed, would you like to take a walk with me?"

"What about Olim? He usually accompanies me on my daily walks."

"Would you rather share your company with him?" she asked with a raised eyebrow.

"No! That's not to mean I don't appreciate him. I like spending time with you, too. Not more than *him*, but it's different. Oh, bother." I covered my face in embarrassment over my befuddled thoughts.

"Don't stress yourself, little gem. If you would prefer to wait for Olim, I won't be offended."

"That's not what I meant at all!" I tossed the bedclothes aside and Laria helped me to my feet. "Let's forget about it. Please?"

"If you wish." Laria was holding back laughter, and I tried my best to ignore her. Laria often found humor in situations I either didn't understand or would rather avoid. She started to help me dress, and I diverted her attention by remarking our roles were now reversed.

"Do you even remember how to dress yourself?" I teased.

"After years of being a lady-in-waiting, I think the ability will come back to me."

"Laria, I know you don't like to talk about your time serving the former princess."

She tensed and her fingers paused on my stays.

"No, I don't." Her tone was firm, a warning I shouldn't continue, but there was something I had to ask.

"I don't wish to know what horrible things they did to you. But was there ever a time when it wasn't completely miserable?"

"Would it soothe your heart to imagine such a time?"

A tremor shuddered up my spine. "I hate to think of you suffering for the entirety of those three years."

"It's true the hardships outnumber any pleasant memories of those years. The princess was extremely cruel, as were her friends and allies. There were some moments I recall with less abhorrence, and a few that give me pleasure. None of them originate from my duties to the royal family."

"How did you manage to plan a rebellion without getting caught?"

She shrugged. "Princess Caelyn thought I was deaf, mute, and stupid. How could such a waif be capable of intrigue?"

We silently walked out of the capitol building arm in arm while I contemplated the bravery of my sister, a trait I could never boast. She'd always been resilient and strong-willed, and her determination helped save Praed.

We strolled in the gardens, the sun hot overhead, until my leg ached. We sat underneath the shade of a large tree with branches heavily laden with quivering silver leaves. A slight breeze stirred the fine hairs framing Laria's face and billowed my skirts around my ankles. She closed her eyes in contentment, and I stole a few moments to study my sister's serene countenance. Freckles dusted the bridge of her nose and cheekbones, and the corners of her eyes were already lined from years of unrestrained laughter. Her lips were full and pink, as was desirable, but her nose was small and rounded instead of straight and sharp. Strands of gold glittered amid her bountiful ginger hair. And her eyes, the color of grass at dusk, held the promise of adventures. She'd never been considered a handsome woman nor even a pretty girl. In my opinion, she had been sorely underrated by our parents and general acquaintances. Laria possessed an attraction that went beyond the canvas to the uniqueness of her soul—a wild, fiercely independent, and brilliant spirit that transcended the classical idea of beauty. She was gorgeous, though she would never believe it even if I told her every day for the rest of her life.

"Would you change any of it?" My voice carried on the wind, mingling with the fluttering of leaves.

Laria slowly opened her eyes, and she turned to me with an enigmatic smile.

"Not a single day. Every harsh word, every heartbreak, every cruelty, and every death brought us to this moment. I wouldn't change that for the world."

Chapter 6

At dawn, I joined Laria and Risteard in a ceremony called "The Blessing of the Crop." We crammed into the small building beside the Capitol, the square stones matching the shade of sun-soaked sand. Though outside it appeared unassuming, the heavy doors ornately carved with twisting vines opened onto a vast space with an arched ceiling and rows of benches. At the far end on a raised platform was a table covered in carvings, goblets, and candles. Behind it, several plushy upholstered chairs curved along the wall. As guests of honor, the three of us sat among prominent dignitaries, including the Lord Protector, on those chairs. With the rising sun, light streamed through the stained glass windows above our heads, bathing those seated before us in shades of red, green, yellow, and orange.

A woman draped in flowing robes in shades of gray stood in front of the table, raised her arms, and asked for silence. Everyone bowed their heads, and the woman lit the candles, reached into a bowl, and dropped a pinch of powder over each flame. The pungent scent of flowers, earth, and musk filled my nostrils, and I buried my nose in the crook of my elbow to stifle a sneeze. Laria huffed out her nose like a horse trying to dislodge an errant fly. Risteard surreptitiously nudged her with his knee, and she rolled her eyes skyward.

"We ask for a healthy harvest," the woman said, and I focused on paying better attention. "May the soil below us be fertile, our crops plentiful, and the rains nourish us. We ask our ancestors to help us reap the benefits of their work, which we continue to this day. May our good wishes channel into our hands that they may pick the best fruit. May our thoughts reach into the ether beyond the veil and bring back good fortune. May our first sips of cider be sweet with it."

She lowered her head, and in the ensuing silence, I glanced at Laria. Her head was bowed respectfully, but her fingers drummed in her lap. I reached over to steady them, but Risteard beat me to it. The woman burned more herbs and walked around the room waving the smoke over the people. The overpowering odor clung to my clothes, the scent lingering in my nose into the afternoon.

Under the low-hanging boughs of a pyrus tree, its long, silver leaves casting cool shade over the warm ground, I sat with my protective knight reading a history on the Ilano Harvest Festival. Among us, the children darted between trees and bushes playing hide-and-seek, their laughter mingling with the singing of birds. A slight sheen of sweat covered my brow, but a cool breeze made the afternoon temperatures bearable. Olim was stretched out on his side next to me watching the children frolic while their nurses looked on vigilantly. Laria complained the fine weather was wasted in endless council meetings, but today she happily toured prominent estates supplying the capital with goods for the upcoming celebration.

"Have you learned about every apple grown in Ilano?" Olim's question pulled me out of my reverie.

"Hmm?"

Olim laughed at my dazed tone, and I nodded and buried my face in the book.

"Perfect. You'll be able to hold a conversation with the elite farmers of Ilano."

"Do I sense sarcasm?"

"Not at all. Crops are generally the only thing farmers can talk about."

I dropped the book in my lap. "Why must you be so cynical?"

"I'm sorry. It's endearing that you're taking the trouble to learn about Ilano, and the people will appreciate it. Don't listen to me."

"Why do you look upon your own people so negatively?"

"It's not *all* the people. Those who work the fields are perfectly respectable. I'm allowing my personal feelings to influence my regard toward the estates again."

"Tell me," I said.

He sighed heavily and lay back on the thick cushion of grass, his arms crossed behind his head. I settled comfortably next to him, propping my head up on my elbow. Above us, birds chittered in the tree, their songs sharp and lilting. The boys' footsteps pounded and scraped as they ran, their shouts mixing in a cacophony of joy. Sulwen's mischievous giggle echoed in the distance followed by Duveesa's pleas to hold still. The other nurses' murmured conversation moved slowly as they wandered among the flowers keeping a vigilant eye on the princes.

"My father worked in an orchard from the time he could lift a spade," Olim said.

"You told me. He's done much to support his family."

"He worked from sunrise to sunset for the same estate for years, learning everything about the soil, the perfect temperatures, the right nutrients to ensure a plentiful crop, and every nuance imaginable to increase his master's profits. You would think after years of such dedicated service my father's work would be rewarded, but those who possess the land and those who tend it have very different views."

"Your father was not compensated fairly?"

"Not remotely. He never took a day for himself in his decades of service, and yet not once has he been acknowledged with the credit he's due."

"Perhaps he doesn't require such accolades. Perhaps the only reward he requires is the comfort of his family."

"My father might agree with you, but I'm certain my mother would have appreciated living more comfortably, especially once her aching hands made weaving more and more painful."

"Have you seen them since we arrived?"

He turned away. "No."

"May I ask why?"

"My duties here have occupied my time."

"Olim, are you avoiding your parents?"

"Not entirely. I'm mostly avoiding a lecture from Father."

"You're in the service of the king! He should be proud of you!"

"Mother is. She wanted more for me than toiling in the orchards, but Father wished for me to follow in his footsteps. He considers manual labor the epitome of honor in Ilano."

"Surely you can set your differences aside and enjoy a reunion?"

"You amaze me. After everything you've been through, you're still so optimistic."

"I have to be since you're so gloomy."

"We complement each other well."

My stomach fluttered and my grin faltered. I lay back and focused on the shivering leaves and swaying branches to avoid Olim's intense stare.

"Maybe I'll follow your advice," he said. "If you would consider joining me so I could introduce you?"

"Surely you would prefer they meet the king and queen? I'm just a lady-in-waiting. That's not very impressive."

"I would like them to meet the king and queen so they understand the importance of my position in Praed. But I also want them to meet my friend."

"Very well, since you're so insistent."

Our voices fell silent, and we became absorbed in our own thoughts, listening to the wind in the trees and the laughter of my nieces and nephews. Duveesa's calm voice grew closer, and I sat up to see her leading Lilias by the hand. The little girl's face brightened when she saw me, and I opened my arms wide to accept her sweet hugs.

"She wanted to sit with her Auntie Ula if that's okay?" Duveesa asked with a sideways glance at Olim.

"Of course!" I gathered the little princess onto my lap and opened the book to the illustrations of the different varieties of apples grown across the country.

Duveesa curtseyed meekly and returned to the other children, her gaze lingering briefly on Olim.

"Stop it," I said.

"What?" Olim asked.

"You're watching me."

"I just wanted to be sure she didn't sit on your wound."

"She's not." I met his eye. "I can manage some things on my own, you know."

"I know." He looked away.

"You've been very overprotective since my fall. I appreciate your help, but I admit that sometimes the attention can be...overwhelming."

"I know. I'm sorry. It's just...I feel responsible."

"For what?"

"For your injuries. I should have been more vigilant."

"Is that what this has been about? Olim, it was my own stupid fault. Please don't feel you need to compensate for some imaginary error on *your* part."

"I don't wish for the king and queen to find me wanting."

"They don't. They haven't questioned your abilities. The queen has been nothing but grateful." I squeezed his shoulder affectionately. "Can you stand down, just a little? I'm doing much better now and don't need to be coddled quite so much." I shook him lightly and chuckled when he grinned sheepishly.

"If you insist." He resumed his relaxed position in the grass.

After several minutes of sitting quietly in my lap, Lilias propelled herself forward with a sharp cry. Fear shuddered through me and I reached out to catch her, then looked up to see the reason for the outburst. Laria was stalking toward us, her features grim. Lilias hurried to her mother, and Laria lifted and squeezed the child in a desperate hug. I tapped Olim on the shoulder. He lazily peered out from underneath his arm, saw the queen, and scrambled to his feet before helping me up.

Laria's troubled gaze met mine. "Come." She beckoned me inside, her lips trembling and skin pale.

She marched determinedly through the gardens, stopping briefly to deposit Lilias into Duveesa's arms. The nurse gave me an inquisitive look as we passed, and I shrugged. Behind her, Risteard was surrounded by the boys jumping around and talking over each other. His eyes followed Laria with evident concern, increasing my apprehension. My leg throbbed when I quickened my pace, but I didn't slow until we were instilled in Laria's chambers.

"Laria," I breathed. I sat down to catch my breath. "What is the matter?"

She paced the room, flinging layers of clothing onto the bed and adornments on the vanity. Her agitation made me nervous. Laria never lost her composure, especially in front of *me*. She collapsed onto the chaise, and I grasped her trembling hand.

"I saw her. I thought after all this time it wouldn't bother me, but look how pathetic I am." Her voice was so quiet I barely heard.

"Saw who?"

She stared blankly ahead. "Who do you think? *Her.*"

My eyes widened as realization dawned.

"Caelyn?"

Her eyelids fluttered closed and she nodded.

"Where?"

"We visited an estate in the west harvesting golden apples. We were touring the orchards, and the manager swept his arm over the workers and boasted some of the heartiest labor in the region. Then I saw her. She was dressed in soiled linens filling baskets with rotten fruit, but I knew her immediately. And it was as if I were her servant again, too terrified to cross her path."

"After everything you suffered, you can't expect to forget so easily. It's only natural for you to be afraid."

"No, it's not!" She rose abruptly and paced the room. "I'm no longer her servant! I'm her queen!"

"Just because you wear a crown doesn't mean you're invincible. Yes, you escaped her, but you're still human with memories and feelings. You cannot expect that to change the moment you're free."

She sat down heavily, crossing her arms. I pulled her close, hoping to break through the wall she raised.

"Did she see you?" I asked.

She shook her head. "I saw her from a distance, then feigned illness and insisted on returning."

"Does Risteard know? He looked very worried."

Laria lowered her head in shame. "No. He tried to ask, but I rode away from the estate and wouldn't answer."

As if summoned, Risteard threw open the door and rushed over to us. Laria's eyes glistened with tears as she gazed up into his anxious face.

"What's wrong? Are you ill?" he asked in a gentle tone he often affected when speaking to the children.

"No," Laria sobbed before hiding her face in her hands.

Risteard knelt before us and tried to coax her into explaining herself, but Laria was incapable of speaking.

"Did she say anything to you?" I didn't recognize the desperation in his voice. My brother-in-law was strong, collected, but my sister's agony reduced him from a king to simply a husband.

I rubbed Laria's back to ease the building tension. "She's upset because she saw Caelyn."

His voice dropped to its lowest cadence. "Oh."

He took Laria's face between his hands and wiped away her tears. "She no longer has power over you," he said.

"That's precisely why I'm crying!" Laria yelled. "It's been years, but when I saw her, I couldn't move and started trembling."

"I told you not to trouble yourself about that," I said. "You've won, but that doesn't erase the pain of what she did to you. Allow yourself time to heal as you would a wound."

Laria continued to weep, and I didn't know how to comfort her. Before I could try, Risteard leaned forward and pressed his forehead against hers. Her cries instantly ceased, replaced by shuddering breaths. For several seconds they remained thus, until Laria calmed down and wiped the tears from her face.

"I hate that she can still make me feel weak," Laria said.

"You should heed your sister's wise words," Risteard said, making me smile.

"I know." Her lips quivered in a tremulous smile.

"Are you recovered?" Risteard asked.

Laria took a deep breath and said, "Yes."

"Good." Risteard rose and put his hands on his hips. "Because you're going back."

"What?" Laria cried and stood to face him.

"You can't allow her to affect you so much that you abandon your duties as queen. Doing so effectively allows her to continue having control."

Laria's green eyes flashed, and I scooted away from their impending argument.

"If nothing else," Risteard continued, "you can see what effect your presence has on *her* and remember you're the one who holds the power now."

"And if she's as defiant as ever?" Laria asked.

"She has no friends, no family, and no allies. What reason does she have to feel superior to you?"

"Her own self-importance?"

"Even if that were the case, it's not as if she can voice her opinion." Risteard's cerulean eyes darkened as he spoke, and Laria smirked in self-satisfaction.

"Perhaps I can handle a meeting knowing she's eternally silenced."

In the ensuing lull, I crept out of the room, aware they may wish to continue conversing in private. I closed the door quietly behind me and edged down the hallway, encountering Olim pacing near the threshold.

"Is everything all right?" he asked.

"Yes," I said.

"You left this." He handed me the book I'd been reading.

"Thank you. I'm going to return this to the library. I'll see you later?"

Olim eyed me dubiously and I reminded him he promised to lighten up. He sighed in resignation and extended his arm toward the library, bowing as I passed. I glanced over my shoulder. He was watching, but he didn't follow. It was a small measure of freedom, but it felt liberating.

When I entered the library, voices coming from the far end of the room alerted me to a class currently in session. Quietly, I shuffled around the bookcases, replaced the book where I found it, then snuck closer to listen. A strong voice projected over the room, and a crowd answered back, repeating a language I didn't understand. Based on the continued back and forth exchange, I concluded the students were learning how to speak the language. I edged around the corner of the last bookcase.

Finton stood at the front of the class beside a large black board with several words written on it. He pointed to each word in turn, pronouncing it so his students could repeat it accurately. I gazed around at the faces, all young, perhaps late teenaged boys and girls. Some were eagerly echoing Finton's voice while others appeared bored, a typical representation of children their age. An hourglass at the front of the room trickled the last bits of sand into the base, and the students shifted to gather their belongings. Finton glanced at the hourglass and declared the class dismissed, reminding them of an assignment due by week's end. I ducked behind the bookcase, and the students filed past, too preoccupied in their conversations to notice me. I turned to follow.

"Ula?" Finton called out. "I did see you, didn't I?"

His uncertain tone made me pause, and I inched backwards until I could see around the bookcases again.

He smiled when he saw me. "I thought that was you lurking at the back."

"I wasn't lurking," I said. "I didn't want to disturb you."

"You're always welcome to join us," he said. "I was giving a lesson on the ancient Ilano language. Many of our early texts are written in the lost language, and anyone who wishes to pursue a diplomatic career must learn it."

My eyebrows rose in surprise. "All of those young people want to be diplomats?"

"Unfortunately, no. Some may have a legitimate interest, but most are being forced to learn by parents who hope their child will become an ambassador or council member."

"Ah." I wandered among the tables, running my fingers over the dark wood. "What else do you teach?"

"History to the young people and biological science to adults wishing to pursue careers in medicine, farmers wanting to better understand their crops, and others simply curious like you."

"Between teaching and being a doctor, you must be very busy."

"I can't bear to be idle." He gathered papers and books into a neat pile on the desk.

"Neither can I, but that seems to be all I've done these days."

"I should examine your injury. If it's healed, the sutures can be removed, and you can resume your duties."

I grinned excitedly at the thought, and without caring that at any moment someone could wander in and see me, I perched on the edge of a table and lifted the hem of my dress. Finton chuckled lightly and retrieved his black medical bag from behind the desk. He knelt in front of me and studied the wound, probing it carefully with his fingers.

"Any pain?" he asked, his tone serious.

I suppressed a giggle at the change in his demeanor and told him the pain was greatly diminished. He straightened, gestured for me to release my dress, and informed me the sutures needed to remain in place for another few days. My heart sank and my smile faded at this news. I mumbled a thank you and dropped to the floor, preparing to leave.

"Wait," he said. "I'm sorry to disappoint you. If it helps, you can start walking without the aid of the stick. It will help increase your strength."

"Thank you." I lay the stick against a table. Dejectedly, I limped toward the doors with Finton close behind.

"It won't be long until you can serve the queen again," he said. "At which time, you will be very busy. Perhaps too busy for yourself?"

I stopped and looked at him with furrowed brows, confused.

"You said once that as lady-in-waiting your time is not your own."

"Yes," I said.

"Well, you've been excused from those duties during your convalescence, effectively freeing you to do as you please."

"In a sense, perhaps. I've certainly filled my days however I wished for lack of anything else to do, though I still find myself bored."

"Maybe if we find something more stimulating to pass the time?"

"What did you have in mind?"

"Would you like to join me on my rounds today?" His expression reminded me of one of the children asking for a special treat and hoping the answer would be yes.

"I would need to ask the queen for permission. If she agrees, then I would very much like that."

His smile broadened, then he looked over my shoulder, searching.

"What of your shadow?" he asked. "Would he have to join us?"

"You mean Olim?" I glanced behind me, expecting the knight to be there. He wasn't, but I didn't doubt he was waiting outside the door.

"I suppose it would be for your own protection."

"Olim is very dedicated to my safety."

"A very honorable cause. I wouldn't wish to place you in danger. If your knight must accompany you, then of course he is welcome."

My mouth quirked in consideration. It would make me feel safer to have Olim with me, but what did I have to be afraid of? The thought of Finton and I alone caused a strange stirring in my stomach, but I couldn't decide if it was foreboding or excitement. Furthermore, it might be awkward for Olim to follow us around, but I also didn't want to hurt his feelings by asking him to remain in the capital.

"I'll ask the queen what she thinks," I said. "I better hurry because she was preparing to leave."

He bowed at my retreating form.

I didn't bother to check her room, knowing how insistent Risteard had been about continuing with their tours of estates. Olim appeared on my way to the stables, and I hurriedly told him I needed to see the queen.

"What's wrong?" he asked. "Did something happen? Have you been harmed?"

"Relax, Olim. I simply want permission to leave the capital."

"By yourself? When I promised I wouldn't hover over you anymore, I didn't expect for you to travel outside the city alone."

"I won't be alone." I was breathless when I reached the stables and hoped I wasn't too late.

"Have the king and queen been here?" I asked the stable master.

"They just left," he said.

My heart sank, and my disappointment at not being able to venture out was palpable.

"Did they happen to mention when they would return?"

The stable master shrugged. My shoulders slumped in defeat and I walked away, ignoring the man's bow. I was stuck until Laria returned.

"Where were you planning on going?" Olim asked.

"Out," I said. I ran a hand down the door frame, wincing as a splinter stuck in my palm.

"With whom, may I ask?"

I picked out the sliver, and a drop of blood welled up in stark contrast to my pale skin.

"Finton. He invited me to join him on his rounds today. I was hoping to enjoy an adventure outside the capital." I didn't notice the suspicious nature of Olim's tone until after I answered. I glanced up at him. His arms were crossed, his face red, and a vein stuck out on his forehead.

"To see sick people? What were you thinking? Were you planning on telling me? Were you even going to take me with you?"

"I was going to leave that decision to the queen." I didn't care for Olim's anger, no matter how well-intentioned it might be.

"But you didn't want me to come. You wanted some privacy? I suppose he told you to leave me behind?"

"It's not like that! He had no objections to you coming. Stop acting like a jealous fool, Olim. You're still my friend and no one will come between us."

Olim lowered his head like a dog who soiled the carpet. His overprotectiveness was irritating, but I knew it came from a place of friendship.

"My apologies," he said. "I know I'm overreacting. The thought of you being vulnerable worries me."

I patted his shoulder. "You can't be with me all the time."

"I know." He offered a crooked smile, and I smiled back with all the affection of a good friend.

"I promise not to do anything foolish. I will never travel alone or speak to strangers."

"A good start."

"It doesn't matter now." My hand slipped down his arm and I stared at the ground.

"I know you're restless and wish to join the queen. I hate to see you miserable." He hesitated, then glanced around and whispered, "Go."

"What?"

"If the queen returns before you do, I'll cover for you. Just be careful and don't catch some contagious disease."

I beamed at Olim and hugged him before I could stop myself.

"Thank you!" I gushed and bounced on the balls of my feet.

He pushed me off and turned away, but not before I glimpsed a rare blush. "You better hurry before I change my mind."

Without requiring further encouragement, I wobbled off to the library to meet Finton. I was elated beyond measure to leave the confines of the capitol, and not even my anxiety over meeting strangers was enough to restrain my excitement.

Chapter 7

Finton sat on the edge of a table, his legs hanging off the ground swinging in time to a beat only he could hear. He pinched his lower lip as he stared intently at the pages of a book open in his lap. He indeed could not remain idle, not even for a minute. He started at the sound of my approaching footsteps and slid to the ground.

"I assume based on your delightful expression that we may proceed?" he asked.

I nodded enthusiastically, choosing to keep quiet about the queen being unaware of this outing. He grabbed his black bag and extended his hand toward the door.

"I made a promise not to contract some horrible illness. Can you ensure my safety in this regard?" I raised an eyebrow and hoped I looked as stern as Mother.

"Not at all. That depends entirely on your ability to restrain yourself from inhaling when someone sneezes."

I curled my lip in disgust. "Ew."

He cocked his head to the side. "Too far?"

"Just a little."

"I seem to offer apologies to *you* more than any other person."

"I'm not offended, as I continually remind you. I will get used to your unique humor in time."

Finton possessed a simple two-person gig pulled by a stout cream-colored mare too short to be considered a horse yet too tall to be a pony. Her large feet shifted, and she munched apathetically as she was hitched to the small carriage. Her ears barely flicked backward when Finton assisted me into the seat.

"She seems very steady," I said as Finton took his place beside me and took up the reins.

"She's been carrying me on my rounds for years." He clicked the old mare forward. "Not a buck or a bite in her entire body. You'll never meet a more unflappable horse."

I closed my eyes and enjoyed the rhythmic pattern of clomping hooves and the comforting sway of the gig. The sun warmed my upturned face, and the smells of the city were replaced by the scent of grass and farmland. I breathed deeply and stretched my legs, placing my feet against the rail in front of me, feeling more relaxed than I had in over a week. Finton remained silent beside me, and I appreciated being able to sit and revel in my surroundings without feeling pressure to converse. When the gig came to a gentle stop, I opened my eyes to a modest stone farmhouse. An older woman with a small child on her hip emerged as we dismounted the gig.

"Dr. Ekhane!" she called. "Welcome!"

"Good day, Mrs. Neace. How is the patient today?"

"I'm not sure who's the worse for wear—him for his injuries or me for having to wait on him." The pair shared a companionable laugh before Finton turned to me.

"I'd like to introduce Miss Ula Audrey. She's—"

"So pleased to be here," I interrupted before he could reveal my title. The last thing I wanted was for my rank to intimidate her. "Dr. Ekhane was good enough to allow me to join him today. I hope I may be of assistance as opposed to a hindrance."

"Not at all, young lady," Mrs. Neace said, casting a cryptic glance at Finton. "Come in and I'll introduce my husband." She turned to the house, and Finton leaned over and whispered that Mr. Neace was the patient we were here to see.

"He suffered a broken arm after a fall from his horse. The bone went through his skin and became infected after the break was set," Finton explained.

His description sent a wave of bile up my throat and I swallowed to suppress it. Laria could watch the births of foals and muck through animal waste right before dinner without losing her appetite, but I was cursed with a sensitive stomach.

We entered the foyer, and to my right was a dining area with a long polished table in front of a large stone fireplace. Cabinets flanked the hearth, and on the far wall was a chest and two barrels. To my left was a parlor simply furnished with two well loved chaises under an open window. Beside one of the chairs was a basket filled with sewing supplies. We followed Mrs. Neace further into the house, and through a passageway I spied two young girls rolling dough into loaves. They looked up as we passed, but a sharp glare from Mrs. Neace was enough to return them to their work. We ascended the stairs near the back of the house and were led into a large bedroom where Mr. Neace lay on the bed propped up on several pillows. One of his arms was in a sling, and his face was fixed in a scowl as he stared out the window. His features brightened when Mrs. Neace announced our presence, and he sat straighter in bed.

"I'm so glad to see you, Doc," Mr. Neace said. "I'm hoping you'll give me a clean bill of health today."

I grinned to myself, understanding Mr. Neace's impatience. He appeared to be of middle age, though it was difficult to be certain as a large, bushy, graying beard covered most of his face. His amber eyes twinkled with anticipation, the laugh lines near his temples deepening. He was a barrel-chested man, his muscled physique carved by years of hard labor.

"Dr. Ekhane brought an assistant today, Armin, so you behave yourself," Mrs. Neace said.

"A *pretty* assistant!" Mr. Neace added, turning his weathered eyes to me.

His wife slapped her forehead with her palm and shook her head. Finton busied himself by removing bandages and jars from his bag, but a small smile suggested he heard the comment and found the exchange amusing.

"Miss Audrey has been kind enough to join us today. She, too, has been recovering from an injury," Finton said.

"Not as significant as yours," I said, bestowing upon him my most sympathetic smile. "It must be incredibly difficult for such an active man to be so constricted."

"You, my dear, are welcome any time," Mr. Neace beamed.

Mrs. Neace nudged me good-naturedly. "Don't encourage him." She winked and turned to Finton. "I'll go fetch a basin of warm water."

Apparently this was not acceptable to the little girl in her arms since it required Mrs. Neace to put her down. The put-out child cried and held out her arms to her mother. Mrs. Neace sternly told her *'no,'* but this only made the tantrum build. Mr. Neace rubbed his forehead and complained of an impending headache as the wailing became louder, and I sensed the poor woman becoming more and more frustrated as she tried to extricate her skirts from the tiny fingers.

"Look!" I knelt before the little girl and withdrew a silver pendant tucked inside my neckline. It sparkled in front of her eyes, and the tears were reduced to sniffles. While the child was distracted, Mrs. Neace snuck out of the room.

The little girl touched the shining jewelry, the metal cool against her dusky skin. Her arms were thin, her fingers long and delicate. She brushed a strand of wavy brown hair the color of rain drenched earth out of her eyes and smiled, her rounded cheeks flushed pink.

"How old are you?" I asked. Suddenly shy, she held up four fingers. "I have a nephew your age. His name is Rian. Can you tell me your name?" She shook her head, and from the bed came Mr. Neace's gruff voice informing me her name was Ionah.

"Ionah is such a lovely name," I told the enthralled little girl. "My name is Ula." She smiled and curtseyed in the clumsy way of a small child. I engaged her in conversation until her mother returned and gratefully thanked me for my assistance.

"Dr. Ekhane was right to bring you along today, Miss Audrey. This one has been in a nasty mood all day. You handled her perfectly," Mrs. Neace said.

"I have five nieces and nephews," I said.

"Then you're no stranger to tantrums." She tsk-tsked and set the basin of water near Finton.

Ionah wasted no time resuming her place in her mother's arms, though her attitude was decidedly more pleasant. Finton was inspecting the wound, and I inched closer for a better look. The flesh was raw, red, and smelled oddly sweet. I breathed shallowly through my parted lips to avoid inhaling through my nose. Finton cleaned the area carefully, but Mr. Neace still hissed with pain.

Finton indicated the bottles lined up on the nightstand. "Ula, can you hand me the vial labeled 'opium' please?"

Mr. Neace waved the suggestion away and gruffly said, "No need."

My hand hovered over the vial.

"Nonsense," Finton said. "No one will reward you for bearing the pain, Armin. Besides, you'll heal faster if you're comfortable."

Reluctantly, Mr. Neace nodded. I handed the vial of opium to Finton, and he dosed out a portion to the large man. Within seconds, Armin relaxed, and Finton was able to clean the wound more thoroughly. After observing Finton remove pieces of decayed flesh, I couldn't watch any longer, and I looked away to quell my rising nausea.

"How did you come by your accident?" I asked Mr. Neace to keep my mind off the putrid wound.

Mr. Neace looked up at me with glazed eyes and smiled slowly.

"Horse spooked," he said lazily. "Damn thing threw me when some bushes rustled as if a bear were after it."

"How awful," I said.

"Meh. Young horse. If you ask my wife, she'll tell you I shouldn't have been riding the blasted animal in the first place."

"An unbroken horse is certainly challenging. They can be quite stubborn and flighty."

"You know something about it, young lady?"

"Miss Audrey is from Praed," Finton said. "She was raised around horses."

"And have ridden a few unruly steeds," I added. "Though my sister was the more accomplished rider."

Mr. Neace leaned forward eagerly. "Maybe you could help me with the damned beast."

"Now, now," Mrs. Neace said. "No sense in putting the young lady in danger."

"Danger? Bah! Ahh!" Mr. Neace cried out painfully when Finton debrided a particularly well attached piece of tissue. I gritted my teeth as I met his eye, but he winked conspiratorially.

I rubbed Mr. Neace's uninjured arm reassuringly. "Once you're well healed, we'll see what we can do about your troublesome horse."

Mr. Neace smiled appreciatively, then his eyes drifted shut and he settled into bed. I shifted my attention to Finton laying out bandage materials, including one ingredient I found particularly confusing.

I looked closer. "Is that…" My eyes widened. "Honey?"

"It is," Finton said. He spread the sticky substance over the wound. "It helps with healing because of its natural cleansing properties and draws out ill humors."

"I don't know if I'll be able to eat any again after today." I covered my mouth with a sweaty hand.

"It's amazing what you can block out and become used to after a time. I could probably eat a honeyed pear right now."

I stared at him, my jaw agape, and he froze. He looked up wide-eyed.

"That was probably more than you wanted to know. And probably makes me look like a lunatic."

I laughed, and his tense shoulders relaxed. "It's strange, but I'm sure it would make sense to me if I shared your profession."

"Your understanding is a relief." He smiled gratefully, then returned to his work, dressing the wound and replacing the arm into a sling.

Once the patient was comfortably situated and already drifting into an opium induced sleep, we quietly left the room and Mrs. Neace escorted us downstairs.

"You're welcome to stay and have a bite," Mrs. Neace said. "Maybe a tumbler of cider to keep from suffering in the heat?"

"A kind offer, but I must decline," Finton said. "I have other visits to make. Unless the lady wishes to partake in some refreshment?"

They turned to me, and I blushed at the attention.

"No, thank you. I don't wish to delay the doctor."

Mrs. Neace walked toward the kitchen. "Let me have something made up for the road."

"You're too kind, Mrs. Neace," Finton called after her. He made a silly face, and I stifled a giggle.

Moments later, Mrs. Neace came out of the kitchen with a bundle, which she placed in my outstretched hands. Whatever was inside was still warm and smelled delicious. I breathed in the aroma, my eyes closing in contentment.

Mrs. Neace nodded toward the gift. "Those are my mother's apple turnovers. Best you'll taste in all of Ilano."

"And that's no boast. I can tell you from experience," Finton added.

"Thank you, ma'am," I said. "I'm much obliged to you. I look forward to passing along my compliments after eating such a treat."

Mrs. Neace waved off the exultation, though the curve of her lips indicated she was pleased. She accompanied us outside, little Ionah quietly observing us from her mother's arms. Finton assisted me into the gig and then spoke a few words to Mrs. Neace while handing her a bottle. Mrs. Neace smiled gratefully, inclining her head in thanks. She glanced at me then leaned close and whispered something in Finton's ear. I couldn't make out the words, but they seemed to discomfit the doctor and he shifted awkwardly, his face flushed. She patted his shoulder and he climbed into the gig without meeting my questioning gaze.

Mrs. Neace waved as we drove away. I smiled and waved back, paying particular attention to Ionah. To my immense joy, she shyly waved back and blew me a kiss.

"Such a sweet little thing," I said. "And such a kind lady." Finton smiled but didn't reply, so I continued. "Have you known them long?"

"Yes," he said. He glanced at me, but turned away again, and I was almost certain his cheeks were a deep red.

"Is everything all right? You seem uneasy."

He shook his head as if to clear his thoughts and adjusted his spectacles. "I'm fine. You'd better try the pastries before they get cold."

I quickly unfolded the cloth covering the turnovers, and the sweet smell of apples and spices wafted toward my nose. I bit into the warm, flaky crust, and discovered Mrs. Neace wasn't exaggerating her abilities.

"It's absolutely delicious!" I took another, larger bite.

"Slow down! And save some for me!"

Crumbs tumbled down my chin, and I wiped them away with the back of my hand. I held out a turnover to Finton, which he ate with equal fervor.

We soon came upon a humble dwelling even smaller than the one we just left. Instead of stone, this home was built of planks, the cracks reinforced with baked mud and straw. We alighted from the gig and Finton strode confidently to the door and rapped his knuckles against the weathered wood. My attention wandered while we waited for an answer. A few dilapidated outbuildings dotted the property, some sagging with disuse. A rudimentary barn opened onto a large pasture dotted with white clouds. I squinted and peered closer, gasping when I realized they had faces.

I tugged at Finton's sleeve and whispered, "Are those sheep?" I pointed to the fluffy creatures grazing peacefully in the sunshine, and he confirmed my suspicions. "We don't have those in Praed, but I read about them. Are they friendly?"

"They're not dangerous, but they aren't sociable either."

The door opened, and a young girl peeked out through a tiny crack. Her eyes widened in recognition when she spotted Finton, and she threw open the door to allow us inside. The girl wore a thin shift washed within an inch of its life, and her dirty blonde hair was plaited and piled high on her head. Her body was all sharp angles and prominent outlines, but her cheeks still retained remnants of youthful roundness. The shade of her blue eyes struck me as somehow familiar.

"How does your mother fare, Enyleve?" Finton asked. He affected a gentleness that spread warmth through the whole room.

"Her hands give her much trouble, Dr. Ekhane, yet she will not admit it," Enyleve said.

She led us through a front room consisting of a great hearth, table and chairs, pantry, sacks of goods, and a bed with a thin mattress, a weathered chest at the foot.

At the back of the room was a curtain draped over a doorway, and the young girl drew it aside to reveal a tiny bedroom. Spools of thread and sacks of wool filled every corner, and a large spinning wheel took up most of the space. An elderly woman rocked in a chair before a small window on the other side of a bed just large enough for two people. A soft clicking could be discerned over the creak of wood. In the woman's gnarled hands was a small loom and lengths of yarn she was weaving into a scarf.

"Mother?" Enyleve called out. "Dr. Ekhane is here."

The old woman looked up in surprise, but a warm smile replaced her startled expression.

"Dear Finton." She made to rise.

Finton held up his hand to stop her and rushed forward.

"Don't bother getting up on my account, Cait," Finton said. "How have you been?"

"Not bad. Enyleve, dear, fetch the pot of water I asked you to boil." The girl left, and the woman, Cait, noticed me at last. "You've brought a guest today?"

"Yes, this is Ula. She's assisting me today," Finton said.

I came closer and curtseyed respectfully, which seemed to amuse the old woman.

"There's no need to be so formal, my dear. I'm only a simple weaver."

"My mother taught me to show respect to the lady of the house. She did not make a distinction regarding their profession." My speech elicited an appraising look and the old woman informed Finton I was always welcome.

"A great compliment, indeed, for the young lady," Finton said.

Enyleve returned with the hot kettle and poured the water into a basin near the bed. Finton soaked some cloth in the water, then wrapped them around Cait's withered hands.

"Not too hot?" he asked.

She shook her head, closed her eyes with a contented smile, and settled back in the chair.

Finton removed a mortar and pestle from his bag then a vial containing what appeared to be seeds. He ground them into a fine powder and added it to a thick salve, creating a pungent odor that tickled my nostrils.

I rubbed my nose and sniffled. "What is it?"

"A salve of comfrey and chili seeds. The combination helps with the inflammation and soothes the pain."

"What's a chili?"

"It's like a fruit, but the taste is spicy, as in it makes your mouth water from heat. Some of the spice lies in the seeds, and it's good for this type of ache."

Once the salve was mixed, he removed the cloth and spread a thin layer on the woman's hands, then covered them again.

"Stings a little," Cait said. "But it keeps these tired hands working for another week."

Finton cleaned out the mortar and added new ingredients—a small, reddish fruit, tiny stick-like pieces, and blue flower petals—and started grinding them together.

"May I try?" I asked impulsively. At his expression, I shrank back and almost retracted my request. Delight replaced his shock, and he pushed the mortar and pestle into my hands. I tried grinding the ingredients together, but it was more difficult than I expected.

"Here, let me show you," he said.

Covering my hands with his, he helped me hold the pestle correctly, then showed me the motions and the proper amount of pressure to apply. His hands were rough and strong over mine, and heat crept up the back of my neck as I tried to ignore the feeling of his skin against mine. Soon, everything was successfully mixed, and he took the mortar and scraped the contents into a thin paper pouch.

"Just like last time, Cait," he said. "Allow the medicine to dry then brew it into a tea."

"Thank you, Finton," Cait said. "And you, too, Ula. Are you learning to be a nurse?"

"No, ma'am. Just trying to be helpful," I said.

"Well, you've helped me forget the pain in my hands," she said.

"Have you been a weaver all your life?" I asked.

"My mother taught me the trade when I was a little girl. I could weave in my sleep." She pointed to the far wall to a beautifully intricate tapestry depicting the progression of the apple from the orchard to the goblet. The colors were vibrant and the craftsmanship impeccable. "That's the first project Mother and I finished together."

I leaned in for a closer look and was impressed by the tiny, perfect stitches.

"I've never seen it's equal," I said. "Does your daughter possess the same talent?"

Cait shook her head with a wistful smile. "Oh, no. Poor Enyleve's fingers fumble too much. She's much better suited to the kitchen."

"Then who will carry on with your trade after you...retire?"

"No lady of my family, I'm afraid. But there are many in Ilano who weave just as well that'll continue the tradition."

"I hope you don't find this presumptuous, but I will be in Ilano for many weeks. Perhaps I may sit with you while you weave. Maybe learn anything you may want to teach? If it would be permitted, of course, to teach someone who is not from Ilano. I don't wish to be an inconvenience, but I do wish to observe your techniques." I was prattling on like an idiot, but the last thing I wanted was to offend the older woman.

Cait chuckled. "Calm yourself, dear. There's no law that says one must be from Ilano to learn how to weave. If you want to learn, then I'll teach you."

I grinned and thanked her profusely. My characteristic shyness vanished. It was wonderful to feel at ease, and I cherished the freedom from my previous reservations.

We left the simple dwelling with another bundle, this time containing savory rolls of bread. I was too full to partake, so I tucked it beside me as the road curved along a large sweep of green pasture.

"You've certainly made some favorable impressions today," Finton said.

"Have I? Well, everyone has been so kind. I thank you again for asking me to accompany you."

"You're welcome any time. Besides, you'll be expected now that you've made promises."

"Which I intend to keep!"

"I don't doubt it." He turned to me, his eyes soft and smile gentle, and I couldn't bear to look away, even as my face flushed.

"Are there many more stops to make?" I asked.

"A few. Would you like to return?"

"I wish to be back before the queen."

"Did she say when she needed you back?"

"Well…" I inspected my hands, the scenery, anything but his inquisitive brow.

"Ula, the queen knows you're with me, right?"

I mumbled, then shifted sharply forward when he brought the gig to a sudden stop.

"Did you ask the queen permission to come with me?" The harshness in his voice made me cringe.

"I couldn't. She was already gone."

"You lied to me!"

"I didn't! I never said the queen gave me permission."

"You made me believe she had."

I'd never seen Finton angry, and my stomach churned to witness the flash in his eyes and redness of his cheeks. He turned the gig back toward the capital with a grim expression on his face.

Don't cry don't cry don't cry.

"Please don't be angry with me. Olim knows where I am."

"That's not the same," he snapped. "What if something happened while we were out? The queen would have my hide."

"Please forgive me. I wanted to come out with you so badly."

"Yes, your boredom was so overwhelming that you would risk the queen's ire and my neck to get your way."

I crossed my arms and turned away so he couldn't see the tear trailing down my cheek.

He flicked the reins and the horse transitioned into a faster gait. We returned to the capitol building in stony silence. He stopped the gig at the front steps, and without waiting for his assistance, I hopped down and stalked into the building. I didn't look back, and I didn't thank him for the wonderful day he'd given me. It was ruined, and it was all my fault. I rushed to my room, ignoring the bows and concerned looks from nobles and knights. Olim loitered near my chambers in case the queen arrived before me, and his friendly smile faded when he noticed my distraught state. Before he could ask what was wrong, I brushed past him and slammed the door behind me with a loud *bang* that reverberated down the hallway.

I threw myself on the bed and buried my face in the pillows. I didn't answer when Olim knocked and asked what happened, if he could come in, what was wrong. After several seconds of trying, he gave up, and I was left to wallow in misery. I wouldn't blame Finton if he decided never to speak to me again. The worst part was I might never again see those dear people I'd met. My disappointment increased when I imagined their dismay at my fickleness. I wept until I was exhausted and drifted into a fitful sleep dreaming of deceit, anger, and betrayal.

Chapter 8

My head and limbs were heavy when I lifted myself off the bed, my mind thick with the remnants of sleep. Rapid knocking filtered through the fog, frantic and insistent. It must have been what woke me.

"Who is it?" I slurred.

Laria's voice came from behind the door. "Ula, may I come in?"

In a surge of panic, I rushed to let her in, straightening my hair and smoothing my gown in the process. Laria bustled inside and gripped my shoulders.

"Are you all right? Olim said you were distressed."

"Did he say anything else?"

"He didn't elaborate." She gestured for me to join her on the settee. "But you do look pale. What happened?"

With a sigh, I sank into the cushions and resigned myself to revealing the truth.

"I've made a terrible mistake."

"Never!"

"Please don't tease me." My throat strained with the effort to restrain my tears.

Laria's grin vanished at my miserable tone, and she wrapped an arm around me. As she rubbed small circles on my back, I confessed that I'd left the capital without her permission and traveled unchaperoned with Finton while he visited patients. I apologized profusely, and when I could no longer speak through the tightening of my throat, I waited for Laria to unleash her fury.

"I can't say I approve of your actions." Laria's tone closely resembled Mother's when she was displeased. "But I can't blame you, either. I know you've been restless these last several days, and I wouldn't have objected to your going if you'd asked."

"I tried, but you'd already gone. I thought I could leave and return before you knew. It pains me to think how I wished to deceive you."

"It pains me as well," she said, and my heart sank further. "But you're a grown woman now, Ula. I suppose that means you should be allowed to live a life outside of mine."

"It's not that simple. I'm your lady-in-waiting. I have no life outside of you."

Laria flinched and she flushed as if I'd struck her. I hurriedly tried to explain that I didn't resent my life and was proud of my title. She placed a hand against my cheek to silence me, and her expression softened.

"There's no need to become agitated. I know the life of a lady-in-waiting centers around her queen, but I want more for you." We remained silent for a moment, and she continued. "I would have preferred for you to have taken Olim for protection, but I forgive you for leaving without my knowledge."

"Thank you," I breathed. I was overjoyed she forgave me, but that was only half the problem.

"You aren't the only person I've disappointed today. When Finton discovered I didn't have your permission to join him, he was furious. I'm afraid I destroyed our blooming friendship."

"Oh, Ula."

I buried my face in my hands. "I don't know what possessed me to act so rashly!"

"It's surprising, but I suppose you were desperate for a little freedom."

"At what cost?"

"That has yet to be seen. I advise you not to allow time to stretch between you and his anger. The longer you wait, the worse it will be for both of you."

I sniffled, dabbed my eyes with a handkerchief, and nodded.

"Before everything turned badly, how was your day?"

Excitement buzzed through me. "Wonderful! I met some very kind, hospitable people, who I wish to visit again. One is an older gentleman who broke his arm trying to train a young horse to saddle and I said I'd help him once he's healed. The other is an elderly weaver and she agreed to teach me some of what she knows."

"That's lovely. I'm happy to hear you're making new friends."

"And watching Finton work was so interesting, though I confess sometimes unsettling. To have to tend wounds and sickness so intimately takes a certain steadiness of mind. And stomach. Did you know honey can be used on wounds to help them heal?"

Laria's eyebrows rose. "I didn't."

"He's been very kind in explaining things and answering all my annoying questions. But I suppose he must be used to such things. Did you know he teaches classes to young people?"

A smile played at the corners of her mouth. "I did. Efram boasted about his ability to teach the ancient language to future council members."

"Finton said I'm welcome to join the classes, but I don't think I could learn a new language."

"Nonsense. You're capable of anything you put your mind to."

"Well, it doesn't matter. Finton said it's only a matter of days until my leg is healed enough to have the sutures removed, and then I'll be able to return to my duties as lady-in-waiting."

"I hope the prospect still makes you happy."

"Of course!"

"Ula." Her serious tone unsettled me. "I do cherish having you near me, and the children adore you, but I want you to know I don't require your services forever if you find another calling."

"There's nowhere else I'd rather be."

"For now." She grinned. "But you may change your mind in time."

I couldn't imagine such a time. After being forced apart for three years, the last thing I wanted was to be parted from my sister. And I adored the children as if they were my own. What could possibly be more important than spending a life with my family?

"Let's talk about something else," I said. "The upcoming ball?"

"You should be healed enough to dance."

My smile faltered.

"Now don't make yourself uneasy. You've overcome much of your shyness."

"I do love to dance," I said.

"And I dearly love to watch you. We'll have a new gown made for the occasion."

Talk of the Capital Ball was a welcome distraction from thoughts of having to make amends to Finton. The look on his face when he learned I'd essentially lied to him pierced my soul. Laria's advice that I not put off speaking to him was valid, but I also felt a little space to cool down could be beneficial as well.

Laria left shortly thereafter and Olim rushed into the room before the door closed.

"He didn't touch you, did he?" Olim's fists clenched at his sides and he tensed like a cat about to pounce.

My jaw dropped in shock, and I instinctively crossed my arms protectively over my chest. "Olim Lemichs, how dare you insinuate such a thing!"

"I'm sorry." He squeezed his eyes shut and hung his head low. "But you looked so upset when you came back, I didn't know what else to think."

"Well, I assure you he was a perfect gentleman. But I let it slip that the queen was unaware we were together. He wasn't pleased. We quarreled." I turned away and busied myself arranging the items on the vanity so he couldn't see how dejected I felt.

Olim's reflection appeared beside me. "I'm sure he'll forgive you. You're impossible to stay mad at."

He shoved me a little, and I smiled up at him, feeling the tension slip off my shoulders.

"Was it worth it?" he asked.

"That's yet to be seen. But I don't regret the journey. I met some lovely people."

The warmth of his smile wrapped around me like a blanket. "Then it was worth it to me."

A few days later, I was convinced my leg was completely healed, so I summoned Finton under the guise of inspecting the injury. While awaiting a reply, I paced the room and practiced a speech I hoped didn't sound too desperate. Time ticked by without an answer, and I sank onto the settee. Finton was still too angry to see me, even as a physician. I'd acted so deplorably I couldn't blame him if he didn't forgive me, but the pain at the loss of his friendship was surprisingly acute, even after such a short acquaintance.

A perfunctory knock startled me out of my thoughts. I hastily arranged my skirts, brushed the hair out of my face, and called out for the person to enter. My breath caught in my throat when Finton appeared lacking his characteristic openness. Black bag in hand, he stood before me blank faced and bowed stiffly.

"Apologies for taking so long," he said, his voice devoid of emotion. "I was teaching a class."

"No need to apologize," I whispered.

"You sent for me?"

I shook myself into an appearance of normalcy. "For my leg. I was hoping the sutures could be removed."

"Ah." He spoke sharply and much too loud, as if he expected me to say something else. Probably the apology he deserved. Without another word, he kneeled, and I pulled up my hem so he could inspect the wound.

"It's fully healed." He rummaged into his bag and retrieved a tiny pair of scissors. A few quick, efficient snips and the sutures were removed with minimal discomfort.

My breath came out in a *whoosh*. "Thank you." I rubbed the leg and saw a scar remained.

"It should fade. The scar I mean." He dropped the scissors into the bag and rose to leave. "There are no further restrictions on your activity."

"Wait!" I called before he reached the door.

He paused but didn't turn around.

"Please, Finton." I winced at the pleading tone of my voice but continued. "I'm mortified that I lied to you. You were so kind to allow me to accompany you, and I repaid you with deceit. I know I don't deserve it, but can you forgive me? I promise it will never happen again."

Don't cry don't cry don't cry.

"I hate that you think poorly of me, but much worse is the thought of losing your respect and friendship. Please, tell me what I must do to earn your trust back."

Finton looked at me. His blank expression was replaced by pain, and my heart shattered knowing it was my fault.

"I'll think on it," he said.

"If it makes any difference, I have confessed to the queen, and she holds no ill will toward you. She blames me alone."

He nodded curtly. "Good."

And then he was gone.

My sorrow at our parting remained while I was fitted for a ball gown later that day. Lilias and Sulwen played around my feet. They, too, were to have new dresses for the occasion, and they busily picked out colors. Lilias chose a beautiful fabric the color of freshly churned butter that complimented her ivory skin and rich brown hair. Even at her young age, Sulwen was perfectly capable of voicing her opinion, and insisted on a dark blue matching Tyrnan's eyes.

"Have you thought of which color you'd like?" Laria asked.

"Green."

"Yes, but what shade of green? Dark? Light?"

"Doesn't matter. Whatever is most convenient."

Laria stared at me for a moment, then asked Duveesa to take the girls to the kitchens for an afternoon snack. Once they were gone, she dismissed the dressmaker to bring whatever bolts of fabric in green they possessed. The moment we were alone, she whirled on me.

"You *have* to stop feeling sorry for yourself. It doesn't do any good to wallow in your misery."

My shoulders sagged. "I know."

"Have you spoken to Finton yet?"

"I have."

Laria frowned. "It didn't go well?"

"He didn't forgive me if that's what you mean. He said he would think about it."

"Well, it could be worse. Give him time." She wrapped me in a tight hug. "Besides, no one could stay angry at you."

I laughed. "Olim said that, too."

"Well, he's right. You're too adorable."

"Stop." I shoved her off me and fought to suppress a smile.

When the dressmaker returned, I chose a soft, green fabric that shimmered like emeralds. Laria nodded her approval, and I ignored the dark cloud hanging over my head for the rest of the day.

The capitol building was decorated beautifully for the ball with adornments of red and green banners, flickering candles in golden chandeliers, and vases filled with pink and white flowers. Freshly pressed tablecloths covered long tables in the dining hall, the centerpieces woven branches from apple trees coiled around shining red and yellow fruits. Along the walls of the ballroom were tables overflowing with delicate hors d'oeuvres made from apples, plums, and ice grapes. Bowls of red punch were available to quench the thirst of children while servants circled the floor with trays of cider and wine for the adults.

The master of ceremonies announced the arrival of the king and queen, and the crowd parted. Laria wore a magnificent gown the color of the sky on a summer day, her hair woven intricately with a scarf embroidered with apple blossoms. Risteard was dressed in his characteristic black doublet and breeches, but a bright red sash with the Elejick coat of arms was prominently displayed across his chest. I followed close behind in the green gown that admittedly flattered my figure and complimented the black hair curled high on my head with ringlets falling across my left shoulder. Beside me was Prince Alyx looking every bit the miniature of his father, and behind us came the Princes Rian and Tyrnan. Princess Lilias held her head as proudly as her mother's, and beside her Sulwen was led by Duveesa's hand. All the children were behaving remarkably, but we were all vigilant for deteriorating moods.

The Lord Protector met the king and queen at the head of the room and bowed. Risteard formally permitted the musicians to play, and the ball commenced. I took my place beside Laria's throne and watched the fluttering gowns and laughing partners twirl during the traditional harvest dance of Ilano. The people believed if the dance didn't occur during the Capital Ball, the crops would dry up and the fruit rot on the vines. Neither Laria nor I subscribed to such superstitions, but we paid respect to the tradition. Even Fynn and Eve Ekhane danced amid the throng of couples, though their performance was wooden and uninspiring. Children chased each other under tables and voluminous gowns, eliciting sharp rebukes from mothers and fathers, but as the night progressed and the parents indulged in the plentiful libations, the threats became less frequent, and the children were waved off as mischievous scamps.

Laria's fingers brushed my arm, bringing me out of a daze.

"Yes? Did you need something?"

"No, no, I'm fine. You don't have to stand by me all night. If you want to mingle and have something to eat or drink, you're more than welcome."

"Thank you, but I'm perfectly content."

She narrowed her eyes. "You're not trying to avoid dancing, are you?"

I shifted and inspected my nails. "No."

"As your queen, I order you to enjoy yourself." Laria's tone brooked no opposition.

"But if you need me?"

"I'll come find you." She turned to Risteard, who was deep in a conversation with the Lord Protector, entwined her fingers with his, and leaned over to say in his ear, "I know I shall disgrace you, but I expect you to dance at least once with me tonight. It wouldn't be appropriate to have a king sit out all night at his own ball."

"Whatever you wish," Risteard replied without a trace of malice at the public teasing. "I am yours to command." They shared a brief kiss and Risteard returned to his conversation with the Lord Protector.

I left the dais to wander around the room and spied Olim out of the corner of my eye. He made a face, one I knew to mean he was tolerating his current company, a gray-haired former knight who loved to share stories of his glory days. I shook my head in sympathy and returned my attention to the people swirling around me.

"Such a beautiful young woman to be standing around without a partner."

I turned toward the unfamiliar voice and beheld the most stunning woman I'd ever seen. She was tall and voluptuous, with flawless skin, dark eyes, and midnight black hair. She seemed older than I, yet younger than Mother, but I was a poor judge of age. She was dressed in a crushed velvet gown of deep burgundy with a plunging neckline and jeweled collar. She looked at me expectantly, one perfect eyebrow raised, and I blinked myself out of a stupor.

"I-I don't know this dance," I said.

"You haven't been taught the traditional Ilano dances? How unfortunate."

"I've learned a few," I hurried to say. "Just not this one."

Before she could respond, Alyx and Rian rushed up to me talking over each other in agitated tones, their faces flushed.

"Calm down, boys." I glanced at the lady. "Collect yourselves for goodness' sake."

"But Alyx wants to fight!" Rian said.

"Fight? Why? Are you boys quarreling over nonsense again?"

"Not me!" Rian said. "He wants to fight Gerrid. I keep saying Mama and Papa will be mad and not to fight but he says he's going to fight even though I told him Gerrid's bigger than he is, but he won't listen!" Just to emphasize his point, he stomped one foot and crossed his arms, his brows drawn in an exaggerated frown.

Alyx puffed out his chest and his mouth fixed in a determined pout, his piercing blue eyes flashing angrily.

"Alyx," I said calmly. "What happened?"

"He was making fun of me," he said.

"Gerrid was making fun of you?"

"Yes."

"Do you think that justifies you fighting with him?"

"Yes."

The children were universally adored in Praed and had little experience with being bullied. It was a tough lesson to learn, but it would strengthen them as they grew into adults.

"Alyx." I knelt to meet his stubborn gaze. "You're going to meet cruel people in your life. They're happy to anger you, to pick a fight, because they're not happy with themselves. You must show them you're stronger by being the bigger man and walking away."

"What if I can't?" His eyes brimmed with tears. I rubbed his little shoulders and felt him shaking with the effort to maintain his composure.

"There will be times when fighting is necessary. But there is always a choice. Do you think it's wise to start a fight with a boy twice your size?"

"No," he mumbled and wiped his face with the back of his arm.

"What do you think Gerrid's picking on a small boy says about his character?"

"He's bad."

"Exactly. Someone probably picked on him when he was your age and he's still angry about it so he's taking it out on you. It isn't fair, and I will have your father speak to his about it. All right?" He nodded, and I stood and grabbed a few pastries from a nearby table.

"Here." I handed them to Alyx. "Take one for yourself and one for your mother. She could use the company and you could use a hug I think."

He smiled, snatched the sweets from my hand, and he and Rian dashed toward the dais.

"Such dear little boys," the woman beside me said.

"They are."

We watched them ascend the dais and climb into Laria's lap. They held out the sweets, and she happily accepted, taking an enthusiastic bite and falling into a fit of giggles when sugar dusted her nose. The boys tucked into her arms and munched contentedly as she swayed back and forth. I smiled at the precious scene and glanced at the woman next to me. To my surprise, she looked sickly pale, her eyes wide with fright.

"Are you unwell?"

"No." She averted her gaze. "I didn't realize those boys were princes."

"The two eldest."

"And you must be?" Her lips trembled as she spoke, and I was convinced she would faint.

"Her Majesty's lady-in-waiting, Ula. I'm also her sister. Are you sure you wouldn't rather sit down?"

"I am well enough to stand, thank you."

"I don't believe I've had the pleasure of your name?" I grabbed a glass of wine from a passing server and handed it to her. She drank the contents in one swallow. Not even a drop remained on her red lips.

"Lady Eveene Sharp."

"Have you held an audience with the king and queen yet, my lady?" I asked. "I can introduce you. Is his lordship here?"

"He is not." Her words were laced with bitterness. "And no introductions are necessary, thank you."

I inched away and eyed her suspiciously.

"Are you sure you're well? I could fetch a doctor if you have need of one."

Her features softened and she managed a tremulous smile. "You're very thoughtful, but I assure you there is no need. Please give my regards to the king and queen on my behalf."

She walked away, her posture straight and poised, but a trace of unease marred her countenance. As I watched her disappear into the crowd, I sensed a presence behind me. I glanced over my shoulder. Olim was also watching the mysterious woman, though with a dark expression that sent a shudder up my spine.

"Why do you look so severe?"

"Do you know that lady?" he asked in a low, troubling voice.

"I've only just met her. Do you?"

"I do. She was not kind to the queen when Her Majesty was a mere servant."

"Oh." I looked back at the crowd of people, searching for her, but she was gone. "She asked me to pass along her compliments."

"Don't. It will only distress the queen."

My eyebrows furrowed. "Truly?" Laria had never mentioned Lady Sharp, though considering this information I wasn't surprised. Laria kept many aspects of her servitude a secret.

"Let us keep this to ourselves then," I said.

A server came by with a tray, and Olim took two glasses and handed one to me.

"Agreed." He took a long drink. "Has anyone asked you to dance yet?"

"Not a single person." I tipped my goblet and allowed the thick, sweet liquid to fill my mouth and ease my tension.

He held out his hand. "May I have the honor?"

I grinned giddily. He enveloped my hand in his and escorted me to the set of dancers. The effects of the potent wine took hold as Olim led me through the motions of a lively tune. The faces of the other couples blurred as we spun, the music uplifting and exciting. Couples passed down the line, and I wiped perspiration from my brow and clapped in time to the music. The ladies to each side of me giggled and made light conversation, their cheeks flushed and eyes shining. The drink eased my shyness, and I felt as carefree as I had when Laria and I ran wild at Riverstone.

Olim reached for me, the sound of boisterous celebration echoing in my ears. We danced down the line of the couples, and we reached the end just as the last notes drifted away. But Olim didn't stop and exuberantly twirled me around, making me laugh until my sides ached. I gripped his hands as I spun and spun, shutting my eyes to keep from getting dizzy, until I collided into someone. My eyes flew open, but the apology froze on my lips when I saw who I'd run into.

"Finton." His name was pulled from my chest in a breathless exclamation.

He smoothed the leather tunic he wore over a navy-blue undershirt and matching breeches. His attire lacked the flourish and adornments of most of the other men in attendance, yet its well-tailored fit and simplicity suited him more than the finest silks or baubles ever could.

Olim tugged at my sleeve, and I snapped out of my haze.

"I apologize," I blurted out. "I hope I didn't harm you?"

"No," Finton said. "Not this time."

My heart sank and I struggled to keep from bursting into tears right there in the middle of the Capital Ball.

"Can we go somewhere and talk?" I asked.

He stared at me, his lips pursed and indecision in his eyes. I feared he would deny me, but his shoulders drooped, and he nodded.

"If the queen desires my assistance," I told Olim, "please let her know I'll be just outside."

He bowed stiffly, and I felt him watching as I led Finton out of the ballroom.

Chapter 9

The heavy doors of the ballroom closed, drowning out the sounds of revelers. I shifted awkwardly, desperately wanting to mend our friendship. The longer he stared without speaking, the hotter my cheeks burned and the more difficult it was to keep from breaking down.

"You dance well," he said, though the compliment lacked genuine emotion.

"Thank you." I took a deep breath and continued. "Please be honest. Is there anything I can do—?"

"No." He waved a hand in frustration. "I mean, there's no need to trouble yourself. You've obviously expressed your remorse, and I've stubbornly refused to grant you forgiveness. I don't know why. I've been unfair."

Hope swelled in my chest as he spoke, and a tentative smile spread across my face.

"Then you...?" I couldn't bring myself to speak further.

He smiled timidly. "Yes, I forgive you. Can you forgive me for being so pigheaded?"

Before I could stop myself, I threw my arms around him, knocking him off balance. The glass of wine had certainly erased my shyness. I was so grateful to have my friend back I didn't care who saw us, but a small voice in my head whispered that *he* might not find this outward expression of affection very welcoming. I pushed myself away and hastily apologized for my forwardness.

"I'm not offended," he said. He smoothed the front of his tunic, brushed a stray lock of hair off his forehead, and adjusted his spectacles. "Perhaps we should rejoin the festivities." He stepped toward the door and opened it.

Another lively dance was underway. I moved closer to watch the couples turn in circles around one another. Finton remained by my side, and we stood companionably together until the dance was over and the couples dispersed.

"Do you know this dance?" Finton asked when opening notes of the next dance played.

"I do," I said. "One of the very few dances of Ilano I'm familiar with. I'm afraid I'm still quite ignorant of many of your ways."

"Will you dance it with me?"

My stomach flipped, and I swallowed down rising panic. I tried to speak, but my tongue stuck to my mouth. Mutely, I nodded, and he led me to the dance floor.

"I don't know the steps very well," I whispered.

"Don't worry," he said. "I'll lead." He winked and I let out a long sigh.

Our right hands came together, palm to palm, and true to his word, Finton guided me expertly in a dance focusing on the intricate movements between two people rather than the coordinated effort of a group. We circled each other, once, twice…then our arms crossed above our heads and we clasped fingers, just barely. Back and forth we moved, and I concentrated so hard on not stepping on his feet I forgot the formality of holding a conversation. He twirled me under his arm, pulled me close, and deftly lifted me in the air.

"Relax," he said, placing me back on the ground. "You're doing fine."

Nervous tension drained from me as our arms entwined. The end of the set was drawing near, and I blushed when I remembered what came next. Finton wrapped his arm around my waist, and I draped my arm across his shoulders. He lifted and spun me in the air. I slid down the front of his body, reaching down with a trembling hand to clutch the hem of my gown, and we circled one last time. I smiled in relief when I finished the dance without making a mistake.

"Did I do it justice?" I asked breathlessly. "I know it's a great favorite."

"Rest assured, Ula, you have not disgraced the entirety of Ilano."

I nudged him for teasing me, but I couldn't be angry. In truth, I enjoyed dancing with Finton, and I was so thankful we were friends again.

The Capitol Ball Feast was announced, and I excused myself to accompany the king and queen to the banquet hall. The family was gathered in preparation to depart, and I sensed the children were on the brink of tantrums.

"Which one is giving us the most trouble?" I asked Duveesa.

"Which do you think?" she said with a wry grin.

Without further ado, I scooped up Sulwen and whispered in her ear about all the delightful treats awaiting her at dinner. Her cheeks were flushed and she tugged at her dress in agitation. She calmed with promises of sweets and we filed out of the ballroom. The situation changed drastically when we entered the banquet hall and discovered the children were placed at a separate table. The boys were happy to mingle with the other children, and Lilias bore every situation with the same equanimity, but Sulwen would have none of it. The king and queen took their places at the head of the grand table, leaving Duveesa and me struggling to contain the tiny bundle of fury.

"Hush now, little one," Duveesa said. "Put some of this delicious food in your tummy, and it will make everything better."

Sulwen crossed her arms and stuck her nose in the air. "No!"

"Sulwen, sweetie, you're hungry," I said, though there was no sense in trying to reason with the toddler. No one noticed the fuss taking place as dishes were served and goblets were filled. Much to my dismay, that was about to change.

"No!" Sulwen said, louder. "Fa-fa!"

"Your father is eating his own food," Duveesa said. "Show him what a big girl you are and eat yours."

"No! Fa-fa! Fa-fa! FA-FA!" Sulwen screamed.

To my horror, the room fell silent, and all eyes turned to us. We hadn't contained the redheaded fury and embarrassed the king and queen. I glanced toward the grand table. Laria started forward, but Risteard placed a restraining hand on her shoulder and rose. The room was more silent than a forest in winter. He stalked to our table and loomed over us, and even Sulwen had the intelligence to hold her tongue.

Instead of issuing an angry reproach, Risteard held out his arms to his anxious daughter. She threw herself at him and wrapped her chubby arms tightly around his neck.

"There's a lot of new people here," he said. "It must be overwhelming."

"Undoubtedly," I said. "She would be much better settled with you."

He turned to Duveesa. "Your efforts are appreciated. I believe you'll find your evening much easier if the queen and I relieve you of Sulwen so you can concentrate on the other children."

"Thank you, Your Majesty." Duveesa bowed her head.

The guests returned to their plates when Risteard carried Sulwen back to his seat and settled her on his knee. Laria wiped away the little girl's tears and made a plate for her between them. She was, indeed, much more content where she was, and the scene was heartwarming.

"Do you need me to stay?" I asked Duveesa.

She glanced around at the other children contentedly eating their food and shook her head.

"You better eat before it all falls apart."

I laughed, though I knew the joke was not far from the truth.

The head table was adorned with sprigs of apple blossoms made from paper, shimmering fruit sculpted in glass, and a woven table runner vibrant with the colors of harvest. Dishes piled with cheese, bread, pastries, and meat covered the table from one end to the other, tendrils of mouth-watering steam rising toward the ceiling like an ethereal mist. I sat beside Laria and piled delicious smelling meat and fruit dishes onto my plate. The dancing had done wonders both for my mood and my appetite.

"You danced very well tonight," Laria said. "Most impressive."

"I'm having a wonderful time!" I took a large bite of a juicy piece of meat.

She laughed. "I noticed. And it makes me happy beyond words. I saw you dancing with Dr. Ekhane. Does this mean you've made amends?"

"Yes. He's forgiven me, and I've promised never to deceive him in the future. I felt so awful when I thought I'd disappointed him so irreparably."

"I can imagine. Let this be an important lesson for you, then."

"Oh, it has been!" I drank deeply of ice wine from my goblet.

Laria eyed my glass. "Be careful, gem. Ice wine is a very potent spirit. Drinking too much too fast can make you ill."

"Can it?"

She smiled slyly. "Trust me."

"Hass that ever happened to you?" I asked, absently noting a strange lisp and slur to my words.

"Once."

"Wha' happened?"

"Ask Risteard."

I leaned across the table toward Risteard, my ability to have any self-control apparently nonexistent, and whispered loudly, "Psst. Your Mashesty!" Again, with the slur?

Risteard looked at me with furrowed brows and Laria stifled a laugh behind her napkin. Sulwen sat between them ignoring the exchange completely and munching on a piece of bread.

"Can I ashk you a question?"

He cocked his head to the side and Laria spit wine.

"Hash my sister ever been drunk?"

Laria slapped the table, startling me, and bit the napkin hard as she tried to control her laughter. Risteard looked at her askance, then back at me.

"Once," he said. He turned to Laria. "I believe your lady-in-waiting has overindulged."

Laria shrugged. "She's a grown woman. I have no fear that she'll disgrace me. I've already cautioned her to be careful."

"I only have so many pairs of boots," Risteard said, which Laria found more amusing than I would have guessed.

"You can borrow a pair of mine," she said.

"Ugh!" I sat back in my chair. "Stop flirting."

A smile played at Laria's lips. "Eat your dinner."

The rest of the evening passed pleasantly as I slipped into a warm blanket of ice wine and roaring fires. I rarely imbibed at home, but the festivities gave me a liberating feeling, and my normally shy reserve tumbled around me. I smiled, danced, engaged in conversations with strangers, and indulged in good food and drink.

A little too much drink as it turned out.

I heeded my sister's advice and slowed down on my consumption of ice wine by switching to cider. In my addled brain, Laria's advice was merely a question of semantics, and I figured if I didn't drink the wine, I'd be fine. By the end of the night, the dancers weren't the only ones spinning.

I managed to maintain a semblance of dignity when the ball concluded, and I followed the king and queen from the room. The children were tucked into bed hours prior, so all I needed to do before falling into bed was tend to the queen's nightly rituals. In her chambers, I stumbled over my feet and clumsily untied her stays.

"Once you help me out of my gown and undo my hair," Laria was saying. "You can go to bed. I can handle the rest if you're too tired."

"S'all right." I hiccupped.

Laria's gown dropped to the floor, and she spun around and fixed me with an inquisitive glare.

"Ula…" Laria said. "Did you ignore my advice and overindulge in ice wine?"

"No! I stopped drinking it as soon as you told me to."

"Did you drink anything else?"

"Only a little cider. But you didn't say I couldn't." I swayed, reached out for balance, but pitched forward anyway.

Laria laughed and caught me. "I suppose not. Come on. *I'll* be tending to *you* tonight."

Despite my protests, Laria donned a dressing gown and led me to my room, where I promptly collapsed on the bed. Laria helped me out of my gown and unpinned my hair.

"Why do people drink so much?" I muttered.

"You tell me," she said.

"It felt nice before it wasn't."

"There's your answer. People feel good when they drink alcohol. The trick is not drinking too much."

"What happened to you when you drank too much?"

"I vomited on Risteard's boots."

My burst of laughter echoed throughout the chamber. I could just picture my brother-in-law's face when that happened.

"Was he angry?"

"I think he was more irritated at my overindulgence while under the service of the old king than anything else. It was foolish and dangerous of me."

"That's why he kept talking about boots." My eyes drifted shut, yet I still felt unsteady.

"Get some sleep. I'll have an ewer of cool water brought up in the morning."

"I saw Lady Sharp," I murmured before I could stop myself. Laria tensed, and I opened one eye to look at her. She was eerily still, and her skin was pallid.

"Did I hear you correctly?" she whispered. "Did you say you saw Lady *Sharp*?"

"I shouldn't have said that." I struggled into a sitting position and leaned against the pillows.

"What did she say?"

"Nothing important. She wanted me to pass along her compliments."

Laria's eyes hardened, and her cheeks flushed. "Anything else?"

I'd seen Laria angry before, but I'd never been frightened of her. I inched my fingers across the bed, torn between sympathy and fear, as if she were an injured animal liable to bite.

I cleared my throat to hide my discomfort. "Nothing memorable. I'm sorry. I shouldn't have told you. Olim said it would be too upsetting."

"No, no. I'm glad you told me. I can be better prepared if I happen to see her. Sleep now."

I relaxed with a sigh when the door closed behind her. Without even sliding down the bed, I fell into a deep sleep devoid of dreams. I could ask Laria questions about Lady Sharp in the morning, but I doubted she would answer them. My sister's pain was a secret she kept close to her heart, and only one person possessed the key to unlocking it. That person was not me, but my brother-in-law.

The next morning I could barely lift my head off the pillow. All the food and drink I consumed the night before settled heavily in my stomach, and it was too much to bear in my weakened state. Groggily, I rolled over and slid off the bed, landing on the floor in a heap. I crawled to the washstand, pulled myself up, and braced myself against the wooden frame. I poured cool water into the basin and splashed my face. It was refreshing on my sticky skin, so I leaned over and wiped my neck with a damp cloth. I stumbled over to the vanity, collapsed into the chair, and looked at my reflection. My haggard visage stared back, and I ran a hand across my face to prove it was mine.

The door flew open and a voice called, "Good morning!"

The sound reverberated against my skull, and I clutched my head. My sister's bright face appeared in the mirror.

"You look terrible!" Laria said. She picked at wayward strands of my hair and started brushing out the tangles. She was already dressed in a dark gray riding habit with burgundy sleeves.

"What's going on?" I grumbled.

"Be more specific, dearest," she said, much too loudly.

"Have I overslept?"

"Not by much."

"I'm sorry." Unable to hold my head up any longer, I dropped it to the vanity with a resounding *thwack*.

"Don't worry about it. You needed the rest. Now it's time to face the day!"

"Why are you speaking so loudly?"

Laria brought her mouth close to my ear. "You don't like it?"

I covered my ears.

"You're doing it on purpose, aren't you?"

"Sorry, I couldn't resist. Have you learned your lesson yet?"

"Yes. I seem to be learning quite a bit lately."

"Well, that's the important thing."

"What are we doing today?" I asked.

"Riding."

I peeked at her reflection in the mirror. "Where?"

"We've been invited to pick the first apples of harvest on the Derville Estate."

"And?"

"What do you mean?"

"I know you, Laria. You're making mischief."

She was silent for several seconds, confirming my suspicions.

"On the first day of harvest," she said, "the Derville's have a magnificent feast with a spectacular display of colored lights in the sky. It's supposed to be breathtaking."

"Lights in the sky? How do they do it?"

"Apparently they're contained until a fuse is lit. Then there's a loud noise and they burst forth into the sky and explode! It's done at night so they can be seen at their best."

"Loud noises? Explosions? Why are you insisting on torturing me?"

"It's not out of malice, I promise. It's all a part of the lesson."

"You're a terrible sister."

"But a very forgiving queen." She hugged my shoulders and proceeded to style my hair. A minute later, there was a knock, and a maid entered carrying a tray with a covered dish and a mug with a paper packet lying next to it. The young girl curtseyed deeply to Laria as she retreated, and Laria removed the lid to reveal a bowl of broth.

She beckoned me over. "Come. Drink some of this broth and gather your strength for today."

I breathed deeply the savory smell of the broth and was grateful not to have solid food before me. I ladled spoonful after spoonful into my mouth, quenching both my thirst and my hunger. Beside me, Laria took the mug and emptied the contents of the paper packet into it and stirred, resulting in a pleasing aroma.

"What's that?" I asked.

"I asked Dr. Ekhane to mix a tonic for bottle ache." She nonchalantly placed the steaming liquid before me.

"You didn't! How embarrassing!"

"I didn't say it was for you."

"You're certain he doesn't know? I couldn't speak to him again if he did."

"I promise he's ignorant of your overindulgence. As far as I'm aware. Did you speak to him at all after dinner?"

"I don't think so. I can't remember."

Laria stared at me with an unreadable expression for a few moments, then carelessly waved her hand.

"I'm sure it's fine."

A vague ache permeated my head, but aside from this, I'd mostly recovered from the night before thanks to Finton's tonic. I shielded my eyes from the bright sun as the gentle gelding Laria chose for me ambled away from the capital. Behind me, a carriage carrying the children rolled forward, the squeaking of the wheels accompanying their voices. I lowered my hand when we traveled under the shade of lush trees lining the road. The dappled sunlight filtering through the leaves reflected off Laria's ginger hair, making it shine like precious gems. She smiled and waved at farmers as we passed, and they lifted their heads and returned the greeting before returning to work. Risteard inclined his head respectfully when people approached and bowed, and children who came out for a glimpse of the royal family were rewarded with coins. Soon, the familiar facade of the Derville estate appeared, and I sighed in relief. The former queen of Praed rushed toward me the second my feet touched the ground, taking my hands in hers with a worried expression.

"I've been so distressed about what happened last time you visited us," Mwiryn said. "Have your wounds healed?"

"It was only the one injury," I said. "And it's fully mended."

"I'm so relieved! Come, the harvest is beginning!" She pulled me toward the orchard, grabbing a basket before we moved deeper into the trees.

Around us, several people were already hard at work, and the trees shook as apples fell into awaiting baskets. The princes giggled as they raced past us, chasing after Mwiryn's niece and nephew.

We came to a large tree swollen with apples, a ladder leaning against the thick trunk. Mwiryn handed me the basket and instructed me to catch whatever she threw down.

"I suppose it's a better idea that you climb this time?"

"I'll not have you falling again! I think your protective knight would be very displeased." She inclined her head toward Olim.

I followed her gaze and saw he was hovering with a watchful eye. I waved him closer, and he reluctantly obliged.

"If you're going to catch me when I fall, you're not going to succeed if you're way over there," I said.

He only offered a half grin in response, not finding my joke as amusing as I did. Mwiryn hitched up her hem and climbed the ladder, a small smile playing at her lips. At least someone thought I was funny.

Shining, red, ripe apples rained down from the tree, and the game of catching them before they hit the ground became instantly entertaining. I laughed when an apple hit the edge of the basket and nearly toppled over, but a swift shift of my weight sent it into the basket. Olim soon participated in the fun, knocking apples in that were about to fall.

Hours passed, and we filled several baskets with the large, juicy fruit. We took a break when the sun was high overhead and gathered around a long table set in the middle of the orchard. We sat alongside farmers and hired hands—the distinction of rank nonexistent during harvest—and ate a hearty meal of roasted birds, fresh bread and cheese, and apple pie. The children chattered excitedly as they stuffed food in their mouths while the adults conversed amiably between healthy swigs from their goblets. I sat back in contentment to observe the scene. The comradery mood devoid of formality made me feel as if this were a gathering of family as opposed to Lords and their employees, royalty and farmers.

I turned to Mwiryn. "Is it always like this?"

"We've had some difficult years in the past, but generally harvest is a jovial time. Especially in the last five years." She smiled and glanced at the king and queen, and I understood her meaning. "We've enjoyed the serenity and prosperity of these times. It was hard for Father to accept a queen who was not from Ilano, but I promise that's no longer the case."

I squeezed her hand reassuringly, and she lifted her goblet. I tapped mine against hers, and we drank to our blooming friendship.

The temperature cooled as the day progressed, and as dusk fell, the first day of harvest was officially declared over. Cheers erupted and everyone congratulated each other with embraces and pats on the back. The apples were transported into storage containers built underground to preserve the fruit before they were conveyed into buildings where they were turned into cider and other confectionery. Guests arrived as the sun set to witness the annual display of colored lights in the sky. My illness resulting from the previous nights' overindulgence was gone, so I no longer anticipated the festivities with a sense of dread.

A gentle slope of grass was especially prepared for the evening with blankets and tables of refreshments, and people chose spots with the best views of the impending show. I stood at the top watching the carriages arrive with Laria and Risteard. Each noble family happily greeted the king and queen before taking their place. The princes were overjoyed to see more children, and even Lilias joined in on the fun, leading a determined Sulwen by the hand.

A large equipage conveying the Lord Protector and his family rolled to a stop. The laughter of the children receded, and I vaguely heard Alyx tell everyone to run away from Gerrid Ekhane. The boy himself emerged from the carriage, a sour look on his face. His mother, Eve Ekhane, followed, a hand clasped to his shoulder. By their body language, I guessed Gerrid had just been issued a lecture, and he wasn't happy about it. The Lord Protector approached the king and queen warmly, and the three moved away together to secure a good vantage point for the evening. Fynn Ekhane and his dour family did the same without a glance in my direction. They whispered amongst themselves, and what few words I could discern were critical of the Derville's decorations and choice of food. I rolled my eyes and ignored their criticisms.

Olim tugged at my sleeve and informed me he found a place for us to sit. Mwiryn and I turned to follow, but I spotted Finton coming up the hill. I waved my arm over my head in frantic arcs and called out to get his attention, which Olim apparently felt was not befitting my station. He pulled my arm down, fixing me with a glare tinged with embarrassment.

I shrugged out of his grasp. "What?"

"People are staring at you," he said in a low voice. "I don't think the queen would approve of your outburst."

"Since when are you so concerned with appearances?"

Mwiryn averted her gaze while we argued, and it was my turn to flush in embarrassment.

"Since last night," he whispered harshly.

If it were possible for my cheeks to redden further, they were now an inferno.

"I'm happy that you're feeling more comfortable, but I'm sure you don't want a repeat of last night."

"I'm not sure what you're referring to," I said. "But if the queen is concerned about my behavior, she will address those concerns herself."

Our conversation ceased when Finton walked up with a characteristically open smile. His eyes darted from Olim and me to Mwiryn, and he shifted uncomfortably in the tense atmosphere.

"I trust I'm not interrupting anything?" Finton asked.

"No!" I said before Olim could answer. "Olim was just telling us that he's found a suitable spot for us to sit."

"Wonderful! I hope you'll enjoy yourself tonight. The Derville's light display is simply spectacular." He bowed toward Mwiryn in acknowledgment, and she inclined her head, a slight smile playing about her mouth and a sparkle in her eye. "Good evening to you all."

Before he could leave, Mwiryn said, "Wait! Would you like to join us?"

Olim's lips pursed, and I couldn't account for his troubling behavior. To make up for my friend's unwelcome appearance, I nodded encouragingly at Finton, hoping he'd ignore the knight.

"I thank you for the offer, my lady, but I wouldn't want to intrude," Finton said.

"It's no intrusion." Mwiryn stepped forward and nudged the small of my back.

"None at all," I added. "Please sit with us."

Finton eyed Olim dubiously, and I elbowed the knight in the ribs. The glare dropped from the knight's face, and he reluctantly gestured for everyone to follow.

"I apologize for Olim," I whispered to Finton. "I don't know what's got into him tonight. He's not usually so hostile."

"I hope I haven't done anything to offend him," Finton said, though his expression held not worry but amusement.

"Not at all. Rather, I believe it's me he's displeased with, though I'm not sure why."

"You?" he asked incredulously. "I don't believe it."

"Despite what you may think, I'm not infallible. Sometimes I make mistakes, as you well know." I grinned wryly. "I've apparently offended Olim with my latest." I wondered what I'd said or done the night before that could have raised Olim's ire. It probably had something to do with the copious quantities of alcohol I'd consumed.

"Don't trouble yourself about it tonight," Finton said as he assisted me onto the blanketed ground.

He settled himself to my left while Mwiryn sat to my right, and Olim sat in front of me so close I had to tuck my knees to my chest. The night was pitch dark, and the stars gradually twinkled to life. Mwiryn shifted, freeing me of the feeling of being boxed in. As it was, I was forced so close to Finton our shoulders brushed together, and he once again asked if I might be more comfortable if he relocated.

"I'm perfectly comfortable," I said. "When does the show usually start?"

As if my words were a cue, a loud *bang* echoed across the estate. Frightened, I kicked Olim in the back and clutched Finton's arm. I barely had time to recover before a brilliant display of yellow light exploded in the sky, showering sparks that trickled to the ground. Another boom signaled the next display, this time in bright red the color of the apples we picked all day. My jaw dropped in awe, and with each subsequent explosion, I became less and less startled. I realized my grip was still settled firmly around Finton's arm, and I turned to offer my apology as I loosened my hold. The words died on my lips when I became mesmerized by the dancing lights reflected in his spectacles and the wide-eyed wonder mimicking my own.

"It's astonishing." He leaned toward me, his eyes never leaving the sky. "How something so insignificant as just a few grains of black powder can produce such a magnificently beautiful vision."

"Yes," I breathed. I returned my gaze to the sparkling white shimmer of light flitting to the ground and added, "A pretty metaphor. If only it applied to people."

Finton studied me in the darkness, but I focused on the sky, ignoring the thudding of my heart and the swirl of confusion in my thoughts. There were many times in my life I felt like the black grains: insignificant, tiny, and waiting for their destiny. My actions and emotions were often subject to the whims of others. Tomorrow, I would have to sort out how I had offended Olim, but tonight was for me. I forced myself to turn my mind as black and blank as the sky before the sparkling of lights illuminated it and focused on the delights of this wonderful day.

Chapter 10

Olim was more amenable the next day, stepping forward the minute I left my room and offering a hasty apology for his behavior the day before.

"I don't know what possessed me to lecture you," he said. "Can you forgive me?"

"I only wish I knew how I've disappointed you," I said. I must have said something inappropriate after drinking too much ice wine. But I wasn't foolish enough to admit to anything outright. He breathed deeply, as if his next words were gravitas indeed, and I was filled with dread.

"I wasn't paying attention to the amount of ice wine you were drinking, and I'm afraid my inattention resulted in your impaired judgment."

"I didn't realize it was your place to regulate me."

"Not officially, but as your friend, I should have been more vigilant. You were enjoying yourself, and it was delightful, so I didn't question it. Then I saw you drinking at dinner and heard you speaking strangely to the king, and I knew the cause of your...exuberance."

"You heard that?" My cheeks heated when I recalled how I'd spoken to the king. "The wine loosened my tongue, but neither the king nor the queen admonished me for it. I believe they understood I'd overindulged, and I drank no more ice wine that night."

"A wise move, but I think the wine had already done its worst. No one else is speaking of it, though. Be assured of that."

"What else did I do?" I asked, my voice barely a whisper. We were standing outside the queen's door, and I couldn't enter without knowing what I'd done.

"To anyone else, you were simply enjoying the evening, but I know you." He looked around then leaned close. "You practically threw yourself on Finton Ekhane. I hope he was a gentleman and didn't take advantage of your impairment?"

The blood drained from my face and my jaw dropped. I remembered dancing and talking with him, but after dinner, the night was fairly a blur. No wonder Olim was so reluctant to allow Finton to join our party last night. Olim's eyes widened in the lingering silence, and I shook my head.

"He was a perfect gentleman as always." Instead of convincing Olim, my words only served to darken his features further. "Please don't look at me like that. I promise Finton has done nothing to deserve such a hostile reception. I danced with him, we spoke, and nothing more. And honestly I'm surprised you think I'd place myself in a position to be disgraced."

He placed his hands on my shoulders and hovered over me. "It's not you I worry about. It's him. These capital people care only for themselves. They can dally about all they want without any consequences to their own reputation. Those they take advantage of, however, live in disgrace the rest of their lives."

I squeezed his hand. "I'm sorry if you've been hurt, but Finton is not the person responsible. He's my friend, just as you are, and you can trust him."

Olim nodded solemnly, straightened, and gestured toward the queen's door.

"I don't want to keep you," he said.

I began to push the door open but stopped when Olim grasped my wrist.

"Ula?"

"Yes?"

"Now that you're healed, I was wondering if you'd accompany me on a visit to meet my family later this afternoon. Would you do me this honor?"

"I would love to!" I smiled warmly at him, and he graced me with a genuine smile of his own. "I'll ask permission from the queen."

He nodded and released my arm. I slipped into Laria's room, my stomach flipping with anticipation at another outing into the Ilano countryside.

What a strange mixture of shame and excitement. One moment happy, miserable the next, and back to enjoying myself. What had I done at the ball?

Laria's face brightened when she saw me, but a frown creased her brow when she undoubtedly noticed my distress. I waved away with her concerns, and she reluctantly sat at her vanity. I pulled a brush through the tangled mess of her hair and ignored her stares.

"Tell me what's happened," Laria said.

I started at her demanding tone and met her glare. I sighed. That look could not be ignored.

"Olim was acting very strangely yesterday, particularly toward Finton."

"Was he? That seems to be a common theme."

"Olim is suspicious of people who live in the capital," I explained. "Anyway, last night he was quite rude, and he alluded to a lapse in my behavior to account for it."

Her hands curled into fists in her lap. "A lapse in your behavior? What could he mean by that?"

"I'm afraid I may have acted...out of character...at the Capital Ball."

She breathed out a laugh. "Oh, that. Did he notice you were...inebriated?"

"He overheard me talking to you and the king." I lowered my eyes and concentrated on styling her hair. "But I worry I may have acted untoward in other respects."

"Come out with it."

"Olim said I was overly attentive to Finton."

"You mean you were enjoying yourself too much and he found this offensive?" Hands on hips, I cocked my head to the side and stared at Laria.

"The most offensive thing to a man," she said, "is a woman who pays more attention to someone other than him."

"But…" I fumbled for words. Not the reaction I expected from her.

"Did you lure him into a dark corner and kiss him?"

My face flushed and I vehemently shook my head. "There are some parts of the night that are fuzzy, but I know with absolute certainty I did not."

"Then you've done nothing disgraceful. A little dancing and perhaps flirting are not punishable offenses."

"I wasn't flirting! At least I don't believe I *meant* to flirt."

"Has Finton said anything that would indicate he found your behavior disreputable?"

"Not at all."

"Olim is very protective, and it does him credit. But you are not his relation. It's not his place to lecture you regarding your behavior. It's mine."

"It wasn't a lecture per se. I believe he spoke as a concerned friend."

"And it pleases me that you have such a friend. But he is still a knight of our kingdom under the employ of the king and as such he must be reminded of his place." Laria's eyes flashed angrily, and I worried she would instruct the king to punish Olim for overstepping his duties.

"I've already reminded him. There's no need for you or the king to say anything."

Laria took a deep breath through her nose.

"My question is," I said, "should I speak to Finton about it? If I need to apologize, I would rather do it sooner than later."

"Did you see him last night?"

"Yes. He joined Mwiryn, Olim, and me for the light display."

"And did he act strangely toward you?"

"No."

"Then I don't think there's cause to say anything. Finton is a very straightforward kind of man. If he's unsettled, he would let you know."

I thoroughly agreed with that assessment based on our recent disagreement. Finton made it abundantly clear he was displeased then, and there was no trace of that attitude last night. My shoulders relaxed and I sighed in relief.

"Is there anything else distressing you?"

I shook my head.

"Then tell me what makes you happy."

I grinned. "Olim invited me to meet his family. May I join him this afternoon? I can take a chaperone."

"Something tells me you have nothing to fear from Olim. He is the epitome of a chaperone."

"Then, may I?"

Laria rubbed a floral scented oil into her pale skin. "When?"

"This afternoon. If that is agreeable to you."

"Efram's impossible eldest son, Fynn, has called a council meeting. I'm afraid Risteard and I will be doomed to remain indoors for most of the afternoon. Please enjoy the day as you wish."

I wrapped my arms around Laria's shoulders and hugged her tightly, then resumed my morning duties as lady-in-waiting. It was exciting to leave the capital once again. I was becoming more and more attached to the beauty of the orchards and the kindness of the people. I was especially looking forward to learning more about Olim's family, to place faces and names to the people I knew so little about. Perhaps meeting them would reveal some insight into the knight I had known for years and explain why he resented the people of the capital so fiercely.

The orchards along the road were dotted with people harvesting the fruits of a year's worth of cultivating. The air was pungent with the smell of earth and the sweet apples filling baskets carried by young women and men. Olim and I rode in companionable silence, taking in the scene and enjoying the afternoon warmth. I was so distracted watching the farmers it wasn't until we were close to a modest house that I recognized my surroundings. My brow furrowed as I glanced around, and then I spotted a shed occupied with white, fluffy clouds with faces.

"Olim," I said. "I know this place."

His eyebrows shot up. "Do you?"

He reined in his horse and dropped to the ground when we arrived at the main building, a small house built of weathered planks. I was too stunned to dismount, and Olim shook my leg to snap me out of my stupor. I allowed him to assist me out of the saddle, but before he could ask me questions, the front door flew open. A skinny girl emerged, her blonde hair flying behind her as she launched herself into Olim's arms.

"Olim!" she cried. "You're home!"

A slight breeze could have knocked me to the ground at seeing the familiar face and hearing her speak to Olim with those simple, shocking words. Home? I gazed around at the house, the outbuildings, and the pasture full of sheep. I recognized them from the visit I made with Finton. It was the house of the elderly weaver.

Olim held the young girl at arm's length and inspected her from head to toe. "How did you get so tall?"

She giggled, her cheeks flushed with pleasure, until she noticed me standing there dumbly.

"Oh!" Olim tidied his hair and blushed when he realized he'd been remiss in introducing me. "Enyleve, this is Ula Audrey, Lady-in-Waiting to Queen Laria. It is my honor and duty to protect her."

The color drained from the girl's delicate face, and her eyes widened. Those eyes that were the exact shade of blue as Olim's.

"Ula, this is my sister, Enyleve." Olim didn't seem to notice the odd way the girl and I stared at one another.

"Pleased to make your acquaintance," Enyleve said in a tiny, shaking voice.

"Likewise," I said.

"Is Father home?" Olim asked.

Enyleve shook her head, and Olim's smile faded.

"No matter," he said. "Come and meet Mother."

My feet were leaden as I followed them into the house, past the familiar hearth and barren table, into the small back room. The old woman sat in her chair taking advantage of the abundance of natural light to darn wool into delicate threads. She looked up at the sound of his boots on the creaking floorboards, and her face brightened so fully it made my eyes well with tears.

"Olim, my dear boy!" She held out her arms, and he embraced her thin frame. He enveloped her small hands in his and asked how she fared. She waved off his questions and tutted.

"We hadn't had a letter in many weeks," she said. "Now I know it was because you were coming to see us in person. What a wonderful surprise!"

"I brought someone I'd like you to meet," Olim said, gesturing toward me.

I stepped forward awkwardly and met the old woman's eyes. If she recognized me, she didn't show it. Perhaps she didn't remember me?

"May I present Miss Ula Audrey, Lady-in-Waiting and sister to Her Majesty, Queen Laria. This is the woman I've told you about, the one I'm sworn to protect."

I curtseyed low, my knees trembling. I lifted my eyes hesitantly.

"Mrs. Lemichs," I said quietly. "This is indeed an honor."

"Pish posh," she said, waving off my remark like an annoying fly. "This lady and I have met before." She held out her hand to me, and I took it timidly. It was warm, the skin thin, yet stronger than I imagined. "I thought you had an air of distinction about you. Sister to the queen, hmm? I'm the one who must be honored, young lady."

Olim looked from me to his mother, scowling. "What do you mean you've met? When?"

"I had the privilege of being introduced to Mrs. Lemichs by Dr. Ekhane. We visited that day I joined him on his rounds," I said.

The old woman smiled. "Please call me Cait. I'm so glad to see you again. Are you still interested in learning my trade?"

I opened my mouth to answer, but Olim swept his hands between us as if clearing a table.

"Let me get this right," he said irritably. "You met my mother and never told me?" He fixed me with a glare, and I pursed my lips in agitation.

"I didn't know she was your mother," I said.

"And I didn't know I was being waited on by such an important lady," Cait said. She turned a narrowed gaze at Olim and squared her shoulders. "But here we are. The day is full of surprises."

Olim's eyes flashed angrily. "Waited on? Was that man forcing you to work?"

"Olim, enough!" Cait said, and even I shrank back at her tone. "Miss Audrey was kind enough to offer her assistance. She was such a comfort. My hands bothered me badly that day. Her sweetness was a welcome distraction."

I blushed at the praise and Olim looked properly abashed. He took his mother's hand again and kissed it lightly.

"I'm sorry, Mother. I had high hopes for this introduction, and I've ruined it."

"There's no need for that," Cait said, her tone softer now. "You always build up a vision of how you want things to be in your head, and when it doesn't work out the way you want it, it's always such a disappointment. Allow that some things are out of your control." She turned to me. "Now. Let me look at this young lady I've heard so much about."

She inspected me closely, more than she had before, yet I didn't feel uneasy. Her gaze was admiring, but not judgmental, appraising, but not overtly so.

"I hope you will take tea with us," she said.

I nodded, and Olim helped her rise and amble the short distance from her room to the dining table. Enyleve had already set the tea service with the humble dishes they possessed, including a large teapot and a delicious looking spread of apple pastries. I inhaled the sweet smell, and my mouth watered instantly.

Cait sat at the head of the table. She indicated the seat to her right, and I obliged. Olim sat across from me and Enyleve filled our cups with steaming, dark brown tea.

I took a healthy bite from a particularly sticky looking treat, and my eyes closed at how delicately it melted in my mouth.

"What do you think?" Cait asked.

"It's the most delicious thing I've ever eaten," I said.

Cait beamed. "That's quite a compliment considering your station."

I thanked Enyleve for serving me, but she wouldn't look at me and nearly spilled the tea when she darted away. She struck me as shy when I met her before, but now she could barely function in my presence. She hurried to her seat beside Olim and kept her head lowered as she sipped her tea and nibbled at her turnover. I looked at Olim questioningly, but he shook his head. That conversation would have to wait until later.

"I hoped Father would be here for tea," Olim said to break the silence.

His mother's smile faded. "Father rarely has time to break for tea these days. But he's always home for dinner. Next time you visit, you must come then. And don't forget to bring the lady." She winked at me, and then settled into her own plateful of pastries.

We passed a pleasant afternoon with Olim's family with minimal embarrassment on the knight's part. Cait shared several stories of Olim's childhood, and while they were endearing, I sensed she saved the most damning ones for when we were perhaps better acquainted. Enyleve remained silent as she moved around the house cleaning and preparing food for the evening meal. Her apparent distrust, or dare I say *fear*, was troublesome. I was at a loss as to how I unsettled her. Regardless, I enjoyed my visit, and promised I would return as soon as I was able. I hugged Cait and could feel every bone in her back. I resolved to speak with Laria about doing something to help Olim's family.

Cait's eyes misted over when Olim said goodbye, and I turned away before the scene produced tears of my own. He bore it well enough, as any stoic knight should, and promised to visit when his duties allowed. Enyleve followed us out, though she still wouldn't look at me. Olim helped me mount my horse, then turned and embraced his sister. She looked up at him with longing, silently begging him to stay. He brushed a stray lock of hair from her eyes and shook his head sadly.

"I'll be back," he said quietly.

"It's been awful without you," Enyleve said in a voice barely above a whisper.

"You're getting the money I've been sending, right?"

She looked away from him, a tear falling from her cheek. "Yes," she said. "But it's not the same as having you here."

"I'm trying to make a better life for myself. For you."

Enyleve's gaze traveled up to my face, and the look she gave me sent shivers down my spine.

"A better life? In the capital?" Her voice held a dark undertone, and I shifted in my saddle and looked away.

"Only for the moment," he said. "We're only there for a visit. And it isn't as bad as it used to be."

"Isn't it?" she whispered.

He embraced her again, and she buried her face in his shoulder, her fingers digging into the fabric of his tunic. Without another word, he pushed himself away and mounted his horse. She watched him, her eyes red and hollow. We trotted away and he turned to wave. She raised a hand but lacked the energy to do the same.

We rode away silently, and I watched Olim. He stared straight ahead, his face impassive, and I didn't have the courage to ask what he was thinking. I distracted myself with the scenery and waited for him to speak first.

He'd said nothing by the time we arrived at the capitol building. We left our horses at the stable and walked inside, but still he remained silent. Eventually, I could bear it no longer, and I placed a hand on his arm to halt his hurried movements.

"Olim," I said. "Talk to me."

"Did you enjoy yourself?" A ridiculously wide and forced smile showed on his face.

"I did, but I don't think your sister was pleased with me."

"It wasn't personal."

"It felt personal."

"Well, it wasn't you specifically but what you represent."

I raised an eyebrow. "The elite class?"

"Yes." He shuffled his feet and lowered his gaze. "Before I came to Praed, Enyleve had a season in the capital. My father saved for months to afford it, but my parents wanted a good match for her." He met my eyes, his expression full of regret. "It did not go well."

"I see," I said. My annoyance disappeared, replaced with a growing dread.

"I know you find it irritating that I'm constantly warning you about the dangers of men from the capital, but it's only because I didn't warn Enyleve enough. And the results were...disastrous." He sank onto a bench tucked into an alcove, and I quietly sat next to him and waited.

"We've always been close, you know," he said. "I'm only a few years older, and I lorded this fact over her our entire childhood. She was such a tiny thing, sickly even, but once she matured and developed a womanly figure, she started turning heads. She was lovely, and I was her stupid older brother absorbed in my own dreams and completely oblivious to her burgeoning womanhood. Mother and Father were hopeful of an advantageous marriage, but though men seemed to appreciate her appearance, none showed any further interest. Except one."

He took a deep, shuddering breath, and I squeezed his hand reassuringly.

"He was a prominent merchant, and Enyleve thought him very handsome," he continued. "She enjoyed many dances with him, and he appeared genuine in his interest, but no proposal was forthcoming. One evening, he arrived at a party and wasn't himself. He was agitated, restless, and impolite, a stark contrast to his usual manner. It was right after the siege."

I shuddered, and without looking at me, he wrapped an arm across my shoulders.

"My kind sister thought he was stressed because of it, and she offered him comfort. He took advantage of her kindness, luring her into his apartments under the guise of a distressed man. He placed drink after drink in her hand, telling her how much he appreciated such a beautiful woman taking an interest in his feelings. He told her his business was in trouble, that his dependent nephews may have nothing to inherit. He showed her a portrait of two boys and lamented their starvation. In her confused state, she offered what little dowry she had. He whisked her away to his solicitor and had the money signed over before she realized what she'd done. When she challenged his honor, he told her no one would force him to marry an impoverished daughter of an apple picker. From that day forward, my family distrusted anyone from the capital, especially the bored people of the upper class who play with lives like toys."

"Oh, Olim, I'm so sorry," I said breathlessly. It was no wonder Olim was suspicious of the wealthy in Ilano.

"Enyleve recovered well enough, but she no longer wishes to pursue a husband."

"I don't blame her."

"I thought to challenge the man, but Father forbade it. He said people of that man's station take what they please without consequence, and to challenge them would be suicide."

"What happened to your sister was reprehensible, but not every man is a scoundrel waiting to disgrace an innocent girl."

"I know, but it's hard to change my opinion." He lay his head in his hands. "I couldn't protect Enyleve. I couldn't bear it if the same happened to you."

"It won't. Between you, the queen, and my own cautious nature, I will be safe from harm."

"If something happened to you…" His voice cracked, and he couldn't speak further.

"I'll always be safe with such a knight as you to protect me." A slow smile graced my lips, and I hoped he saw all the confidence and trust I held in him.

My words seemed to please him, but he looked so tired he could barely muster a grin. I gave his hand one last squeeze and rose from the bench.

"Thank you for today," I said. "I enjoyed my visit with your family. I hope in time Enyleve can learn to trust that I'm no threat to her."

"I'll speak to her," he said. "She may have been wounded, but that's no excuse for being rude to a guest, especially one of such 'distinction.'"

I shoved him playfully, then left him to his thoughts.

"Arella," the captain's voice moaned in her ear. He moved against her, his arm tightening around her waist and pulling her closer. "Keep moving that way and you'll never leave this cabin."

Nothing would give Arella more pleasure than to remain in her current state, with him, forever.

I closed the book and lay back against the pillows, my eyes heavy with the effort of staying awake long enough to read a few more pages. I set the book aside, wondering how Arella would get herself out of this mess. I couldn't condone lying with a man out of wedlock, especially when she was destined to marry someone else, but it made for some interesting entertainment. What would she do if the man she was traveling to meet was just as good and handsome as her beloved captain? How would she choose between them?

Chapter 11

A week into harvest, I was the most exhausted I'd ever been, but at night when I rested my weary head, it was with a satisfied smile. Laria wasn't the type of queen to sit in the shade while others worked and fully participated in the harvesting of apples and ice grapes. Muscles I'd never dreamed existed were sore after long days climbing ladders and carrying heavy, fruit-laden baskets. The manual labor gave me a healthy respect for the working class. I'd thinned in the hips and thighs, and a bulge of muscle was forming on my upper arms. The growing strength in my body made me feel less the pampered lady and more the well-rounded woman.

The Lord Protector's golden and red apples were coveted by bakers and cider brewers alike, and it was here we spent one of the hottest days of the season. Sweat trickled down my back before the carriage stopped at the doorstep. We'd donned our thinnest frocks, even the queen, in preparation for a hot day of work. The orchards were dotted with laborers, their wide brimmed hats shading their faces from the harshest rays of the sun. The children were sequestered into the house so their delicate skin wouldn't burn, especially Sulwen's. I pointed out that Laria was just as pale and prone to sunburn as her ginger-haired daughter, but she simply pulled a bonnet over her head and stalked away with Risteard into the orchard. Fynn Ekhane's wife, Eve, and his sister, Fidelma Patel, remained behind in the shade of an awning, their fans working harder than they were.

"I do so admire the queen for joining in on the harvest," Fidelma said. "It shows a great appreciation for our economy."

"Indeed," Eve said dryly. "Why don't you sit with us, Miss Audrey? It's so dreadfully hot."

"Thank you for the offer and the refreshment, but as you can see, I'm dressed for work as well." I gestured to my clothing.

Eve's eyes roamed over my figure critically.

"Well, when you've had your fill, come and join us in the shade." She flicked her fan open to cover her face and hurriedly waved cool air across her skin.

"I suppose your husbands are already hard at work?" I asked.

Fidelma tittered behind her fan and said, "My brother doesn't exactly *work*."

Eve raised her chin haughtily and said, "My husband is better suited for diplomacy in the capitol building. But that doesn't mean he shirks his duties here." She pointed with her fan to where Fynn was directing the laborers and inspecting the incoming crops. Despite the heat, he was still dressed quite formally. Better *suited* was the correct word indeed.

"I sincerely hope he doesn't overheat," I said.

Fidelma giggled.

"Shouldn't you be picking apples!" Eve huffed and crossed her arms.

I shrugged off her irritation and skipped into the orchard, my happiness at being outside stronger than their attempts to impress me with their snobbery. I grabbed an empty basket and headed for an unoccupied tree. After I made sure no one was looking, I lifted my hem. I ran a finger along the faded edges of the wound running down my leg. It wasn't sore, so I climbed the ladder and started tossing down the ripe fruit.

"I certainly hope your tree climbing ability has improved these past weeks because I left my bag in the house."

I looked down toward the source of the voice, slipping on a branch in the process. Finton laughed up at me, his arms outstretched to catch me.

"Don't worry," I called down. "I'm dressed much more appropriately for climbing today, and I don't intend to fall."

"Thank goodness." He relaxed and picked up the basket to catch the apples I tossed down. "I don't think I'm as strong as your knight. If you fell, I'd probably break my own neck trying to save you."

I poked my head through the branches. "Are you saying I'm heavy?"

"Even an apple falling from a great distance can cause significant damage. It's all about height and velocity, not necessarily weight."

I threw an apple at his head, but he intercepted it with the basket and gave me a triumphant grin. Unlike his brother, Finton was dressed properly for work in tan breeches and a light linen shirt. The sun reflected off the lenses of his spectacles, temporarily blinding me. I rubbed my eyes until the flash of lights faded from my vision, then reached for another apple. Together, Finton and I soon had the basket brimming with delicious fruit. I glanced down to toss one last apple and caught Finton with one in his mouth.

I pointed a finger at him and yelled, "Ah ha!"

He froze in mid bite, his eyes wide.

"It seems some things never change."

He finished his bite with a satisfying crunch and munched happily, the juices running down the front of his shirt. He held a finger up to his lips. I climbed down and stood before him with the apple still in my hand. He looked at it, and we both stared as if it held the answer to an important decision. I flashed a cheeky grin of my own and sank my teeth into the fruit's sweet flesh.

"I won't tell if you won't." He took another bite.

"Deal."

We devoured our contraband apples, occasionally casting about glances to ensure no one noticed. The fruit was refreshing on such a hot day, and it gave me energy to finish out the work.

Finton left to deliver the full basket into the storage warehouse, and Laria drifted over looking as tired yet content as I was.

"Your face is flushed," she said. She linked her arm with mine, and we walked toward the shade of the awning. Eve and Fidelma inclined their heads respectfully as Laria approached.

"You look in need of a cool drink, Your Majesty," Eve said and handed a tall glass to Laria. I was left to serve myself, and we gulped down the refreshingly sweet, juicy draught as fast as our parched mouths would allow.

"I hope you haven't become overheated," Laria said. She touched a cool hand to my forehead.

"Have we been working you too hard, my dear?" the Lord Protector asked.

"I think she should stay in the shade for a while," Laria said.

"If she's in desperate need for a cooldown, there's a pond through those trees." The Lord Protector pointed in the direction of a small copse of thick-leaved trees amid a field of grass. "It's quite refreshing if you want to dip your head in." He smiled, the expression fatherly and gentle, and I couldn't help but smile back.

"Sounds wonderful! Just like at home," Laria said. She shooed me toward the trees, and I hurried as quickly as the heat of the day allowed in anticipation of the cold water washing over my sticky skin.

The trees were densely packed, the bark weathered and flaking, and branches twisted and tangled together. I wove through them, their leaves bright green and soft, and the temperature dropped, the air alive with moisture and the scent of earth. A grassy bank sloped toward the pond. A few stones rose out of the ground, but unlike the rocky Rhyvor, the shore around the water was soggy. I lifted my hem and rushed toward the water's edge. I knelt on a patch of soft grass, cupped my hands, and splashed my face with cold water. It trickled down my chest and neck, cooling my heated skin. My eyes slipped shut in contentment, and I reached up to slide the dress off my shoulders.

A loud splash echoed across the pond, and my eyes flew open. The naked back of a man emerged from the water, and I scrambled up the bank, making more noise than I thought possible in mud and grass. The man turned. *Finton.* My eyes widened in astonished mortification, flickering over the damp locks framing his face as he squinted toward shore before traveling down his chest.

More hair than I would've expected.

I regained my senses and turned around. "I'm so sorry! I didn't see you. If I'd known you were here, I wouldn't have come." And I will immediately cease reading the blasted novel that prompted such an inappropriate thought. My cheeks flushed again, not with heat but wretched embarrassment.

"Don't berate yourself so much," Finton said. The water lapped and sloshed around his hips as he waded through the murky water. "Keep your head turned."

He rose from the water with a *whoosh* and cascade of water flowing off his body. I shifted awkwardly, wishing the ground would open and swallow me whole. The rustle of clothing lasted forever. How many layers was he wearing?

"It's safe."

I startled from the close proximity of his voice, swallowed, and hesitantly turned to face him. Fortunately, he was clothed, wiping his spectacles on the linen shirt clinging to his wet skin. The red hue of *my* skin deepened, and I turned away again.

"The Lord Protector said I could come here," I said stupidly, as if the pond were a secret, forbidden place.

"A wise suggestion. You look as if you may have sunstroke. Are you feeling dizzy or lightheaded?"

"No," I said, too loudly even for my own ears. "I'm fine." I nodded enthusiastically, probably maniacally.

"Are you sure?" He donned the spectacles and regarded me with his physician's eye. "Your skin looks burned. It's really red."

Without answering, I walked stiffly away, through the trees, and back to the house. I found Laria still enjoying the shade with Eve and Fidelma. Forgetting all manners, I grabbed her arm and pulled her into the foyer.

"What's wrong?" she asked.

"I need to leave," I whispered.

"Are you ill?"

"No, I'm dying of embarrassment! And I can't stay another minute."

"What happened?"

"I went to the pond as the Lord Protector suggested, but when I got there, I wasn't alone. Before I could leave, I saw Finton. Naked!"

"Naked!" Laria's outburst could surely be heard all the way to the orchards.

"Shh!" I hissed, but a quick glance determined that only a few servants shared the space.

"You saw...everything?" Laria whispered.

"No, thank goodness. Just everything above the waist. The rest was underwater."

"Then what's the problem?"

"What do you mean? How can I look him in the eye after this?"

"Did you avert your gaze as a lady should?"

"Yes."

"Then what do you have to be ashamed of? It was an accident, and you only saw his chest. You're both adults, after all. You can move past this."

I regarded Laria warily, not quite convinced I could pretend nothing happened.

"My sister's first glimpse of an unclothed man!" Laria gushed, her hands framing her cheeks.

I frowned at her mocking tone.

"A truly momentous occasion!"

"Laria…" I let slip a twitch at the corners of my mouth.

"Was his chest very hairy? I can't stomach the thought of a man as furry as a beast."

I tried to resist her jests, but a laugh crept up my throat and the tension eased from my shoulders.

"Not very," I said. "Though I have no reference for comparison. He was more muscular than I would have guessed an intellectual man to be."

"Well, he works in an orchard as well," Laria said, her hands on her hips. "Such hard labor would keep any man in good shape."

I sighed, though not the wistful kind the character in my story would have uttered.

"So it'll be all right?" I wondered aloud.

"It could have been worse." Laria turned serious. "It could have been *Fynn* Ekhane you saw shirtless. Think how awful that would have been."

Our laughter filled the foyer and echoed through the entire manor.

Despite Laria's assurances, I felt a little distance would be beneficial after such an intimate encounter. I'm not proud of such a childish response, but the next day I avoided Finton. I told myself this was for his benefit, that he needed time to regain his dignity. But that, as Laria would say, was absolute rubbish.

I was being a coward because I didn't know how to speak to Finton without picturing him in the middle of the pond, rivulets of water tracing down his chest to places I wasn't about to consider. In retaliation for my devious thoughts, I threw the scandalous book in my trunk and slammed the lid shut. Before reading Arella's sordid tale, I would've never had such lascivious thoughts. To avoid picking up the book again, I read a history of cider making from cover to cover. In under five hours.

The children were a welcome distraction. We spent the hottest hours of the day inside reading and putting on theatricals, while the cooler morning and late afternoon were for exploring the hedgerows and watching the nobles train their birds. The children were fascinated by the large eagles. Risteard told the boys that when they were old enough, they would enter the practice yard at Praed and be paired with their own eagles. The girls would be matched with falcons. Laria was quick to add they would also be trained to be expert horsemen, a perfect blend of Ilano and Praed culture. Lilias showed little interest in any animals.

Laria and I leisurely strolled under the densely leafed trees blanketing the far end of the gardens in welcome shade. The princes and Sulwen watched a noble exercise his bird while their father explained the maneuvers. Lilias and Duveesa sat on a cushion of lush grass and played with dolls. Laria paused momentarily to listen to the little princess' narration of the toys' tale.

"They all have such vivid imaginations," I said.

"It doesn't matter how different we are from each other as long as their minds are rich with ideas."

"I would be surprised if they weren't so opinionated. Considering their mother."

Laria smiled, a lovely, peaceful smile. She closed her eyes and enjoyed a slight breeze stirring the small hairs framing her tranquil face. She'd earned the respite, not only after working so hard in the orchards. After surviving three years as an abused servant, Laria deserved every moment of peace.

A pained look flashed across her face, and her eyes darted around in confusion.

"Laria?" I said. "Are you all right?"

Her features relaxed and she nodded, but the next moment, a sharp cry was pulled from her body, and she buckled, clasping her abdomen and dropping to the ground.

I caught her up in my arms, falling beside her. "Laria! What's happening?"

"Ula…" Her voice was strangled, as if hands were literally tightening around her throat. "It hurts."

She cried out again, clutching her stomach, and our eyes journeyed downward. A bright plume of red appeared on her dress and spread across her front. All the warmth left my body.

"Olim!" I cried.

His blonde head appeared from behind a stand of trees. He saw the queen on the ground and took a step forward, but before he could speak, I yelled, "Get the king!"

Laria breathed in quick, shallow gasps and slumped in my arms, her skin eerily pale. I shook her, hoping to revive her, but she wouldn't open her eyes or answer my frantic questions. Footsteps thundered behind me, and I turned to see Risteard running toward us.

"What happened?" Then he saw her, the pale face and the blood-stained dress, and his complexion faded to match hers.

"I don't know," I said. "She grabbed her stomach and said it hurt."

"Oh, nooo…" His voice was low, mournful. He gathered her in his arms and carried her into the capitol building, saying her name.

I followed, waving away the children and telling them their mother was tired while giving the nurses a meaningful look.

Risteard carried Laria to her chambers, ignoring the stares and questions. He laid her on the bed, cupping her cheek and begging her to answer. Her eyes opened at last, but they were glossy and unfocused.

"Risteard," she said in a weak voice and clutched at his tunic. "What's happening? Is it…like Ailis?" Tears glistened in her eyes, and she cried out again in pain.

I looked from Risteard to Laria. "Who's Ailis?"

Risteard's jaw clenched and he pressed his forehead against Laria's. "My darling. No."

"I'm going to get the doctor," I said before rushing out the door.

Olim was waiting, his features strained. I told him to stay outside the door and not to let anyone enter, and he assumed his post gratefully.

I hoped Finton would be in the library and not out on rounds. I burst through the door, heard voices, and breathed a sigh of relief. I rounded the bookcases and leaned against them to catch my breath.

"Finton!" I gasped.

He looked up and all the students turned to eye me curiously.

"Emergency," was all I managed.

That was all he needed to act. He grabbed his black bag and hastily dismissed the class. I ran ahead, knowing he could keep up.

"Who is it?" he asked.

"The queen."

His speed increased and he outran me, reaching the queen's chambers first. Olim opened the door, and we dashed inside to witness Laria moaning in agony on a bed soaked with blood.

"Help me," Finton said.

I nodded, and he instructed Laria to lay on her back with her knees bent. She lolled from side to side, but Risteard was able to position her. Finton set his bag aside and tried to sort his way through Laria's gown. I grabbed the hem and ripped the bottom of the dress to shreds, exposing my sister's body. Risteard and I stared expectantly while Finton silently examined her.

"I'll need you to hand me instruments," he told me quietly.

Laria spoke incoherently in Risteard's arms, and he tightened his hold. His jaw clenched and his brow furrowed, the effort to control his emotions slipping the more Laria groaned and writhed. Finton described the instruments so I could pass them quickly. I tried to avert my eyes, but I found myself drawn to the movement of his hands as he worked. There was so much blood, surely more than a person could lose and still survive...

"Dr. Ekhane." Laria's voice was clear, distinct, and matter of fact. "Am I going to die?"

My heart seized and I looked to Finton for reassurance. My sister cannot die. If she dies, so will I. He held my gaze, then he met Laria's eyes over the tops of her knees and said, "Keep breathing. We'll talk soon."

"Finton is an extremely accomplished doctor," I said. "You couldn't place your life in more capable hands." I stared at Risteard pointedly, and his hold tightened.

I continued to hand Finton instruments and rags used to wipe the blood so he could see. I squeezed Laria's leg, hoping she would know I was there. Shadows gathered in the corners of the room, and the air became oppressive with tension. I focused on a bead of sweat at Finton's temple and watched it glide down his face. His hands were steady, his expression determined. I waited.

Laria's breathing grew stronger. I looked up and was relieved to see a pink tinge to her cheeks.

"The bleeding has stopped," Finton said. There was relief in his tone, and something else, something sad. He finished cleaning up and lowered her legs.

She stared at him expectantly.

"I'm so sorry," Finton said. His voice broke on the last word. He swallowed and looked away, but not before I saw his eyes were brimming with tears.

I'd never seen a grown man cry before, and it broke my heart. But nothing prepared me for his next words.

"Your pregnancy has miscarried."

The most agonizing sound escaped from Laria's mouth before her wails became muffled in Risteard's tunic. My heart shattered, and I struggled to maintain my composure in the face of her grief.

"How far along?" Risteard asked hoarsely.

"Did you not know?" Finton asked.

"No. Can you tell what it was?"

"No," Finton said, shaking his head solemnly. "It was too early. But she will live and be able to bear more children should you wish it."

Risteard nodded curtly and wrapped his arms around Laria more securely. Quietly, Finton gathered his supplies before we slipped out of the room. Olim waited outside, and I collapsed into his outstretched arms. I steadied myself in his enduring strength, my arms grasping his.

"Ula?" Olim said.

"Olim." My voice trembled. "People will have seen us hasten the queen inside. Many saw me summon Dr. Ekhane with great urgency. You must let it be known the queen survived her sudden onset of illness and will recover. Anything more that needs to be said will be announced by the king."

He squeezed my arms and I looked up. Questions rippled across his worried face, but I could explain no more. He seemed to read my expression, nodded, and left.

Finton sagged against the wall, looking defeated, and I could no longer bear the gravity of what happened. I clamped a hand over my mouth to keep from crying out, but I couldn't hold back the tears falling in torrents down my face.

"She loves children so much," I managed to say.

"She may have more in time," he said.

"You saved her life," I choked out past the anguish tightening my throat.

"She will live," he pronounced like a vow.

My knees shook so violently they could no longer support my body. I leaned forward, my head hitting Finton in the chest, and wept loud, bitter tears. His arms came around me, but I was too distraught to appreciate the comforting gesture. I barely registered him stroking my hair or the words he spoke in my ear. There was nothing that existed outside the despair of losing Laria and Risteard's child, a niece or nephew I would never have the privilege of meeting. How strange to love something you never knew was alive in the first place, but I mourned as I would any of my family. I couldn't imagine what Laria was feeling, but I knew it would be a long journey toward her recovery.

A few hours later, I stole a glance into my sister's room to check on her. She and Risteard lay in each other's arms, the emotional torment of the day engulfing them in a deep, bone-weary sleep. I pulled a blanket over them and touched Laria's cheek. Her skin was warm, yet pale, and her breathing ragged. She suffered the greatest loss any mother could bear, and the toll upon her physically and emotionally would be great indeed. She shifted in her sleep, and Risteard drew her closer into his protective embrace. My poor brother-in-law's eyes were red-rimmed and swollen.

I moved to the window and gazed out into the city, watching people go about their day. They walked blissfully through the street without a care, going blithely about their business. Yet how many of those people were living a nightmare they hid in order to function? How many of them suffered heartache and loss and pretended it didn't affect their daily lives? I turned to the sleeping pair. They would be forced to wear masks in public, to hide their grief and conduct themselves respectfully to rule their countries. How long would they be allowed to mourn?

For the next several days, I instructed the staff to leave the needs of the king and queen to me. There were questioning looks, but no one inquired as to the reason for their confinement. The children were particularly curious since their parents usually spent many hours a day in their company. I confided in Duveesa that the queen was quite ill without going into details, and with infinite wisdom, she was able to distract the children.

Laria didn't leave her bed, eat, nor drink following the loss of her child. Risteard remained at her side, and I could tell his frustration at her apathy was a greater burden than his mourning. I did everything in my power to coax her to eat, but she stared blankly ahead and wouldn't acknowledge me. Finton may have saved her life, but I feared his efforts would be for naught. If this continued for much longer, I worried she would follow the child beyond the veil.

Thus, my hesitancy at the door, a tray of food in my hands. My despondent sister lay on the other side, and I dreaded facing her expressionless face once again. Her cheeks were hollow, her eyes dull, and even her ginger hair lacked luster. She was fading before my eyes, and I feared one day I would open the door and find her lifeless. Though she never so much as glanced in my direction, I knew she needed me. I took a deep breath, ever so lightly rapped at the door, then quietly stepped inside.

Laria's bed was empty. My heart seized, and I almost dropped the tray. Risteard was slumped in a chair asleep, and I carefully set the tray next to him. My gaze traveled around the room and halted on Laria's still form sitting in front of the window. I took a few tentative steps forward, calling her name. I touched the tips of my fingers to her shoulder, scared I would find her cold and stiff beneath them. My breath *whooshed* as if a weight lifted off my chest when she turned to look at me.

"You're out of bed."

"Yes," she said quietly.

"Won't you come and eat?"

She blinked slowly and stared apathetically at the tray of food.

"I'm not inclined to eat just now," she said. "I was wondering if you could summon Dr. Ekhane. I'd like to speak with him, preferably before Risteard wakes up."

I glanced at the king uneasily then met Laria's eyes. They were clear, decided, and determined. An encouraging sign.

"Yes, Your Majesty." I gave a low curtsey.

I didn't care if I had to look for Finton at the bottom of a pond. If Laria needed him, I would present him, with or without his clothes.

O lim was stationed outside the door as usual, and I grabbed his arm before hurrying down the hallway.

"I need your help," I said. "I need to find Finton. For the queen."

"How is she?" he asked.

"She's requesting to see the doctor. I'll check the library if you go down to the stables and find out if he's left the city."

Olim nodded shortly and hastily ran off.

I gave no thought to my appearance as I ran down the corridor, my arms pumping and skirts flying around my ankles. I dodged nobles and servants, calling out hasty apologies over my shoulder and 'beg pardons' as I dashed through the hallway. I threw open the door to the library. The room was quiet, the tables empty, the only sound my harsh breathing. I slammed a fist onto the polished wood and cursed, thankful I was alone so no one could hear me. I spun on my heel and hurried to join Olim at the stables.

Drawing stares and troubled whispers, I skidded to a stop at Olim's side. My face was hot and flushed, and my chest burned with the exertion of running.

"Well?" I asked breathlessly.

"He left mere minutes ago," Olim said.

"Did you happen to notice which direction he was headed?" I asked the stable master.

He pointed in a direction out of the capital, his face awash with concern.

"Bring me a horse," I ordered. "Hurry. It's urgent." Doubtless my abrupt behavior would result in rumors, but I didn't care.

"Just give me a moment to saddle her," the stable master said.

"There's no time. Bridle a horse, a fast one, and bring it out."

The stable master glanced at Olim, much to my annoyance, and the knight nodded. Within seconds, a tall chestnut was produced wearing only a bridle. Olim gave me a leg up, and a *thank you* barely escaped my lips before I dug my heels into the animal's sides. We raced out of the city. Finton traveled at a leisurely pace on his rounds, but I wouldn't lose a second.

The city gave way to rows of trees and a smattering of farms. I reached a crossroads and pulled the horse to a stop. The animal tossed its head and frothed at the mouth as it danced beneath me, waiting for me to decide. There was no sign of Finton's gig. Hoofprints in the dirt headed in both directions. If Laria were here, she would have been able to determine how old they were, but I was a dunce at tracking. I growled in frustration, my thighs squeezing against the agitated beast. Then, I saw it. Down the road to my right was a fresh pile of manure, and when I looked closer, a plume of dust. I reined my horse in that direction and galloped toward it.

On the other side of a hill was a simple dwelling with several people milling around a familiar gig pulled by a cream-colored horse. I urged the horse faster with a swift kick and a yell, sending us flying over the road, my hair blowing free from dislodged pins.

We arrived at a mad pace at the front of the house, sending up a torrent of dirt. A man, most likely the owner of the house, clutched his chest in surprise.

Finton cautiously approached the fidgeting horse. "Ula? What's wrong?"

"You're needed back at the capital. Can you come?"

The desperation in my voice prompted a shift in Finton's confused features. He turned to the man, begged his forgiveness, and excused himself for an emergency. The man, despite the scare he received, was very understanding and granted his leave.

I jerked my head toward the passive mare harnessed to the gig. "How fast can that horse go?"

He paused, considering briefly before glancing up at my frantic expression.

"Not fast enough." Finton hopped off the gig and held his bag out to me. While I situated it in front of me, he hauled himself onto my horse.

"Hold on," I said. Finton barely had time to wrap his arms around me before I kicked the horse hard, and the beasts' hooves dug into the earth as it launched itself forward. I hoped he could keep himself on the horse's back without falling and sending me crashing to the ground. He seemed to have a good seat. I didn't allow myself to consider his tight hold around my waist had anything to do with it.

"Is it the queen?" Finton yelled over the pounding of the hooves.

"Yes," I said over my shoulder. "She's out of bed and asking for you."

The horse faltered when the capitol building stables came into view, and I silently begged for the animal not to stumble. Sweat poured from its neck and flanks, and its breathing was ragged when I brought it to a halt before the wide-eyed stable master. Finton leaped off and reached for me in one fluid motion, and the moment my feet touched the ground, we ran into the building. Olim appeared as if he had been awaiting our arrival and waved away the concerned citizens.

"We should go by the servant's entrance," Olim said. "To keep the wagging tongues at bay."

As one, the three of us veered toward the back of the building and entered via the kitchens. Though our appearance must have been startling, the cooks barely raised an eyebrow as he wove our way through. I was out of breath and my knees were shaking when we made it up the stairs, and Olim had to propel me the rest of the way to Laria's room. I stopped at the door and the two men nearly bumped into me. I held a finger up to my lips.

"The king is asleep, and the queen prefers he stay that way," I said. Quietly, I opened the door. Finton and I entered, leaving Olim to stand guard outside.

Laria was seated at the window, just as I left her, while the king slouched further in the chair. I swallowed past the tightening of my throat, my heartbeat steadily decreasing. We took a few tentative steps closer, and Laria turned to face us.

"Dr. Ekhane," she said calmly. "You seem out of breath."

"You asked to see me, Your Majesty?" Finton said between gasps.

"Yes." She rose and moved into an alcove further away from the king. She sat on a plush chair and bid Finton to sit across from her. I stood beside him, leaning onto the chair as the heat in my cheeks faded and my breathing returned to normal.

"Are you in much pain?" Finton asked.

"No," Laria said, shaking her head. "I wish to have a frank discussion with you, Dr. Ekhane. Can you accommodate me?"

"I will answer any question you ask using my objective medical opinion," he stated.

"That's just what I hoped. Tell me then, doctor, could I have prevented the loss of my child?"

My heart sank at such a devastating question. I prepared to argue that this wasn't her fault, but Finton spoke first.

"I cannot say for certain, Your Majesty. But I will tell you the facts as I know them. You are young and healthy and have carried five pregnancies to term. Statistically speaking, the odds that you would suffer a miscarriage due to any deficiency on your part is highly unlikely."

"I have been working in the orchards. In the heat," she said, her eyes welling with tears.

"I have seen women in their eighth month work during harvest with no ill effects. If your body is used to working, it will not affect a pregnancy. It's not always the popular opinion amongst medical professionals, but I believe a woman should keep herself fit as opposed to remaining confined during her pregnancy. It helps maintain her strength and stamina for the labor."

A smile crept along Laria's lips, but just as quickly faded.

"Furthermore," he said in his clinical tone. "You were not very far along. When a pregnancy miscarries at such an early time, it is often because the fetus itself is not viable. It's nature's way."

My fingers dug into the fabric of the chair, but Laria seemed to find comfort in his detached tone.

"I appreciate your candor, Dr. Ekhane," she said.

"Your Majesty," he said. "This was not your fault. A child in its mother's womb is built to withstand many of the outward traumas we as adults face. Have you been stressed during any of your other pregnancies? Beyond the normal rigors of life, I mean?"

The corner of Laria's mouth twitched. "A little."

"And the child is now well and healthy?"

She smiled, a real, genuine smile. "He is."

"There's no plainer way to express myself than that, Your Majesty."

Laria looked away and struggled to maintain her composure. I wanted to go to her, to embrace her and tell her she was the strongest woman I'd ever known. But I knew she would brush me aside in a bid to regain control of her emotions, so I willed my feet to remain still, and watched as she resumed her cool demeanor.

"You have bestowed upon me the frankness of which I asked for." She faced Finton again. "And in return I will be just as candid with you. I am able to conceive more children, correct?"

"Yes, Your Majesty," Finton said.

"How soon?"

I opened my mouth to protest, but a sharp look from my sister stilled my tongue.

"I recommend waiting until after you have a normal monthly cycle. And if you will permit me to say, Your Majesty, I suggest you recover some of your health first. You are quite pale and thinner than when I last saw you." His voice was low, almost mournful, and Laria nodded in understanding. "I recommend a diet consisting of red meat at least three days a week to replenish the blood you lost as well as plenty of fresh air."

"Anything else?" she asked.

Finton shifted and his eyes darted in my direction. Laria sensed his unease, and it amused her. She extended a hand, inviting him to continue.

"Your body should be allowed time to heal. I would suggest refraining from marital relations for the next few weeks as well."

Heat bloomed from my cheeks to the tips of my ears. Laria's mouth quirked. Her eyes drifted toward her sleeping husband and a full-fledged smile spread across her face.

"That is a request I'm not sure I can abide," she said. Though her words made me blush, I was grateful to hear the humor in her voice.

"I can examine you next week and hopefully shorten the sentence," Finton teased.

"That would be greatly appreciated." Laria rose from the chair and walked toward Risteard's prone form. She placed a hand on his shoulder, and he was instantly awake.

"Laria?" His voice was heavy with sleep.

She smiled down at him, and he grasped her hand as if she were the last glass of water in a desert.

"Risteard." Laria's voice was clear and confident. "Dr. Ekhane and I have been speaking. He has been very informative." She met Finton's steady gaze with an equally strong eye. "He has saved the life of your queen. He should be compensated."

Risteard hastily gained his feet, his eyes only for Laria. He cupped her cheek and saw a face devoid of helplessness. She lay her hand over his, and the tension drained from his face.

"Dr. Ekhane," Risteard said. "If you would accompany me to my study."

He stalked out of the room. Finton looked at me with uncertainty. I motioned for him to follow and moved to comfort Laria.

"If you would help Dr. Ekhane find his way," she began, "that would be best. You know how Risteard hates to be kept waiting. I would like to rest now."

"Of course," I said. My eyes blurred with unshed tears. Laria squeezed my shoulder and asked me to inform the cook of her updated diet. I nodded, then accompanied Finton into the hall.

Finton wrung his hands on the handle of his black bag when we entered the study and approached the king. He gestured for Finton to take a seat across a vast desk, and I propped myself against the opposite wall to keep out of the way.

"Dr. Ekhane," Risteard said. "You have not only given a kingdom back their queen, but me back my life. If there is anything I can offer to repay you, it is yours."

My gaze flickered to Finton. He considered the king's words, then smiled.

"Your Majesty," Finton said. "I have performed my duties as a physician. I would have done the same for any lady requiring my help. I don't need payment, but I appreciate your thanks."

"Surely you must make a living."

"I live comfortably enough, Your Majesty."

"There is nothing I can give that would adequately express my thanks?"

"I don't perform my services in hopes of a reward or accolades. There is nothing more I need than to see the queen fully recover."

"He wants to study in Hrgun," I blurted before I could stop myself.

Both men turned to me, Finton wide-eyed and Risteard inquisitively.

"Hrgun, as I understand it, is a great center for learning. Some of the brightest minds study at the universities there," Risteard said.

"Yes, Your Majesty," Finton said nervously. "And Miss Audrey is correct that I wish to study there, but I don't have the means, and I believe my father would prefer I remain in Ilano."

"He's said this for certain?"

"Well…" Finton looked up at the ceiling and shrugged. "Not in so many words."

"Dr. Ekhane, I would be glad to sponsor your studies in Hrgun, including any living expenses you may incur, for however long you require to become the surgeon you wish to be. Consider it a payment for services rendered."

My heart swelled at the king's proposal, and I excitedly turned to Finton to gauge his reaction. His eyes were wide, and he couldn't speak, though his mouth moved to form words.

"Consider it," Risteard said.

"I will, Your Majesty."

Risteard nodded and rose, and Finton nearly toppled over in his haste to get up.

"If you will excuse us, Dr. Ekhane," Risteard said.

Finton turned his wide gaze on me, and I was sure my features mirrored his own. The king and I rarely spoke alone, and my speaking out of turn might earn me a reprimand. Finton bowed toward the king and shuffled backward out of the room, his eyes never leaving mine. I worried I would soon be issued a verbal lashing from *him* as well.

"Hrgun?" Risteard asked once the door closed.

"Yes," I said, still uneasy. "He wants to study there, but he feels family obligations necessitates his remaining here. To be honest, I think his brother has guilted him into staying."

Risteard nodded, and I could see his mind working behind his blank expression. I relaxed when no reprimand was forthcoming.

"Laria looked well," he said.

"Yes. She needed someone to release her from the burden of believing the miscarriage was her fault. Someone other than us, I mean."

"And Dr. Ekhane was able to convince her of this?"

"He didn't just tell her what she needed to hear. He told her the truth in a way she accepted—in detached, clinical terms."

"Then I will be forever grateful to him."

"Me, too."

"I've been neglecting the council."

I curtseyed, knowing his words signaled the end of our meeting.

"I will check on the queen after I report to the kitchens."

Risteard extended his arm for me to precede him out of the study, and I happily obliged, a relieved smile on my lips.

In the following days, Laria's health and spirits gradually returned. She started eating again, resumed her daily walks in the garden, and spent most of the afternoons with the children, overjoyed to have their mother back. There were a few inquiries regarding her absence, but Laria distracted them with play and stories until the questions ceased and only the fun remained.

I watched her from underneath the boughs of a tree chasing the princes in a game of tag and reveled in the sound of her laughter. I braided flowers into Lilias' hair, and she clapped her pudgy hands when Laria caught Rian and twirled him in circles. Alyx danced around them singing a song, very poorly, causing Tyrnan to fall over laughing. Sulwen took advantage of her brother's vulnerability and jumped on top of him, eliciting an 'oof!' from the victim and more laughter from the other children.

"It's so good to see everything returning to normal," Duveesa said. "We were so worried about Her Majesty's health."

Lilias jumped off my lap and ran off to join the fun.

"Yes," I said. "I was afraid I'd never get my sister back."

"Can you tell me what was wrong? There's been speculation, but no one knows for certain."

"I can't. The king and queen didn't make the malady public knowledge, so I must respect their privacy and say nothing."

"I understand," Duveesa said. We watched the family in companionable silence, both of us grateful they were once again whole.

"I've heard a rumor about *you*," Duveesa said with a sly smile.

"Me?" I was incredulous. "Why would people want to gossip about me?"

Her smile widened. "It's in regard to a certain gentleman."

"Oh?" I brushed flowers off my gown and flattened the creases. "I don't know why that would be." Were people talking about me and Finton? I couldn't say I was entirely surprised, especially after the way we rode frantically into the city on the back of the same horse several days prior. Now I was going to have to quell any rumors before they reached *his* ears.

"You have to admit you spend an awful lot of time together."

"Not so much time."

"You're practically joined at the hip!"

"That's a little exaggerated, don't you think?"

"Ula," Duveesa laughed and grasped my shoulder. "Calm down! No one is accusing you of anything scandalous. I think it's rather sweet actually."

"I don't want people to talk about me!" Panic rose in my chest, and I placed a hand against my heart to still its fluttering.

"That can't always be helped," she said.

"How do I make it stop?"

"You can't. All you can do is make sure your behavior is above reproach."

"Has anything been said in that regard?"

"Of course not. People are merely talking about how close you appear to be and how well you look together. It makes sense, if you think about it. You're always together and he's very attentive."

"Do you think he's heard the rumors?"

"I don't know. Do you think he would act differently if he did?"

"It's hard to say. We haven't spoken in a few days."

Duveesa's brow furrowed, and she cocked her head quizzically. Her gaze briefly flickered to Olim where he stood ever watchful several feet away.

"How can that be?" she asked. "He's right there."

I followed her stare, and when my eyes fell on my vigilant knight, I turned back in surprise.

"Olim?" I whispered loudly. "He's the man?"

"Who did you think I meant?" she whispered back.

"Not him! How mortifying! People are talking about me and *Olim*? He's my protector!"

"It's only natural to develop feelings for someone you're so close to."

"He's my friend!"

"Isn't that as good a basis as any to begin a relationship?"

"There is no relationship!" I cried as I cradled my face in my hands.

"Ula, relax!" She rubbed my back. "There's no reason to become so defensive. It's only talk after all."

"What should I do?"

"Don't let the rumors trouble you, but perhaps consider their perspective."

"What do you mean?"

"Well, you said yourself that Olim is your friend and you've never considered him more than that. Until now."

I eyed Duveesa warily and she laughed at my expression.

"Just think about it. He's handsome, brave, and a good friend. A man worth considering as a potential suitor if you ask me."

I looked at Olim standing stoically in the sunshine, constant as always even in the blistering heat. I'd never studied him as a man. His blonde curls shone like fresh straw in the sunlight, his skin tanned from exposure to its rays. He did indeed have a handsome face with a strong chin and soulful blue eyes. Funny that I never noticed before. My gaze traveled the length of his body, noting his wide shoulders, muscular arms, and firm stance. He was an excellent example of a manly physique to be sure.

"I don't have any interest in suitors," I said, though my tone lacked the intensity from earlier.

"All women want suitors," Duveesa said. "Even women who don't want suitors."

"I'm certain Olim has no such intentions toward me."

"Are you?"

I started to answer, but paused, considering. Olim and I had been friends for a long time, and I assumed we shared the same level of esteem. But what if he didn't? He always treated me with kindness and respect, and those times we quarreled it resembled that of a brother and sister as opposed to lovers. At least, that's what I always thought. He could be critical, it was true, but I attributed this to his protective nature, especially considering he believed he failed his sister. The stare I fixed upon him next was contemplative. Olim didn't talk about his personal feelings very often, so how could I be sure of his regard for me?

"Pretty sure…" I said.

"I wouldn't discount him outright if I were you," Duveesa said with a glint in her eye. "He is very pleasing to look at."

She raised an eyebrow, and I couldn't help a giggle from escaping my lips. We laughed together, our voices joining in the echo of the royal family dodging in and out of trees and bushes as they played.

After a while, Duveesa said, "Wait. Who did you think I was talking about?"

"No one," I said. Too quickly it would seem. Duveesa eyed me suspiciously. "I think I'll join in on the game." I hurried to my feet. "How about you?"

"Sure," she said slowly as she rose, the odd look remaining.

She asked no more questions as we walked toward the romping children. Olim smiled and inclined his head as we passed. I turned away so he couldn't see me blushing. I roughly elbowed Duveesa when she covered her mouth to muffle a laugh, and I lamented that from this day forward I would not be able to look at him without remembering our conversation.

Several people crowded the docks, some waiting for loved ones and others for deliveries of supplies. Arella scanned their faces, wondering which man was waiting for her, knowing he may possess her hand, but he would never possess her heart.

One man stood apart from the rest, and her mood sank further as she surveyed his appearance. He donned fine clothing, but of a fashion that was at least two years old. He was short in stature, much shorter than she, and was at least twice her age as evidenced by his balding head. Bile rose in her throat, and she took a hesitant step forward. He looked up at her and wiped perspiration from his wide brow. She gulped, her throat dry, and spoke.

"I beg your pardon," Arella said through trembling lips. "Are you perchance Lord Griffith?"

A deep voice resonated behind her. "No. I am."

Arella spun around and discovered all her expectations did not prepare her for reality.

I closed the book I promised myself I would no longer read. But like Arella, I was powerless to resist. Escaping into a fantasy was much easier than reflecting on the strange developments of real life. The rumors Duveesa revealed to me were troubling, but what was more intriguing was my reaction to them. Perhaps the people could see something I didn't? Was I closing myself off to the possibility of Olim having affection for me simply because I couldn't believe it? And if he did, how did I really feel about it? Could I return those feelings? I slid the book onto the night table and wondered if there had been signs I was too oblivious to notice. As my eyes drifted close, I resolved that I would heed Duveesa's advice and keep an open mind.

Chapter 13

The apple harvest was waning, but soon the cultivation of pears and pumpkins, which I was informed tasted very good baked in pastry, would commence. An outdoor assembly was planned where farmers would present their finest examples from the harvest to the Lord Protector, a tradition hundreds of years old. In return, the Lord Protector would take these offerings and use them to feed the guests at a grand party at the end of harvest. Ilano certainly enjoyed their celebrations.

Laria resumed attending council meetings and visiting neighboring orchards, returning my days to normalcy. Not only was I grateful to have my sister back, but it was also refreshing to have a change of scenery. In addition to some of the greater estates, Laria also insisted we visit some of the lowlier farms. The Lord Protector was impressed with her idea, but his son was not pleased.

"Forgive me, Your Majesty," Fynn said, his words dripping with condescension. "But I would advise against such a venture. You've been treated to the best comforts on the larger farms and the more...destitute ones might come as a shock. I would hate for the conditions to unsettle Your Majesty, especially after recovering from an illness."

I sucked a sharp hiss through my teeth and looked to Laria for her response to this impertinent remark. The king shifted in his seat, his fist curled into a ball on the table. Laria's neck reddened and her green eyes flashed in barely restrained fury, but she maintained her composure with all the patience of a mother of five. The Lord Protector's face was pale as he looked from his foolish son to his queen, but he wisely said nothing.

"Though I appreciate your concern both for my welfare and my sensibilities, I am not unfamiliar with the conditions of those less fortunate than us. We will visit these farms, Fynn Ekhane, and there will be no further discussion on the matter. Do I make myself clear?" Laria's cool tone sent a shiver up my spine.

I could practically hear Fynn's teeth grinding.

"If you insist, Your Majesty," he said, inclining his head. "I would recommend a strong showing of knights."

"A trusted few will suffice," she said.

"Make all the necessary arrangements." The king rose. The men scrambled to their feet and bowed as he escorted the queen from the council chambers.

"Insufferable!" Laria muttered once the doors closed behind us.

"I know," Risteard said.

"Is he like that with all women or just me?"

They were walking so quickly I stumbled trying to keep up. Laria glanced back and slowed her pace.

"Fynn Ekhane is equally intolerable to both men and women. He makes no distinction."

"How can such a sweet man produce such an awful son?"

"He's the product of his own making."

"And he hopes to be Lord Protector someday."

I nearly choked when Laria spoke those words. Surely that would be a disaster.

"Not as long as I am king," Risteard said, his voice a low growl. He stopped to level a meaningful look at Laria, and she looked up at him with a powerful gaze of her own. They continued to stare at each other, and the tension left Laria's body, replaced by a different kind of intensity. I focused on my feet and shifted awkwardly.

"Ula," Laria said, making me jump. "Would you be a dear and check on the preparations for the party this evening?"

"Yes...if you wish," I said. Such a mundane task was not one I usually performed, but I guessed her real motivation in asking was to get rid of me based on her quick smile and apathetic wave before she dragged her husband down the hall. I rolled my eyes at their retreating backs.

If they'd wanted to speak in private, they could have told me.

The sun hadn't reached its zenith, but the temperature was already approaching a sweltering pitch. People were already at work transforming the gardens into a welcoming assembly. White tents were erected to cover long tables for dining and banners were shifting in the gentle breeze delivering relief from the heat. A platform for musicians was built at one end of the gardens in front of a vast lawn. There were no thrones, for at this assembly everyone was equal. Even from outside, I could smell the enticing aromas from the kitchens. I closed my eyes and inhaled the pleasing scents of pastries, bread, and meat and sighed in satisfaction.

"It's going to be very hot today, but that should make for a comfortable evening."

My stomach twisted at the sound of Olim's voice, and a slight blush crept across my cheeks. Hesitantly, I looked up into his smiling face and wondered if he'd heard the gossip I'd been made privy to. He didn't act any differently toward me. He didn't shift awkwardly or avert his gaze nor blush. His eyebrows raised expectantly when I continued to study him silently.

"Yes," I said and hastily looked away. "I do look forward to tonight. I understand everyone in Ilano is welcome."

"Well, anyone who owns land and farms," Olim said. "This is for those that harvest, which does exclude much of the population."

"Nevertheless, it will be a diverse gathering."

"Does that frighten you?"

"Why should it?"

"New people," he teased as he waggled his eyebrows.

I shoved his shoulder and smirked.

"I think I've done very well speaking to strangers on this visit."

"You have. You should be proud of yourself."

My heart swelled with satisfaction. "I am." It was very kind of him to say so, and I thought it would stir something inside of me if indeed I had some hitherto unknown affection for him. But while I appreciated his words, they did not move me as I would have expected were I... besotted with him.

"I wish your sister would come and indulge in the festivities like any young woman."

"I know," he said. "But Enyleve will not come back here. Too many bad memories."

"I understand."

"I would like for the two of you to get on better, though. Perhaps you could join my family for dinner? You could meet my father."

My face brightened and a tremor of anticipation stole up my back.

"I would really like that, Olim. I do want Enyleve and me to be friends."

He smiled. "Me, too."

I took a moment to really look at his face, something I never bothered to do before. He was quite young, only a few years older than I, but he already had a few lines of worry about the mouth and eyes. I wondered if his having to protect me had anything to do with that. His short blonde curls were still unblemished with gray, and when his smile extended across the whole of his face, the slightest dimples appeared on his cheeks. Strange that I never noticed before. Duveesa was right. Olim was indeed handsome.

"Let me know when," I said in a daze.

The sun crawled across the sky and would soon start setting, leaving behind its warmth. Torches were placed around the gardens for when the light faded, but for now the last rays of the sun illuminated the assembled nobles and farmers who gathered to compare stories and toast to their prosperity. Children waved ribbons and stuffed treats into their mouths, and even straight-laced Lilias found a few girls her age to romp with.

Only once did a fight have to be prevented when Rian "accidentally" dropped a fruit tart on Gerrid Ekhane's head. The older boy promptly climbed the tree where the little prince was hiding with threats of poundings, and Rian nearly broke his arm jumping out of it. He raced to hide behind his father, but the king was in no mood to indulge in his son's mischief.

"What did you do?" Risteard demanded.

"Nothing!" Rian whined.

At that moment, the angry custard and berry-stained victim came stalking forward and the prince shrank backward. I took a long sip of punch to hide my amused expression. The king eyed the fuming ten-year-old and looked down at his son.

"Your work I presume?" he asked the boy.

"It was an accident!" Rian said.

"You were accidentally eating up a tree?" Gerrid yelled.

Laria spoke up. "Rian Elejick, were you climbing trees again after you were told not to?"

The prince nodded sheepishly, shuffling his feet. He was in trouble now.

"Apologize," his father ordered.

Rian at least had enough self-preservation not to argue any further and mumbled, "Sorry," without meeting Gerrid's eye.

"Like you mean it," the king demanded, and even *I* would have with that tone.

Rian met Gerrid's twisted little face, his hair plastered to his head and custard dripping down his cheeks. The prince's green eyes were glossy, but he jutted out his chin and restrained his tears.

"Apologies," the prince said in his most authoritative voice. He opened his mouth to say more, glanced up at his father, then thought the better of it.

"Come on," Laria said before leading Gerrid away. "Let's get you cleaned up."

The young boy's murderous glare never left Rian's, and I knew this wouldn't be the last quarrel between them.

"Rian," I started, my voice conveying my disappointment. "Didn't we have a conversation about fighting? You were so upset when Alyx was going to fight. What possessed you to do the same?"

"He was saying bad things about Sulwen," he said, his lower lip trembling.

Risteard and I looked at each other in confusion.

"What could he possibly have to say about a toddler?" I wondered aloud.

No longer able to maintain a brave exterior, Rian broke down and wailed, "He said it must be her red hair that makes her so bad!"

The king's eyes turned dangerously black, and his right hand twitched at his side.

"You can't listen to what he says," I said hastily, speaking to both the prince and his enraged father. "It's only words, and he's just a boy trying to get attention." I knelt before Rian and grabbed his shoulders. "It is admirable of you to defend your sister, but you must ignore him! Do you understand?"

He nodded, sniffling and wiping his eyes. He buried his face in his father's tunic, and the king placed a gentle hand on the boy's head.

"Listen to your aunt," Risteard said, his voice quiet. "Words certainly can hurt us, but we have to overcome the anger they cause. Otherwise, those who speak them will win." He lifted the prince and wrapped him in a tight hug, meeting my eyes over the boy's shoulder. I inclined my head, and he carried the prince away, no doubt to find a sweet treat to cheer him up. Well, one he wouldn't drop on anyone's head. I hoped.

The dancing was lively and loud, with laughter and voices lifting into the sky as dusk fell. The torches were lit, and candles reflected from within the tents, creating a shadow dance of people as they served themselves drinks and delicious food. There was no formal dinner tonight. Dish after dish was brought out and placed upon the long tables, and one would serve themselves at their leisure.

I avoided the ice wine.

People moved in rhythm to the music, not as a set but individually, as if there were no steps at all. Olim pulled me into the fray, and I protested I didn't know the steps.

"No one does!" he said. "You just dance!"

I allowed the music to move me, and together Olim and I twirled and leapt among the other couples, all of us enjoying the freedom of the night. I was breathless with exertion and laughter by the time the music faded, and I was thankful for the proffered glass Olim placed in my hands.

"It's only punch," he assured me when I eyed the contents.

I emptied the cool liquid in only a few swallows.

"I would love one of those myself," Duveesa said between gasps. Her face was flushed from dancing as was her partner's, little Prince Alyx.

"Me, too!" he added.

Olim left to retrieve some refreshments, and Duveesa elbowed my ribs and gave me a meaningful look.

"You danced well tonight." Her eyes darted in Olim's direction and sly smile spread across her face.

"Stop it," I said.

She muffled her laughter, turning her face toward the throngs of people to avoid my glare.

"It's getting late," Duveesa said. She rubbed lazy circles into the base of her neck. "The children should be put to bed."

"Would you like my help?" I asked.

"No, we can manage," she said, referring to the other nurses. "You enjoy the rest of the evening." She hugged me tightly and went to round up the royal brood.

I moved around the edge of the assembly content to observe rather than participate. The party was coming to an end, but many still danced and drank, especially the older farmers who indulged in this one night of the year. I didn't recognize anyone, but I smiled and inclined my head to those offering a kind eye. My belly was full, so I retreated into the shelter of a tree with low hanging branches, the torchlight casting flickering shadows across my face. I leaned against the tree and closed my eyes, listening to the last notes of a pleasing tune.

"You look as if you're enjoying the festivities," a familiar voice said.

My eyes flew open and there was Finton in a wrinkled amber tunic. He brushed back his messy hair and flicked a speck of dirt off his hem.

"Where have you been?" I bit my lip in embarrassment at my impertinence.

His mouth curved into a lopsided grin. "I didn't realize I'd been expected."

"You weren't. I mean, I didn't intend to make it seem that you were and that I was displeased. Because I'm not."

"I was sent for. Not that you require an explanation." He quirked an eyebrow.

"I don't!" I shuffled my feet and was grateful the darkness concealed my inflamed cheeks. "Are they all right? The patient, I mean. I assume that's what you were sent for."

"It was. An accident on one of the farms, but he'll recover. Thank you for your concern."

I took a few breaths through my nose to steady my nerves. Finton was silent for several seconds and didn't meet my gaze. By the drooping of his shoulders and neutral expression, I sensed he was preparing to broach a serious subject.

"Ula," he began in a quiet tone. "Would you do me the honor of accompanying me on my rounds tomorrow? There's something I wish to discuss with you."

A shudder passed through my chest, and I inhaled sharply. I couldn't speak with a frozen heart, so I nodded mutely.

"With the queen's permission of course." He winked.

"I'll ask her tonight." My mind was abuzz with the possibilities of the nature of this 'discussion.' Was it regarding my presumption when he spoke with the king? Or some other offense? Or could it perhaps be something else, something...less disagreeable?

"Well, I know I've only just arrived," he said, "but I'm afraid I must wish you goodnight. It's been a long day."

"So soon?" I cringed at the evident disappointment in my voice. "Can't you stay for a little refreshment? Perhaps one dance? After all, the assembly is almost over."

His eyes drifted toward the dwindling number of revelers enjoying the last of the evening's entertainment. He adjusted his spectacles and again ran his fingers through his hair.

My insistence had been inappropriate. "Forgive me," I said. "I shouldn't have—"

"Would you dance with me?"

My words froze on my lips, and I stared dumbly at him. The firelight illuminated his features, and the nature of his expression was intriguing. I was not familiar enough with his moods to be able to decipher what he was thinking, but I could at least deduce he was not annoyed or simply placating me. I took his proffered arm and he led me among the last dancers of the evening.

The music remained lively, and the excited movements of the people as they enjoyed the remnants of the evening soothed my anxiety. As Finton and I joined in the circle of dancers spinning and kicking their feet, my trepidation completely vanished, and I gave myself up to the motions and notes moving us. The young woman next to me laughed and exclaimed she'd never had so much fun at an outdoor assembly. I smiled back, and it was then I noticed how tired I was. Too tired to engage in conversation at any rate. I looked down at our clasped hands as we followed the serpentine chain we formed, and I hoped he didn't notice the dampness of my palms. Self-conscious, I slipped my hand out of his grasp, and when he glanced at me in confusion, I excused myself from the dance.

"Is something wrong?" His brow furrowed in concern.

"The queen will be preparing to retire." My voice wavered.

"Of course." He flashed a good-natured smile. "Tomorrow then?"

"I'll meet you in the library if I'm able."

He bowed and I retreated, and I was further ashamed of my rudeness in not returning the gesture. What had come over me I couldn't say, but my legs felt heavy, and my head spun. As I approached the queen, I was certain at any moment I would retch. Being an astute observer, she immediately noticed my distress.

Laria grasped my shoulder. "What's wrong? You look like you're going to be sick."

My thoughts couldn't keep up with my mouth, and I shook my head to sort the jumbled mess. I met her eye and forced a smile, then asked if she might be ready for bed. She studied my face, her green eyes roaming over me intently.

"I think that would be best," she said evenly, and she linked her arm with mine. She strode over to the king staring ahead placidly while Fynn Ekhane prattled on in his ear. His cerulean eyes softened at our approach, though he stood just as rigidly. Fynn bowed clumsily when he noticed us, and I stifled a grin.

"I'm going to bed," the queen said.

The king's eyes flickered to me briefly before he nodded, and I was pulled toward the building without another word exchanged between them.

"Won't he wonder at your abruptness?" I nearly tripped over my hem.

"No."

The queen remained silent when we entered her bedchamber and I assisted her out of her gown. She sat at the vanity, still quiet as I removed the pins from her voluminous hair and started brushing out the thick strands.

"Laria, may I ask you a question?"

"Of course."

"Finton invited me to accompany him on his rounds tomorrow. May I join him?"

She turned and looked up at me, a small smile on her face. "Did he? I'm glad to be aware of it this time." I pursed my lips at her teasing, and she laughed lightly. "You don't need my permission, Ula. I just like to know where you are. If you wish to go, then of course you may."

"That's just it, I'm not sure I do want to go."

She spun around and fixed me with a strange look. "Why not?"

"I have a strong suspicion that I'm being invited so he can lecture me."

"About what?"

I averted my eyes and said, "For being presumptuous."

She raised an eyebrow. "In regard to?"

"When the king asked about compensating him for…his service to you, he said he wanted nothing in return. I spoke up and informed the king that Finton wanted to study in Hrgun."

"Risteard told me about it. He said he offered to sponsor Finton's career there. He has yet to give his answer."

"Finton hasn't spoken to me much since. I don't think he appreciated me saying that."

"Why not?"

"He doesn't want to disappoint his father by leaving. I'm afraid I may have intruded into his personal affairs."

"Perhaps, but if he wasn't going to speak up for himself, you may as well have. No one is forcing him to accept Risteard's offer."

I contemplated her words, and a small smile spread across Laria's face.

"What?"

"What did Finton say exactly? When he invited you out tomorrow."

"He asked if I might accompany him on his rounds as there was something he wished to discuss with me."

"And you assumed the worst?"

"Well, what else could he be referring to?"

Her eyes traveled up and down my body, and she turned back to the mirror.

"Take all afternoon if you wish. I trust you without an escort trailing after you if Finton can ensure your safety." The small smile remained on her lips as I finished preparing her for bed, and she ignored my inquisitive glances. She settled into bed and retrieved a book from her nightstand, still avoiding my gaze.

"Laria? Are you hiding something?"

She looked up at me, eyes wide and innocent.

"I have nothing to hide, gem," she said.

"You're thinking about something. I can see your mind turning. You had the same look when you were trying to figure out how best to sneak from the house without Mother and Father noticing so you could ride before breakfast. And I know how that turned out."

She smirked. "It worked."

"So? What new mischief are you planning now?"

"None, I promise. I just had a thought, but that doesn't mean it's true. Don't trouble yourself about it."

"It worries me more when you say things like that!"

Laria closed the book and rolled her eyes. "Ula! It's nothing!" She sighed and regarded me warily. "I would hate to say something, have you fret about it, then have nothing come of it. I don't want to influence you. We'll talk about it tomorrow night, though. I promise."

"Very well." I stomped off to bed.

Chapter 14

My anxiety was high, and my hands trembled violently while I helped the queen dress. She asked if I needed a glass of wine.

"No, I'm all right," I said.

"Are you nervous about today?" A sly grin crept onto her lips.

"A little. Laria?"

"Mm-hmm?"

"Do you know Olim's family?"

"He never introduced them. We extended an invitation that went unanswered."

"They don't trust the people here."

"Don't they?" She raised an eyebrow.

"Nothing against you or the king! Olim's sister had a bad experience. That's such a simple way to put it." I rested my hands on my hips and tapped the hairbrush against my thigh. "A man extorted her dowry from her."

"Did he?" Her eyes darkened, her voice low, cold, and frightening. "What's his name?"

"I don't know. Olim never said and his family never pursued it. I can't believe they just let him get away with it! He wronged them." I was aware of my petulant tone, but I didn't care. "Why wouldn't they come forward, even in confidence, if it meant seeing him pay for what he's done?"

"Privacy? Family honor? Shame? There are many reasons. Even for the sake of justice, you cannot ask a woman to relive the most traumatic moment of her life."

Laria's eyes sparkled verdant in the sunshine streaming through the window, and though her expression was passive, in her steady gaze I sensed a deeper understanding of the situation.

Silence stretched between us as I styled her hair. I glanced at her reflection in the mirror, and her eyes were far away—not in distance, but in time.

"How much longer do you think we'll remain in Ilano?" I hoped a change of subject might bring her out of her dark reverie.

"I don't know. I imagine we'll stay until the end of harvest at least. I would prefer to travel home before the winter. Have you enjoyed our visit here?"

"I have." I nodded eagerly. "I was nervous about meeting so many new people, but I'm glad we came."

She smiled, but it didn't reach her eyes.

When I finished with her hair, she asked, "You will let me know how today went?"

"I will. Laria?"

"Hmm?"

"I'm sorry if I upset you. Please forgive me."

"You haven't upset me." She smiled, genuinely this time. "There is much on my mind at present. There have been some...developments."

"What do you mean?"

"I can't say right now. They could only be rumors. Regardless, the news is troubling."

"If there is anything I can do to ease your burdens, please let me know."

"Just having you here is a comfort. Now go enjoy the day."

Laria had always been careful to disguise her concerns, so whatever disturbed her must be something dire if she couldn't steel her features and hide her worry. It struck me again how resilient my sister was, that she could bear the weight of the world upon her shoulders and maintain her composure.

I eased open the library door, not wishing to disturb any occupants. The murmur of voices grew louder as I moved further into the room, and I peeked around the last bookcases and saw Finton conducting a history lesson. I slipped into a chair and listened to a story about the first settler in the area, describing how the man built a strong house but struggled to grow the familiar crops from his previous country. The man worried his family would starve, until he had a vision of trees bearing red fruit growing from tiny, dark brown seeds. He spent months searching for the source of the dream and found a single tree growing amid dense forests. He picked a few of the fruits, and from those seeds, the entire economy of Ilano grew. It was a nice folktale, but more than the story, I was mesmerized by Finton's engrossing abilities as a narrator.

The last grains of sand ran through the hourglass, and Finton dismissed the class. A few students glanced curiously at me as they passed, but none lingered. I watched them file out of the room, and when I turned around, Finton was staring at me.

"Am I right in assuming you've secured the queen's permission to join me?"

"You assume correctly."

With his black bag in hand, Finton gestured for me to lead the way to the stables. My knees shook in nervous anticipation, and I surreptitiously studied Finton's face for any clue to his mood. He stared ahead, relaxed, but when I looked down, I noticed he fidgeted with the handle of his bag and tapped his toes. Was he impatient to leave or anxious to get our conversation over with?

An age later, Finton's gig appeared, and I was assisted into my seat. As we departed the capital, I saw Olim in the yard training and waved. He fixed me with a hard stare and didn't return the greeting.

"He doesn't look pleased," Finton observed.

"I cannot think why," I said.

"Can't you?" He barely restrained a smile.

"I hope he's not having a bad morning."

"Maybe one of the other knights beat him in combat."

"Doubtful. Olim is very good with a sword." My eyes drifted away from Olim's grim expression, and I chewed my lower lip wondering what could have my friend so discomposed.

The following silence was tense, and my back ached from sitting so rigidly. I wrenched the fabric of my dress and nervously waited for Finton to reveal the purpose of his inviting me out today.

"Are you all right?" he asked.

I nearly jumped out of my seat.

"I'm fine," I breathed. I darted a quick glance and saw him looking at me strangely. It was not concern nor the normal open friendliness he usually carried, but something unsettling. He looked...uneasy. The blood drained from my face and my hands became icy cold.

"I suppose you're wondering what I wished to speak to you about," he said.

"I was. I can guess what you're going to say."

Up ahead, the road widened, and grass spread toward an open field on one side. Finton maneuvered the gig toward the widest point and reined in the stout mare, bringing us to a gentle stop. He relaxed and the horse dropped its head to munch on the green shoots, and we sat watching her for several seconds without speaking.

"I'm sorry," I whispered hoarsely.

"What for?" he asked.

"I spoke out of turn when you were with the king. I should not have pried, especially since you already said you couldn't leave Ilano. Can you forgive me?"

"I'm not angry with you about that. Yes, I was surprised, but never angry. Actually, I wanted to thank you."

I looked over at him, startled, and saw open kindness behind his spectacles.

"Thank me?" My heart lifted as I slowly realized we were not about to have a fight.

"You spoke up when I couldn't. I would've never presumed to ask the king for such a generous gift." He took a deep breath. "I wanted to tell you first that I decided to accept his offer."

In a matter of seconds, I went from complete despair to utter joy at those words. I gasped and clapped my hands in excitement.

"That's wonderful!" I exclaimed. "But what about the Lord Protector? You were so concerned about his needing you here."

"He's actually the reason I'm accepting. I don't know if the king spoke to him, but he hinted that if I wanted to pursue a life outside Ilano, I would have his support. He assured me Fynn could manage things well enough at home."

I sighed. "Then it's really happening! You're going to Hrgun as you've always dreamed."

"I owe it to you," he said. "I wouldn't be going if you didn't have courage where I did not."

I shook my head. "You owe it entirely to your own merit. I just opened my big mouth."

His eyes dropped then met mine again so quickly I nearly missed it. I lowered my gaze to my tightly clasped hands, blushing furiously, wondering if he'd glanced at my lips as I suspected.

"Ula—"

"When—" We had spoken simultaneously, but Finton politely bid me to continue.

"When will you be leaving?" I asked.

"After harvest."

"So soon?"

"I suspect that's when you'll be leaving, too."

"I'm not sure. The queen would like to travel before the winter. It snows quite a lot in Praed, and the roads can become treacherous."

Finton nodded in understanding and lifted the reins, directing the mare back onto the road.

"I wish you a safe journey," he said. "In case I leave before you."

"Likewise." Though I was elated he was going to pursue his ambitions, I felt inexplicably sad.

Chapter 15

The temperature was already warm, and it promised to be another sweltering afternoon. I breathed in the sweet smells of fruit filling baskets in the orchards, and when we passed a cidery, I could hear the calls of workers and the crushing of apples even from the road. I waved at some children running alongside us, and one called out that she recognized me as an attendant to the queen. Audible gasps followed, and I laughed at their curious faces and wide eyes. I asked Finton if he wouldn't mind stopping, and he obliged me with a smile.

"Is it true?" a dirty-faced boy asked. "Do you work for the queen?"

"I do," I said. "I'm her lady-in-waiting."

The children murmured amongst themselves excitedly.

"What's she like?" a little girl asked. "Is she really as nice as she seems?"

"She's very nice," I said. "And very funny."

The children giggled.

"Is the king as scary as *he* seems?" another boy asked in a whisper.

I bit back a grin and mustered my best serious face. "Not *as* scary." Finton started to laugh, and I nudged him with my elbow. "He may not appear so, but he's very kind. Don't tell anyone."

"Is that your beau?" the little girl asked, pointing to Finton.

"No!" I said. My cheeks warmed and my heart pounded.

"Is he your guard?" the youngest boy asked.

"No." Finton leaned forward. "She's mine." He winked, and the children fell to the ground laughing. He flicked the reins, and they waved excitedly as we drove away.

"You're very good with children," Finton said.

I smiled wryly. "I've had a lot of practice."

"I suppose you have. How is the queen by the way? She appears well in public, but I know that façade may just be for the people's benefit."

"She's much better, thank you. I would not say she's fully recovered, but she is more herself now."

"I don't imagine one gets over such a loss quickly."

"I don't think she ever will. But the pain has lessened."

***

We traveled further, and I started to recognize my surroundings. A modest stone farmhouse appeared around a bend in the road, and we came to a stop as a familiar woman emerged from the house.

"Well, what a pleasure to receive you again, Miss Audrey," Mrs. Neace said.

Finton helped me off the gig and turned to Mrs. Neace. "I'm happy to see you again. How are you and Mr. Neace?"

"Come on in and see for yourself."

The three of us entered the house, and the familiar odor of fresh-picked fruit filled my nose. Mrs. Neace led us into the dining area and crowded around the small room were scores of baskets filled with apples. The two young women I'd seen on my previous visit and little Ionah were sorting through the baskets, setting aside the bruised and worm-nibbled apples and arranging the suitable ones by size. Mr. Neace, his arm still in a sling, was overseeing the work. He looked up when we entered, and a broad smile crossed his bearded face.

"Dr. Ekhane! So good to see you brought your young protege this time. We've missed your pretty face here, Miss Audrey."

"You mean you miss her pretty compliments and promises to help you with that blasted horse," Mrs. Neace clarified. She looked over her shoulder at me with a knowing smile. I grinned back.

"Oh, don't listen to her." Mr. Neace waved off his wife's comments.

Finton helped take his injured arm out of the sling and unwrapped the bandage. I was amazed at how much better the wound looked after the last time I saw it.

"That's incredible!" I said. "You must be so relieved to have healed so completely."

"Dr. Ekhane is a miracle worker," Mr. Neace said. "Now if only he could tell me the bone is healed."

"Nearly," Finton said, our compliments having no effect on his concentration.

"I don't feel near as much pain as I used to," Mr. Neace said.

"He certainly complains less, which I'm thankful for," Mrs. Neace added.

"The wound shows no more signs of infection," Finton said. He removed fresh bandages from his bag and started rewrapping Mr. Neace's arm. "However, your arm must remain in a sling for a while longer. The bone is healing well but isn't strong enough yet to bear stress."

Mr. Neace huffed gruffly and said, "I suppose half good news is better than no good news."

I could tell by her expression that Mrs. Neace was just as disappointed as her husband. He sat dejectedly while Finton finished dressing and fastening the injured limb into a sling, and my heart went out to the poor man.

"Perhaps you can introduce me to this troublesome horse of yours," I said lightly.

Mr. Neace looked up at me with glistening eyes and a wide smile. Then he slapped his hand on the arm of the chair and stood up with a flourish.

"Well, come on then, young lady!" he called, waving me toward the door.

Mrs. Neace shook her head reprovingly for indulging her husband, but her silent reprimand was tempered with an indulgent smile.

The older man led Finton and me to a humble barn with a few stalls opening onto a vast pasture. True, it was smaller than many of the Praed estates built to accommodate extensive horse breeding operations, but it was suitable for one or two animals. A brown horse grazed in the distance, and as we approached the weathered barn, the walls shook from the stomping of hooves. Mr. Neace opened the top of a split door, and a large reddish-brown head with a wide, white stripe down its nose thrust through the opening. The horse's nostrils flared as it inhaled our scent, and its ears flicked back and forth when it peered around the barn toward the pasture.

"Why do you keep it stalled?" I wondered.

"Can't catch him if I don't," Mr. Neace said.

I silently stared into the beast's eyes, making no move toward it until both of its ears pricked toward me. Laria was amazing with horses, and she taught me a few tricks that served me well in the past. I blew into its nose. Once I had the horse's full attention, I reached out and ran my hand from its muzzle to the middle of its forehead and rubbed tiny circles between its eyes. The horse nickered at me, and I stepped away from the door.

"Open it," I said.

"Pardon?" Mr. Neace asked.

I met the man's eye. "Open the door to the stall and let him out."

He looked at Finton in confusion, which irritated me, but my friend made no effort to influence the man's decision. Mr. Neace shrugged, unlatched the door, and allowed it to swing open. I stepped aside as the great beast bolted out of the stall and galloped into the pasture toward the brown horse. The pair lifted their tails and pranced together for several minutes before turning their attention to the lush grass.

We watched the horses swish their tails contentedly. "He's been lonely," I said. "He needs to be reminded what it means to be a horse. Once he becomes reacquainted with his own species, I'll show you how to encourage him to trust you."

Mr. Neace regarded me skeptically. "Trust?"

"Yes. How can you expect him to listen to you if he doesn't trust you?"

Mr. Neace nodded with evident approval before returning his attention to the beautiful animals shining in the late morning sunshine.

"How long do you think he needs?"

I turned to Finton. "When will you next need to attend to Mr. Neace?"

"Next week if that's convenient."

Mr. Neace nodded in agreement.

"With Dr. Ekhane's permission, I will join him next week," I said. "That should be a sufficient amount of time to assess our progress."

"Don't disappoint me and tell her she can't ride with you, Doc," Mr. Neace teased.

"I wouldn't dream of it, Armin," Finton said with a bow.

Mrs. Neace joined us carrying a tray with cups of cider, which Mr. Neace gratefully downed in one swallow. Finton held up a hand to excuse himself, but Mrs. Neace insisted, promising it was low in alcohol.

"Just one then, thank you," Finton said. He took a cup and sipped hesitantly, as if he didn't really believe in Mrs. Neace's assessment of the drink's intoxicating ability. I took the remaining cup to avoid appearing rude, and the liquid filled my mouth in a delicate blend of sweetness and spice.

"It's a recipe of my own making," Mrs. Neace said, nodding toward my cup. "Best on a hot day, don't you agree, Miss Audrey?"

"Whole-heartedly, ma'am. It's almost as delicious as the apple turnovers you gave me on the last visit."

"Just as my husband says," Mrs. Neace said to Finton, a slight rosy hue to her cheeks. "You're welcome to bring Miss Audrey to our door anytime."

The four of us laughed companionably, and then Finton announced we had to attend to other patients. I thanked Mrs. Neace again for her hospitality and wished them a plentiful harvest before taking my seat next to Finton in the gig. As we pulled away, little Ionah peeked her head out of a window. I waved and was rewarded with a brilliant smile. I watched the house fade from view, sighed, and faced forward. Finton was watching me, his mouth quirked in a half smile.

"Why are you looking at me like that?" I asked. "Do I have something on my face?" I reached up to wipe my cheek, but he shook his head.

"You've become very popular," he said.

"No, I wouldn't say that." I blushed furiously. "Everyone has been very kind and polite, of which I am grateful. It's funny. I was so afraid to come here, and now I can't imagine what my life would be like if I'd never met these people."

"Why were you afraid?"

"I've never left Praed. I lived a very comfortable life until...we were invaded." I shifted uncomfortably and avoided looking at Finton. "I gradually learned to trust a few people after my sister became queen, but I was still nervous to leave home. I've never been easy with strangers."

"If that's the case, you've performed beautifully."

"It's not a performance, I assure you!" I said, but his slight grin told me he was teasing again. I nudged him playfully.

"Anyway," I continued. "I've enjoyed my time here and will be sad to leave."

"You will return, though, on visits with the queen?"

"Perhaps. But I cannot say for sure."

"I know many people would be disappointed to never see you again. I'm certain Mr. Neace will be anxious to exhibit his success with his troublesome horse."

"Yes."

I watched the landscape ease by at the pace of a languid stream. The thought of saying goodbye to the friends I met depressed me. Would we return to Ilano? It was the birthplace of the king, so it was reasonable to assume we would. However, he had no family here, no ties aside from it being his place of origin, and the king did not appear the sentimental type eager to relive old times. Any business he needed to conduct with the Lord Protector could be accomplished via letter, but certainly he would make public appearances and attend council meetings in person *sometimes*. At least, every five years…

At the next stop, I tried to appear unaffected, but the prospect of only visiting Ilano every five years, if at all, hung like a thick smoke around me. My chest was tight, and tears welled in my eyes. I couldn't remember the names of the people Finton introduced me to, couldn't even describe the house or the reason for our being there. I saw the world through a haze, but the roar in my ears was not fire. It was a rising panic. Inexplicably, I felt the need to act, but how or why I couldn't say.

Finton darted concerned glances in my direction, but the people didn't notice my distress. I hadn't even registered that we'd left until a wheel of the gig struck a hole in the road and I bounced roughly from side to side.

"Are you all right?" Finton asked, his voice full of gentle concern.

I looked down. In the tumult, I'd not only gripped the side of the gig but his forearm as well. I released my hold, mumbling an apology, and shifted away.

"Have I said something to offend you? You haven't been yourself since we left the Neace house."

"No, it's not you. I've been in my own head. I'm sorry." I shook to clear my mind and plastered a smile on my face.

"It must be difficult having to constantly hide behind a smile. I hope you know you don't have to. Not…"

When he hesitated, I met his stare and waited expectantly. Whatever he meant to say, if indeed he intended to elaborate, I would never know. Behind us came the distinct sound of rapidly approaching hooves. We turned and spotted a figure urgently riding toward us. Finton pulled the cream-colored mare to a stop just as the rider pulled up his horse so abruptly its feet skidded to a stop in the dirt, sending dust and rocks flying.

"Olim!" I yelled when I recognized the man atop the frothed animal. "What's wrong?"

"The king has called a special council," he said through raspy breaths. "I don't know what it's about, but the queen requested your presence. Many of the nobles are being called to the assembly as well."

My eyes widened. Something very important must have happened. Perhaps whatever had unsettled Laria?

Finton was turning the gig around to take me back to the city, but Olim moved his horse to block us and raised a hand.

"I do not wish to disturb your business," Olim said. "Allow me to escort the lady back and you can go about your day."

The two men stared at each other, immobile, and pensive. I looked from one to the other, confused at this odd exchange. Finton met Olim's intimidating glower impassively. A lesser man would have withered under such scrutiny, and I braced for an explosion of Olim's temper.

"Of course," Finton said slowly. He lay down the reins and jumped off the gig.

Olim watched him intently as he came around to help me down. I gave Finton an apologetic look, thanked him for the day, and climbed behind Olim's saddle. I gripped the back of his tunic, and he kicked the animal forward.

I peered over my shoulder at Finton standing beside the gig. He didn't move as the distance between us lengthened, and I watched his still form until he disappeared. I ducked my head to avoid the wind whipping around us as we galloped past humble stick-built houses. Everything blurred as the horse sped down the road, the slap of hooves and howling wind so loud Olim couldn't hear when I asked if he knew what was going on. We slowed when we approached the stables, and Olim brought the horse to an easy walk before reining it to a stop.

"What's happening?" I asked when he helped me dismount.

"The king told the knights and soldiers to be prepared for an announcement," he said.

I could barely keep up with Olim's long strides when he entered the capitol building and ran up the stairs. Beads of sweat trickled down the side of my burning face as we hurried past curious soldiers and nobles on their way to the council chambers. I was completely out of breath when we burst through the heavy doors and encountered the scores of people milling around waiting for the meeting to come to order. I scanned the room for Laria's distinctive locks, and saw her pacing before the thrones on the raised dais. I mustered my composure and rushed toward her.

"Thank goodness you're here." She sighed, her features washed in relief, and reached for me. I grasped her hands and was shocked to feel them quake in my grip.

"What's going on?" I asked.

"I don't know. Risteard asked all the estate holders, council members, and high-ranking knights to gather here as soon as possible." She paused when a group wandered by and took their places at a head table. "I have a horrible feeling, Ula."

Before she could speak more, Risteard strode in with the Lord Protector. The room fell silent. He glanced at me, then indicated for Laria to be seated. I took my place beside her, our eyes meeting anxiously. The king lowered himself into his chair, and as one, the entirety of the assembled people took their seats and waited for him to speak.

"We have received some disturbing news," the king said. "News which affects all of us, so I cannot in good conscience make a decision based solely on my own opinion." The people nodded appreciatively, and he continued. "Our neighbors to the south have informed me that Karne, the heir to the throne of King Tuar, has gathered his forces in a bid to defend his father's honor after the defeat of Crif many years ago."

Voices rose in alarm, and he held up his hand for silence. I turned to Laria, and by her pallid complexion, I guessed this was news to her as well.

"He already threatens the border of Torshul. Their king has written begging for help from the northern countries. They are nearly defenseless." His voice dropped and the edges of his jaw tensed. Laria clutched his hand, and he took a deep breath. "I would like to answer their call, but not without your consent. It is your sons and husbands who will fight to protect them, to protect all of us. For we all know Torshul is a simple country, and when they fall, Crif will come for us next."

People began talking amongst themselves, their voices echoing in the large room. The king stared resolutely ahead, waiting. Laria had eyes only for him, but he didn't look at her. The Lord Protector stepped forward with a bow.

"Your Majesty," he said. "We have fought the desert people before and suffered irreparable losses, but we proved victorious. There is no reason to believe the same cannot be accomplished now."

"Here, here!" a knight called. He was joined by other men, but the women looked doubtful.

"I do not wish for us to fight the desert people alone," the king said. The cheers were silenced, and the Lord Protector cocked his head questioningly. "Yes, we defeated them before, but King Karne has had many years to prepare, and even if we beat him into a retreat now, we risk them coming back. We must end this."

"What do you propose, Your Grace?" the Lord Protector asked.

"We must stop fighting as divided countries," the king said. "Praed and Ilano are a united kingdom. As king of these countries, I will enlist Hrgun, Faqur, Kuste, and Berg. Together, we will destroy King Karne, and keep Crif off the continent forever."

Shouts erupted from the room, and it was difficult to determine if they were displeased or excited about the king's proposition. I placed a hand on the queen's shoulder and felt her trembling violently beneath it.

"Your Majesty," the Lord Protector said over the din of the crowd. "Berg has always kept to itself and does not join in other countries' fights."

The king rose. "This is not just our fight." The talking ceased as his imposing figure loomed over the assembly. "Crif is a threat to us all. If Berg doesn't see that, then they'll all die if we fail."

The beat of each person's heart could be heard after such a declaration, and several people stood proudly and nodded approvingly.

"I'm tired of fighting Crif," the king said empathetically, a tone I'd never heard from him before. "Aren't you?"

I heard nothing more over the 'hurrahs' and cries of 'Long Rules the Crown' erupting from the crowd. There was so much excitement and fervor that I was the only one who noticed the queen bolt from her seat and escape the council chamber, ducking around groups of men patting themselves on the back as if the war were already won.

Chapter 16

"Wait!" I called out to my sister's retreating form, but she didn't falter. She didn't so much as glance over her shoulder when I pleaded for her to stop. She reached her chambers and threw the door open so forcefully it bounced off the wall and nearly slammed into my face. She stomped around the room, wringing her hands and struggling to control her rapid breathing.

"Laria." I cupped her face in my hands. "Calm yourself."

She took several deep breaths, her face flushed and her lower lip trembling, and squeezed her eyes tightly shut.

"We're going to war," she whispered.

"I'm scared, too. Do you think we should return to Praed?"

"I don't know. I don't know how safe the roads will be. If we leave, we should leave immediately."

I nodded and dashed around the room gathering gowns. Laria remained fixed in place, gazing into a distance I couldn't begin to traverse.

"Should I have the king's wardrobe packed as well?" I asked.

"He will not be joining us," she said quietly.

I straightened. "What do you mean?"

Risteard burst into the room, eyes trained on Laria. She met his stare calmly, but her clasped hands shook with the effort it took for her to control her emotions.

"You're going to fight with them, aren't you?"

I gasped before I could stop myself. It hadn't occurred to me that the king himself would be joining the fray.

"If you ask me to stay, I will," he said.

Laria turned away, her features pinched in thought. My heart pounded as I waited in wide-eyed astonishment for her answer. My father never considered staying behind in a war, nor asked Mother for her opinion. His position as First Knight meant he had no choice, even if he wanted one. It was understood he'd leave and it was our duty to accept his absence. The king's deferment to my sister was an unprecedented sign of respect. For a few agonizing moments, the room was silent save for the rush of blood in my ears and Risteard's ragged breathing. Laria straightened and met his gaze resolutely.

"I can't ask you to do that," she said. "Your family may need you here, but your countries need you more. You're the best knight we have. Send those people back into the desert, then come home."

A tear trickled down her cheek, and I felt answering moisture on my own face. I could live a thousand lifetimes, and I could never be as strong as my sister. My heart swelled with pride and sympathy as she stood solidly before her husband, knowing she may lose him and letting him go anyway. He nodded once, took a step forward, and pressed his forehead against hers.

"I have to end this," he said.

"I know," she said. "No more children losing their fathers. But what shall we tell ours?"

"The truth." He pulled away and gazed down into Laria's wide, green eyes. "Come." He took her hand. "The people need to see this campaign has your support."

She allowed him to lead her from the room, and I followed behind, rubbing my face to cover the tears.

I saw very little of my sister over the next few days as plans were discussed for the impending war with Crif. Dispatches carried by the fastest horses were sent to the northern countries of Hrgun and Berg, and west to Kuste and Faqur. We did very little in the way of trade with these countries since Praed historically kept to itself, but the king was confident they could be convinced of the worthiness of our cause. Hrgun and Faqur fought against the desert people in the past, but I knew nothing about them, and my ignorance was embarrassing. When I asked Olim, he said Berg was isolated at the apex of the continent and didn't involve themselves with other countries, and the Kuste were generally nomads who followed the migrations of herds of beasts as opposed to building cities and castles. He wasn't convinced that either of these countries would heed the call to arms, but he believed that if anyone could accomplish the impossible, it was our king.

The children were told of their father's impending departure, and their reactions were heartbreaking. Their little faces fell, and the tears ran in torrents. The king and queen comforted them as best they could, but no platitudes helped assuage their fears.

There were many questions over the days that followed, and we answered as honestly as possible without frightening them more. Alyx bravely assured his younger siblings their father was a good fighter and would come home with exciting stories to tell. Rian, spurred by his confidence in his father and older brother, pretended to be a knight every waking hour. He ran down the halls brandishing a sword and declaring no enemy was too great for a prince of Praed and Ilano. Tyrnan tagged along, but in private he seemed uneasy and confused. Lilias responded by attaching herself to Laria and refusing to leave her side, even when her mother was needed in council. The stability of the royal family was crumbling before my eyes, and it tore me apart.

Laria and Risteard decided we would meet with the leaders of the other countries who answered the king's summons in Praed. The Lord Protector said he would follow us shortly, leaving his son, Fynn, temporarily in his place.

A slight breeze rustled the papers spread across the ground where Sulwen and I were stretched out in the afternoon sunshine. I glanced up at the yellow blossoms in full bloom along the garden path, and then back down at the painting I'd been working on for the past hour. Sulwen had long since abandoned her brush and was spreading colors around her paper with her fingers. She waddled over a few times to present her work, paint oozing down her arms, and I dutifully gushed over her use of bold strokes and imaginative color combinations. Her little chest would puff out, and with a satisfied grin, she would snatch a blank piece of paper to create another beautiful masterpiece. The three boys were engaged in reading lessons, and I could hear Alyx reciting from his primer over the buzzing of insects while Tyrnan practiced his letters by my side. Duveesa dedicated herself to distracting the children from their anxieties and bringing as much joy into their troubled lives as possible.

Over the days that followed, the training of the knights and soldiers intensified, and beyond the sounds of the children, I could hear them practicing their drills. Olim had been in a state of restless anticipation since the declaration of war. He was anxious to distinguish himself in battle, but my stomach was in knots at the thought of never seeing him again.

"Mama!" Tyrnan leapt from his seat as Laria sat beside me and scrambled into her lap. She shifted her permanently attached daughter to her hip. Despite Lilias' protests, Tyrnan snuggled into a comfortable position and popped a thumb in his mouth, a new habit.

"Any news?" I asked Laria.

She wrapped her arms around her children. "Torshul is sending their king, and the Admiral of the Fleet of Faqur also responded to our invitation. We anticipate Hrgun will as well, based on their history with Crif, but they haven't said officially. No word from Kuste or Berg."

"From what I hear, we aren't likely to receive any reply."

"Berg, I am told, is a rocky, desolate place surrounded by mountains. The people make their homes atop monoliths of stone. They have always kept to themselves for fear of outsiders. Even those who visit to chronical their history are turned away, so little else is known about them. No one knows how they live, their customs, nothing."

"How frightening." A chill wiggled up my spine. "How do we know we can trust them if we know nothing about them?"

"We don't," she said.

"And the Kuste? Olim said they're nomads without homes."

"They travel, yes, but they bring their homes with them. They're simple people who hunt and live off the land. Risteard said his father met a chief once when he traveled to Faqur. The man was there to trade and apparently was an intimidating, well-muscled fellow with dark skin and eyes. He carried all his belongings, everything he owned in the world, on his back. When Risteard's father offered his assistance, the man smiled, set his pack on the ground, and beckoned for him to lift it. According to the story, the young, well trained knight couldn't lift it past his knees."

"Impressive," I said, and even I could hear the apathy in my tone.

Laria squeezed my shoulder. "I'm sorry we'll have to leave so soon."

"What do you mean?"

She stared at me with an unreadable expression for a few moments before shaking her head.

"Nothing," she said. "Perhaps I was mistaken."

I waited for her to explain, but instead she said we should pack for our journey. I rose, and she had to shift the children so she could join me.

"I *will* be sad to leave," I said, gazing around the gardens and the capitol building beyond. "I've enjoyed my time here. Thank you for forcing me to overcome my fears."

"My pleasure. You've come into your own over these last few months, Ula. Can you feel it?"

"I can. I don't think I shall ever be the same."

I was organizing the packing of the queen's trunks when someone knocked against the door frame. I looked up to see Olim standing awkwardly in the entryway, shifting his feet and keeping his eyes lowered. Suppressing a smile, I asked the other ladies to excuse me and bid Olim to step out into the hallway.

"Afraid you'll see something unmentionable?" I teased.

By the red hue of his cheeks, I deduced I'd guessed correctly.

"I know you're very busy," he said in a rush. "But I was hoping you could spare an evening to dine with my family. Tonight, perhaps? It may be the only opportunity we'll have before leaving."

"That would be wonderful! And a welcome distraction."

He bowed quickly, his eyes darting into the queen's chambers, before hurriedly striding down the hallway. I shook my head in wonderment. Here was a brave knight, ready to fight for his country, afraid of ladies' undergarments. Men were truly a separate species.

Laria was in council all morning, and I didn't see her until midday. She appeared with Lilias asleep on her shoulder. She handed the precious bundle to Agnus, and the older nurse carried the little princess to bed to finish her nap. The queen linked her arm with mine, and together we strolled into the dining hall for the afternoon meal. I examined her, and my heart sank when I noted dark circles under her eyes, pale skin, and dejected expression. She uttered a long-suffering sigh as we took our seats and made no move to eat when plates were placed before us.

"Your Majesty," I ventured. "Are you not hungry?"

She looked down at her plate as if she hadn't realized it had been there. She picked at the food, a morsel or two made it into her mouth, but it was clear she was merely going through the motions and not really tasting the food.

"Rough morning?" I asked.

"Hrgun has committed to sending an ambassador to Praed," she said.

"That's good news."

"Still nothing from Kuste or Berg, but no one is surprised about that." She took another bite and chewed thoughtfully.

"I can't imagine how difficult this must be for you," I said, squeezing her hand. "If you need to talk, I'm always here to listen."

"Oh, Ula." She sucked in a shuddering breath and shut her eyes. "I'm so afraid."

Her face dropped into her hands, and I waved away the servants so we could be alone. Once the doors closed, I moved closer to my distressed sister and wrapped my arms around her. She pressed into my shoulder and wept while I rocked her.

"You don't have to be brave all the time. Let it all go."

I'm not certain how much time passed with us embraced in this manner, but eventually the tears ceased, and Laria drew away, wiping the remnants of her grief from her tired face.

"It's been so peaceful," she said. "We've never had to face anything as awful as a war before. What if we fail?"

"You can't ask those questions." I was more apprehensive about my sister's doubts than the prospect of war. She had always been so confident, so true to her purpose, that to hear her voice such fears was like a kick to the stomach.

"I can't lose him."

Her voice was small, vulnerable, such as I'd never heard it before. I lay my head on her shoulder and listened as her shuddering breaths became steadier.

"You once told me you believed the king was the other half of your soul. If that is the case, how can you ever lose him?"

"A sword to the gut comes to mind," she said bitterly.

"Your soul, safe at home, will sustain his if he's injured," I said.

"Superstitious nonsense," she snapped, though I could tell there was humor behind her words.

"Have you spoken to him about your concerns?"

"No," she said firmly. "The last thing he needs is to see me falling apart. I must be strong for him. I can't say anything that may potentially distract him if he's to keep his head."

"The curse of being the wife of a king, I suppose."

"Not of a king. Of a knight. In his heart, that's what he'll always be."

I lifted my head to meet her eye, and I was relieved to see the familiar spark. She smiled and focused on eating her meal. I watched her for several minutes until I was sure she took in a proper amount of nourishment.

"When will we be returning to Praed?" I asked.

"A few days. Efram is holding a farewell celebration the day after tomorrow and we will leave the following morning. So, try not to overindulge." She winked.

"Ilano does enjoy their parties."

She laughed. "They do. Efram regrets that we'll miss the big Harvest Festival in a month. I understand it's impressive."

"It's very kind of him to honor us," I said. She nodded and returned to her meal. It was now my turn to pick at my food.

"Laria? I know this isn't the best time, but I was wondering if you could spare me for dinner tonight."

"Spare you? For what purpose?"

"Olim has invited me to dine with his family. May I?"

"Oh." I couldn't account for her disappointment, but she quickly recovered.

"I promise I won't be late."

She waved dismissively and said she was perfectly capable of taking care of herself if my evening proved long.

Most of the packing for the royal family and their entourage was complete by day's end, and I felt as drained as my sister. I worried I would not make a very desirable dinner companion for Olim, but I didn't want to disappoint him. Plus, I was eager to meet his father and try to endear myself to Enyleve before I left.

While I brushed out a day's worth of tangles from my hair, I glanced at my nightstand. The salacious novel was sitting there, innocently closed. Absently, I styled my hair in a simple plait, then walked toward the book, wondering what sort of nonsense Arella was going to get into now that she was on solid ground. I opened it to the last page I'd read and found myself pulled into the familiar fantasy that at present was much easier to stomach than reality.

Arella stood with evident shock, staring at the man before her. This was not the Lord Griffith of her imagination. Gone was the vision of an old, fat, bald man, to be replaced with a tall, young, and decidedly handsome gentleman. His eyes were nearly as dark as the brown, wavy hair sweeping across his forehead. He stared intently as she inspected every strong line of his jaw and soft curve of his lips. Traveling further, she noted his fine blue jacket fit tightly to his wide shoulders. This was not the physique of a man who sat idly at gaming tables. He wore tight gray riding breeches and tall black boots polished to a perfect shine.

"Do I meet your approval?" the deep voice of Lord Griffith asked.

Arella blushed and met his gaze, but she could not formulate a reply.

"You must be exhausted from your journey," he continued. "I do hope you did not meet with any trouble?"

She shook her head numbly. "No trouble, sir."

"Come then," he ordered, extending his hand. Tentatively, Arella set her delicate, white-gloved hand in his and noted how much larger they were than hers...than the captain's. His fingers closed, enveloping her in their warmth. A shudder ran up her spine and her stomach tightened. Blood rushed through her ears, and she swayed slightly. He clutched her shoulder to steady her, bringing his body closer, and she could smell leather, sandalwood, and a distinctly earthy, masculine scent that tingled her nose and made the hairs on the back of her neck stand erect.

"I'm fine," she said and shook her head to clear the sudden heaviness. "It has been a long journey, though. I will be happy to sleep without feeling the world rock beneath me."

"Let me take you home then," he said before pulling Arella to a waiting carriage. "But I must warn you. You may no longer be on the sea, but that doesn't mean you won't feel the earth move."

"Rubbish," I muttered and tossed the novel into a trunk. A woman doesn't find herself drawn to two men at once.

Halfway to pinning up my hair, I froze, considering the character in my story, the way she felt when a man was close. How unsettled, confused, and strange she acted. It seemed oddly familiar, but I brushed the thought away as fanciful.

I heard a light tapping at the door, and Olim called out asking if I was ready.

"Coming!" I opened the door and stopped short.

"Olim! You're wearing clothes!"

He checked to make sure no one heard and glared hard at me.

"Yes, I am," he whispered harshly.

I grinned to soften the awkwardness. "Proper clothes, that is. I meant to say you look very handsome."

He indeed was dressed quite nicely. Where he normally donned the garb of a knight—simple, light blue tunic often with chainmail, dark breeches, and a sword at his hip–tonight he wore a red doublet over brown breeches, tall black boots, and a matching half cape.

"Thank you." He extended his arm. "Shall we?"

I eyed him nervously before taking his proffered elbow. Several people glanced our way, and I had the urge to hurry out of sight to avoid their stares. I was oddly uneasy, as if I needed to justify our closeness when we'd been friends for years. I shook off the feeling and pushed it to the back of my mind, determined to enjoy an evening away from the politics and stress permeating the capitol building.

We trotted leisurely out of the city, and the familiar sight of rolling valleys covered with apple trees spread out before us. My vision blurred at the thought of never seeing this beautiful landscape again, and it struck me how completely my opinion of leaving home changed over a few short months. I'd been reluctant, afraid, and so convinced that nowhere other than Praed could hold a place in my heart. Now, I considered Ilano as dear to me as Praed.

Olim was speaking beside me, but I was so absorbed in my own thoughts I didn't acknowledge him, and eventually he grew quiet. I glanced toward him and noticed his scowl.

"What's the matter?" I asked.

"Oh, are you speaking to me now?"

I shrank at his angry tone.

"I'm sorry," I said. "I didn't realize I was ignoring you. I was lost in my head."

"I've been talking to you since we left the city. You didn't hear a word I said, did you?"

I lowered my eyes guiltily. "I was thinking about how sorry I will be to leave Ilano."

His features softened, but the sharpness of his tone remained when he said, "Yes, it seems to have made quite an impression on you."

I narrowed my eyes, my ire piqued. "What's that supposed to mean?"

"You so badly wanted to come out of your shell. Though I'm happy you're pleased with Ilano, I hope it was worth it."

"I don't understand what you mean. I already said I was sorry for not listening. There's no need to continue quarreling with me."

Olim clutched his reins and squeezed his eyes tightly. He remained silent for several minutes, and my frustration increased with each silent mile. With an exasperated sigh, I kicked my horse forward, and told him we'd revisit this discussion later. The pace of his horse increased behind me, and I dug my heels into my mount's side until we were galloping down the road. Olim's family home appeared, and I slowed to a walk. Olim rode up beside me looking placated.

"Forgive me," he said. "I don't wish for us to quarrel before we visit my family."

"Nor do I," I said. "But I have no intention of letting you off easily. Something is on your mind that is clearly bothering you, and I insist you explain yourself."

We dismounted and Olim took my horse and led it into the stables. I crossed my arms and waited for him to return, and when he did, he met my gaze resolutely.

"We've always spoken plainly to one another," he said. "I will grant you that courtesy. Later."

I nodded shortly and stalked toward the house. At the front door, I plastered a pleasant smile on my face before Olim knocked.

Enyleve's face appeared in the open doorway. She beamed when she saw her brother and rushed forward to throw her arms around him. Despite my waning anger at Olim, my heart warmed to see their touching greeting.

"Father said you were coming to dinner," Enyleve said. "I've been watching for you for hours!" She spied me over Olim's shoulder, and her excitement vanished. She pushed away from her brother, curtseyed in my direction, and mumbled "Your Ladyship" so quietly I barely heard.

"I'm so happy to see you again," I said in the kind tone I used with the children.

She stared at me blankly, then gestured for us to enter the house. I glanced up at Olim, and he shrugged at her continued coldness.

"I tried talking to her about her rudeness last week," he whispered. "But it appears she didn't listen. I must not have anything to say worth hearing to young ladies."

I shot him a glare, but he was already moving into the house to embrace his mother.

"Dear Olim," she said with a fond gaze. "What a wonderful gift to have you here tonight." She looked past him to me and extended a weathered hand. I took it, grateful that at least one of Olim's family was glad to see me.

"You're looking very well this evening, Mrs. Lemichs." I squeezed her hand, feeling both her strength and warmth.

"That's Cait to you, young lady," she said with a wagging finger. "Please allow me to introduce Olim's father. Ron," she said loudly and tapped his shoulder. He turned, and she practically yelled, "This is Miss Ula Audrey, the girl I was telling you about."

The man stood, yet his body did not straighten. His frame hunched, as if years of working in the orchards permanently altered his posture. His light blue eyes shone against his tanned skin, and his white hair and beard glistened in the firelight. He smiled, and I noted several teeth were missing, and the lines about his eyes and mouth were deep furrows.

"We are honored," he said with a tremulous bow of his head.

"It is I who am honored," I said. "Thank you for inviting me into your home. Olim speaks very fondly of you."

"Does he?" Olim's father glanced at his son with a sparkle in his eyes. "And here I thought he believed me a foolish old man."

"Don't you start," Cait said. "Come and have a seat, my dear."

The tension at the table was palpable as Olim and his father eyed each other across the expanse between them. I glanced from one to the other, noting they sat as far apart as possible. Enyleve watched them nervously as she placed platters of food on the table, and even Cait shifted anxiously.

"Is there anything I can do to help?" I asked to break the silence.

Cait placed a weathered hand over mine. "Don't trouble yourself. You're our guest. Ron, did I tell you Miss Audrey is the queen's sister?"

Ron reluctantly tore his gaze from his son.

"You did," he said.

"What a great honor for our son to be trusted with protecting her," she continued.

"It must be a great honor for 'im."

I bristled at his sarcasm. "It is a great comfort to *me*. Olim is an accomplished knight, and I feel very secure knowing my life is in his hands."

Olim and his father stared at each other, and us women held our breaths as time ticked by without a response.

"The king's favor and the lady's praise is a credit," Ron said. "I hope he knows how proud 'is family is of 'im."

All eyes turned to Olim, and the shocked expression on his face was almost comical. His wide eyes fell on me, and I smiled brightly as if to say 'I told you so.'

"Now," Ron said, breaking the spell. "Are we going to eat this good food or talk?"

The rest of the meal passed more pleasantly. I answered the inquiries of Olim's parents regarding my family and enjoyed Ron's stories about his life. Unlike Cait, he was all too willing to reveal embarrassing secrets about Olim's childhood, including the time he tried to smuggle a lamb into the house because he wanted it to sleep with him. I giggled behind my hand as Ron described hearing the lamb's bleats Olim tried to pass off as snoring. Olim flushed red and grumpily shoveled food into his mouth, but even Enyleve relaxed enough to tease him.

"You could cover the sounds well enough," Enyleve said. "But not the smell!"

All of us burst into laughter.

Olim covered his face and muffled, "Can we talk about something else, please?"

"When do you go back to Praed?" Ron asked.

Enyleve's smile faded, and I resented her father's changing the tone of the evening.

"A few days," Olim said. "The great leaders of the surrounding countries will meet there within the week to discuss the upcoming war."

"How frightening," Cait said, clutching a hand to her breast. "I can't stand the talk of another war."

"We have no choice, Mother," Olim said. "Crif is threatening the south. If we don't stop them, the desert people will come here next."

"You were just a babe the last time they came," Cait said, her gaze faraway. "You don't know what it's like to live in dread every minute of the day. Why do men always resort to violence to solve their problems?"

Olim slammed a fist on the table, making me jump. "This isn't a simple land dispute. These people cannot be reasoned with. We have to protect our own."

"Watch your tone with your mother," Ron warned, but Olim didn't flinch.

"Once we win this fight," Olim continued. "Ilano and all the other northern countries will be free of Crif at last, and we'll never have to worry about an uprising again. Isn't the peace of mind of every generation after us worth it?"

My heart stirred at Olim's passion, but Cait's features were passive.

"I suppose," she said quietly. "And will you be joining in this fight?"

"I intend to," he said.

"Then may the spirits of our ancestors watch over you." Cait resumed eating, leaving the tense conversation to linger over the table.

Chapter 17

Olim's father signaled the end of the evening meal by pushing away from the table and inviting Olim to join him for a measure of brandy. Enyleve started clearing the dishes, and despite Cait's protests, I helped in the hopes of endearing myself to her. She didn't acknowledge me when I followed her into the yard to scrape the leftovers into a trough for the animals, nor when she retrieved a pot of hot water off the hearth to soak the soiled plates, cups, and cutlery. Together, we washed the dishes, completing the task in a heavy silence that pressed against my chest as if a boulder were lodged there. I could no longer tolerate her unfair treatment of me, and I turned squarely upon her as she dried the last of the plates.

"I'm not the one who hurt you," I said.

She froze. Droplets of water trickled down her arm and dripped rhythmically off her elbow.

"I only want to be your friend," I continued. "And you're punishing me for something I haven't done."

She resumed drying dishes and wouldn't look at me. "Olim told you?"

"He wanted me to understand your coldness toward me. What happened to you was reprehensible, but do you think it's fair to treat everyone with the same contempt you feel for that man? And what about the damage to your own soul? To live with such hatred cannot be healthy for your heart."

Slowly, she set aside the plate and raised her eyes to mine. They flashed sharply, and I self-consciously took a step backward.

"You people are all the same," she spat. "You think everyone below you should bend and scrape whenever you're nearby. You want the poor to simper and smile and make you feel good about your superiority. Well, I'm sorry if I don't wish to oblige you."

"That's not what I want! I simply wish for a chance for us to get to know one another. As equals."

She pounded a fist against her thigh. "But we're not equal! You're the queen's sister!"

"Yes, I am a sister. And a daughter. Just like you."

We stared at each other, unmoving, for a heartbeat. Two. Three. She slowly blinked and lowered her gaze. A tear fell from her eye, and my chest tightened. I wanted to comfort her, but I feared she might pull away.

"My life hasn't always been as privileged as it is now."

She sighed and her shoulders relaxed as she said, "I'm sorry I've been so awful. I should've at least been polite for Olim's sake, but I see someone from the city, and I instantly become suspicious."

"It's wise to be on your guard, but as your brother's friend, I mean you no harm."

"Is my brother in love with you?"

I flinched. "I-I cannot say that he is. We're friends. That's all."

She studied me intently, and as her blue eyes searched my face, I wondered at her words. Did she know something? Had Olim confided in her? Nothing in Olim's behavior indicated he felt more than friendship for me, but my ignorance in such situations proved I couldn't make an accurate assessment of his true feelings. The hair prickled on the back of my neck as Enyleve stood there watching my reaction to her startling question.

"If you say so," she said. She shook her head and turned her gaze to the fields beyond the house.

"Is he really as good of a knight as you claim?" Her eyes shone with unshed tears as her earnest face met mine.

"He is. I know it won't alleviate your worries, but Olim is a strong fighter. His chances of survival are high." My words emerged weakly through the tightening of my throat, and I turned away lest my eyes betray my thoughts.

I sensed a shift in her mood, and I peered over my shoulder at the sound of approaching footsteps. Olim hesitantly walked toward us, his eyes darting from Enyleve to me.

"I hope I'm not interrupting," Olim said.

"No," Enyleve said. "I was just going back inside to clean up." She rushed past me, squeezed his arm affectionately, then retreated into the house.

The moment the door closed behind her, Olim focused his attention on me. I couldn't bear for him to see my distress at the thought of his fighting in the upcoming war, so I moved away, strolling toward the edge of the stables to peer out into the pasture. The sun was setting, and the orange glow illuminated the sheep clustered in the field dozing contentedly.

"We should leave before it gets dark," Olim said.

"Olim, have I done something to displease you?"

"No! Why would you even think that?"

"You've been acting so strange lately. I didn't dwell on it, but after our argument earlier, every dark glare and harsh word came rushing back." I dared a glance over my shoulder. He was staring at me incredulously, pain evident in his eyes.

"I didn't realize I was behaving so badly," he said. "It wasn't because of you."

"I thought perhaps it was the stress of the war, but then there have been other moments before then. Are you sure I haven't done or said anything to upset you?" I maintained a steady composure, but my heart pounded so fiercely against my chest it nearly sent me off balance.

He looked away, abashed, and kicked at the dirt, sending a plume of dust and rocks skittering across the grass.

"You've changed since we've been here, and I confess it worried me. At first, it was refreshing to see you so open and able to overcome your shyness, but then...I'm ashamed to admit I became jealous of the other friendships you formed. I worried you would forget about me."

"How could you think that? I've told you countless times how important you are to me. I could never forget you."

"I've been an idiot, I know, and there is nothing I can say to justify myself." He picked up a stone and threw it into the field.

"Well, we'll be leaving soon, and everything will return to normal." At the thought, a sharp pang pierced my heart.

"Normal only in relative terms," he said.

I raised one eyebrow. "Enyleve is very afraid for you."

"I knew she would be, but I have a duty to Praed and Ilano."

"*I* understand, but I'm not sure *she* does."

"She doesn't have a choice," he said bitterly and chucked another rock. It whizzed past a stray sheep, nearly striking it in the head, and we both cringed.

"You don't have to take your frustrations out on that poor creature."

"Come on." He grumbled irritably, but the corner of his mouth twitched upward. "We should take our leave."

Watching Olim's family bid him farewell, perhaps for the last time, filled me with agony, and brought sharply into light the fact that soon I would be standing in their shoes. What would I do without Olim to watch over me? His presence was as constant as my family's, and soon there would be a vacant space where he stood, ever vigilant. No more would I see his kindly smile or hear his voice. No more would I see him practice his drills or tease him for shrinking away when I handed him one of the children. And if he did not return, I would feel empty without my trusted friend.

Cait's eyes shone adoringly at her only son, his face framed in her gnarled hands. Her lips moved, but no words escaped her strained throat. She kissed his cheeks and turned away before she lost her composure. Ron stepped forward and pulled Olim into a brief yet firm embrace, pounding his fists against his son's back. He grumbled, "Safe journey," before moving away himself, leaving Enyleve to say goodbye to her brother.

"Try not to be a hero," she said with a tearful smile before wrapping her arms around his waist.

"I'll try to resist," he muttered.

When Enyleve showed no sign of pulling away, Olim carefully extricated himself from her embrace. He kissed the top of her head, smiled reassuringly, and escorted me outside. The family followed and watched as we mounted our horses, Ron's arms draped across the ladies' shoulders.

Cait hobbled forward, and I expected her to wish Olim one last farewell, but instead she approached *me*. She grasped my calf, and I leaned closer to hear her speak.

"Dear girl," she whispered. "Whatever you decide, you are always welcome at my hearth."

My brows furrowed in confusion, but before I could ask her to clarify, she patted my thigh and stepped away. Olim kicked his horse, and we swiftly cantered away. We did not speak on the return trip to the capitol building. We left our horses with a groom, and I followed Olim, still patiently waiting for him to speak. He stalked to the barracks where the knights slept and paused.

"I'm fine," he said, waving his hand in the air between us. "But I'm tired. I bid you goodnight until tomorrow."

He opened the door and stepped through it before I could blink. I sighed, knowing Olim didn't want me to see how acutely he felt the pain of parting with his family.

The next morning, Laria was informed her presence was required at an early council meeting, and her heavy sigh echoed off the walls.

"There'd better be good news," she mumbled as we trudged down the hall.

We stopped at the entrance to the council chamber, and she turned her weary gaze on me.

"Oh, Ula." She blew a stray lock of ginger hair off her forehead. "Sometimes I wished I lived a simpler life."

"I know." I smiled and re-pinned the rogue strand. "But we would be lost without you."

She grinned wryly before stepping inside.

I wandered down the hallway and expected to be inundated with swirling thoughts of the days to come. But my mind was blank. I absently pushed open the door to the library and was immediately comforted by the familiar smell of old pages, leather, and aged wood. I moved through the room with half closed eyes, trailing my fingertips along smooth bindings. A voice came from the back of the room, and I peered around the corner of the last bookcase to see Finton, a large map displayed behind him. Hands were raised in the air, waiting patiently to be called upon. I sank into a chair at the back and realized with shock he was teaching a lesson centered around the topic at the forefront of everyone's mind: Crif.

Finton pointed to one of the students, and the young man rose and said, "Dr. Ekhane, can you explain how people who live in the desert can support a population much less an army? Where do they get their water to drink and grow crops?"

"An excellent question," Finton answered. "In Ilano, we are lucky to have ponds and underground springs and rivers to tap into for our orchards and vineyards, our livestock, and to quench our own thirst. Crif is not fortunate enough to boast such sources. They must draw moisture through other means. There are the simple methods of following birds and digging into the ground where they gather. Beasts can smell water under the surface of the sand, and even a small hole can collect a decent amount of water for a single person. Certain plants are also rich in moisture, but digging in the ground and eating succulents can only go so far. The Crif have developed a system of collecting water that harnesses a natural phenomenon: morning dew. Miles of netting spreads over Crif like fences, and when the morning fog heavy with moisture settles upon it, tiny droplets form in the mesh and trickle down onto a collection duct that funnels the water into a central area where families can take what they need. These pools can become large enough to water hundreds of people and their animals."

I listened with the rest of the class, intrigued, as he answered several more questions until the last grains of sand fell through the hourglass. The students prepared to leave, but Finton held up a hand to stop them.

"This shall be our last meeting for a while," he said. "I know many of you have family and friends who will be leaving you soon. Spend as much time with them as you can."

Somberly, the students filed out of the room. Many recognized me at this point and offered a respectful incline of the head as they passed, but my focus was solely on the large map behind Finton. My eyes wandered over the borders of the desert country in amazement until the door closed on the last person.

"I had no idea Crif was so big," I said. My eyes traveled northward, and a thought struck me.

"You have questions?" Finton asked.

I frowned. "I don't understand. It's such a large country, why would the king...what was his name?"

"Karne."

"Right. Why would King Karne want to invade us when he has so much already?"

"The usual reasons: resources, subjects, greed, expansion of their territory. A modicum of revenge also motivates him, I imagine."

"But if he did manage to conquer all the countries north of Crif, how does he expect to rule them all? That's a lot of ground to cover."

"A good question," he said. "He would probably establish a centralized capital and place trusted allies in positions of power at points around the continent. He would have to travel quite a bit to remind the people he's in charge and sit in council."

"How exhausting."

"It's a small price to pay if you want to create an empire."

I studied the map again, and a troubling question arose: "How many people do they have in their army?"

"I can't say," he said. "Father would know better than I, and I haven't the strength to ask."

I looked at Finton then, and he had such an expression of sorrow it broke my heart to see it. I rose shakily, and we stared at each other over the empty tables that may not see students for many months, perhaps years.

"I don't wish to keep you." I took a steading breath and cleared my throat. "Will you be at the Farewell Assembly tomorrow?"

His hazel eyes shimmered behind his spectacles. "Unless I'm—"

"Yes." The word escaped my lips in a throaty laugh, tightened by the thousand words I longed to say but couldn't articulate. "As long as you aren't called out on an emergency." My stomach twisted in knots, and I couldn't bear the intensity of the situation and turned to leave.

"Ula?"

I paused and slowly faced him. He was several steps closer and seemed about to speak, but he lowered his eyes to the ground, searching for the right words. He drummed his fingers on a nearby table and shuffled a foot across the polished floor.

"What—" He swallowed, then met my eye. "What should I tell my patients when they ask about you?"

Warmth spread across my cheeks and tears pricked the corners of my eyes. "If you would be so kind as to thank them for their kindness and hospitality, I would greatly appreciate it. Please tell them." I gulped down the urge to cry. "I shall never forget them."

He nodded, and I took a deep breath.

"Please tell Mr. Neace to be patient with his horse. He should spend as much time with the animal as possible, even if it's just sitting in the pasture. The nearness will help build trust. Tell Mrs. Neace I shall miss her apple turnovers."

He smiled warmly, and I faltered. I pictured the little girl smiling sweetly when she waved goodbye. I reached behind my neck and unclasped the necklace hanging there.

"Please give this to little Ionah," I whispered and placed the necklace in Finton's open hand. His fingertips brushed my palm, and I stilled, my heart pounding as our eyes met.

"That's very generous of you," he said strangely, as if the words had to bend and twist to escape his lips.

The tips of my fingers grazed his as I withdrew my hand, and a flush of heat bloomed from my neck to my cheeks.

"Until tomorrow then."

I retreated before a sob escaped my lips, and I was equal parts grateful and disappointed that Finton did not follow.

The queen was in a reflective mood when I helped her undress and unpin her hair after dinner that night. Her expression was not pained nor sorrowful, but rather nostalgic, as if she were replaying every moment of the past several years. She twirled the silver band on the third finger of her left hand, a ghost of a smile gracing her lips. On her vanity was a picture Sulwen painted for her earlier that day next to a bundle of flowers Lilias picked. A stick curved into a bow made by Rian sat alongside a quiver fashioned out of an old knapsack Alyx had filled with handmade arrows fletched with eagle feathers. A sheet of paper scrawled with Tyrnan's first attempts at writing his letters was propped against the mirror. She ran a hand reverently over these precious objects, and my jaw ached with the effort to hold back tears.

"I wish we had time to have portraits made of the children," Laria said. "Pocket ones. For Risteard to take with him."

I massaged away some of the tension coiled in her shoulders. "I'm sure he'll hold their memories in his heart," I said.

"I'm certain he will, but it would give him something to hold onto and look at when he misses them."

"I wish I knew what I could say to comfort you, Laria." I resumed brushing out her long hair. "I could never be as strong as you."

"We all show strength in our own way." She met my eye in the mirror. "Yours may not be as obvious as mine, but it's just as formidable."

"How was the council meeting today? Any news?"

"Kuste has replied to our invitation to Praed. Several scholars were brought in to translate their message, but essentially, they expressed a wish to also be rid of the

Crif threat. A Great War Council has been called and the chief of the tribes will be joining us."

"It already has a name?"

She smirked. "You know how men are. They'd give their privy pots titles."

We laughed in the easy manner we did as children, the kind of laugh that erased the stress of responsibility. Laria's eyes lit up like beacons when she laughed this way, and I hoped it wouldn't be the last I'd see it.

Laria rose and took my hands. "I have a favor to ask."

"Anything!"

"Don't agree before you know what it is. You may regret it."

"Go on then."

"Tomorrow at the Farewell Assembly, will you sing for me? Something from all of us. To say goodbye."

I paled and my smile faded, not at the prospect of singing in front of hundreds of people, but because it felt so final.

"You don't have—"

"Yes. Of course, I will."

Laria's eyes glimmered and she pulled me into a fierce hug.

"Thank goodness for you, Ula," she said in my ear. "I don't think I could bear what lies ahead without you."

I knew she could, but it warmed my heart to hear her say otherwise.

Chapter 18

If one were to ask me, even that evening, what I'd done the morning of the Farewell Assembly, I could not answer with any certainty. The day was a whirlwind of activity from the loading of trunks for our early departure the next day, to last minute alterations to our dresses, to finalizing the details of the menu. Anyone who wished to attend was invited, and the kitchen staff were diligently preparing to ensure there was enough food. The queen had me sending messages all over the capitol building, including the lower mews because an aerial display was planned for a proper send off. The gardens in the evening were becoming colder, and several fire pits were constructed for everyone's comfort. The seamstresses were relieved the queen didn't require new gowns on such short notice, but they did tailor some of the older pieces into newer styles.

The queen was absolutely stunning in an ivory gown with three-quarter sleeves billowing in delicate organdy that almost reached the ground. The bodice was embellished with soft, pink threads from Ilano sheep embroidered to resemble lace. I chose a light blue gown I discovered too late had a very low neckline. Despite my sister's assurances that no one would stare, I insisted on wearing a light wrap across my chest and shoulders.

The children were excited at the prospect of yet another party but their happiness at returning home the next morning eclipsed the delights of the evening festivities. They enjoyed their time in Ilano, but their young hearts yearned for the familiarity of Praed, especially under the circumstances. They prattled on about being able to sleep in their own beds, seeing their grandmother, and their eagerness to inspect every inch of their home for changes. Their childish innocence tempered my anxiety, and their excitement fueled my own.

I grew more and more queasy the closer it came time for the Farewell Assembly to begin. The afternoon supper tasted bland on my tongue, and the smells of serving platters drifting from the gardens nearly brought the contents of my stomach to the forefront. I swallowed the rising bile in my throat and fixed my features into a pleasing countenance as the royal family and I gathered to present ourselves formally to the crowd of people waiting outside.

Laria lay a cool hand on my arm. "You look a little ashen. Are you nervous about singing?"

I shook my head. "Just anxious."

"I know the feeling." The king appeared beside her, and she took his arm as we left the capitol building and marched into the waning light of a crisp evening.

The beauty of the evening should have awed me and filled my heart with joy, but my trepidation regarding the events surrounding our departure dulled my perception of the festivities. The voices of the guests gathered in finery and tapping their glasses together were warped in my ears. All I could hear was men talking, leaning over a large table with a map, and planning the upcoming war. I looked at the delighted faces illuminated by the last glow of the setting sun and grimly wondered how many of the men would be joining the fight and how many women would be in mourning this time next year.

I pressed my palms to my eyes to keep the tears at bay and focused my attention on the children. They were worried about what was to come, but they lived in the moment and were able to enjoy the delights of the assembly. The princes giggled as they dodged around dresses and servers while playing games and sneaking treats, a few other boys their age joining in the fun. The boys easily made friends in Ilano, and they already expressed remorse at leaving their playmates behind.

The sun dipped below the horizon, and torches and fire pits came alive. I was startled to realize how much time passed while I wandered in a daze. Absently, my fingers closed around a morsel of food from one of the trays displayed on a series of long tables, but I didn't taste it when I placed it in my mouth.

"You look as if you're about to pass out or throw up." I looked up at the sound of the familiar voice. Olim's blue eyes were filled with concern.

"I'm fine," I said. "A little tired, I'll admit."

"I know how you feel." He stretched his head from shoulder to shoulder. The joints cracked and popped, and he rubbed the muscles at the base of his neck. "I'm sorry I've been remiss in watching over you, but we've been running drills from sunup to sundown."

"Don't worry about me," I said. "You have more important things to do than make sure I don't fall out of trees." I smiled reassuringly, and as I gazed into his grinning face, I noticed the dark circles under his eyes and lines about his mouth. What must it be like for him and the other knights having to prepare themselves to go to war, knowing they may not survive? My chest tightened at the thought of never seeing my friend again, and I turned away so he couldn't see the moisture welling in my eyes.

Laria caught my attention and waved me over, and I was relieved to have a reason to excuse myself before I started blubbering like a fool. She grasped my hand when I reached her, and her eyes narrowed.

"Your hands are like ice," she said, "and you're as pale as the moon."

"I'm just…" I met her worried stare and knew I couldn't lie to her. "I'm frightened."

"I know." She pulled me into a firm embrace. "I am, too. But right now, we must put on our masks and be brave."

I nodded as I drew away and wiped the tears from my stained cheeks.

"Come on." She rested a hand on my back. "If you're ready, it's time to say goodbye."

I squared my shoulders and allowed her to lead me to a raised dais. Behind me, musicians were waiting to play lively tunes that would carry the feet of eager dancers. The king raised his hand, and one by one, the conversations ceased, and the gardens fell silent as all eyes focused on us. Laria stepped forward.

"Dear ladies, gentlemen, and children of Ilano," she said, smiling. "This shall be the last time we meet for some time, and words cannot adequately express how grateful we are for your support. We are only as strong as you, our people, have made us, and we are honored by your resilience. It will sustain our brave knights and soldiers and shield our king as they face our greatest enemy." She paused when the people cheered, and she struggled to maintain her composure. "We will miss you. Your welcoming, kind nature has made Ilano as dear to me as my own home." She swallowed, her eyes shining in the firelight. I searched the faces of the crowd and noticed many of them were also struck by the emotional moment. Risteard wove his fingers with hers, and she inhaled deeply.

"To signal the start of the dancing, my lady-in-waiting shall sing for you," she said. "To say goodbye. From all of us."

All eyes turned to me, and my hands shook upon seeing the sheer number of people. I'd never performed for so many before, and I doubted if I had the fortitude to continue. Shakily, I looked to my sister, and she smiled and mouthed 'go on' as the first notes of the song played behind me. I squeezed my eyes shut and listened to the music. I pretended I was in the drawing room at Riverstone, and the only people there were my family, a far less nerve-wracking prospect. The notes signaling my cue were struck, and my lips opened automatically to release the song.

I sang the opening lines to a song about a bond that grew so strong the thought of breaking it was grievous. I sang about how nothing could compare, could be enough, to fill the hole left behind. I opened my eyes as my voice carried over the crowd and became stronger as I contemplated the meaning of those words. I felt their impact down to my toes, and my hands shook as I raised them toward the people and told them how important they were. My sister was right. Ilano had become a second home. I was certain I would miss it, but until that moment, I hadn't felt how devastating it would be to say goodbye.

I sang as if I were singing to my family, to close friends, for that is what they'd become. I'd never sung so passionately as I did to their open, honest faces. The last lines drew near, and I powered on through the strain in my throat, not just from the high notes but the emotions boiling to the surface. I closed my eyes to force back tears, and when I opened them, I saw Finton. My chin trembling, I uttered the final notes as a lone tear escaped to burn a trail down my cheek. The crowd erupted in clapping and whistling, the sounds muffled behind the pounding of my heart. In a daze, I walked off the dais, and the musicians played the first dance of the evening.

Laria was smiling, her hands clasped before her and tears in her eyes, but I did not hear her praise. I walked past her as if I were a ghost. Vaguely, I sensed a presence step beside me, but I did not acknowledge them. Someone shook my shoulder, and I lifted my eyes.

"Are you all right?" Olim asked.

"Yes." I brushed him off. "I just need a moment."

I left him befuddled and strode into the capitol building, the sounds of laughter and music drifting into nothingness as the doors closed behind me.

I started to climb the stairs, gripping the railing tightly to keep from shaking. I breathed deeply through my nose and released it through my bloodless lips. I admonished myself for losing my self-control in front of so many people, but no amount of chastisement stopped the agony in my chest.

"Ula?" The quiet voice came from behind me.

Slowly, I turned, keeping my grip on the railing to keep from tumbling. Finton stood at the bottom of the stairs, his hazel eyes shifted to deep brown in the low light. Tears flowed down my cool cheeks, and I lost the ability to contain the uncertainty building since I learned we were going to war. Wordlessly, Finton opened his arms, and I rushed into his comforting embrace.

His arms encircled me as I buried my face against his chest and wept without restraint. I cried for my sister who dreaded losing her husband, for Olim who was so ready to go to war, for all the knights and soldiers, and all the people of every country who would be fighting as one for the first time in history. I cried for my own miserable self and my worries that I would never see my friends and family again. I cried until there were no more tears, until I made no sound except for a few sniffles, and for the entirety of my mournful display, Finton said nothing. He held fast, stroking the back of my head and rocking me gently.

I pulled away and rubbed a hand against the spot on his chest left damp from my tears.

"I'm sorry." Heat bloomed across my face to the tips of my ears. "I hope I haven't ruined it."

"It's only fabric," he said, wiping away the last of my tears with his thumb. "It'll wash."

I took a step away and raised my eyes to meet his tender gaze, a soft smile on his lips. His hand was warm on my face, the pad of his thumb rough as it stroked my cheek. My pulse fluttered and my heartbeat became erratic.

"You sang beautifully tonight," he said.

"Thank you." I took another step back and ducked my head to dab at my eyes with a handkerchief.

"You don't always have to be so strong."

My eyes widened as the words I spoke to Laria echoed in my ears. I stared at Finton in shock, blinking rapidly before regaining my senses.

"I'm not strong," I said. "But I can't very well go around sobbing like an idiot in front of everyone, can I?"

"I suppose not," he agreed with a crooked grin. "Perhaps a drink will help?"

"Oh, no," I said, shaking my head vigorously. "I don't want to overindulge. Not after…"

Finton's eyes narrowed, then with a mischievous grin he pointed at me and said, "The bottle remedy was for you, wasn't it?"

I groaned at the memory. "How embarrassing."

"Don't worry. I won't tell anyone."

"I didn't do anything foolish, did I? That night I mean?"

"Not that I can recall. You appeared to be enjoying yourself immensely."

"You're sure? I didn't do or say anything to offend you?"

"Of course not! But if you're really worried about it, limit yourself to one drink. If nothing else, it will help you forget about your worries for a while."

"I'll consider it."

His features fell, the camaraderie of our previous topic vanishing, and his voice was hoarse when he asked, "You leave tomorrow?"

"In the morning."

"Then this is, perhaps, the last time we shall be alone together."

"Perhaps." I held my breath, each beat of my heart like a drum against my chest.

"Ula, I want you to know." He swallowed, looked down at his feet, then shuffled closer. I didn't move, didn't blink, didn't breathe as he met my eye with an uncertainty I'd never seen in him before.

"Know what?" I whispered.

"That I shall…That I shall miss you."

"Oh," I breathed as my shoulders relaxed. "I'll miss you, too."

"Do you think," he said, still shifting nervously. "That's there's even the smallest chance that you—"

Heavy footfalls made him pause, and Olim appeared walking briskly toward us. The knight stopped short in surprise at seeing us, and if I wasn't mistaken Finton rolled his eyes in exasperation.

"Ula," Olim said. "I was just coming to see if you were well." His eyes shifted from me to Finton. "I'm not intruding, am I?"

"Yes, actually, you are," Finton snapped before I could reply.

My eyebrows shot upwards at his irritated tone, and even Olim was struck speechless.

"My apologies," Finton said to me as he ran a hand roughly through his hair. "It appears your knight has come to summon you."

I could not muster a reply, and Finton bowed respectfully and turned to leave.

"Wait," I called out.

Finton stopped but didn't face me.

"Would you save a dance for me?" I asked his rigid back.

He turned, his expression less severe than it had been moments before.

"I'll come find you," he said. "If there's room on my dance card." He winked and I suppressed a laugh as he disappeared from the building.

"What was his problem?" Olim asked.

"I don't know." I took the knight's proffered elbow. "We're all under an inordinate amount of stress. Surely Finton is as well."

"What could *he* have to be stressed about? He's not going to war."

"We're all going to war."

"You know what I mean," he said with a wave of his hand. "He's not going to the front."

A fact which flooded me with relief. I squeezed Olim's arm tighter, wishing the same was true for him as well.

We stepped out into the cool night, and I breathed in the warmth of firelight and mixture of perfumes. "I think I'd like a drink. Could you get me a glass of cider, please?"

Olim eyed me dubiously. "Are you sure? After what happened last time?"

"One drink shouldn't be a problem, right?"

He continued to look doubtful, and I was on the verge of rolling my eyes myself.

"All right then. One drink only."

I shook my head at his retreating form, half annoyed and half amused at his overprotectiveness.

"Your singing was absolutely enchanting," a smooth voice commented.

I stilled when I recognized the low, sultry tone, and cautiously turned to look up into the face of Lady Sharp.

"Your Ladyship," I said warily, dropping a slight curtsey.

"In fact," she continued, "I can't say that I've ever heard your equal. And I congratulate myself on having a very melodic singing voice. My praise does not come lightly."

"I thank you, then, for your praise." I glanced around my immediate surroundings, and my heart sank when I saw how isolated we were.

"I understand the royal family returns to Praed tomorrow."

"Yes, my lady."

"Well, I wish you all a safe journey. Will the king join the knights at the front?"

"I believe so, my lady."

Her expression became almost wistful as she stared ahead, the corner of her perfect mouth upturned.

"I do wish him well," she said quietly. "We've known each other a long time, the king and I. Did you know?"

"I've been acquainted with some of your history."

Both Lady Sharp and I turned in surprise. There stood the queen, poised and regal in her beautiful gown, her green eyes flashing angrily at Lady Sharp.

Lady Sharp hastily curtseyed. "Your Majesty."

The queen watched her closely, her mouth set in a firm line.

"Your husband, Martyn?" the queen inquired coldly. "Is he here?"

Lady Sharp shook her head, her eyes downcast. "Lord Sharp does not attend assemblies with me, Your Grace."

The queen cocked her head inquisitively as she regarded the tall woman, and my eyes flickered nervously from one to the other.

"I know I have no right to," Lady Sharp said. "But I wish to offer an apology for our behavior toward Your Grace many years ago. I know I cannot offer an adequate explanation—"

"Try."

Lady Sharp was clearly unsettled, so acutely I almost felt sorry for her. I didn't know what offenses she spoke of, but they were terrible enough to leave her pale and glowing from a sheen of sweat. She gathered herself and met the queen's steely gaze, took a deep breath, and unfolded the story.

"Many years before Ilano invaded Praed," Lady Sharp began, "I lived in the capitol building. My father was a friend and trusted advisor to former Lord Protector Davian. I was thus very aggressively sought after." A sly smile stretched across her face as she remembered. "Every man wanted me, but soon I grew tired of the sport of conquests so easily won."

I listened with undisguised interest while Laria continued to stare blankly.

"I became acquainted with Risteard, apologies—" She held up a hand before Laria could issue a sharp retort, "—the king, through a close friend."

That friend was former Princess Caelyn, and I appreciated her not mentioning the woman's name.

"He was distant, stoic, and never looked at a woman. There was talk that the last time he showed the slightest interest in a lady, his cousin seduced the girl, resulting in the pair coming to blows. I cared not for his past, but in him I saw a challenge. Many ladies found him attractive despite his taciturn nature, and I vowed I would lord my conquest of him over their heads."

The queen sneered. "So, that's it? You were jealous of me?"

"Not jealous. My vanity was damaged when he rejected me. It was my wounded pride that led me to revenge. You see," Lady Sharp explained as she looked at me. "He never so much as glanced at another woman, and no matter how boldly I pursued him, he paid little attention to me. I, who was considered a great beauty who could give a man endless pleasure, was cast aside. Not to give up so easily, I followed him to Praed, where he ignored me again. I began to consider rumors of his preferring the company of men, until I saw the way he doted on a simple, skinny, ginger-haired servant." She returned her attention to Laria, and if she was intimidated by my sister's dark glare, she didn't show it. "I thought perhaps it was pity for your disabilities that drove him to be so protective or your position in the royal household, but the more I saw the two of you together, the more I realized the awful truth: he was fond of you."

"Enough," the queen said. "I don't wish to hear more. Your insulted pride is no excuse for what you did to me."

Lady Sharp lowered her head and whispered, "I deserved to be punished. I wonder why you didn't come after us after you were crowned."

"It wasn't out of mercy," the queen said, her eyes full of a hatred I didn't recognize. "You owe your life to the king."

Lady Sharp's eyes closed, and she smiled contentedly. "He wished to spare me?"

"No. He didn't want me to appear vindictive. It was for my sake you were spared."

Lady Sharp frowned. "Well, you may not have enacted revenge against me, but it may please you to know I haven't lived blissfully. His Lordship and I have no children. It seems I am barren."

The queen's hard expression softened. "That is regrettable. I would not wish childlessness on any woman."

"Because I have displeased him, Lord Sharp chooses not to attend public appearances with me and finds comfort in the arms of other women."

"I would be shocked if this truly inconvenienced you. You never had any trouble taking lovers."

"I'll admit keeping lovers has lost its appeal," Lady Sharp said in a pitiable tone.

The two women stared at one another, one with an open, appealing face and the other with a fury that had been restrained for years.

"Please," Lady Sharp said. "Forgive me, Your Majesty. No matter our personal history, Ilano has prospered under your rule, and despite how this affects me personally, the country is grateful to you."

The queen's face was impassive, but I knew she was considering her words, and I hoped she would forgive her for her own peace of mind at least.

"You contributed to the misery that was my life," she said. "But it seems you have suffered since, and that is punishment enough for anyone. I will endeavor to hold a grudge against you no longer."

"You are truly magnanimous, Your Majesty." Lady Sharp released a relieved sigh and curtseyed.

"Not really," the queen mumbled. She fired a glance toward me. I stifled a smile as Lady Sharp met her eye once more. "I expect for you to keep the king and his knights in your thoughts during this trying time."

"Of course, Your Majesty."

"Your *pure* thoughts."

I shot Lady Sharp a narrowed glare.

"You don't have to worry about that any longer, Your Majesty, I promise." Lady Sharp smiled sweetly, and my lip curled to see its insincerity.

"I don't normally consider myself a petty woman, but I want you to know how thoroughly you've lost."

The hairs at the back of my neck prickled. I'd seen many sides of Laria, but this unforgiving woman was a stranger to me.

"I feel it keenly, Your Majesty. The king has found himself the perfect queen."

The queen's eyes flickered briefly, so quickly only the most perceptive person would have noticed. Lady Sharp proved to be incredibly astute. She looked over her shoulder, and there stood the king, his eyes narrowed menacingly at her. I don't know how long he'd been standing there, but his presence disturbed the lady immensely. Her eyes widened, and the color drained from her face. Clumsily, she curtseyed low, almost stumbling over the hem of her tightly tailored gown.

"Your Majesty," Lady Sharp breathed shakily. She did not rise nor lift her head to look at him as she waited for him to address her.

"Lady Sharp." The king's tone froze the blood in my veins, making me shiver. "Does Lord Sharp join you tonight?"

"No, Your Majesty. He does not join me any night," she said, her voice steady with bitterness. It seemed her husband's infidelity was more insulting than a bruise on her vanity.

Risteard and Laria locked eyes over her prone form. The tense silence stretched between us, punctuated by Laria breathing heavily through her nose. I shifted uneasily, waiting for someone to speak.

"I'm so grateful to Your Majesties," Lady Sharp said, "for the prosperity you've brought to Ilano. Your rule has been truly inspiring."

"Get up," Risteard insisted. "You're wasting our time."

I'd never heard him speak so callously before. Whatever offenses Lady Sharp committed must have been grievous indeed to incite such wrath.

Slowly, Lady Sharp rose to her feet and inched her gaze up toward the king's stony countenance. For a moment, she regarded him from beneath her long eyelashes. But she remembered herself and raised her chin innocently.

"Your Majesty," Lady Sharp said with astounding composure. "I wish you well on the journey to Praed, and both Lord Sharp and I send our good thoughts to you and your soldiers for your health and safety."

"That is much appreciated," the king said dryly. "Give my regards to Lord Sharp when you see him."

By the look on Lady Sharp's face, this was not a request that would bring her husband joy. Without another word, the king extended a hand toward the queen, and together they drifted off to mingle with the assembled crowd. We watched the queen clutch the king's elbow to lift herself toward his ear to whisper something and his answering nod. My ears perked up at the sound of the children running toward their parents, Sulwen with her arms outstretched toward her father. The king lifted her into the air, and the sweet sound of her giggles permeated the night. Alyx and Rian were animatedly telling their mother a story and she dutifully laughed and gasped at the appropriate parts before they dashed back into the throngs of people. The king became engaged in a conversation with the Lord Protector, Sulwen's sweet head resting contentedly on his shoulder as her eyes drifted closed. A few noblewomen held the queen's attention, and the three women stood smiling in an amiable discussion. The king and queen had their backs to each other, their focus appearing to be solely fixed on the people before them, when the king dropped an arm and stretched an open hand backwards. As if instinctively sensing the movement, the queen reached back and entwined her fingers with his, and the pair stood holding fast to one another without pausing their respective conversations.

I glanced at Lady Sharp to gauge her reaction to this touching display. She stood transfixed, her face blank but her eyes glistening. I did not know her well enough to ascertain if it was sorrow, envy, or anger that flashed in her dark gaze, but were I in her position, I imagine it would be a mixture of all three.

Lady Sharp turned her cool gaze on me. "They have a true affection for each other."

"Yes." I couldn't tell if her statement was a question or simply an observation. "I hope to be as happily married one day."

"It's almost as shocking as hearing the queen's voice. For as long as I'd known her, I never heard her speak. Until now."

Laria pretending to be mute for the three years she served Princess Caelyn was almost as remarkable as her organizing a rebellion.

"A fact I find difficult to imagine." The tense atmosphere was not fitting for a night of celebration, and though I wasn't fond of Lady Sharp on principle, I did not wish for any of the guests to be unhappy. Her red lips curled in a slight smile, and she looked down her perfectly straight nose at me.

"They have been rewarded by providence for their patience and good deeds," she said, "while I have suffered for my actions against them. A fitting ending, but it does not always happen that the honorable win and the villainous lose."

"Not always. But luckily that's what happened in this case."

Her eyes narrowed. No words passed between us for several seconds, until she shook her head, and the hateful stare was replaced with a mask of pleasant propriety.

"Well," she said.

I expected her to continue, but she said nothing more as she watched people dance and avoided looking toward the king and queen.

Questions teetered on the tip of my tongue, pressing against my teeth, eager to escape, but I was too timid to speak.

"Has the queen told you what I've done?" Lady Sharp asked as if reading my mind.

"The queen prefers to keep the past in the past."

"She is wise to do so."

"Why…" I swallowed and licked my lips to quench my parched mouth. "Why pursue the king if he didn't return your affections? It couldn't only have been a matter of pride." Heat burned my cheeks and I wiped my hands surreptitiously on the sleeve of my gown.

"You sweet girl." She smiled down at me as a mother to a naïve child. "You are lucky to be ignorant of the dealings of those in pursuit of pleasure." Her smile faded, and her gaze grew distant. "You're right, though. He was the First Knight to the former king, but he was also the king's nephew, the grandson of the former Lord Protector, and the son of Ilano's most cherished knight. I'll admit his lineage held great appeal for a single woman hoping to raise her fortunes. I didn't even care if he preferred the company of his own sex. Not if it meant elevating myself to the status afforded to me as his wife."

I was speechless, and though I was conscious of my open-mouthed stare, my jaw was too heavy to snap shut.

"The king made it clear in no uncertain terms he did not desire my attention. And he said it right in front of the queen, though at the time I didn't know she could hear. My reaction in that instance alone was enough for the queen to order my death after her coronation."

I shivered, my clacking teeth echoing in the silence left in the wake of her confession. Though part of me curiously wanted to know more, my stomach sickened at the possibilities. My expression must have reflected my thoughts, for Lady Sharp averted her eyes and assumed a nonchalant attitude.

"Do you think there's any reason the queen might change her mind in that regard?" she asked, the slightest tremor in her voice.

"Hard to say," I said with a coldness unfamiliar to my tongue. "You never can tell what a redhead will do."

She turned sharply, and I met her startled dark eyes with an icy glare. Her perfect ivory skin turned ashen, and her mouth opened and closed several times without uttering a word. Feeling a little protective and admittedly vindictive, I raised an eyebrow and shrugged as if to imply her fate could still be uncertain. Shortly thereafter Lady Sharp took her leave, and I was content to never see her perfectly composed face ever again.

The moment Lady Sharp was out of sight, I vowed for my sister's sake to never think or speak of her. I went in search of Olim and discovered him deep in conversation with an older knight, a drink in each hand. Quietly, I extricated one of the drinks from his grasp, and he barely glanced at me in acknowledgement. The other knight was a war-seasoned veteran, and he was giving the younger knight advice. Not wishing to interrupt, I wandered into the crowd.

I took a sip of the sweet cider and rolled the cool liquid around in my mouth. A bloom of lush tartness filled my nose at the first taste. Tiny bubbles popped along my tongue and slipped down my throat, leaving behind a hint of flowers. The emotions of the evening and the prospect of leaving in the morning were overwhelming, so I tipped back my head and drank the entire glass in a few swallows. Within minutes, my head was fuzzy, I forgot my worries, and accepted dances from familiar faces whose names I couldn't remember. Eventually, I dragged Olim into the festivities and danced with him until I spotted Duveesa struggling with Sulwen.

"Are you giving your poor nurse trouble?" I asked the toddler as I approached the pair, towing Olim behind me.

Duveesa huffed, blowing a strand of hair off her damp forehead. A red streak stained the front of her bodice and her shoulders sagged.

I took her hand and placed it in Olim's. "Have a dance and I'll take over."

She chewed her lower lip, looking from Olim to Sulwen. Olim smiled pleasantly and tugged her toward the dancers. She looked back, flashed a toothy grin, and skipped beside Olim.

"'Ssert!" Sulwen's insistent voice broke through the fog in my brain.

"How many have you had already?" I asked.

With an impish grin, she held up one finger. I raised an eyebrow. She pursed her little lips and reluctantly held up another finger.

"And how many did Mama and Fa-fa say you could have?"

She didn't answer, but her scowl was enough to convince me the second dessert was ill-gotten. One more sugary treat and she would probably bounce around the gardens causing trouble before crashing in a heap under a table.

Sulwen's eyes glittered with anticipation when I placed a caramelized apple slice in her hand, and she greedily stuffed the confection into her mouth. I wiped away the sticky residue from her lips and cheeks and whispered that this was our little secret. She giggled and gestured for me to chase her around the gardens in a game of hide-and-seek. I laughed at her exuberance, breathing in the cool night air as we dodged around trees and bushes at the periphery of the party. Her high-pitched squeals pierced the darkness, giving herself away and defeating the object of the game, but she still seemed surprised when I found her tucked behind the trunk of a large tree. I captured her in my arms, tickling her and enjoying the precious sound of her laughter, when a shadow flickered in the periphery of my vision. I stilled and strained to hear beyond Sulwen's delighted giggles and peered into the darkness. The little girl wiggled out of my arms to run off and find another hiding place, and in the ensuing quiet, angry voices filtered through the trees. I feared Sulwen might stumble blindly into a fight, so I hurriedly found her and scooped her into my arms before going to investigate.

When I rounded a hedge, I saw in the dim light of nearby torches a group of children, their voices mixing as they argued and shouted. A familiar weeping caught my ear and I dashed forward, setting Sulwen on the ground when I recognized Tyrnan's cries. I moved children aside, and when they realized an adult was now present, many ran off. Tyrnan was sitting on the ground, his brother Rian standing protectively over him. Alyx was toe-to-toe with Gerrid Ekhane, looking defiantly up at the older boy whose fists were clenched tightly at his sides.

"What's happening here?" I demanded.

The remaining children fell silent, and all eyes turned to me in shock. Gerrid's eyes were darkly hostile as they met mine. He roughly pointed a finger toward Rian. "It's his fault. He was hiding in a tree again getting ready to attack me."

"I was not!" Rian protested.

I raised a hand for silence and turned back toward Gerrid.

"And then what happened?" I asked.

"Well, I wasn't going to just let him humiliate me again," Gerrid said. "I threw a rock into the tree to let him know I saw him. It's not my fault the other one got in the way."

That explained Tyrnan's tears. I beckoned to the little prince, and he came over so I could inspect him. A trickle of blood ran from his temple down the side of his face, but the wound wasn't deep. I turned a hard glare at Rian.

"Were you planning mischief again?" I asked him.

"No!" he said. "Not this time, I promise!"

"Stay out of trees!" His red face turned away, and I looked back at Gerrid. "I don't blame you for being worried, but you had no proof they were going to bother you. And you certainly didn't have to act so violently." By the boy's grim expression, I guessed he disagreed. "And you," I directed my attention at Alyx. "What do you have to do with all this?"

"I heard Tyrnan crying, and Rian told me what happened, so I hit Gerrid in the stomach."

"Alyx Elejick! Why would you do that?"

"He hurt my brother," Alyx said as if this was a perfectly acceptable explanation.

"Then you get a grown-up! He's bigger than you are, Alyx. Stop picking fights with him."

"He started it!" Alyx cried, tears welling in his eyes. "Father said I have to look out for my brothers." His chin trembled, and he bit his lip to keep from crying.

"I'm sure he did," I said. "But that doesn't always mean the correct course is violence. You owe Gerrid an apology for hitting him."

Alyx's eyes widened incredulously. One look at Gerrid's smug expression, and his piercing blue eyes darkened.

"I don't want to," he grumbled.

"Show him that despite your age difference you're the bigger man."

The corner of Alyx's mouth twitched, and he looked at Gerrid askance.

"Sorry," the prince mumbled.

"Your turn," I told Gerrid.

"No," he said, crossing his arms across his chest. "This is all their fault. I don't care if they're princes. I was defending myself."

"You're twice their size." My anger rose. I stopped myself from yelling by remembering he was a child. "You could have just walked away. It's not defending yourself when you feed into the mischief of little boys and lose your temper."

"I can't wait for them to leave!" He gestured a fist toward Alyx, but he was wise enough not to strike the boy. "Everyone thinks they're so wonderful, but they're monsters!"

A shriek came out of the darkness, then Gerrid buckled over with a cry of pain. I looked down in horror and saw a flash of red, and for a moment I thought it was a plume of blood. My brain caught up with my eyes, and I realized it was Sulwen grasping Gerrid's lower leg, her teeth sinking into his calf.

"Sulwen!" I pulled the toddler off the poor boy and restrained her as she swung her fists toward Gerrid. "Stop!"

The commotion drew the attention of the children's nurses. Poor Agnus came panting toward us, her hand clutching her chest.

"There you are! Little tricksters gave us the slip and we couldn't find them," she explained.

"It's your job to watch them!" I snapped. They gaped at me in shocked silence. I shook my head and handed the tiring redhead to the younger nurse and placed Alyx's hand into Agnus'.

"I'm sorry," I said hastily. "Please put them to bed. Rian, go with Agnus. Tyrnan, come with me." I led Tyrnan by the hand and pushed Gerrid back toward the assembly. He resisted at first, but I grasped his sleeve and practically dragged him into the crowd.

"What's going on?" I heard Eve Ekhane's cool voice ask when I passed her.

"We're going to speak to the king and queen," I said.

"Gerrid," she said as she joined us. "What have you done now?"

The boy didn't answer, but began exaggerating a limp on his injured leg. His mother noticed and frantically asked questions, to which I told her everything would be explained.

The king and queen regarded us quizzically when I towed the boys forward, Eve on our heels. The whole tale unfolded from my lips, and the queen's expression alternated between distress, disappointment, and concern while the king remained impassive as always. The queen inspected Tyrnan's wound and decided it wasn't worth getting upset over, but suggested the doctor look at it just in case. The same was said for the crescent shaped welts on Gerrid's leg. Eve boxed Gerrid's ears and begged forgiveness on his behalf for harming the prince, and the queen diplomatically expressed remorse that their children continued to quarrel. Everything was handled properly, but I sensed the king was not satisfied, a steely glare marring his stoic countenance.

"You have been tormented, indeed, and that is regrettable," the king said, and Gerrid's face paled under the weight of his stare. "However, your response to the games of children much smaller than yourself is deeply disturbing. From one man to another, I strongly advise you to learn how to control your temper."

"Oh, he will, Your Grace," Eve interjected. "Won't you, Gerrid?"

The boy nodded mutely, but though he appeared compliant, rage still sparkled behind his eyes. He had a healthy regard for the king, but time would tell if he was smart enough to heed the wise words. The king turned his attention to the queen, and the pair regarded each other with unreadable expressions.

"Come on," Eve said sharply. "Let's have your uncle take a look at that leg." She bowed respectfully at the king and queen and stalked away, leading her son by the ear. I excused myself as well so Finton could also examine Tyrnan, leaving the king and queen to their silent exchange.

I had to carry Tyrnan to keep up with Eve's long, quick strides, but I kept a respectable distance so she could lecture her son without an audience. Tyrnan and I looked at each other, and even at his young age with a wound on his head, I saw sympathy in his eyes.

"I feel sorry for him, too," I whispered.

The little prince covered his mouth to stifle a giggle, and we both jumped when Eve's prickly tone called out to her brother-in-law.

"Finton!" The man himself barely had a moment to acknowledge her when she added, "I need you to examine Gerrid. That ginger-haired devil bit his leg. *Bit* him for Artur's sake!"

"After that," I said as I joined them. "Could you please look at Prince Tyrnan? I'm afraid a stray rock has struck him in the temple." I fixed Eve's wide-eyed gaze with a thunderous expression, and the woman at least had the decency to look ashamed.

"Of course," Finton said, smiling at the two boys. He gestured toward a well-lit area, and we followed, Eve casting a furtive glance in my direction. Probably wondering if I'd tell the queen and king about her callous comment. I stared at her impassively and let her fret over it.

Meanwhile, Gerrid pulled up the leg of his breeches so his uncle could examine the wound.

"Good news is you'll keep the leg," Finton teased.

The boy wasn't amused.

"You should go wash it immediately, and I'll bring over a salve tomorrow to be applied a few times a day."

"Will it scar?" Eve asked.

"Not likely, as long as you leave it alone," he said to his angry nephew.

"It won't become infected, will it?"

I rolled my eyes at Eve's frantic tone.

"Not if you follow my instructions." He then focused his attention on Tyrnan.

"Is that it?" Eve demanded. "My son suffered a bite wound from a *person* and all you do is look at it and tell him to wash it? Fynn was right about how worthless physicians can be."

My mouth dropped open. Eve never raised her voice or spoke so viciously before. I could easily explain her behavior arising from worry, but to insult her own family so horrendously was inexcusable. Finton fixed her with a calm, almost bored expression, and explained in intricate detail the current state of her son's skin.

"There are many layers that make up the skin," he said. "The outer layer is the body's protective covering. Below that are connective tissues and tiny capillaries. And deep to the surface of the skin is fat and larger vessels before you reach the muscle. Your son has been bitten by a tiny child through breeches, the equivalent of being bitten by a small, elderly dog. The only layer of skin to be broken is the first, and the wound is not bleeding, though it may bruise. These factors contribute to my medical opinion that the injury is in no danger of becoming gangrenous. With proper washing and application of the salve of which I have promised, your son will recover without permanent damage. Would you prefer my evaluation be different?"

Her chest moved rapidly, and her nostrils flared, but she didn't answer.

He pointed to Tyrnan. "This child, however, has suffered a blow to the head, and therefore warrants a full neurological examination. He could have sustained permanent cognitive dysfunction as a result of his injury, and thus is placed higher on my list of concerns than whether tiny pinprick welts on a strong, healthy boy are going to scar. Now, may I proceed?"

Eve pulled her son into the capitol building and mumbled about washing the filth off his skin. I stared at Finton, my eyes wide with worry.

"Do you really think Tyrnan might have permanent damage?" I asked.

"Was it Gerrid who threw the stone?"

I nodded, and he grinned. "Then no."

I smirked and set Tyrnan down for an exam. Finton inspected the wound and concluded it didn't require sutures, but it may scar.

"Battle wound," he told Tyrnan.

The little boy shied away, but he couldn't hide a smile. Finton held out a finger and asked Tyrnan to follow it with his eyes without turning his head, then held the finger out in front of him and asked Tyrnan to touch it. He covered one of Tyrnan's eyes, then the next, his focus intent on the boy's deep blue gaze.

"Did you fall asleep after the rock hit you?" Finton asked.

Tyrnan shook his head.

"Do you see two of everyone?"

Another negative response.

"Do you feel sick to your stomach? Like you're going to vomit?"

"No," Tyrnan muttered.

"You're sure? If I offered you a sweet, would you take it or say no?"

Tyrnan smiled. "Take it."

Finton stood and looked at my anxious face.

"I think he'll be fine," he said.

I breathed a sigh of relief.

"Keep an eye on him, though. If he forgets simple things or has trouble speaking, he should see a physician immediately."

I drew in a shuddering breath and released it slowly through parted lips. Thinking about Tyrnan suffering permanent damage sent a stone crashing through my stomach. I ran my fingers through his soft, wavy brown hair, and his big blue eyes met mine. They were clear and focused. I hoped this would be the last time Laria's children tangled with Gerrid Ekhane.

"Thank you. I'm going to send him to bed now." I turned to leave, but Finton raised a hand to stop me.

"I've found I am quite free to dance the next if you are," he said.

I grinned. "I haven't filled my dance card yet. I'll be right back."

I led Tyrnan into the crowd and searched for Duveesa. I scanned the faces of the people twirling and spinning to the music and spotted her still dancing with Olim. I smiled at the sight of her enjoying herself so thoroughly and waited until the music faded before approaching her.

"You dance beautifully!" I told her.

She blushed. "Hardly. Poor Olim had to guide me the whole time so I wouldn't run into anyone."

"Or step on my toes," Olim added.

I pulled Tyrnan forward and placed his little hand in Duveesa's.

"He's had a long night," I said. "And an early start tomorrow. I've already sent the other boys and Sulwen to bed."

"I'll go see if Princess Lilias is still attached to the queen." Duveesa bid Olim and me goodnight and ushered the little prince away.

"May I have this dance?" Olim asked with a gallant bow and a flourish of his extended hand.

"You're not tired?"

"It may be the last night of leisure I have for a while. I intend to enjoy every moment."

My smile faltered, but I regained a pleasant expression to match his own to keep the mood light.

"As you should, but we'll have to find you another partner as this one is spoken for."

"Oh." He straightened and opened his mouth to continue, but I excused myself before the music started in case he was about to ask the identity of my dance partner. I didn't want Olim's unfounded jealousy to pollute his good mood.

Finton took my hand in his sure grip and led me among the couples gathering for the next set. As the first notes played, I recognized the music from the first time we danced. It seemed like a lifetime ago, and I wished for the same feeling of carelessness without the gloom of an impending war hanging over our heads.

After enduring the stress of the last few days, I was happy to close my eyes and surrender to Finton's lead. The music filled the spaces between my thoughts, and I concentrated on the feel of Finton's guiding hands. A wave of emotions overcame me. Between the children fighting, Eve's comments, and the threat of war, I was completely drained. When I thought I could face the world without crying, I opened my eyes and met Finton's tender gaze.

"It's all right," he whispered. "I've got you."

My eyes drifted shut, and I choked back a sob. For the remainder of the dance, I felt like a ghost drifting aimlessly on the wind. And because I didn't have the strength to resist, I allowed it to take me, to spin me and to lift me into the air, and to set me back to earth.

The next morning dawned much too quickly. Before breakfast, servants loaded the carriages with our trunks and prepared for our departure. The king and queen preceded the family from the capitol building, and gathered on the steps were the Lord Protector, his family, the council members, and the other noble residents. The entire city turned out for our departure and lined the streets in droves to bid us goodbye, and I was once again touched by their welcoming generosity.

The Lord Protector informed the king he would follow him to Praed within the week, and I glanced over his shoulder to see Fynn puffed up with pride at having Ilano at his disposal while his father was away. The queen hugged the Lord Protector warmly and thanked him profusely for everything he had done. By her tone, I knew she meant so much more than his hospitality while we resided in Ilano. The Lord Protector then patted the princes on their heads and wished them a pleasant journey before kissing Lilias' tiny hand and pinching Sulwen's nose. I bit my lip to keep from laughing when the toddler looked past the Lord Protector to shoot Gerrid a dirty glare.

Duveesa and I regarded each other with mournful gazes while the children piled into the carriage. She put a hand on my shoulder, glanced around at the masses of people gathered along the street, and her shimmering eyes met mine. A tremulous smile touched my lips, but I lacked the strength to sustain it. I clutched her hand, gripping it as if I were about to faint. She squeezed back, inhaled deeply, and mouthed, "We'll be all right," before ducking into the carriage.

The king assisted Laria into another carriage, then placed Lilias in her outstretched arms. Sulwen whined behind me, crying out for "Fa-fa" and struggling to break free from Agnes. The older woman shushed and soothed, but the toddler dissolved into tears when her father mounted his black stallion and cantered to the front of the procession with a perfunctory wave.

I placed one foot on the carriage step, but a strange clench in my heart made me pause. I turned and surveyed the people standing proud on the capitol steps. The Lord Protector smiled warmly while Fynn and his wife, Eve, were as placid as ever. Fidelma waved a handkerchief and pretended to cry, her husband draping a comforting arm across her shoulders. My eyes alighted on Finton. His face was devoid of expression. He didn't smile when our eyes met, and it pained me to see him so despondent.

Duveesa touched my arm. "Come on. Let's go home."

Without a second glance, I took a seat inside the carriage next to the window. Tyrnan sat on my lap so he could see as we left the city. The people cheered and waved as we passed, and the children dutifully waved back. I leaned back in my seat, unable to watch the beloved landscape of Ilano fade while we traveled out of the city into the vastness of the orchards. If I saw the roads to farms where I picked apples or visited patients with Finton, I would break down and frighten the children. So, I kept my eyes averted and didn't look out the window for the entirety of our journey back to Praed.

While the journey to Ilano filled us with excited anticipation, the mood upon our return to Praed was decidedly more subdued. A dark cloud hung over our heads threatening to dampen our spirits. Even the children sensed the tense atmosphere and were less exuberant. But as the landscape changed from vast greenery to rolling fields of golden prairie, a thrill of longing shuddered in my breast. The children pressed their tired faces to the carriage windows and pointed out familiar estates. After days of traveling in the cramped space, Market Town came into view, the White Mountain looming in the distance.

As in Ilano, the people of Praed crowded the streets and welcomed us home with applause and cheers. The children smiled brightly and enthusiastically waved their little hands. The king and queen led the procession on horseback up the mountain, passing underneath swaying branches of ancient trees hanging over the road. Praed Castle emerged before us surrounded by knights and soldiers. Waiting on the front steps were the council members, and accompanying them, standing as regal as a queen, was Mother.

"Grandmama! Grandmama!" the children cried. They jumped from the carriage and bounded up the steps toward Mother. She opened her arms and gathered them into a warm hug, and my heart swelled to see such an openly affectionate display from an otherwise cold and composed woman.

The council members bowed low to the king and queen and wasted no time filling them in on what transpired in their absence. The king gestured to the castle and stated that since there was no time to waste, they may as well call a meeting. I moved to Laria's side and linked my arm through hers.

"Perhaps you should skip this meeting," I said. "You look like you're about to fall over."

She sighed, her shoulders sinking heavily before she pulled herself together again. "I am. The journey there felt much shorter than the journey back."

"You should rest. You're so pale."

"Though I would like nothing more than to sleep the rest of the afternoon, I'm afraid there is much to do."

"Can't the king handle everything on his own?"

"He could." She grinned, a sparkle in her green eyes. "But I don't want him to."

We walked into the castle, the children's voices chattering behind us as they described their visit to Ilano in detail to Mother. I breathed in the familiar smells of aged wood, the lingering odor of straw, hints of the evening meal, and realized how acutely I'd missed home.

"No matter what happens next," I said as we approached the council chamber. "I'm glad we're home."

She embraced me briefly and smiled. "As am I." She disappeared into the room, the heavy doors closing behind her in a deafening *thud*.

The rest of the day sped by in a blur of regular duties, leaving me dizzy. After being gone for so long, I had to reacquaint myself with the castle and our routines. The children were ushered into bed for naps while their trunks were unpacked. Once I was satisfied the queen's rooms were ready, I spent several hours in the kitchens discussing the upcoming menus and ensuring we were prepared for the number of guests expected to arrive. Afterwards, I hurried to the stables to make sure Laria's mare was well settled and munching happily on hay. By the time I met the queen in her chambers to help her dress for dinner, my energy was spent.

Laria met my reflection in the mirror with widened eyes. "And I thought I looked done in."

"I've been playing catch-up today," I said. "I haven't stopped moving since we arrived."

"I know the feeling." She absently toyed with a feather I was to place in her curls. "I haven't been able to relax all day. I don't suppose any of us will for a long time. We've come home only to start a war."

I put a hand on my sister's bowed head and waited for her to compose herself. She would need my strength and support in the next few weeks, so I buried my own worries and sadness so I could be the pillar she needed.

"We've survived worse," I said quietly.

Her green eyes shined as they met mine in the mirror, and she offered a small smile. We remained silent while I finished preparing her for dinner, and together we entered the banquet hall full of joyous laughter and the clinking of glasses. The king held out his hand, and Laria reached for him as if she were adrift at sea and he was the only rock for miles. It broke my heart to see her cling to him so fiercely, as if this may be their last moments together.

I made sure Laria's favorite dishes were passed around frequently and distracted her with casual observations whenever I sensed her mood shift. Mother watched silently beside me, placing delicate bites between her thin lips. A few boisterous knights started singing, and soon the whole company joined in. With the king and queen thus distracted, Mother took the opportunity to lean close and whisper in my ear.

"How does she fair? She looks quite unsettled."

"Her country is going to war. How would *you* fair?"

I shook my head and mumbled an apology in response to Mother's shocked expression.

Her lips formed a grim line. "I understand she's under some stress. I only wanted to inquire after her health. I know she won't tell me herself."

"She's tired," I said. "And she worries for the king."

"Naturally. But she must maintain a strong front. If the people see her crumble, it will present a poor image of our ability to conquer our enemies."

"I'm sure she's well aware of that, Mother."

I looked toward my sister and studied her smiling face. She clapped appreciatively at the completion of the song and appeared in every way the regal, poised queen. Only those close to her could sense the tension behind her sparkling eyes and the slight tremble on her lips. The king didn't betray any unease as he conversed with those around him, the very picture of a stalwart leader.

"How did you find Ilano?" Mother asked.

The entirety of our trip rushed over me, and I became so overwhelmed I couldn't catch my breath.

"Friendly," I managed to say. "Everyone we met was very kind."

"I find that difficult to believe," Mother said bitterly.

"I know, but it seems you cannot judge an entire country based on the practices of a few evil people."

"Perhaps not." She sipped her wine. "But I confess I'm glad you're away from the influence of that place."

"It's a place full of people living their lives, just like any other country." There was nothing I could say to erase the anger Mother still clung to after the siege on Praed. She would always see Ilano as the country that birthed King Conall, the man who killed her husband and enslaved her family. I hoped over time her bitterness would ebb, and she would accept we were no longer at war with Ilano, but she could hold a grudge as steadfastly as Laria could.

"Even so," she continued. "I'm relieved you're home."

I surreptitiously rolled my eyes and took a long drink from my own cup. My mother's words could fill me with sadness if I allowed it, but truthfully, I pitied her inability to overcome her prejudices. There were good friends to be had in Ilano if she would only open her mind to the possibility. But Mother was staunchly loyal to Praed at the behest of everything else and nothing, not even her half Ilano grandchildren, would change that.

Before climbing into bed, I saw to my own neglected trunks. A maid unpacked most of my clothes, but I sent her away to attend to other duties. As I removed each gown, I recalled what I'd done in Ilano while wearing it, and after the third or fourth time of disintegrating into tears, I abandoned the project. I opened the trunk containing my underclothes and accessories in search of a nightgown when my hands closed around something hard. I moved some garments aside and withdrew the novel I hadn't opened in weeks. I sat on the edge of my bed and moved to crack open the cover when I realized reading the salacious story no longer held any interest for me. Laria told me several times that what we read in stories does not always mimic real life, but a part of me secretly wondered if what I read of poor Arella could be possible. I'd never thought seriously about romance for myself, but I could no longer deny that I thought about it now. I was inexperienced when it came to men, but I was no fool. Feelings of which I'd never known stirred inside me, and nothing I read in a novel could help sort them out. I opened the drawer of my nightstand, slid the book inside, and watched it disappear without the slightest hesitation.

The time would come for me to analyze the confusing emotions within me, but now was not that time. There were more important matters to be concerned with: an impending war and my sister's resulting distress. The last thing either of us needed was for me to dwell on the inconsequential musings of my own heart. Like the novel in the drawer, I locked away my feelings for the present and immediate future.

The castle settled into a semblance of normalcy when the first guests arrived. We stood on the front steps in all our finery to greet them, the children bouncing anxiously on the balls of their feet. An enormous carriage ambled up the mountain flanked by an impressive show of soldiers dressed in gray linen uniforms and riding delicately boned horses with high tails and dainty, nervously twitching ears.

"Who are they?" Rian whispered.

Light gray banners bearing a black anchor surrounded by a circle of fish rippled in the chill wind. Recognizing the standards, I leaned down to whisper, "They're the ambassadors from Faqur."

The great carriage stopped, and a perfectly poised soldier opened the door and pressed a stiff hand to his forehead.

"What's he doing?" Rian asked.

"Saluting. It's what sailors do to show each other respect," I said.

An imposing gentleman emerged from the carriage dressed in a dark blue wool coat with shining gold buttons. His chest was ornamented with medals and gold trappings. The collar was high, and the cloth clutched tightly to his broad frame and ended just at his knee. His breeches were startling white and his tall boots black as coal. A strange black hat trimmed with gold fabric sat like a sail across his head. There wasn't a stray thread or a fleck of dirt upon him. I self-consciously wiped my hands down the front of my gown, brushed a stray lock of hair out Rian's eyes, and wiped my sleeve across Tyrnan's cheek.

The gentleman approached with his hand resting casually on the hilt of a thin sword sheathed in black leather, removed his hat, and bowed respectfully to the king and queen.

Duveesa elbowed me and grinned slyly when I met her gaze. At my confused head tilt, she nodded toward the gentleman whose face was now clearly visible. He was tall and lithe with tanned skin and sun-bleached golden hair flecked with white. His blue-green eyes sparkled like a pool in afternoon sunshine, but his expression was severe. By the lines about his eyes and mouth, he looked old enough to be my father. I darted Duveesa a pursed look and shook my head, disagreeing with her assessment of his attractiveness. She hid a giggle behind her hand, a sure sign *she* disagreed with *me*.

The king addressed the man in his usual deep timbre. "Admiral Volppe. You are welcome here."

Admiral Volppe stood straight and still, and I had a sudden urge to poke him with my finger to see if he would move.

"Have any of the others arrived?" he asked.

"You are the first," the queen said. "Please come in and settle yourselves. Have some refreshments after your long journey."

"My thanks, Your Grace," the admiral said with a short bow.

The king and queen led him inside and several sailors followed. One, a young man less embellished than his superior, roamed an appraising gaze over Duveesa and me as he passed. He smiled and winked. I turned my nose up at him so he wouldn't get any ideas about our receptiveness to any flirtations.

"Keep your eye on that one," I whispered to Duveesa. "No doubt these sailors will be looking for a warm bed to comfort them while away from home."

Duveesa gasped, and a hand flew to her mouth to hide a smile. "What a shocking thing to say!"

"One can't be too careful."

"Ula." She wasn't doing a very good job stifling her giggles. "A little flirting never hurt anyone."

I pursed my lips and glared at the sailors' straight, ordered backs.

"Relax," Duveesa whispered with a gentle nudge. "What would Arella do?"

My eyes widened, and I burned from the tips of my ears to the base of my neck. Duveesa feigned a coughing fit to hide her laughter, and I twisted my hands into the soft folds of my lavender gown to keep from hiding behind them. I wasn't surprised she'd read the book, too, but I thought I'd been discreet. We turned toward each other at the same time and locked eyes, then quickly covered our mouths to muffle giggles.

The next morning, Lord Protector Ekhane arrived, and it was a comfort to see his warm, smiling face again. He brought with him a sense of calm that permeated the castle, and the queen visibly relaxed as she took his hand and thanked him for making the journey through the driving rain.

"A little water never bothered me," the Lord Protector said good-naturedly as he shook droplets off his greatcoat.

"You left your family well, I trust?" I asked.

"All are in good health. Thank you," he said.

Before I could speak further, he was led away to be introduced to the Admiral of the Fleet, and I was left awkwardly standing alone in the foyer.

"A shame the poor man had to make the journey alone," Olim said before emerging from the darkness of the corridor.

"Yes," I said. "It's quite tedious. How have you been, Olim?"

"The training has been exhausting. Drills from sunup until sundown, lectures about Crif terrain and tactics, and never enough time to relax in between. I'll be glad to leave and get on with it."

"I see." I could not match his eagerness. Once again, I was filled with anguish over the possibility of losing my friend. I walked to the window and breathed in the scent of rain and earth to mask my discomposure.

"How is the queen?" he asked.

"Well enough. Having so many distinguished guests arrive is a welcome distraction. She's kept too busy to dwell on the war."

I'd always been in awe of my sister's fortitude, but she would be sorely tested in the coming weeks and months.

That afternoon, the ambassadors from Hrgun arrived, and I was delighted to find my vision of them as elderly intellects was not far off. They were a pair of middle-aged scholars dressed in brown robes with long crimson sashes wrapped around their heads and forming a hood that draped down their chests. The gentleman with piercing dark eyes, a crooked nose, and steel-gray hair was introduced as Ambassador Andor. The lady, presented as Ambassador Sarika, surveyed the great hall with soft russet eyes and moved with dignified grace, her small hands clasped before her. I watched them curiously, wondering if some day they might meet Finton. At the thought, I inexplicably became resentful of the pair, knowing they would see him, converse with him, perhaps even become friends, whereas I'd said goodbye forever. Scowling, I didn't speak to the ambassadors unless absolutely necessary, which wasn't difficult since they mostly kept to themselves, sneering at average folk and only engaging in conversation with the king, queen, and other diplomats.

That evening, however, I found myself seated next to Ambassador Sarika. I peered desperately down the table at the queen, but she was too preoccupied to notice. The ambassador soundly ignored me and spoke in quiet tones to Lord Protector Ekhane seated on her right. I focused on my plate and allowed my thoughts to wander, perfectly content to be left alone.

I was so self-absorbed that it took several seconds before I realized someone was talking to me. Startled, I looked up into Ambassador Sarika's sharp gaze.

"I beg your pardon, ma'am?" I asked in a tiny voice.

"I understand you're Queen Laria's sister?" Her voice was resonant, as if she were speaking to a room full of students.

"Yes, ma'am. I'm Ula Audrey."

She looked me up and down critically, and I shrank under her scrutiny.

"You're very pretty," she said, though it was less a compliment and more an observation. "The queen says you're quite an accomplished artist and musician."

My cheeks flushed. "She's very kind."

"Have you considered coming to Hrgun to study? We have an exceptional program for people of your caliber. If you're as good as the queen says, that is. We would have to judge for ourselves, of course. But if you're deemed worthy, you can study with some of the finest masters in the known world."

"I thank you," I said, bristling under her condescension. "It would be an honor to be deemed worthy enough to study in Hrgun, but I have no wish to at present."

"If you change your mind, be sure to tell the Master of Students I vouched for you."

"I'm truly honored, ma'am, and thank you again."

She turned away and waved a hand carelessly at my words, as if dismissing a student.

Before I could stop myself, I said, "Pardon, ma'am. Would it be possible for you to take a message back to Hrgun for me? I know someone who is going to be a student there. He should be there by the time you return."

She slowly turned her gaze on me. "There are many students at Hrgun. I cannot be expected to know all of them."

"No, I would expect not, but perhaps you may be able to find someone capable of looking him up?"

"What is the name of this student?"

"Finton Ekhane."

Her eyebrows shot up in surprise and she glanced to her right.

"Yes. The Lord Protector's son."

She straightened and her eyes brightened with interest. "What is his area of study?"

"He is hoping to become a surgeon."

Her lip curled and her shoulders dropped. She obviously disapproved of this profession. She covered her distaste by saying, "Hrgun has the most distinguished medical college in the world. He will find great satisfaction in his studies there. If he can handle the rigorous and challenging coursework that is."

"He can," I said through gritted teeth.

She took a sip of her wine, set it carefully on the table, and arranged the rest of her place setting so everything was equally spaced. "Tell me your message then."

"Tell him." I paused, my throat tightening as I considered what to say to Finton through this stranger. "Tell him I wish him well and that he must remember to take care of himself."

Her chin tilted toward me, but she didn't look up. "Is that all?"

"That's all." My words were spoken through rising emotion threatening to overwhelm me, and I focused on my food so Ambassador Sarika couldn't see my eyes fill with tears. I felt her stare and cautiously watched her out of the corner of my eye. She studied me impassively, and after an interminable amount of time, she nodded and agreed to deliver my short message. She resumed her conversation with the Lord Protector and didn't speak to me for the rest of the evening.

When the queen retired, I was anxious for her opinion regarding our guests.

"Ambassadors Andor and Sarika appear displeased with everything around them," I said. "I found the lady to be very condescending."

Laria stared at me wide-eyed. "I'm surprised at you. It isn't like you to give a negative opinion so freely."

"I'm sorry." I lowered my eyes and fiddled with Laria's hair. "I shouldn't be so harsh."

"No, on the contrary. I find your frank observations refreshing. Everyone has been on their best behavior with me, of course. What was it about Ambassador Sarika that you didn't like?"

"She offered me a position in Hrgun to study art and music, but in a very underhanded way. And she cast aspersions on Finton's ability to handle his studies there."

"She's obviously a monster. Would you like me to have her flogged?"

I pushed her shoulder. "Stop teasing me."

"So much for considering Ambassador Sarika as a lifelong friend. What do you think of Ambassador Andor?"

"He seemed very severe, but I don't know him well enough to formulate a solid opinion."

"What about Admiral Volppe?"

"He certainly doesn't strike me as someone to be trifled with, but as with Ambassador Andor, we haven't spoken."

"We'll have to remedy that."

"Why?"

"If you're willing, I would like for you to get to know our guests over the next few days. I'm curious to find out how they behave outside my presence."

"They'll hardly misbehave much with me. I'm your lady-in-waiting and sister after all."

"That's apparently enough separation for some. Ambassador Sarika was nothing but endearing graciousness to me."

"If you think it will help, then I'll chatter their ears off."

"How progressive of you." Laria smiled. "My little sister is a full-grown woman at last."

We laughed companionably at Laria's joke until she laid a hand against mine and went very still. Her eyes narrowed and she gestured toward the window. I held my breath as we listened. Nothing. Before I could ask what was wrong, the clatter of wagon wheels drifted into the room. We hurried to the window and peered into the gloomy night. Torches flickered to life below, but we couldn't see what caused the commotion.

"Who do you think has come at this hour?" I asked, intrigued yet frightened at the same time.

"I don't know." Laria strained to see what was happening outside.

Heavy footfalls sounded in the corridor and moments later the door flung open, and the king marched into the room.

Laria hurried to his side. "Who is it?"

"A group of men have asked to be admitted," he said. "Come. Make yourself decent."

Laria looked down at her simple nightgown and smiled up at him.

"I don't suppose this is the right time to make a joke?"

"Save it for later."

I draped a heavy cloak over her shoulders, and she drew it tightly around her as we followed the king to the castle entryway.

The soft padding of our feet and clomping of the king's heavy boots echoed in the wide space as we approached a sodden party of men shaking water off their patchwork leather coats. One man's dark eyes lit up when he saw us, and he stepped forward to extend his hand toward the king.

"Your Majesty, I presume?" the man asked, his words thick with rolling *R*'s and drawn-out *S*'s. He wore layers of leather on his stocky frame, from his coat to his breeches and silver-tipped boots. He twirled a felt hat in his free hand, and candlelight glittered off the gold rings on his fingers.

The king glanced at the man's outstretched hand and made no move to take it.

The man laughed. "You must wonder who these crazy men are that come in the night. I am Qoyahdii, King of Torshul." He indicated two men I guessed were around my age if not a little older. "These are my sons, Nosusluv and Fusvolam. And this is my jewel, Elasha."

A striking, round-faced woman with dark curly hair, amber eyes, and a colorful scarf wrapped around her head stepped forward and curtseyed. She was young, olive-skinned, and dressed in a heavy raincoat like the men, but underneath shone a flash of bright pink fabric. She kept her eyes to the ground as her father spoke, and I took the opportunity to study the group.

The young men weren't very tall, barely taller than I, yet their short stature accentuated muscular arms and sturdy legs. Well-worn leather boots and baggy pantaloons peaked out from beneath coats dripping with rain. If they carried weapons, they were well hidden. In their hands were leather hats, and their long, wavy black hair glistened with sweat. They must have ridden for days. My cheeks reddened when I noticed one of the brothers was watching me, but he didn't smile nor appear angry.

"We were not expecting you so late," the king said, and I could hear the irritation in his voice.

"Apologies, Your Majesty," King Qoyahdii said, still smiling. "We stopped in the city to do some entertaining."

I couldn't help but smile at his pleasant expression, remembering the troubadours that came to Riverstone to entertain us with music and magic shows. Perhaps some traveled from as far as Torshul for the chance to line their pockets with our coins.

"Indeed," King Risteard said flatly. He indicated his wife. "Queen Laria." Then he pointed to me and said, "Her sister and lady-in-waiting, Ula Audrey."

The King of Torshul bowed to both of us, the fatherly smile never leaving his face.

"Please allow my steward to escort you to your bedchambers for the remainder of the night."

"We thank you for your graciousness," King Qoyahdii said. "We look forward to seeing you in council tomorrow, and perhaps my daughter may entertain you at dinner? She has been practicing a performance especially prepared for Your Majesties."

"We would be delighted," the queen said with a glance at her husband. "You've had a long day. Please rest well tonight."

Laria linked her arm with mine as the Torshul party followed the steward to their rooms and remarked that they seemed a pleasant lot.

"It's very late," her husband grumbled.

"Since when did you concern yourself with that?" Laria asked with a glimmer of mischief in her eye. "As I recall, the best castle intrigue happens in the dark."

He shot her a pointed glare and she grinned innocently.

Usually when Laria flirted with her husband, I'd roll my eyes and tease her. But this time, a twinge of envy twisted my heart. A wave of emotions overcame me, and I pressed my hands to my ears and squeezed my eyes shut to drown them out.

"Ula?" Laria's fingertips touched my shoulder, and I ducked away.

"I can't listen to this right now." Without another word, I ran from the foyer, my face burning with embarrassment. I rushed to my room, and the moment I threw myself onto the bed, I burst into tears. What was wrong with me? Whatever war threatened on the horizon, I hoped it would be over before the one igniting in my soul consumed me.

The next morning, I was determined to be myself again. My resolve shattered when I saw the distressed look on my sister's face when she rushed toward me with outstretched arms.

"I'm so sorry for my carelessness. I wasn't thinking about how much you're hurting right now."

"I'm fine," I said "I shouldn't have spoken so harshly. I was tired."

"Yes, but…" she hesitated as our eyes met, and I stared back without a trace of the anguish I felt the night before. A small smile crept over my lips, and I squeezed her shoulders reassuringly. She shook herself, nodded, and we commenced our morning routine.

I pinned up the last curl of ginger hair and asked, "Do we expect the emissaries from Kuste to arrive today?"

She sighed and tapped her fingers on the vanity. "Yes. And then the Great War Council will begin."

"No word ever came from Berg?"

"None, though no one was surprised."

We walked in silence to the breakfast room where the children were noisily being served food. Lilias attached herself to her mother when we entered, and I helped the nurses settle everyone in their seats before serving myself. I sat next to Duveesa, my food untouched, and observed the family. They appeared the picture of idyllic domestic bliss. Sulwen and Tyrnan were chatting away, each trying to speak over the other. Lilias waited patiently as her mother sliced her food into easy bites, her little legs swaying under the table. Risteard and Alyx were intently playing a board game while Rian leaned over his brother's shoulder and advised him on the best moves between bites, his cheeks full to bursting.

"I'll miss this," Duveesa whispered sadly.

"Yes." I took a deep breath to cool my emotions. "But we must try to keep the mood positive for all their sakes."

After several moments of silence, she asked, "I heard we had some late-night visitors. Is it true?"

"Yes. It was the King of Torshul, his two sons, and his daughter. Apparently, they became distracted on the journey and stopped to entertain the people in the city."

"I've heard the people of Torshul are excellent musicians and storytellers."

"They plan on putting on a show for us tonight. Then you can see for yourself."

"What's troubling you, Ula? Besides the obvious. You seem cross."

I sank lower in my seat. "I'm sorry. I'm not myself lately."

"Everyone is under so much stress." Duveesa covered my hand with hers. "You're not alone, and you don't have to suffer in silence."

"Suffer? What is my suffering compared to the queen's?"

"Her cost for this war is high, indeed, but you do not have to bear the weight of her suffering as well as yours."

Tears welled in my eyes, and I clenched my jaw to restrain them. "She's my sister. She would do the same for me."

She nodded in understanding, and we resumed our meal, passing the time with idle conversation and ignoring the tension I'd created.

After breakfast, the children were ushered into the schoolroom while the king and queen met with the ambassadors in the assembly room. The King of Torshul had been introduced to the other dignitaries and was proving to be the most interesting character of them all. Where the Admiral of the Fleet and the Hrgun Ambassadors were stoic and serious, King Qoyahdii was boisterous and gregarious. His hands flew about as he regaled the Lord Protector with stories of his travels, and he was quick to laugh when the older man covered his head and teased that he didn't expect to have to be on his guard. The two sons smiled pleasantly when they were addressed, but they were not as talkative as their father. I found the daughter tucked in a corner of the room practically being interrogated by Ambassador Sarika, the poor girl shaking her head every time the older woman asked her a question.

Ambassador Sarika huffed and smoothed her hands down her robes. "You have no idea what I'm saying, do you? I'll go find a translator."

Once she'd stalked away, I tapped the girl on the shoulder to get her attention and signaled for her to follow me into a secluded corner.

"You should be safe here," I said. "You're Elasha?"

She nodded vigorously. "Elasha."

I placed a hand on my chest. "Ula."

"Oo-La," she mimicked, deliberately exaggerating each syllable.

I nodded my approval, and her wide eyes brightened. Her features relaxed the longer we stayed away from the rest of the group, and I sensed she found the crowd intimidating.

"You dance?" I asked as I pointed to her and twirled around.

She nodded and spoke quickly in her own language, a dialect with soft consonants and lilting vowels. Her hands moved as she spoke, like her father's, but her movements were graceful, and with each lift of her arms, a gentle melody sounded from colorful wraps with tiny bells adorning her wrists. I became mesmerized by the brightness of the fabric and the tune of the trinkets. I pointed to my eye and indicated the bands, asking if I could take a closer look. She nodded enthusiastically and held up her arm. I ran the fabric between my fingers and was amazed at how soft it was, like feather down. They were intricately embroidered, and the tiny bells were intermingled with shining beads, creating a delicate music with every movement of her body.

"Beautiful," I said in a hushed, reverent tone.

Elasha spoke enthusiastically, removed one of the colorful wraps, then took my hand and started weaving it around my wrist. I withdrew my arm and shook my head, saying, "I couldn't possibly accept," but she was insistent, and I relented lest I insult her generosity. She beamed up at me after finishing tying the band in place and I moved my arm around to inspect the fabric and listen to the gentle music it made. Wanting to return the kind gesture, I reached up and unclasped my necklace and held it out to her. She ran her fingers along the smooth chain and her eyes widened at the sight of the large jewel nestled in an elaborate pendant.

"Allow me."

I moved behind her and draped the necklace around her neck. She gathered up her hair so I could fasten the clasp, and the pendant settled against her chest. I stood before her, remarked that the adornment suited her, and her face brightened further. She took my hand and said something that sounded like a question based on her tone and the rise of her eyebrows. She placed a hand to my heart and then to her own, said our names, then repeated one phrase with a nod of her head. I could not understand the words, but the meaning was clear.

"Yes. Friends."

She squeezed my hand and then tugged it toward the crowd with a jerk of her head. I nodded and followed as she led me through the people. A few turned their heads and watched us curiously, and for the first time I felt not embarrassment but pride. I succeeded in communicating with an outsider and gained her confidence. A pretty fine accomplishment for a formerly shy lady-in-waiting.

Elasha stopped in front of her brothers and introduced them to me. I curtseyed respectfully and the young men bowed their heads while speaking. One of the men turned to his sister and said something that even I could tell was derisive, and the pair began to argue. I shifted uncomfortably, and Elasha made a sweeping motion with her arm to end the discussion. She glared at her brothers as she led me away. I hoped my presence hadn't caused a rift between them. I tried to apologize, but she wouldn't hear of it, repeating a phrase over and over with an annoyed expression.

"*Dahdro*," Elasha said to King Qoyahdii.

The older man ceased his conversation with the Admiral of the Fleet to smile at his daughter, though his eyes glimmered with a dark undertone at the interruption. She proceeded to introduce me, and I curtseyed low.

"An honor, Your Grace," I said with my head down. "I hope we are not intruding."

"Not at all, sweet lady," the king said. He touched my shoulders and drew me up to face him. "And please do not speak so formally. To you, I am simply Qoyahdii." He smiled pleasantly, no trace of anger in his dark eyes, and I couldn't help smiling back at his warm expression.

Admiral Volppe remained stoic as he watched our exchange, and my skin tingled under his intense scrutiny.

"We are so grateful that you are here. All of you," I said, looking from King Qoyahdii to Admiral Volppe. "Never have so many countries gathered together as one before."

"Yes, we are the history makers now," King Qoyahdii said. "And the songs they write will be sung by my grandchildren's grandchildren."

"I don't doubt it. We look forward to Elasha's performance tonight." I smiled at my new friend, and she looked to her father for a translation, which he hurriedly gave.

"My people have written a song to honor the King and Queen of Praed and Ilano," he said.

"But will anyone understand it?" Admiral Volppe added gruffly.

I was taken aback by his rudeness, but King Qoyahdii met the question with unwavering affability.

"I believe music can be understood by all who choose to listen," King Qoyahdii said, the kindly expression never leaving his face.

I was impressed by his diplomacy, especially coming from a man whose people were comparatively uncivilized. Admiral Volppe made no reply nor did his severe countenance waiver. His critical eyes met mine, and though a shiver raced up my spine, I didn't look away.

"I understand there will be some dancing before dinner. For everyone, I mean," Admiral Volppe clarified with a quick glance at Elasha. "Would you do me the honor of dancing the first set with me?"

I blinked in stunned surprise. The Admiral of the Fleet didn't strike me as a dancer, but I accepted to avoid insulting him. He bowed stiffly and took his leave of us, and my eyes followed his retreating form until he stopped to converse with his sailors.

"I don't believe that man ever smiles," King Qoyahdii observed once he was gone.

"He frightens me," I said.

"Bah," the king scoffed with a wave of his hand. "Such as he looks dangerous as a rule. It is his duty to be strong and protect his people. I believe he is honorable and is no threat to you."

"You speak very highly of a man whom you've only just met. Looks may deceive, but they may also prove correct. He could be a villain in disguise."

"If that were the case, then King Risteard would not have allowed him into his country."

"He may not know."

King Qoyahdii waggled a scolding finger. "You are a very suspicious lady. It is not good for you."

"I didn't used to be. But I have learned to be cautious."

"This is a good thing but be careful your caution does not lead you to fear that which you do not know. I choose to see people with open eyes and regard them as friends waiting to be met. Sometimes I am disappointed, but mostly not."

"You don't think it's dangerous to be so trusting?"

"Well, I am not telling them where to find my family's fortune!" He laughed with his whole body, from ruddy cheeks to bobbing knees. "I risk nothing in being kind. It is up to them to show who *they* really are when I am freely showing them who *I* am. Easy for me, you see?"

"I see. I hope *I* will not disappoint you."

"In having made a friend in my daughter, you have made a friend in me. I will forever be at your service, my lady." He bowed low. "I hope the next time we meet shall be a happier one."

Chapter 21

The excitement of the day was only beginning. The entirety of Praed Castle, our guests, and most of the populace gathered outside in anticipation as several people on horseback meandered up the mountain. The rain relented to a foggy mist that soaked through my simple gown and chilled me to the bone. Wrapped in my cloak under one arm was Rian and in the other was Tyrnan, their large eyes peering out into the gloom as the seemingly unaffected travelers from Kuste came to a stop and leisurely dismounted at the bottom of the steps. Their horses were sturdy and dappled with splashes of white, their tails and manes short and wispy. The earthen shades of their clothing blended together, making it difficult to distinguish one person from the other. A group of three, two men and a woman, broke away from the group and climbed the steps.

The tallest of them glided forward with an air of authority, his wide mouth set as he looked down his straight, aristocratic nose. Black, shining hair was pulled back in a long queue woven together with strands of rough fibers. His hair was longer than mine, almost reaching the waist of his tight leather breeches. Straps of deeply tanned leather decorated with silver and blue baubles crisscrossed the chest and middle of his prairie yellow, long-sleeved shirt rippling in the breeze. The sun-warmed skin of his square jaw was shaved smooth, his long-fingered hands unadorned. Sheathed on one side and peeking from behind his back were enormous knives, and on the opposite hip what could only be described as an elaborately carved hatchet. What was most startling about his appearance were his eyes. One was the dark brown of rain-soaked earth and the other was as blue as a summer sky.

His elderly companion looked cross as he surveyed the gathered crowd, the lines of his skin deep from age. His torso was swathed in layers of soft green fabric, making the bright white of the necklaces falling in waves down his neck stand out blindingly, even in the mist. From the numerous belts at his waist hung pouches of varying sizes. He bore no weapon that I could see. His eyes were black as were the woman's, and he frowned when King Risteard took a few steps forward and bowed.

"We are honored you have made the journey to join us," the king said.

The woman turned to the taller, younger man and spoke in a guttural language full of soft vowels and harsh consonants. One wouldn't think such a mixing of sounds would be pleasing to the ear, but I found myself drawn to her words. Her hair matched the shade of her dark eyes, cascading in waves from underneath braided bands of faded blue fabric and strips of brown fur. Her nose was small and rounded, her lips full and soft. Her clothing was similar to the men's, but the neckline of her light shirt was low to accommodate the intricate adornment at her neck. From just below her chin, dried strands of wide green, yellow, and blue grasses were woven together until they ended in a 'V' at her throat. Her leather skirt hung low on her hips and moved easily when she walked.

The man spoke confidently to the King of Praed and Ilano, did not bow or offer a hand, and gestured toward the castle.

The woman translated. "Chief Wakashda is glad to be here. He has high hopes for the war talk. For now, we are tired and our horses thirsty. He wishes to talk of other things."

"Of course," King Risteard said. "Someone will show you to your rooms and look after horses. There will be celebrations and dinner tonight. Tomorrow, the Great War Council will begin."

Chief Wakashda nodded in approval at the king's translated words and allowed himself to be led inside. Many of the people gathered to welcome them had never seen a person from Kuste before. We stared unabashedly at the trio until they disappeared into the castle, and the murmur of conversation immediately commenced.

Behind me, people were saying the Kuste people were great warriors, and it was a relief to have them as our allies. Others commented on the strange attire. I blocked the gossiping from my mind so my perception of the people would not be tainted and focused on ensuring the children were well behaved. It was late in the afternoon and their moods were beginning to deteriorate, so I advised Duveesa and the other nurses to take them to their rooms for naps since it was going to be a very long night.

"It's all very exciting, isn't it?" Duveesa's cheeks flushed. "I never thought I would see so many people from different countries."

"Yes." I surveyed the gathered crowd. "I only wish the occasion wasn't so solemn."

Duveesa's smile faded, and I regretted souring the mood. I offered a wavering smile and showed her the wrist adornment Elasha gave me. She admired the bright colors and became sufficiently distracted enough to forget my earlier comment before ushering the children to bed.

I wandered around the room listening to snippets of conversation and not hearing anything of note. I was conscious of the queen's request to garner an honest opinion of the people. So far, I'd formed a favorable impression of the Torshul and was less than impressed with the Hrgun ambassadors. The Admiral of the Fleet appeared haughty, but I would reserve judgment until we shared our dance. The Kuste, not surprisingly, were being interviewed by the aforementioned Hrgun in their pursuit of knowledge.

"What materials is your attire made from?" Ambassador Andor asked the chief. His translator explained they made their clothes from plant fibers and hides of beasts they hunted.

The ambassador leaned close to inspect the clothing, making the older man shift nervously.

"The Chief of the Five Tribes must have a circle of space surrounding him," the translator said sternly.

Ambassador Andor straightened and glared at the young woman, but he maintained his distance.

"We would like you to consult with the translator we brought," Ambassador Sarika said, her nose in the air. "There are currently no references in regard to your language and it would be most informative if you would help start a written translation."

The young woman eyed Ambassador Sarika and briefly passed the request to the chief. A frown marred his passive features. He swept an arm across his chest, a firm, decisive movement that even *I* could easily interpret.

"Our language is not to be traded so freely," the translator said firmly.

"Surely you can make an exception," Ambassador Sarika said. "In the interest of diplomatic relations?"

"No," the young woman said.

"You speak our language. Don't you think it's fair that we learn yours? It might make our discussions easier. We can speak directly to the chief without the bother of a translator."

The young woman's eyes hardened, and her next words dripped with anger.

"You are not worthy to speak to Chief Wakashda using our tongue. Only those born to the Kuste may have the honor."

The ambassadors bristled at the insult to their dignity. Before they could argue further, the chief signaled the talk was over and the three took their leave. I trailed behind at a respectable distance until they paused outside the periphery of the room. I approached demurely and curtseyed low before meeting the chief's intriguing stare.

"My respects, Chief Wakashda," I said. Despite his relaxed manner, I found myself unsettled when I stared at his bright blue eye. I blinked rapidly and tried to appear as casual as he when I introduced myself as the queen's lady-in-waiting. The young woman translated, and the chief smiled and inclined his head.

"Chief Wakashda sees your importance to the queen," the young woman said. The chief ran a hand over his face, spoke a few words, and the woman asked, "Are you family? Your faces look alike."

My eyes widened in surprise. "Chief Wakashda is very astute. Not many people notice any similarity between us. I am indeed her sister."

The chief smiled in approval once the young woman confirmed his suspicions. I looked closer at the decorative neckpiece and noticed tiny white beads interspersed within the blades of grass. Her ears were pierced with multiple thin, polished rings. The entire outside of her ear was rimmed with them, and from the largest dangled a red stone. Finished with my examination of her, I glanced into her eyes and flushed when I realized she'd been staring at me.

"Apologizes," I said, shifting nervously. "I was just admiring your attire. What are your earrings made from?"

"Bone," she said without a flicker of emotion.

"They're quite extraordinary." I hoped the compliment would lighten the tense mood, but she continued to stare expressionless. "I don't believe I had the pleasure of your name."

The young woman looked at the chief uneasily and translated my request. He listened, considering, then nodded and waved a hand in my direction.

"Wicoya," she said quickly. "I am the keeper of words."

I smiled. "You may call me *Ula*. And the gentleman here is?" I indicated the old man.

Wicoya spoke to the chief, presumably to ask for permission to reveal his identity, before turning back to me.

"Wechagalah," she said. "Closest advisor to the chief."

"It is a pleasure to meet you all," I said. "The king and queen are very grateful you're here." They inclined their heads in acknowledgement, and I left them to their own company hoping I'd made a favorable impression.

People dispersed from the room in search of afternoon refreshments and rest before the evening festivities, which made it easy to spot Olim lurking in the shadows. I frowned at his dark expression, and my heart pounded with worry.

"Olim, what's wrong?" I asked. "You look cross."

"I'm frustrated," he said, and I recognized his petulant tone. "Several knights are boasting at having already received their orders for combat."

"And you have not received yours and are feeling left out?"

"I've been serving the king for years. I should have been considered first."

"Perhaps he has something especially important in mind for you. You should be honored he's taking his time and not throwing you into some arbitrary position."

"I know." He shuffled his feet. "I'm just anxious."

"I wish you wouldn't be," I mumbled and leaned against the wall next to him.

"I know it's difficult for you to have to stay behind to worry and wonder while we go off to war."

"Yes," I said.

Olim wrapped an arm around my shoulders and hugged me against his side.

"I'll come back. I promise."

I melted into the warmth of his embrace. "Take care not to put yourself into a position to break that promise."

"I'll try not to, but if I have to protect the king, I'll have no choice."

"I know. You'd give your life to save the king."

"Or any of his family."

My head shot up in surprise. His clear blue eyes burned with the same intensity I'd seen when he wielded a sword. The weight of his arm draped across my shoulders grew heavier and heat flushed from my neck to my cheeks. I shifted away, but my insides twisted into tense knots. I rubbed my stomach to settle my nerves and diverted my attention to the people milling around. King Qoyahdii was in an animated conversation with his sons, Elasha trailing dutifully behind. She smiled at me when our eyes met, and I waved.

"You've been making new friends again I see," Olim said.

"Elasha is very sweet. Though we don't understand each other's language, we've found a way to communicate."

"I understand she'll be entertaining us tonight."

"She'll perform a dance especially for the king and queen."

"A pleasant distraction from the reason we're all here."

My irritation was piqued, but the half grin on his face stopped the scolding reproof on my tongue. I shoved him good-naturedly and he held out his arm to escort me to the queen's side. There was much to prepare for, but tonight my goal was to keep the queen's mood light and ensure she was distracted from thoughts of the days to come.

✦ 🐎 ✦

Keeping the queen's mind delightfully occupied was hindered by her distant manner. She barely spoke when I dressed her for dinner. A gown with sheer sleeves and full skirt the color of morning fog lay on the bed, and I asked if she might prefer a brighter color. She shook her head, her gaze fixed out the window. Admittedly, the dim shade made her ginger hair glow like a flame.

The overwhelming silence as I tightened the laces and adjusted the gown was unnerving. It wasn't until I was styling her hair that she spoke.

"Can you leave a few strands loose in the back?" she asked. "Risteard likes to twirl them around his fingers sometimes."

207

"Of course." I finished pinning up her braids, leaving a length of hair to trail down her back, then leaned over and hugged her. She grasped my arms, clinging to me as if she were teetering on a precipice. I squeezed her tighter, and she shivered.

She released a shuddering breath, patted my arms, and disentangled herself from my embrace. Though no tears marred her pallid complexion, they nevertheless shimmered precariously in her eyes. She perused my attire, smiled tremulously in approval, and asked me to summon the king to escort her to dinner. I didn't have far to go. He was always waiting close by. The two were inseparable these days, and it pained me to imagine how agonizing it would be for them to say goodbye.

Finton's face flashed in my mind, and I couldn't shake the heart wrenching memory of our last moments together. Music drifted through my mind, through my veins, adding a sway to my step. I closed my hands over the sensation of his fingers brushing against my skin. A breath whispered against my ear, and I almost felt the warmth of a hand against my waist. Though I'd tell Laria I didn't believe in ghosts, I swore I was surrounded by them. The sensation remained as we processioned into the banquet hall full of distinguished guests in their finery. A flutter of shyness broke the spell, but I buried those feelings beneath my duty to the queen.

An impressive array of dishes accommodated the tastes of everyone present. From delicate fish platters to hearty meat and tuber plates, the aromas filled the room with a delicious and complex blend of exotic spices. Colorful drinks were poured into waiting goblets, and as the night progressed and libations continued to flow, the conversations grew louder. I darted a glance toward the queen on several occasions to gauge her mood, but each time she appeared perfectly content. She smiled and spoke pleasantly to those who addressed her and passed the finest courses to our special guests. I noted with a wry smile that she instructed the glasses of the Hrgun ambassadors to be filled throughout the night to loosen their rigid demeanors. Even my usually taciturn brother-in-law engaged people in conversation to improve relations with our new allies.

The quiet background noise of the musicians eventually ceased, and the King of Torshul rose from his seat.

"We thank you for the generous hospitality of Your Majesties," he said. "We now wish to please your eyes and ears with the music and dancing of my people."

He gestured to his sons, and they started playing, one with a stringed instrument and the other a circular drum with bells attached. Elasha emerged wearing a red form-fitting dress over a white, billowy shirt. The skirt was ankle-length and multi-layered with silver strands strung throughout the fabric. Tiny bells attached to the skirt added a delicate melody to the lively music her brothers played. Her hair flowed freely from beneath a red sash, and her feet were bare. She danced, slowly at first, her hips barely twitching, arms crossed over her face. As the music grew more intense, her arms spread wide, and her body undulated with the music.

Her performance was captivating, and my breath quickened as the music reached a crescendo as she flew around the middle of the room. The queen leaned forward in her chair, her eyes tracking Elasha's frantic movements. The music rose to a feverish pitch, and with a wide sweep of her arms, it abruptly ended. Silence permeated the room. We watched with bated breath when the music started again, the tune light and pleasant. Elasha smiled dreamily, her chin held high, and gracefully glided around the room. She extended her hand toward the king and bowed. His eyes darted from her bowed head to delicately outstretched hand, searching for a clue as to what he was supposed to do. He looked toward the queen for help while Elasha remained poised, and my sister gestured toward the girl encouragingly. Reluctantly, the king reached out and limply shook Elasha's fingers before hastily withdrawing as if they were covered in thorns. Unaffected, Elasha danced toward the queen and extended a hand again, which my sister enthusiastically kissed with a dramatic flourish that pleased the crowd immensely. We clapped as Elasha danced toward the center of the room, twirled impressively, and struck an exotic pose when the music ended.

The king and queen dutifully showed their appreciation by applauding for an extended period, the queen's cheeks flushed with pleasure. The King of Torshul's pride at Elasha's well received performance was the topic for the remainder of the meal.

After the last dishes were served, the guests were invited into the grand ballroom for more music and dancing. The children flitted around my feet in an excitement fueled by sweets and the prospect of staying up past their bedtimes. The boys were encouraged to praise the attending ladies, which at their age was akin to breaking a stallion to saddle. Alyx accepted the task with equanimity, but Rian and Tyrnan required...persuasion.

Bribes. We bribed them.

The boys bowed and kissed the hands of several ladies, including Ambassador Sarika, eliciting coos and adoring gazes even from the strictest countenance. Lilias observed the crowd wide-eyed from behind Duveesa's skirts while Sulwen endeared herself by play-fighting with some of the Faqur sailors. The first notes of the opening dance played, and the king and queen took their place in the set. It must have taken all of Laria's powers of persuasion to convince her husband to dance. He tried valiantly to cover her poor rhythm, but my sister was hopelessly clumsy.

"Miss Audrey?"

The voice was like the muffled roughness of the hull of a ship scraping against rock in deep water. It was Admiral Volppe, dressed impressively in a dark blue uniform with gold buttons and decorations of valor. He inclined his head and held out his hand. I took it and he placed me beside Laria. I suppressed a grin when she mimicked the Admiral's rigid stance.

Even when dancing, the admiral was stiff and formal and moved without taking a step out of turn. I was pleased to discover I no longer found him intimidating, but his cold demeanor made me feel like I was dancing with a block of wood.

"Your presence here is very appreciated, Admiral," I said, hoping to break the silence between us. "There has been much unease in regard to the Crif threat, and you cannot imagine how comforting it is to have the support of so many countries."

"I'm here in the best interest of Faqur," he said. "We have faced the Crif before and suffered great losses. It makes good military sense to ally ourselves with other countries to reduce costs and loss of life."

"It may be a war with Crif that brought you here, but I hope our countries remain allies afterward."

"If such a relationship can be mutually beneficial."

My jaw clenched but I shook off my ire. "I wish to know more about Faqur. I understand it has the largest port on the continent."

"It does. Our ships are many and built by the best craftsmen in all the kingdoms. They are moored on the south shore of Brasdemer Sound. No one has defeated a Faqur fleet in five generations."

"There is a great fishing trade there as well I've heard."

"Yes." His tone dripped with condescension. "Many families have built their lives around the sea whether as fishermen or sailors."

"Are there other forms of trade the people engage in?"

"Not really."

"Well, it must be exciting to live on the sea. I've never seen it before. Is it very beautiful?"

"If you respect it. The sea can be dangerous."

"I don't think I could sail on a ship. But I would like to visit someday."

"The king and his family will be welcome in Faqur as honored guests if we succeed in this war."

"And if we do not?"

He looked down, meeting my gaze, his eyes flashing like lightning across a dark ocean.

"Then may the gods welcome our bodies into the sea's embrace and our children forgive us this folly, for Crif will surely show them no mercy."

The blood drained from my face and my hands went cold at his words. I knew very little about Faqur beliefs regarding the afterlife, but the thought of lying at the bottom of the sea for all eternity was almost as unsettling as the thought of life amid defeat. I didn't want to picture Praed as a wasteland of razed homes and bodies left to decay under the snow. A memory flashed through my mind of the walk from Riverstone to Praed Castle after the Ilano siege. I remembered the shells of burnt stables and the rubble of bricks and stone that once held neighbors. I pictured the faces of children covered in blood and soot and their parents sifting through the wreckage to find supplies and precious mementos. There would be nothing left and no survivors should we lose a war to Crif.

I attempted idle chatter, but the effort was minimal. The admiral's morose attitude soured my mood, and I had no desire to satisfy my curiosity about Faqur if his answers were going to be so bleak. My partner was just as happy to pass the remainder of the dance in silence. To be honest, I think he much preferred me mute.

After the dance ended, I reported the entirety of the conversation to Laria. She rolled her eyes.

"He could at least hold his cynical tongue in the presence of my lady-in-waiting. Surely, he realizes you'll pass everything he says to me," she said.

"I don't think he cares," I said. "He would probably repeat everything he said to your face without shame."

"Sailors are simple people. They don't believe in mincing words or practicing delicacy. Although I confess, I find their bluntness refreshing. You never have to wonder if they're concealing some hidden agenda or secret opinion. One knows exactly where they stand with a Faqur sailor."

I danced nearly every set, fumbling through the ones held in honor of the foreign dignitaries. My partners were mostly patient and kindly showed me the steps, and I hoped my willingness to learn reflected well on Praed. The language barrier was inconsequential when it came to moving with music, but I couldn't glean any information about Torshul when I danced with one of Elasha's brothers nor Kuste when one of the young warriors pulled me into a vigorous dance with pounding drums and stomping feet. By the end of the evening, I was worn out and could barely shuffle after the queen to assist her to bed. I helped her out of her heavy gown and unpinned her hair with half-closed eyes and barely registered her talking until she lightly shook my arm.

"Go to bed," she said. "I'll need you here early in the morning. It's the first day of the Great War Council."

"Do you think it will last long?"

"I think we all want the same thing. It's only a matter of organizing the best way to work together. These are reasonable men and women, I think. No one will want to waste time."

Idly, I rubbed the soreness out of my right shoulder. I'd danced so much my body ached, but it was the satisfying ache of a long day of hard work. Instead of harvesting apples to feed a family, I'd endeared myself to ambassadors. Though my part in bringing about peace was relatively small, I reveled in being included, and I didn't want to miss anything.

"I think I will join you in council tomorrow."

"Absolutely! We should prepare ourselves, Ula. We're about to witness history in the making."

Mandy Schimelpfenig

Chapter 22

Menacing clouds gathered over Praed during the night, and by the next morning, the whole country was blanketed in darkness. The rumbling of distant thunder woke me in time to witness a flash of lightning illuminate my bedroom. Reluctantly, I emerged from the warmth of my bed and peered out the window at the gray sky as torrents of rain were released from the clouds. When I lived in the bowels of the castle, the heavy droplets sounded like an army pounding against the walls trying to get inside. I would cower under the covers and tremble so violently my teeth chattered, and I wouldn't fall asleep until the noise subsided. Now, I reached out a cupped hand to collect the rain soaking my skin, reveling in silky coolness I once took for granted. When one lives in solitude essentially underground, even the feel of cold rain and icy snow are gifts to be cherished.

I hurriedly donned a simple forest green gown with sheer sleeves, styled my hair into a long, thick braid I curled around my head and pinned to resemble a crown, then rushed to the queen's rooms. She was already awake and helping the king with the last buckle of his black doublet before stepping back to examine his appearance.

"Acceptable?" he asked, his arms wide.

She rushed into his arms and buried her face against his chest. In a muffled voice she said, "You'll do."

His deep laugh permeated the room, and he kissed the top of her head.

"Now it's your turn to make yourself presentable. Try not to keep us waiting."

My sister poked her husband in the ribs and stuck her tongue out at his turned back. He strode toward the door without so much as a wince. I curtseyed low and he nodded perfunctorily, his expression characteristically blank.

Laria turned to me. "What do you think?" She held up two equally lovely gowns. "Should I wear the dark blue one with the gold belt or the ivory one with the embroidered bodice?"

"The blue one. In case one of the children spills something on you."

"We'll be in council while they're at breakfast."

"Well, then in case *you* spill something."

She opened her mouth to argue but conceded the point. The sapphire blue gown perfectly complemented the glow of her ginger hair. I braided two small strands on either side of her face then joined them in the back. The rest of her hair fell in cascades down her back like the rain continuing its barrage against the castle walls. I curled the wavy locks, then settled her crown firmly on top of her head.

"An interesting approach," she said.

"We're not preparing for a ball. We're preparing for war."

She arched an eyebrow. "And you thought to make me appear a wild savage?"

"Something like that."

We broke our fast with an impressive serving of bread with honey, eggs, blood sausage, sweet fruits, and chilled milk. I looked at the queen in astonishment at such an uncharacteristically vast platter.

"We'll be behind closed doors most of the day," she said. "We might as well fortify ourselves."

When we ventured into the council chambers, my stomach roiled, and I feared the delicious offerings were in vain. Laria and I never visited these rooms as children, nor did I as a prisoner, but Laria said she'd been inside "once or twice" during her tenure as lady-in-waiting to the previous princess. The table where council members usually sat was too small for such a large gathering, so in its place was a large, round one so everyone could look each other in the eye as equals. The rain pattering against the vast stained-glass windows cast eerie shadows about the room, lending the people gathered a mysterious air of intrigue. In the corner whispering were the Hrgun Ambassadors, and in another was Chief Wakashda and his companions from Kuste. The Admiral of the Fleet and a couple sailors peered out at the weather scowling as if they had to sail in the storm. The King of Torshul and his sons arrived shortly after us, followed by Lord Protector Ekhane. He took Laria's outstretched hand and covered it with his own. She relaxed against him, and I was struck by how she regarded him like a father.

"Now that we're all here," King Risteard's voice boomed over the chatter. "Gentlemen, Ladies, please be seated."

After the clamor of chairs scraping against polished wood subsided, Ambassador Andor remained standing.

"Did you have something to say before we begin?" the king asked tersely.

Ambassador Andor gave a slight bow. "With your permission, Your Grace." The king nodded, and the ambassador addressed the council. "I'm sure you are all aware of the historical significance of this gathering. Never have so many kingdoms joined together in pursuit of a common goal. With this in mind, I hope you will all give your permission to have what is said in this council documented for posterity."

"You mean, written down for everyone to read?" Wicoya asked.

Ambassador Andor sniffed haughtily. "If one is able."

"A good idea," King Qoyahdii said. "I give my permission and ask for yours in return. My people will want to sing songs about this day. Music that every class and country can enjoy."

Ambassador Andor's face reddened, but he said no more. Everyone granted both his and the King of Torshul's requests with approving nods.

"Does anyone else have anything to say before we begin?" Risteard asked.

There was silence around the table, and he opened his mouth to speak again when a commotion arose outside the door. A few men rose from their seats amid the shouting of knights, their hands poised at their weapons. Laria grasped my hand, both of us shaking at the recollection of the last time we were disturbed by shouts of angry voices. Just as quickly as the raucous began, it ceased, leaving behind a chilling stillness. Suddenly, Olim burst through the doors, and my heart caught in my throat when I saw his pallid complexion and trembling lips.

"What's going on?" Risteard demanded.

"It's..." Olim whispered, his voice weak and strained.

"Speak up!"

"Your Majesty, they say they're from Berg."

Quizzical murmurs circulated around the table, and Laria and I looked at each other in undisguised shock.

"Let them in then," King Risteard said as calmly as if he were admitting an old friend. "They were invited."

Olim nodded numbly and cast me a quick glance before opening the door wide. A man and a woman entered with casual grace, as if their very presence wasn't an earth-shattering occasion. The moment their feet touched the inner chamber, Olim removed himself from the room and closed the doors soundly.

The man was thin with light blue eyes, the golden undertone of his skin in sharp contrast to the dark, wavy hair swept back over his ears and tied neatly in a short queue. A thin black beard traced the line of his jaw and thin lips, accentuating his sharp features. His eyes darted about the room, settling momentarily on each of our faces before examining the next person. His knee-length, slate-gray tunic had sharp shoulders, long sleeves, and a short collar. It was made from a thick fabric with a strange sheen, tailored tightly to his lanky form, and devoid of any embellishments. His black breeches were made in the same oddly shimmering fabric, and his feet were covered with simple thick-soled leather boots. Based on his humble appearance, I guessed he was a lower noble.

The man captured my attention so completely I failed to notice his companion, but the rest of the room hadn't been so distracted. All eyes were fixed in stunned silence upon her unusual mien. Her skin was pale, not in the sense of an unblemished complexion kept out of the sun, but completely devoid of color. Her full lips held the only sign of life in their pink hue, and her shoulder-length straight hair was so white it was translucent. It was pulled back with elaborately decorated pins, a few wisps framing her face. She wore a gauzy, shimmering white dress trimmed with feathers and an intricate necklace with perfectly round white and ivory beads. Her remarkably pale blue eyes met mine for an instant before scanning the room, and I clapped a hand over my mouth to smother a gasp when the color of her irises shifted from icy blue to lavender. A small smile crossed her lips and she leaned over to whisper in the man's ear. I looked around the table and was not surprised to see everyone staring in open-mouthed shock.

"My lord and lady." Even my even-tempered brother-in-law sounded awestruck. "You are both welcome here. I am Risteard, king of Praed and Ilano." He indicated my sister. "This is my queen, Laria."

Laria's mouth snapped shut and her cheeks flushed in embarrassment.

"A pleasure," the man said in a high, hoarse voice. "I am King Arkyn, and this is Mistress Dalyah."

Laria and I shared a wide-eyed look. She seemed to find his identity unexpected as well for neither of us expected a king to dress so plainly. King Risteard introduced the others, who gradually recovered their senses by the time the two newcomers took their seats.

"We were just about to get started unless you would like to address the council beforehand?" King Risteard said to the King of Berg.

"We do not wish to delay the council," King Arkyn said. "Please continue." He waved toward his host with a delicate, long fingered hand, and I saw he didn't even wear a ring.

"You all know why we're here," King Risteard began. "King Karne has moved northward and will soon be threatening the borders of Torshul. King Qoyahdii has asked for help in defending his country, but instead of beating back Crif to return another day, I propose we join our forces and meet them before they cross the border at the Voet Foothills and decimate their armies so soundly, they won't be able to rise again."

"Do we have any idea how many the Crif number?" Admiral Volppe asked.

"We sent scouts to meet with contacts arranged by King Qoyahdii. Together, they estimated over eight hundred thousand warriors."

A stunned silence followed this revelation. Their army outnumbered the total population of Praed.

"We can offer two hundred ships crewed by two hundred men apiece," Admiral Volppe said without missing a beat. "I agree with King Risteard. We cannot allow Crif to pick us off one by one. Surely between all of us we have enough men to match their numbers?"

"The unified Praed and Ilano forces number around four hundred thousand," King Risteard said.

"Hrgun does not have a large standing army," Ambassador Andor argued. "We are a place of learning with enough soldiers to protect our borders."

"Hold a draft then," Admiral Volppe said dryly. "Recruit able-bodied men who are willing to volunteer."

"It is a difficult thing to ask men to do. Not very many would willingly sign up for their deaths."

"Explain to them that if they do nothing, their deaths will come for them anyway if we fail," King Risteard said.

Ambassador Andor pressed his lips into a firm line while Ambassador Sarika mumbled they would do whatever they could to increase their numbers should the council decide to ally and go to war.

"'Should'?" King Qoyahdii echoed. "I suppose the ambassador is right. We should vote first before we speak of numbers. There is no point of worrying we are too small if we don't all agree to join. Everyone knows my position. Torshul is a peaceful country without an army, but we will provide goods and shelter to any man who fights for our cause."

"Praed and Ilano have both suffered losses in past battles with Crif. I do not wish for my children to live in fear of another threat. Therefore, my armies are yours," King Risteard said.

"Faqur has also fought Crif," Admiral Volppe said, "but never with the numbers Praed and Ilano can offer. My ships are at your disposal. May the Gods grant us favor."

We looked to the Kuste as Wicoya finished translating and waited while Chief Wakashda contemplated his decision. After several tense moments, he addressed the council.

Wicoya translated as the chief spoke. "Chief Wakashda would like to express how good it is that we are all here. Never in any of his memories was there a time people from all countries came together. He hopes this is the beginning of friendship between us."

"But," she continued. "Chief Wakashda knows sometimes war must happen before there can be peace. Though it hurts his heart to think of the widows and orphans of his fallen warriors, he must think of future generations as King Risteard does."

Chief Wakashda consulted briefly with his advisor, Wechagalah. The elderly man gestured wildly as he spoke, and based on the scowl on his face, I guessed he was arguing against joining us. I couldn't blame him. No one wanted to face an army as large as Crif's. Chief Wakashda held up a hand, spoke softly, and Wechagalah quieted. The chief addressed the council once more with Wicoya translating.

"Kuste offers their nineteen thousand warriors," she said. She glanced sideways at her chief, who swept an arm across the table in finality.

"I am interested to hear what King Arkyn has to say," Ambassador Sarika said.

The Berg king steepled his fingers, and when he spoke in his curiously hypnotic, hoarse voice, he made eye contact with everyone at the table.

"No foreign army has ever breached the Black Mountains bordering our lands," he said. "The Crif have never threatened us, so we have no past grievances to avenge. We found your invitation intriguing, but we intended to ignore it. Then Mistress Dalyah had a vision."

Laria tensed. She regarded visions as 'superstitious nonsense.' The previous queen of Praed claimed to have visions as well, further blackening Laria's perception of those who profess to have the power of the sight or unspeak. To her credit, Laria kept her opinion to herself. At least in front of the council.

"I was walking on soft ground, my feet sinking deep," Mistress Dalyah said, her melodic voice also somewhat raspy. "It was so bright I could not see, and I thought I was walking in snow. Then I tripped, and my hands fell to the earth. Then I knew it was not snow, for my hands were hot. I raised them, and sand ran through my fingers. Then the sand turned to blood and blackness spread over the ground. I believe this is a warning that the sand people are coming, and they will bring death with them. Berg has always been protected, as my king says, but when people are angry enough, they will go to great lengths to extinguish that anger with the blood of their enemies. Crif not only saw defeat in your countries, they saw humiliation. What will stop them from coming for us if they conquer you? The thirst of revenge does not quench so easily. Even the Black Mountains cannot stop it."

We waited with hopeful anticipation as Mistress Dalyah took several cleansing breaths, as if her speech expended all her energy. King Arkyn watched her intently until she composed herself and inclined her head towards him.

"Berg is not a large kingdom," King Arkyn said. "But our knights are great warriors with the strength of two men each."

"That's quite a boast," Admiral Volppe interrupted.

"I do not boast," King Arkyn said through gritted teeth. His blue eyes flashed like dagger blades at the Admiral's impertinence, and the other sailors shifted away from their commander. "I tell the truth. My knights were born and live in the stone. It makes them as strong as the mountains that shield us. If you insist on mocking us, we can leave."

"I'm sure Admiral Volppe meant no disrespect," King Risteard said with a dark glare of his own.

The admiral offered a hasty apology and bid the King of Berg to continue.

"Berg offers eight thousand men to keep the desert people from spreading the death Mistress Dalyah has seen," King Arkyn concluded.

I mentally tallied the number of men to fight for our side, and my heart sank when I realized how outnumbered we were. All eyes turned to the Hrgun Ambassadors whispering among themselves. King Risteard's fingers rapped impatiently on the table, and the pair turned toward the rest of the council.

"Ambassador Sarika and I find these numbers...disappointing," Ambassador Andor said. "We hoped to have a stronger showing with such a union of great kingdoms. However, we are aware that alone we certainly have no hope to defend ourselves from Crif a second time."

"A relief," Wicoya said for Chief Wakashda. "It would be cowardly to use our armies as a shield to hide behind."

The ambassadors from Hrgun narrowed their eyes at the Kuste, but continued without marking their insult.

"We believe we can amass an army of forty-four thousand," Ambassador Sarika said. "It will be such a pity to have such learned men fall, but we're also capable of acting for the good of posterity."

Laria's shoulders relaxed and my mood reflected her relief. Well-trained soldiers from Hrgun would narrow the gap between our numbers and those of Crif considerably. If the estimates of the scouts were correct, they still outmanned us, but we had the advantage of soldiers of varying disciplines and the ability to attack from land and sea. With Hrgun's declaration, the decision to go to war was unanimous. King Risteard proceeded to unfurl a large map of the northern countries and Crif and started strategizing the movements of armies. My mind drifted as technical terms were bantered about and pieces representing each force were moved around the map. I focused on the blocks representing Praed and watched King Risteard place them along the southern border of Torshul just outside the boundaries of the Orkyef Forest and the Voet Foothills. Beyond those natural defenses lay Crif, and on the map it appeared to place our knights and soldiers directly on the front line. My hand found Laria's under the table and squeezed firmly. Her skin was chilled, and she was trembling, though her face remained passively engaged in the discussion. She'd doubtless done the math as well.

The council meeting lasted for several hours, and I honestly only heard snippets of the conversation. Chief Wakashda advised the king to place his men amid the trees as his warriors could move silently enough to ambush any stray Crif that wandered too close. Their archers would man the foothills to send well-aimed arrows sailing down from above the fray.

Admiral Volppe would divide his warships along the coast and into Bluvert Bay. His only concern was the Lochmal Gulf that bordered the eastern shores of Torshul and the northernmost point of Crif. He lamented he had no time to sail any ships around the continent and through the strait to defend our forces from that quarter. There was a large island at the mouth of the gulf, but it was unexplored and considered uninhabited due to its sheer, non-traversable cliffs. No one ever met a soul claiming to live there.

Hrgun soldiers were tasked with patrolling the shores in case the Crif became brave enough to sail their rudimentary boats into the gulf to bypass the front line, but most agreed this would be a foolish move on their part. The overpowered Berg knights were relegated to the front line at King Arkyn's insistence as anywhere else would be "a waste of their talents" as he put it.

Seeing a map with pieces laid out like a game board brought the war to life for me. Now it became truly real. Sweat broke out on my skin and I swallowed bile. I couldn't stay any longer.

I whispered to Laria. "May I please be excused?"

Her brow furrowed.

"I just can't stay here anymore," I said.

She nodded and permitted me to leave. The moment I rose, the room vibrated with the scraping of chairs as the gentlemen stood and bowed politely at my retreating form.

Once out of the council chamber, I leaned against a wall and took several deep breaths to settle my nerves, but my stomach still roiled. I feared I would lose the bountiful breakfast I enjoyed that morning. Of those thousands of soldiers, how many would return home? The people in council spoke so dispassionately, as if they weren't sending men to their deaths. One must truly close off their hearts when it comes to war.

"Ula?" Olim's voice cut through the fog of my dizzy brain. A strong hand clutched my shoulder. "You don't look well."

"I—" The words caught in my throat, and I clamped a chilled hand over my lips and leaned into Olim. He practically carried me down the corridor, found an empty sitting room, and lowered me onto a settee. The nausea subsided, but my knees and hands trembled violently. Olim knelt before me and took my shaking hands in his, gripping them hard to still their movements.

"What happened?" he asked.

I raised my head, stared into his soft blue eyes, and found I couldn't comprehend what he was saying. I watched his mouth move, but his words were silent. The blood rushing in my ears was too loud, my heartbeat too quick, my breathing too rapid to be able to hear his voice. But I could feel his hands, their warm strength covering mine, and his breath stirring the few tendrils that escaped my braid to dangle over my face. My eyes traveled over his familiar features, and I remembered Duveesa once called him handsome. It seemed so long ago, but it came back clearly now. His mouth was still, his jaw set, and his eyes were no longer gentle. A faint flush spread over his cheeks, and he gripped my hands tighter. I pulled away from his grasp and stood, ignoring the residual light-headedness. He towered over me, but not in the intimidating way he sometimes did when he was about to deliver a lecture. The darkness faded from his eyes, and I saw the friend I'd known for five years. He was indeed handsome, and soon he would be gone.

Tears filled my eyes, but I didn't care. I was tired of saying goodbye and tired of leaving things unsaid.

"I don't want you to leave." I took a step closer. "I watched the king place our people at the front line. I cannot bear to think of you being the first to meet Crif."

He shrugged one shoulder. "We're many. It makes sense to have a strong showing to intimidate our enemy."

"Stop being so logical!"

He pursed his lips, but there was only pity on his face. Nothing I could say would convince him to stay. He was a dedicated soldier, a young knight ready to prove himself in battle, and a devoted protector of the crown. His loyalty was one of the qualities I most treasured in him, and it was leading him to death. What would I do without him? I'd grown accustomed to having my shadow watching over me, making me feel safe, and always willing to lend a listening ear.

The tears dried on my face and I continued to contemplate my ever-vigilant knight. Olim looked down at me quizzically since I'm sure my strange behavior was both troubling and confusing. Instead of breaking the silence, I allowed myself the freedom of consideration, for I might never get this chance again. So many more important matters had been at the forefront of my mind lately, but now I would unwind my thoughts regarding Olim. How did I really feel about him? He was dear to me as a friend, but did I feel more? Sometimes when he would gaze at me intently or touch my hand, I felt certain I did, but now I wasn't sure. What was it Laria told me about the moment she realized she loved Risteard?

"Are you feeling all right?"

"Don't move." I gathered my courage, placed my hands against his cheeks, and pressed my lips to his.

My eyes closed at the warmth of his breath, and for a moment we both stood frozen. Then he moved his mouth against mine. His lips were chapped but gentle, almost shy against mine. His hands settled lightly at my waist, and mine dropped to his chest. My mind was a jumble of thoughts, and I concentrated on naming the feeling of that moment.

It was...nothing.

His lips against mine wasn't unpleasant, but it didn't stir my heart, and the longer we remained thus the more uncomfortable I became. I stopped abruptly and pushed Olim away.

"What's wrong?"

"I'm sorry," I whispered around the tightness in my throat. He kissed sweetly, but it left me in no doubt.

I did not love him.

His jaw clenched and his eyes narrowed. "Are you?"

"That wasn't fair of me." I tucked a stray strand of hair behind my ear. "Can we forget about it?"

"I don't think I can. Why did you kiss me if you were just going to pretend it didn't happen?"

"Please don't be angry. It was an impulsive thing to do, and I don't want it to ruin our friendship."

"Maybe I don't want to be *friends*! Maybe I *want* you to kiss me! Have you considered that?"

"I don't know!" I buried my face in my hands. "I thought you only saw me as a friend!"

"Well, I don't!"

"Well, I do!"

Our voices rose to an alarming level, but there wasn't time to stop and consider that people might hear us.

"Then why did you kiss me?" Olim shouted.

"Because I wanted to know for sure!"

"For sure? You thought you'd kiss me to figure out your feelings for me?"

"It sounds so awful when you say it like that!"

"It is awful, Ula! You can't play with people's emotions like that!"

"I didn't think I was…playing," I sobbed. "I only thought it was my feelings I was risking."

"And you've discovered that, in fact, you find me unworthy?"

"No! I just don't love you!"

He stared at me as if I'd just told him someone died. I covered my mouth with my hands as if to stuff the words back down my throat. I'd never felt so horrible in my entire life. Did I hurt Olim irreparably and lose his friendship?

"I see," he said. "I'm glad you were able to clear up any confusion."

"Olim, please," I pleaded, but he left the room without a backward glance.

I sank into the cushions of the settee and wept fiercely. Had I intentionally pushed Olim away so it would be easier to say goodbye? It didn't feel any easier. My sides ached and eyes burned from crying, and I rubbed my chest to ease the sharp pain of my heart breaking. Everything around me was falling apart, and not only was I helpless to fix it, I was making it worse.

Chapter 23

Late into the evening the Great War Council adjourned for the day—so late Laria asked to dine in her room. Her shoulders drooped and she fell heavily into a chair when I presented her meal. She dragged her food around the plate while I prepared her nightclothes. She asked about the children, and I told her they were long in bed. She sagged further, and though I assured her they understood her absence that day, she still nibbled dejectedly at her meal.

"How did it end?" I asked.

Her knife clattered onto the plate. She languidly finished chewing and swallowed the tiny morsel that managed to make it past her lips. "Well enough. There was a lot of talk about strategies and weaponry, and everyone agreed on the position of each army and when to determine a time to retreat. Very cut-and-dried. These men aren't new to this sort of thing."

"Is there much more to talk about?"

"Not really. They wanted to cover as much as possible today because tomorrow many will return to their home countries to start organizing their people. They'll settle on an exact date to meet in the morning."

"It won't be long now, will it?"

"No."

She looked up at me, and her eyes narrowed when she noticed my red-rimmed eyes and puffy cheeks. I averted my gaze and tried to ask about the war again, but she wouldn't have it. She straightened and placed a cool hand against my face.

"What's wrong? You look like you've been crying."

Did I dare tell her the truth? I was ashamed of what I'd done, and the last thing I wanted was for my beloved sister to think poorly of me. On the other hand, it was eating me up inside, and she may have some advice. I took a deep breath, but before I could speak, tears flowed down my checks.

"Little gem!" Laria guided me to a cushioned settee. "What's the matter?" She brushed away the tears, and for a moment it was just me and my sister at Riverstone. My parents adored me, loved me in a way they never loved Laria. But they were horrible when it came to conflict. Their policy was to ignore the problem until the emotions ran their course. Laria always dried my tears, tended my wounds, and hugged me when I was scared. My older sister comforted me in a way Mother and Father could not.

I rested my head on her shoulder as she wrapped her arms around me. A part of me felt guilty for burdening her amid her grief. But Laria was always selfless when it came to me, and I needed her to fix the mess I'd made.

"I've done something awful!" I cried.

"Nonsense," Laria said in the tone she used on the children when they were exaggerating an alleged injustice.

"It's true. You'll be so ashamed of me when I tell you."

"Go on." She unpinned my hair so she could run her fingers through the thick locks.

"I won't waste time explaining what led up to it, but the awful truth is, I kissed Olim."

Laria's eyebrows shot up and her jaw dropped.

"You...you kissed him?"

"Yes." I squeezed my eyes tight and covered them with my hands.

"How was it?"

I dropped my hands and stared at her incredulously.

"How do you think? I've felt awful all afternoon."

"So...bad then?"

"Laria, please be serious."

"I am. You didn't enjoy it?"

"You're not angry?"

"Why would I be angry? Olim is a good man and if you like him, I wouldn't begrudge you a potential husband."

"Well, there's no chance of him becoming my husband." I tucked my knees into my chest and wrapped my arms around my legs. "It wasn't unpleasant, but I realized he wasn't for me. Afterward, he was very angry and accused me of using him."

"Did you?"

I hesitated. "Yes." My voice was as tiny as I felt. "I remembered what you said about a kiss being all it took for you to realize you loved Risteard, and I thought it would clear up the confused mess in my head if I just kissed Olim and figured out how I really felt about him. It didn't end well between us."

She rubbed my knee. "You're sure you weren't just afraid?"

"I wasn't afraid. I was uncomfortable. It was like I was forcing something that shouldn't be. Off and on, I've felt this strange knot in my stomach and a flutter of my heart, but not when I kissed Olim. I expected a stirring of my soul. Instead, I felt only the need to stop what was happening and make sure it never happened again."

"A sure sign you're not in love." Laria sighed. "After I overcame my initial embarrassment, I couldn't stop thinking about kissing Risteard again."

"What do I do? I apologized profusely to Olim, but he was so angry."

"He needs time, Ula."

"He said he didn't want to be *just* friends! How can we go back to where we were?"

"You will not be easy to overcome." She smiled and stroked my hair. "A little distance will be good for you."

"Distance," I whispered. Distance would mean Olim going to war. I feared for his safety, but guiltily looked forward to his leaving so I wouldn't have to be reminded of his disappointment. "I wish I'd never been so impulsive."

"I can't judge you too harshly. I made the same impulsive move years ago."

"But yours ended so differently. I shouldn't go around kissing men to sort out my feelings for them. Mother would call that wanton behavior."

"She would. And it certainly would not reflect well on your reputation. But you're not one to flirt shamelessly with random men. I would rather you steal one kiss than marry a man and discover your true feelings too late."

"I'll never kiss another man again!"

"Don't despair. Recover from this disappointment and mend your friendship with Olim. One day, you may change your mind and find a man that your heart and lips will cry out for."

She smiled encouragingly, but I was in no mood to be placated.

I shook off her hand and stood. "Come on. It's late and you have another big day tomorrow."

"You won't join us in council?"

"No. Though I'm curious, I can't handle all the details involved in planning a war. It's too depressing."

"Yes," Laria said distractedly and sat at the vanity. "Preparations are already being made to mobilize our armies. It takes a lot of food and supplies, and most of our horses and wagons will be employed. Efram will leave in the morning to organize Ilano. Risteard is confident our combined forces will set off for Torshul by week's end."

"He's very efficient. I'm sure they will have a safe journey. Our knights are very well trained."

"Risteard has personally overseen their training." Laria's chin lifted proudly. "We are sure to see victory with them on the front lines."

I admired her fortitude and the defiant sparkle of her green eyes. I rested a hand on her shoulder and detected a slight tremor, as if her skin was about to burst with restrained energy. I squeezed, and she reached up and gripped my hand.

"Oh, Ula," she whispered through trembling lips. "I've been keeping a secret, but I'm not sure I'm ready to tell."

"What secret?"

She shook her head. "I can't say."

"You can tell me. I won't breathe a word of it."

"I know." She released a shuddering breath. "I'll tell you. But not now."

My heart twisted, and I tried to keep my fingers from shaking as I unpinned her hair. She'd been carrying the burden of a secret on top of her despair at watching her kingdom go to war. My disastrous venture into love seemed a trifle in comparison. The last tendrils of ginger hair fell as the door opened and the king strode into the room. Laria hastily wiped her eyes and plastered a smile on her face, a mask to keep him from worrying about her. He tossed his doublet carelessly onto a chair and rummaged through a dresser.

"What did you think of the King of Berg and his mysterious lady?" Risteard asked Laria's reflection.

"A strange pair," she said. "You know I don't subscribe to superstitious visions, but the result was favorable. I admire King Arkyn's confidence, and I hope his army is as strong as he boasts."

"I got the feeling he spoke practically as opposed to bragging," He donned a black linen tunic trimmed with silver embroidery. "It would make sense that men raised in the mountains would be strong, and they're so isolated they wouldn't have much else to do besides training."

"Speaking of which, how are our men doing? Do you think they're ready?"

"Yes. The knights are performing at top form and every man knows his place."

I darted a glance at Laria, and she met my eye in the mirror.

"You have issued all the assignments then?"

"Yes," he said distractedly as he finished fastening his belt.

"I suppose you have your most loyal knights serving alongside you," she continued.

He looked up, his dark brow furrowed, and the queen stared impassively back. He glanced at me, but if he noticed my unease, I wasn't certain. I kept my focus solely on brushing out the tangles of my sister's hair, and hastily braided the thick strands.

"Who?" he asked.

"Olim," she said, and my face flushed. "We've been worried for him and wanted to know where he'll be assigned."

"I've given Olim a very important assignment."

He came closer, hovering over me, but I was too self-conscious to look him in the eye.

"Though it took some convincing, he ultimately accepted my decision."

Laria pursed her lips and huffed out her nose. "What decision was that?"

"To keep him here."

The blood drained from my face and the floor dropped out from under me. Olim was staying? My heart leapt for joy that he would be safe from harm, but my stomach twisted knowing I would have to see him every day after I've potentially ruined our friendship. Laria stared open-mouthed, her jaw working but forming no words.

My tiny voice broke the silence. "Why?"

"To protect my family," he said. "Should the worst happen."

"I'm sure he considers it a great honor," Laria said as she rose. "Where are you off to now?"

"I'm meeting with Efram. He's leaving early tomorrow and wanted to settle a few details first. I won't be too late."

Laria smiled. "Give him my regards. And take your time if you wish to talk about other things."

The barest of smiles played at his mouth before he leaned forward to place a brief kiss upon my sister's lips. Instead of averting my eyes as I normally did, I studied their faces. Though the moment of affection took mere seconds, I observed so many subtle nuances that sent an unusual pang shooting through my heart. Laria's eyes closed, a contented smile gracing her lips, and she looked up into her husband's face with an expression one might have after waking from a pleasant dream. My brother-in-law's eyes were soft as he brushed a hand down her cheek, but in the next instant, he was once more the stoic king. He nodded shortly at me as he left the room, and I turned back to Laria. The sweet smile remained as she crawled into bed and reached for the book on her nightstand. I sighed and settled myself next to her.

"It can be quite wonderful, can't it?" I asked wistfully.

"What's that, little gem?"

"Kissing."

"When it's with the right man."

"I'm relieved Olim will be safe, but now I'm afraid we'll be forced to deal with this awkward situation sooner rather than later."

"Just act naturally. If he thinks you pity him, it will only make him angry. For a while, only speak to him if necessary. You told him in no uncertain terms that you do not return his affections?"

"I'm afraid so," I muttered. "I left him in no doubt with horrible bluntness."

"It's for the best not to give him any hope. It may be painful now, but it will be easier for him to move forward if he knows there's no chance for him to win you."

I ran a hand over my face and uttered a frustrated groan before bidding my sister goodnight. The stress of the council meeting coupled with the incident with Olim served to not only drain my spirits but my body as well. I left my dress where it fell on the floor and didn't bother to brush my hair before slipping under the covers. I considered retrieving the novel from my nightstand, but I was too tired to bother.

The sordid tale and Laria's own story swept me up in a fantasy, resulting in this mess I currently found myself in. I hoped Olim would forgive me and in time we'd learn to be friends again, but until that time I embraced misery.

Avoiding Olim wasn't difficult since he spent the next day practicing drills and training with the other knights while I occupied my time playing with the children. They were in pleasant moods except for Alyx, who was despondent and removed from the rest of his siblings. He refused to engage in any activities or lessons and only spoke when asked a direct question. The weather deteriorated drastically over the last day, which prevented us from taking the children outside for fresh air. However, I didn't fool myself into believing this was the source of Alyx's upset. As the eldest child, he was sure to understand more of what was happening around him than the others. While the younger children were curious about our visitors, Alyx regarded them with dread, as if he knew they were deciding the fate of his country behind closed doors. The nurses and I exchanged concerned looks, but we did not press the young prince into confidence.

By the afternoon, the council was still in session. Lord Protector Ekhane left before dawn followed shortly thereafter by Admiral Volppe, leaving the Hrgun ambassadors, the Kuste, the King of Torshul, and the King of Berg and his companion to discuss the final details with our king and queen. I kept the children far away from the council chambers, but their repressed energy was reaching the breaking point. I bundled them up and led them into the inner courtyard. The rain lightened to a drizzle, and I estimated we had approximately thirty minutes until their coats were soaked.

"Won't they catch a chill?" Duveesa wondered.

"It's not very cold out," I said. "They need to burn off some energy. We can put them in hot baths afterward."

Duveesa was skeptical, but the children were delighted to splash around in puddles and chase each other in the rain. Everyone but Alyx. For a moment, I couldn't find him, and I frantically searched the courtyard before discovering him at the threshold looking down the castle wall toward the distant mews. I approached slowly and shook his shoulder, but he didn't look at me. I followed his gaze and saw a horde of black shapes circling and diving through the sky. Above the drumming of the rain, I could hear the clash of steel and shouts of men.

"It's just the knights training their eagles," I said.

"I know," Alyx said quietly.

When he continued to watch silently, I carefully led him to a private corner of the yard.

"Alyx." I knelt before him. "Do you want to talk about anything?"

He shook his head and averted his reddened face. I placed a hand against his warm cheek and turned him to look at me.

"Please, Alyx, let me help."

"No one else cares!" he said, his shimmering blue eyes filling with tears.

"Cares about what, sweetie?"

"That Papa is leaving! Rian, Tyrnan, and Lilias are still playing. Sulwen is too little to care. All the grown-ups are acting normal. Even Mama!" He cried in earnest, and I wrapped my arms around his trembling shoulders.

"Oh, Alyx! Of course, they care! You're right. Sulwen doesn't quite understand, but your brothers and Lilias know something is happening. And I promise your mother cares. She cares very much. But if grown-ups show you how sad they are, it makes it harder. We want to be brave for you."

"I don't want him to leave," Alyx wailed, his voice muffled against my shoulder.

"I know, little prince." I hugged him tighter. "And it's all right to be sad. We just need to make sure you give Papa extra hugs before he leaves."

"Why does he have to go?"

I disentangled the distraught boy and held him at arm's length. He rubbed his red-rimmed eyes and sniffled before fixing me with such a forlorn gaze that I tried not to cry myself. In many ways, he was so like his father: dark hair, cerulean blue eyes, and sharp features. But when he let his guard down and became vulnerable, he reminded me of Laria when our parents disciplined her unfairly. I dried his tears with a handkerchief and took his little hand in mine.

"You know there are bad men who want to fight?"

He nodded.

"Well, your father has organized the other countries to join us to defeat them. They need his leadership."

"But Papa said not to fight!"

"He did. Except when you must. And unfortunately, they must, otherwise these men will hurt everyone. Your father leaves to protect us all, and he needs our support to help him stay strong. Can you be Papa's big helper, Alyx? It's especially important that he has you standing behind him. Do you know why?"

"Because I'm a prince?"

"Not just a prince. You are his first-born son and heir to the throne. Not only do the people need to see you're following in his footsteps, but *he* needs to know you're willing to put aside your personal feelings to do what is right. I know this is a lot to think about at your age, but you've always been a smart boy."

Alyx dragged his sleeve across his nose and his eyes filled with pride.

"Papa needs me?" Hope filled his voice.

"Very much. So does Mama. You'll be the man of the family once Papa leaves."

A smile slowly spread over his face and his chest puffed out. I gathered the small boy into a fierce hug, and his arms wrapped around my neck. A blanket of melancholy draped over me as I thought about all the turmoil spoiling my life, and I found solace in my nephew's embrace. At some point, it was no longer me consoling *him* but rather him comforting *me*.

Alyx pulled away and tilted his head in concern. "Are you sad about Papa, too?"

"Yes. And I'm sad for you and your brothers and sisters because I know how much you'll miss him."

He nodded sagely, but I could tell he wasn't completely satisfied with my answer.

"How do you stop missing someone?"

"You don't," I said before I could form a more encouraging reply. "I mean, when someone's gone, you miss them. But you learn not to think about it all the time so you can carry on."

"Is that what you do?"

"I suppose." I shook off any errant thoughts. "Come on now. Let's go inside and see if the council meeting is over."

He smiled brightly and allowed me to lead him by the hand. I summoned the other nurses and instructed them to prepare the children in case their parents were free. As they bounced excitedly into the castle, I considered my nephew's question. How do you stop missing someone? I rarely had occasion to 'miss' anyone in my life. I missed Mother and Laria when I was stuck working as a laundress, and of course I missed Father, but I never dwelled on 'missing' them because so many other emotions and events surrounded those instances. When Father went to war, I admittedly never missed him because we were never close, and fighting was such a large part of his life it was strange to have him at home. For an instant, I thought perhaps I'd never truly experienced feelings of loss for anyone, but then there was an ache in my stomach and a pang in my heart I couldn't account for. In the past, I would have ignored these sensations in favor of concentrating on more important matters, but I was weary of neglecting myself. All the way to the council chambers I wondered about what prompted my unease, but no answer was forthcoming.

I pressed my ear against the heavy door and listened, but I couldn't hear any voices. Tentatively, I pushed it open and peered inside. No one sat around the large table still strewn with papers. My gaze drifted around the room and settled on a small group clustered before one of the large stained-glass windows. I recognized Laria and stepped inside. She turned at my approach, revealing the other people in the room. I froze, uncertain, but Laria smiled and beckoned me closer.

"Come," Laria said. "Everyone else already left, but King Arkyn and Mistress Dalyah wished to have a private word."

I could detect a hint of annoyance in her eyes and prepared myself to meet the strange pair.

"Your Grace," Laria said to King Arkyn as I curtseyed. "My lady-in-waiting and beloved sister, Ula."

King Arkyn barely inclined his head and the pale lady smiled, but neither said anything.

"Was there anything else?" King Risteard prompted.

Laria darted a sharp glare in his direction, but he continued to stare ahead expectantly.

"We do not wish to trouble you any longer, Your Grace," King Arkyn said, and I cringed at his venomous tone.

"I hope we meet again," Laria said. "We wish you a safe journey and send our best regards to your knights."

"I thank you, Your Majesty," he said with a gracious bow.

"If we survive this trial," Mistress Dalyah said. "I believe it will usher in a new era for our people. I foresee a great alliance of kingdoms."

"Ensuring our children live in peace and securing a lasting friendship between our countries would make this war truly worth it," Laria said.

The men nodded in agreement, and it was then I noticed Mistress Dalyah regarding me with calm intent. I met her mysteriously colored eyes with more confidence than I felt, and she smiled kindly, as a mother would to a child.

"Young woman."

Her crystalline voice captured every fiber of my being, as if every cell of my body needed to hear what she had to say. Though everyone turned to look at me, I was not self-conscious. When she spoke, they faded into the background, leaving only me and this enigmatic lady.

"The answer to that which troubles you will soon become clear. You only need to listen to the words of your king."

My brother-in-law and I looked at each other in confusion and waited for further explanation. When none was forthcoming, I politely thanked Mistress Dalyah for her advice.

"We shall return to Berg now," King Arkyn said. "We will see you again soon on the borders of Torshul."

Laria and I curtseyed respectfully while Risteard escorted our guests from the room. The moment the door closed, she turned to me.

"What do you think she meant by that?" she asked.

"I have no idea."

She wasn't fooled.

"Ula." Her eyes narrowed. "What's troubling you? Is it about Olim?"

"The situation with Olim does trouble me, but there's something else gnawing at me that I can't quite name."

"Well." She linked her arm with mine as we left the room. "Apparently paying attention to Risteard will reveal the answer."

"Then it's hopeless."

"Why is that?"

"He never speaks."

Her laugh echoed down the halls. I didn't find the situation amusing. I'd only been half joking.

"You *kissed* Olim!"

I covered Duveesa's mouth and raised a finger to my lips. "Keep your voice down!" We were sitting on my bed in the middle of the night and I didn't want the rest of the castle hearing about the huge mistake I'd made.

"Sorry." Duveesa shook her head in amazement. "But it's just so wonderful. I knew there was something between you two."

"That's just it. There isn't anything between us. At least, there's nothing on my side."

Her smile fell. "What do you mean?"

I sighed. "I don't love him, Duveesa. And now I've ruined our friendship."

"Are you sure? Maybe you're just confused."

I shook my head and met her sympathetic gaze. "Have you ever kissed anyone?"

The color of her cheeks took on a rosy hue and she glanced away. I nudged her and she reluctantly raised her eyes.

"Yes," she said. "Once."

Silence stretched between us until I couldn't bear it. "And?"

"And…Nothing." She pulled her knees to her chest and wrapped her arms around her legs. "He was a squire. He was so excited to become a knight someday. He wouldn't shut up about it." She sniffed and rested her cheek on her knee. "I loved him from the moment I saw him at the Harvest Festival when I was thirteen. All my friends were swooning over the big knight, but I couldn't help staring at the skinny, curly-haired boy trailing after him. I cornered him for a dance and we were inseparable until…" She inhaled deeply and I covered her hands with mine.

"What was his name?"

"Tavin." Her voice broke and she buried her face in her hands.

"What happened?"

"Some bastard tried to extort a marriage from me and ruined my reputation. Tavin's father forbade him from seeing me, and I moved here."

"Oh, Duveesa. I'm so sorry." I could blame the man who accused her, but Tavin and his father were equally responsible for believing the vicious rumor.

"When Tavin kissed me, I felt warm, and I didn't want him to stop." Her eyes drifted shut and she hugged herself.

"When Olim kissed me, it couldn't stop soon enough."
Her eyes opened, and her whole body sagged.
"I guess that means I can't tease you about him anymore."
She rested her head on my shoulder and a sob shuddered through me. For my friends, for my family, for me, all I wanted was happiness. Was that too much to ask?

Chapter 24

The king's time with his family was ending, so over the next couple days, they spent as much time together as possible before he left for Torshul. Alyx adopted a brave countenance and stood by while his brothers played games with their father, watching over the scene to learn from Risteard's example. Lilias clung to her mother whenever possible, perching herself in Laria's lap to play the piano or practice sewing. The rain prevented any outdoor activities, which I knew the queen lamented. She was terrible at indoor pursuits, but she tried valiantly to teach her daughter what little she knew. Sulwen was too young to understand what was going on, but she surely sensed the tension in the air and spent much of the time curled up in her father's lap.

When the boys grew tired of table games, they played hide-and-seek around the castle, and the king read stories to his ginger-haired daughter. At these times, I would lean in close to listen, remembering Mistress Dalyah's cryptic message. He glanced at me once or twice, but he said nothing about my proximity. Not surprisingly, no great mysteries were revealed.

The king was scheduled to depart with our armies at week's end, and as the time grew near, my sister became more and more frantic behind closed doors. To the public, she was poised and supportive of the war effort, but once she was in her chambers, she would collapse onto the settee and cry for several minutes before bed. I held her tightly, stroking her hair and rocking her until she composed herself. My heart broke for her, and I felt inept as her sister because I couldn't bring her comfort. The king retired earlier than usual so they could spend every spare moment together. A few nights he caught Laria crying in my arms, and I'd relinquish her to his embrace and leave them to their privacy.

Olim moved about the castle with a thunderous expression. Whenever we passed each other in the castle corridors, he passed by as if we were strangers. It was upsetting to be ignored, but also a relief that I didn't have to deal with him quite yet. There was enough on my plate without worrying about mending our friendship. There would be time for our inevitable argument soon.

Late one evening, two days before the king's scheduled departure, the children were in bed and the king, queen, and I were in the library enjoying a few quiet moments before turning in for the night. Laria and I were seated before the hearth reading novels while Risteard caught up on correspondence, a pile of letters on a small table beside his chair. Periodically, he would flick a missive into the flames, and less often he would tuck a letter next to him to save. One letter captured his attention longer than the rest, though I didn't notice how closely until I heard Laria's voice.

"What is it?"

My head jerked up, and I saw how intently she studied her husband. I turned to him, glanced at the letter in his hand, then at his expression. It was, as usual, unreadable to me, but my sister obviously inferred differently.

"A letter from Finton Ekhane." His eyes flickered to me briefly and settled back on the letter.

The book I was reading fell from my hands and my heart thudded painfully.

"Oh?" Laria said casually as she took my hand. "Is everything all right?"

"Yes," he said. "He says he wishes to offer his services as a physician. He states he is no soldier, but perhaps he can lessen the loss of life by tending to those who fall in battle. He requests permission to commission a hospital near the front line at Torshul."

"That's very gracious of him," Laria said, squeezing my hand. "How will you answer?"

"I won't deny it would be beneficial to have a surgeon accompany us." He tucked the letter next to him. "I will grant him his request."

"Then," I started, my lips trembling. I could barely speak past the lump in my throat, and I swallowed audibly before continuing. "You'll allow Finton to join the war?"

Risteard met my eye steadily. "I have no cause to deny him," he said. "And he may save many lives. It would be prudent to have a hospital as he suggested."

"He won't be fighting," Laria reassured me.

"But he'll be on the front lines!" I cried. "In the midst of danger!"

Risteard's eyes darkened. "So will many other men."

I shrank back at his tone and lowered my eyes.

"It is very admirable of him to offer his services," Laria said. "Many injured men will be saved due to his selflessness."

"Yes," I said. "He is a very good physician, and he cares very deeply for people." Pain stabbed through my chest and stomach, and tears burned my eyes. An overwhelming depression settled over me, fogging my mind and making my limbs feel as heavy as stones. I'd barricaded memories of Finton behind a wall, unwilling to visit them. Now, his smiling face flashed in my mind, and every muscle of my body ached. Without caring about my duties as lady-in-waiting, I hurried to my room.

The door slammed shut behind me and I threw myself upon the bed and wept into the pillow. For weeks, I'd ensured the children and my sister were well attended and only concerned myself with *their* feelings. Now, I had no choice but to confront my own, and I wasn't sure I could bear it. The thought of Olim heading off to war filled me with sadness, but this level of despair was something entirely different. The knock at my door and the sound of someone entering were drowned in my grief. A hand touched my shoulder, and I stilled.

"Ula?" Laria. I relaxed, but not completely.

"I don't want to talk about it."

"That's all right." She rubbed my back. "Go ahead and cry."

I did, for what seemed like hours, until I was gasping for breath. Laria said nothing, even after many minutes of silence. In those moments, I recalled the words of Mistress Dalyah.

"She told me to listen to him." My voice was muffled by the pillow and strained from crying, but I knew my sister could hear me.

"She did."

"I miss him." Acutely. I missed Finton, a fact I hadn't admitted until now. I missed his kindness and his humor, but also the little things, like the way light reflected off his spectacles and his authoritative voice when he taught lessons in the library. "What if something happens to him?"

"He won't be fighting, gem. You should be proud that he's offering his services to save lives."

I rolled over onto my back to look at my sister's determined face. Her expression was a mixture of sternness and sympathy, and I felt guilty for burdening her with my own problems.

"I'm sorry," I mumbled. "You have enough to worry about—"

"Nonsense." She shook her head and waved a hand before her face. "Your feelings are just as valid. We are all being affected by this war. None more so than another."

She brushed a stray lock of hair out of my face and smiled down at me, and my heart swelled with gratitude to have such an affectionate sister.

"What if I never see him again?" My voice was so small and disparaging I barely recognized it.

"You can't dwell on those thoughts. Trust me, it does no good."

I lapsed into a contemplative silence and tried to heed Laria's advice, but I found the task difficult. My face flushed and my chest tightened when I considered that the last time Finton and I spoke was indeed the last time.

"What do I do to make them stop?"

"I think of happier times, a particularly wonderful memory, or little things I don't want to forget. It still makes me sad, but it keeps me from wondering 'what if' quite so often."

I eased myself up into a sitting position and offered Laria a weak smile before gaining my feet.

"I'll try to do as you say. You must wish to go to bed soon."

Laria lay a restraining hand on my shoulder. "Don't worry about me. Rest yourself now. You have much to think about, I believe."

"I don't think so. I'm fairly certain I've discovered the source of my discomfiture."

"Which is?"

"That I miss Finton. Well, and worrying for his welfare."

"Is that all?"

"Isn't that enough?"

She eyed me critically, as if she didn't quite believe me. After a long sigh she rose from the bed.

"I'm going to give you a piece of advice you once gave me that helped tremendously when I found myself in a confusing situation. Ask yourself a question, and what follows immediately is the truth."

I nodded mutely and bid her goodnight. Once the door closed, I lay back against the bed and stared up at the ceiling. It was good advice, but it only worked if you knew the right question to ask. I thought the truth had already been revealed, what answers still awaited me? My mind swirled with all the sources of my unease: the impending war, Olim, Laria and the children, my brother-in-law leaving, Finton…like strands of hair tangled in knots, I was going to pick out each to analyze before moving forward. If nothing else, it would occupy my time in the dark days to come.

Risteard's last day in Praed passed with heartbreaking speed. He spent the morning organizing the soldiers and knights for their morning departure and ensuring his trunks were packed. The horses and eagles were prepared as well, and wagons were loaded down with provisions and were already on the move. The rest of the day he reserved for his family, and the weather had blissfully cooperated. Though the roads were still muddy, the rain relented, and the king ordered a carriage for his family. The nurses were dismissed as were the protective contingent of knights, much to their consternation. The knights argued against this plan, but the king sternly insisted his family be allowed their privacy. And, he pointed out dryly, he was fully capable of protecting them should the need arise. We were subsequently loaded into the carriage and trundled off the mountain.

By the afternoon, we'd arrived at our destination: Laria's swimming hole. It was a small pool branching off the Rhyvor via a small waterfall. Laria and I spent hours during our childhood swimming and sunbathing there. The weather wasn't warm enough for the latter, but it wasn't so unpleasant as to preclude the children from splashing in the water. I chased Rian, Tyrnan, and Sulwen around the periphery of the pool with Laria while Lilias laughed from the shore, and Risteard taught Alyx to skip stones. The stone skipping evolved into all four boys–the king included–having a contest to see who could throw the farthest, which ended up a challenge to see who could throw as far as Risteard. The sun miraculously made an appearance at midday while we picnicked, and I lay back on the grass to enjoy the warm rays. Lilias and Tyrnan lay beside me and Sulwen curled onto my lap, and soon thereafter all three children fell asleep.

Alyx and Rian's laughter followed by the king's incredulous, "What are you doing?" prompted me to sit up. Laria had stripped down to her underclothes and was heading into the water. She threw a mischievous grin over her shoulder at Risteard and arched an eyebrow daring him to stop her. The boys fell on the ground laughing when their father rose to the challenge, kicking off his boots and pulling off his tunic and undershirt before taking off after her. Laria splashed water to keep him at bay. He reached her when the water was waist high, wrapped his arms around her waist, and pulled her under the waterfall. Laria's gasp echoed over the land as icy water flowed over her ginger hair and she struggled against the king's grip. Mingled with her protests was his deep laughter and the delightful squeals of Alyx and Rian. Risteard loosened his grip and Laria spun around and slammed a fist into his chest. He merely chuckled and pulled her into his arms. The laughter of the boys turned into exclamations of "Ew!" and "Gross!" and they covered their eyes as their parents became lost in passionate kisses. I diverted my attention to the toddler asleep in my lap to give them some privacy.

Instead of remembering this day as the last the royal family spent together, I would recall the thrilling laughter of the children, the autumn sun on my skin, the warmth of Sulwen sleeping contentedly in my lap, and the beauty of the love shared between my sister and her husband. These were the things I would remind her of during the lonely days ahead.

Rain fell in gentle drops, pattering rhythmically on the steps of Praed Castle where we stood to bid farewell to the king and his knights. Despite the inclement weather, the streets were lined with people showing their support and offering well wishes. The children were already crying, but Laria stood stoically beside me. Well-ordered knights waited at the bottom of the steps, their banners fluttering in the slight breeze. One by one, the children embraced their father and bravely said goodbye amid their falling tears. Sulwen wrapped her arms tightly around his neck, refusing to let go, and had to be pried off him. Her loud cries pierced the air, and she was so inconsolable, Duveesa retreated with her into the castle. Alyx wished the king a safe journey and whispered that he'd watch over Mama, which broke my heart. Risteard smiled warmly at his first-born son, thanked him for being a good boy, and kissed the top of his head. He looked at me next, his gaze steady. A cry stuck in my throat.

"I'll take care of her, too," I whispered around the emotions threatening to break free.

He nodded shortly, and his eyes drifted over my shoulder. I turned and saw Olim standing stolidly behind me. Despite the awkwardness between us, I was grateful for his silent strength.

The king stood before the queen, and she looked up at him proudly. She did not weep or tremble nor throw herself in his arms and beg him to stay. She showed Praed how a queen behaves in the face of heartache, how she puts aside her personal feelings and holds her head high. A queen cannot afford to appear weak, for her people need her guidance, especially in times of war. She understood this better than anyone, and by all outward appearances she was calm and collected. But those of us who knew her best could see how desperately she clung to this facade. Her eyes were bright, feverishly so, and her jaw clenched. Her knuckles were white from clasping her hands tightly together to keep from shaking. The minute he left, she would collapse.

"Laria," Risteard whispered. He brushed a hand down her cheek and rested his thumb on her bottom lip. He opened his mouth to speak, reconsidered, then took a deep breath through his nose. Laria's hand covered his and she smiled.

"Would it be inappropriate to make a joke?" she asked.

"No," he said, his gaze loving and soft.

"Sorry," she said, shrugging one shoulder. "I can't seem to think of one right now."

"There's always a first time for everything."

She made a sound somewhere between a laugh and a sob and closed her eyes to compose herself. The king framed her face in his hands, placed a brief, gentle kiss on her lips, then pressed his forehead against hers.

"I love you." His voice scraped over his emotions like a rake over gravel. I'd never heard it so raw before.

"I love you, too."

Like a bubble on the surface of a babbling brook, he was there one moment and gone the next, descending the stairs and mounting his horse with purposeful haste. The crowd waved and cheered as the Elejick banner disappeared down the mountain, until they were nothing but specks in the distance. Laria clutched my hand, and I squeezed back reassuringly, moving closer to her side.

I felt a hand press lightly on my shoulder. I glanced over and met Olim's eye. There was no trace of anger there, though I could sense his regret at not being able to join his fellow knights. He looked at me sympathetically, and this small gesture was meant to comfort me. I covered his hand with mine and mouthed, "Thank you." He nodded, the corner of his mouth lifting ever so slightly. It was a small moment, but I hoped it signaled the reconstruction of our friendship. I would be relying on it heavily in the months to come.

The mood in the castle was mournful for the remainder of the day, and most of it was spent consoling the children. Laria had no time to grieve herself since she was too busy being the strong, comforting mother they needed, holding them close and answering their questions as best she could. The one which she could not answer was the one that plagued her thoughts as well: "When is Papa coming home?"

She answered them honestly: "I don't know."

Laria didn't leave their sides the entire day, not even after they went to sleep. She moved from bed to bed, sitting beside each of their sleeping forms in silent watchfulness. When she turned in herself, her eyes were heavy lidded and red-rimmed.

She stared silently out the window, her arms wrapped protectively around herself, while I tidied up the room and turned down the bed. She was already in her nightgown with her hair braided, but she still didn't seem prepared to sleep. I came up behind her and laid my hands on her shoulders and attempted to guide her toward the bed, but she merely turned and gave me a melancholy look.

"Come and get some sleep," I said. "You're exhausted."

"Yes." She glanced at the bed. Her shoulders trembled under my hands. "I don't think I can sleep without him next to me."

"Do you want me to stay?"

She squeezed her eyes tightly and her body shook as she nodded. She allowed me to lead her to bed, and we tucked under the covers. Tears flowed down her cheeks, her sobs echoing in the space as if she were screaming at the cliffside. I held her close, whispering quietly those platitudes I knew meant nothing at times like these, but we say them anyway. At last, she inhaled a few shuddering breaths and released them in a *whoosh*, then all was silent save our steady breathing and the rain falling outside.

"Ula?" Her voice was heavy and hoarse from crying. "If I tell you something, will you promise to keep it to yourself for now?"

"Of course," I said. "Is it your secret?"

She nodded sadly, took a deep breath, and said, "I'm pregnant."

I blinked in surprise. "Are you certain?"

"Yes. Absolutely certain."

"Does Risteard know?"

"No," she said, the words sounding as if they were painfully extruded from her mouth.

"Why didn't you tell him?" I didn't mean to sound so accusatory, but I was shocked that he didn't know.

"It would have been a distraction he can't afford to have right now."

"He might have stayed if he'd known!"

"And he would have regretted it for the rest of his life."

There was nothing more I could say. I saw her point. He loved his wife, but he was a king, and therefore the people sometimes had to be his priority. And first and foremost, he was a warrior, and on the battlefield was where he belonged.

I stroked her tear-stained face. "How far along?"

"Two months. Perhaps a little less." She absently laid a hand against her flat stomach. Soon her secret would be plain for all to see.

"I'll take care of you. Until he comes back."

She smirked. "I'm your big sister. *I'm* supposed to take care of *you*."

I smiled broadly at my brave sister, whom I loved and admired. She had indeed taken care of me from the moment I was born, through the worst time of our lives, and I owed her my life.

"Now it's my turn," I said.

Chapter 25

Olim leaned close to my ear and asked, "How's the queen?"

Two months ago, the king and his knights left to fight Crif at the borders of Torshul. We've received very little news since then.

"As well as can be expected."

The first snows of winter had fallen over the last several days, and we were gathered in the courtyard watching the children play. They threw snowballs at each other and caught snowflakes with their tongues, their laughter echoing in the white stillness of the morning. The queen, who usually delighted in such games, sat perched on a bench watching with a delicate smile on her face. She hadn't announced her condition publicly and so hid behind layers of fur. She knew she couldn't conceal the truth for long, but she held out hope that it could wait until her husband returned. I didn't have the heart to contradict her.

"Any news?" Olim asked.

"Not since the last letter confirming all the countries kept to their word and their forces were in position."

"I'm sure it doesn't signify anything. There are armies to move, strategies to plan, and battles to fight. This leaves little time for writing letters."

I gave Olim a brief, appreciative smile. Over the last weeks, I worked hard to mend the breach that formed when I made the horrible mistake of kissing him. At first, he barely acknowledged my apologies, and I resorted to begging to get him to speak to me. Gradually, he relented, though our discussions were generally one-sided. He only recently started initiating conversations with me, and I was relieved our relationship was returning to normal.

Part of his reticence stemmed from having to stay behind despite the honor of his assignment, and I teasingly suggested I fall out of a tree to make him feel less idle. He didn't appreciate it.

The queen rose from her seat, and we hurried to her side. She gave us a wan smile and declared the children should be taken inside for some warm chocolate drinks and a snack. As if by magic, the children stopped playing and rushed toward the door with their nurses in tow. All the children except Alyx, who took his promise to take care of his mother very seriously and hadn't wandered far from her side since his father left. I took her arm on the opposite side, and together the three of us went inside. Olim trailed behind.

"Are you feeling all right?" I whispered in the queen's ear.

"A little queasy, but that's all. I think I'd like to lie down."

"Of course."

I transferred Alyx's hand to Olim and informed them the queen was tired and wished to rest. Alyx fixed us with a wide, worried stare as he was led away, but his mother gave him an encouraging smile and a wink that set him to rights.

Once we were in the queen's rooms, I helped her remove the layers of clothing and remarked they must have made her over warm.

"I was fine," she said with a dismissive wave.

"Laria, you can't hide forever. You certainly cannot wear these many clothes indoors or you'll pass out from the heat."

"It's cold out. It's not unusual to wear heavier clothing in winter."

"No, it's not."

She pulled on a nightgown, the fabric accentuating the already noticeable swell of her belly. It was only a matter of time before her pregnancy was too obvious to ignore. I'd concealed her new ritual of morning sickness and changed her diet without much questioning, but I couldn't very well explain away a large belly. I'm sure she knew this as well, but she chose to keep the secret.

"Don't let me sleep for too long." She settled under the covers.

Her eyes closed before her head hit the pillow.

I brushed a stray lock of hair from her forehead. "I won't."

"Wake me if there's a messenger." Her voice was drowsy and drifted away as she spoke. She was asleep before I could answer.

I sighed and left her in peace, casting one last glance toward her sleeping form. I'd never seen a pregnancy take so much out of her, and I was convinced the added stress of the war and having the king so far away was detrimental to her health. I was helpless to do anything but sit and wait. It was agonizing.

While the queen stole a few minutes of sleep, I wandered into the library. In our free time, Olim and I made it our mission to pour over the books searching for any information we could about our new allies. It gave us purpose aside from waiting and helped pass the idle days. Regrettably, there wasn't much to learn regarding Kuste and Berg, but there were several volumes detailing the history of Hrgun and Faqur. Olim was already in the library when I arrived and glanced up from his book to offer a lop-sided grin before returning his attention to the open pages.

I retrieved my own tome and settled into my favorite overstuffed chair. "Anything useful?"

"Did you know Admiral Volppe was actually born on a ship? Apparently, his mother greeted his father aboard the vessel, *The Dangerous Ranger*, upon entering port after an extended expedition and the excitement sent her into labor."

"Really? How interesting. You could say Admiral Volppe was literally born to sail!"

"You could." He flipped another page without smiling.

I rolled my eyes and opened the chapter on the areas of study offered at the universities in Hrgun.

The only sound for several minutes was the fire roaring in the hearth and the turning of pages. I was fascinated to learn about all the colleges available in Hrgun from visual arts to medicine to history to business. I read everything I could about the college of art, a little enviously I'll admit. Great masters in all aspects of art taught classes in watercolors, music, composition, and even weaving and architecture. I read a brief transcript on a class in oil landscapes and felt wholly inadequate. I could barely comprehend the type of brushstrokes and had never heard of the color "malachite." Once I overcame my initial envy, I drifted into a daydream where I was a student learning with masters. Ambassador Sarika offered me a place provided I was deemed worthy. Perhaps when this was all over I would seriously consider it.

My attention continually wandered to the section on medicine, but I kept finding other subjects to occupy my time. Now, I scanned the topics of discussion for those who studied to be surgeons. Many of the words I couldn't begin to understand let alone pronounce, but I was impressed to learn how much study was required. My thoughts inevitably drifted to Finton, who would one day be studying these very subjects and sit in on these classes. If he made it through the war.

Tears pricked the corners of my eyes. I worried about Finton and found him often in my thoughts. Were his skills already being used? Were men falling in battle and being placed in his capable hands? Was he staying safe? Laria assured me repeatedly that he was out of harm's way, but was there such a thing when one skirted along the front lines of war? Did he ever think of me? The time we spent together was brief, but we formed a dear friendship I would cherish for the rest of my life. I squeezed my eyes shut to keep the tears from falling and took several deep breaths. When I opened them again, I became entranced by the flames and focused solely on the mixture of reds, oranges, and yellows in the hopes my mind would clear of all dark thoughts.

"What are you thinking about?" Olim's voice registered through a thick fog.

"Finton," I said before I could stop myself. I blinked when I realized what I said and hurriedly explained, "He's at the front, too. I was just wondering if there were many injured men he was treating." It was a half-truth. Hesitantly, I looked at Olim, who was glaring angrily.

"I see."

He returned his attention to his book, but I could see the veins pulsing at his throat and his jaw clenched. I chose to ignore it. I didn't feel the need to defend my friendship.

"Are you going to continue to insult me and pretend you don't have feelings for him, or don't you realize it yourself?" Olim asked.

"What? I don't know what you're talking about."

"So, the latter then."

"You don't have to be so confrontational." I sank deeper into the cushions to bury my face in the book.

Olim sighed heavily and the loud *slam* of his book closing echoed throughout the room, making me jump. I peered at him from over the top of the pages detailing courses in anatomy to regard Olim's dark expression. A chill ran down my spine at how angry he appeared, angrier than when I kissed him and broke his heart.

"Please don't look at me like that," I said.

"It's one thing to lie to me, but why do you insist on lying to yourself?"

I dropped the book in my lap.

"I don't know what you're talking about, honestly!"

He rose and moved to loom over me. "Well, allow me to explain it to you."

I shrank further into the chair to escape his ire.

"It's obvious to everyone except you that you're in love with Finton Ekhane."

My eyes widened and I straightened in the chair.

"I don't know why you think that. He's my friend."

Olim stared at me silently. I shifted uncomfortably under the intensity of his gaze, then looked away, brows furrowed, considering his words.

"Ula," he began, his voice more tired than hostile. "I'm sorry. I don't mean to attack you, but enough is enough."

My vision blurred, and I kept my gaze averted. Olim knelt before my chair and hesitantly reached out to rest a hand on my arm.

"Look at me."

I looked down at his hand, but I couldn't meet his eyes.

"How can you know for sure?" he asked, his voice pained.

I peered at him sideways and saw him struggle to keep his composure.

"You didn't know the true nature of your feelings for me until..."

My cheeks burned when he faltered, but I didn't stop him.

He shook his head. "All I'm saying is that you're obviously uncertain about how you really feel until you face things head-on."

"He's my friend." My voice wavered.

"Yes. And I am, too."

I smiled, relieved he once again considered himself as such.

"But," he said sternly. My smile disappeared. "You've never looked at me the way you look at him. As much as it pains me to admit it, and no matter how much I tried to ignore it, you always glowed when he was around."

I opened my mouth to argue, but paused. He used my silence as an opportunity to press his point.

"I know you care about what happens to me, and that you were worried about the possibility of my going to war, yet you still functioned. You're hiding it well, but you're a wreck over him. You know how I know for sure you love him? Because you deceived the queen in order to spend time with him."

"You helped me!"

"I did. Because even then, I knew you were developing feelings for him, and I stupidly wanted to please you."

"I'm sorry." I could no longer look him in the face and turned away.

"Ask the queen," he said, squeezing my arm. "I'm sure she knows as well."

I grasped his hand to stop him from rising. "Olim, I hope you know I never meant to hurt you."

"I know," he said, reluctantly. "You can make it up to me by getting over yourself." His mouth curved in a rueful smile, and I released his hand.

Olim left the library, and I took advantage of the ensuing stillness to analyze the thoughts swirling in my mind. Though I staunchly disagreed with Olim's assessment of my feelings, I couldn't help wondering at their validity. A strange sense of relief flowed through me, and a weight pressing down on me lifted. I sank back against the cushions in complete relaxation. An inexplicable sense of freedom filled my heart, and without restraint, I allowed my mind to wander.

Every moment I'd spent in Finton's company replayed in my mind. From the moment we met, he'd been friendly and open, making me feel at ease and able to be myself. I rarely felt comfortable with strangers, but with Finton, I immediately let my guard down. I'd been drawn not only to his humor, but his intelligence, kindness, and exuberance. From teaching students to tending patients, he gave all of himself.

The beginnings of a headache pulsed at my temples. I rose from the chair and moved to the window. The bright whiteness of the snow made me squint, reminiscent of the few times I became blinded from lights reflecting off Finton's spectacles. I pressed a hand against my forehead as blood throbbed through my veins, and I rushed out of the library before I became sick.

Gently, I shook my sister awake, and from the moment she raised her head from the pillow, I forgot my troubles and focused on being the pillar of strength she needed to get through the day.

"Any messages?" she asked.

I shook my head, and her disappointment was heartbreaking.

"You know what we should do?" I asked brightly as I fixed her hair. "We should all gather around the fire and tell stories like we used to on cold nights at Riverstone. The children love your stories."

"That would be nice," she said. She rested a hand lightly on her stomach and absent-mindedly trailed her fingers across the slight swelling.

"Are you feeling better?"

She nodded but remained lost in thought. I wished there was something I could say to lift her spirits, or at the very least distract her. I figured if I talked about myself, she would put aside her own troubles to comfort me. No matter how she suffered, she would always revert to being my big sister whenever I needed her. I didn't particularly wish to discuss what Olim asserted in the library, but I was willing to broach the subject if it meant keeping her mind off the war and her absent husband.

"Can I talk to you about something? If it's not too much trouble. I know you're preoccupied with other things—"

"What is it?" She seemed as eager to turn her mind to other things as I was.

I sighed and dropped onto the settee in front of her, and she leaned forward expectantly.

"There's no sense in dodging around, so I'll come straight to the point. Do you think I'm in love with Finton Ekhane?"

She drew back as if she'd been struck and blinked before recovering from my blunt question.

"Well. I have to admit I had my suspicions."

I blushed furiously, but I resisted the urge to change the subject.

"Why?" I asked, genuinely curious. I wasn't aware of any changes in my behavior toward Finton and was intrigued to know what she saw.

"Little things. Your cheeks turn pink when you hear his name, and you become discomposed. Mostly, you enjoy his company so much you risked my wrath to spend a day alone with him." She was smiling wryly, but I knew she wasn't joking.

"That's what Olim said."

"Did he? What's he to do with it?"

"He accused me of not admitting I'm in love with Finton. He was very cross about it."

"Not surprising given your recent history."

"Yes."

She placed her hand lightly on mine and smiled. "*Are* you in love with him?"

I tried to speak, but the words caught painfully in my throat, so firmly they burned. A hoarse voice I didn't recognize squeezed through the cracks, "I don't know. How can I?"

"You could always kiss him like you did Olim."

A laugh escaped my mouth, and with it some of the tension, but the thought of kissing Finton made my stomach flutter and my chest tighten. I inhaled deeply, rubbing a hand over the area above my heart and tried not to cry.

"I can't—" I choked on the words and turned away.

Laria squeezed my hand reassuringly. "You've spent too much time thinking about everyone else, Ula. I know it's hard, but you have some questions to ask yourself."

"I don't know if I'm ready. So much could change."

"It can, but I think the time is coming for you to fly on your own."

For the last five years, my life revolved around Laria and her family. Who would I be without them? No longer a lady-in-waiting, an aunt, a sister. I'd just be Ula, and I wasn't sure if I was prepared for that.

Not yet, but almost.

Chapter 26

For several days I was filled with restless energy. We received no word from the front, and though a low rumbling of anxiety about the war rolled through me, this wasn't the source of my unrest. My veins buzzed and my nerves vibrated in anticipation, but no matter how often I went on long walks or brief rides, I couldn't dispel the feeling. Soon, I became edgy and irritable, snapping whenever someone startled me. Laria eyed me anxiously but said nothing. Duveesa was not so wise.

"Has something happened?" she whispered when the children were occupied with their painting lessons.

"Many things have happened," I said.

She drew back in alarm at my acerbic tone, and I immediately apologized.

"I know you've worn yourself thin lately," Duveesa said. "Unburden some of your stress."

With a sigh, I moved to the window and stared down the mountain. I could just see the northern border of Market Town, and though we were too far away to make out the shapes of people, the rising smoke from chimneys and shops conveyed a bustling city ripe with activity. Sunlight danced on the tributaries feeding the Rhyvor, and mist rose from the trees in delicate tendrils. It would be warm today, warm enough to take the children outside.

"It's strange," I said. "I have this odd sense that I'm supposed to be doing something, and it's driving me mad trying to figure out what it is."

"You do more than anyone else in the castle," she said. "What more can you do?"

"I can't explain it, but I don't think the answer is here."

"In the castle?"

"In Praed."

She tilted her head. "Where is it then?"

"I don't know." I squeezed my eyes shut and repeated her question silently in my head. "Not here."

She raised her chin defiantly. "You should go find it then."

I crossed my arms over my chest. "I wouldn't even know where to start."

"You could start by leaving the castle." Her tone was strong, but her eyes shone at the prospect of my leaving.

I gasped. "I could never do that! Especially now. I'm needed too much."

"You *are* needed. But the longer you wait, the less useful you'll be. You're absolutely stewing these days."

"There's too much snow on the ground."

"True. What will your excuse be when it melts?"

I narrowed my eyes and glared at her.

"I've learned time is precious," she said, "and you never know when it'll run out. It's better to act than wait and live with regret."

"Who would watch over the queen?" I blinked back tears.

"She's a strong woman. She'll survive."

I shook my head. "She needs me now more than ever."

"I know she misses the king and worries about the war."

"Exactly." I nodded enthusiastically.

"But it's not as if you'll be gone forever. You just need space to sort things out."

I inhaled deeply through my nose and turned away from my friend's intense stare. The children chatted amongst themselves between the nurses critiquing their techniques and use of color. Lilias used delicate strokes while the boys made sweeping motions with bold colors. Sulwen abandoned her brush entirely and was painting with her fingers, her lips puckered in concentration. A small smile played at my mouth when I imagined a sixth child at the table. Would it be a boy or a girl? Would it take after their father, or would the royal family be graced with another redhead? Unexpectedly, a pang of longing twisted in my heart. For six years, I watched my nieces and nephews grow, walked beside them during their milestones, and shared in the joy with their parents. I loved every moment of it. But for the first time, I wished for children of my own. I wiped a hand across my eyes and met Duveesa's stoic stare once again.

"We can sit here and discuss this until we turn blue. But it doesn't change anything. There's no chance the queen will grant me leave at such a time. For several reasons."

"You waste nothing by asking."

We let the subject drop and concentrated on the children for the remainder of the afternoon, but it tugged at the back of my mind.

During Laria's nightly routine my conversation with Duveesa continued to nibble at my mind. Laria kept an intent eye on me, but I smiled encouragingly as she tucked into bed. She wasn't fooled.

"Ula," she said sternly. "What's troubling you? Is it about Finton?"

"Maybe. But maybe I'm just sick of winter."

"Rubbish." She crossed her arms and raised an eyebrow.

"Let's not do this now. It isn't good for you."

"I'm not made of glass. And I'm no green mother. I've carried children many times before if you recall."

"But never by yourself," I shot back before I could stop myself.

She turned away, the color rising in her cheeks.

"I'm so sorry! That was an awful thing to say! Please forgive me."

"I forgive you," she mumbled. "I wish there was something I could say to bring my sister back."

"I'm here!" I grabbed her hand and pressed it to my heart. "I'm here for you, Laria."

She turned to me, and her expression melted into sadness. She released a heavy breath.

"Oh, Ula, I've been so selfish."

"No. You have carried the weight of the world these past few months. If anyone has earned the right to lose themselves in despair, it's you."

"I shouldn't have. I am a queen."

"You're a woman and a mother," I said firmly. "You deserve to break down every now and then." I smiled reassuringly, but her eyes hardened.

"I've been acting as if I'm already in mourning. I may as well wear black."

"No one thinks that. You've shown the country nothing but strength."

"It's only a mask," she said, her eyes shining. "And I'm tired of wearing it. It's not fair for you to wait anxiously for the moment we're behind closed doors for me to fall apart. I've been taking you for granted."

I opened my mouth to argue, but she glared darkly and I kept quiet.

"I know my secret has weighed on you. I've been living a fantasy that Risteard will return before the truth is revealed. Today, I was thinking about what he would see were he to return right now, and I'm ashamed to realize how disappointed he would be. Yes, I have maintained a mask for the people, but it's only believable if you're committed fully to the lie. He would see immediately that I've been wallowing, and that is not the woman he married."

"He married a very determined, stubborn woman," I said.

A smile bloomed on her lips, and her eyes sparkled. "Exactly."

"Go to sleep now. Tomorrow is a new day."

She snuggled into the covers, and I silently left the room, not only satisfied that her fire returned, but that she forgot about interrogating me about Finton. There were some decisions to be made about my life, and for the first time, I didn't want my sister's opinion to influence me.

Laria surprised the castle by wearing a gown without the multitude of layers she previously donned. Though her pregnancy was still quite early, her lower abdomen bore an unmistakable prominence. She resolved to hide her condition no longer, but to bear it proudly. Her strategy negated the need to make a formal announcement, for simply taking a stroll along the corridors left no doubt she was with child. She drew many surreptitious stares and whispers as she passed, but she paid them no heed and walked with her head held high.

When she entered the council chambers, the nobles' eyes were immediately drawn to her swelling middle, and I almost laughed at how ridiculous their faces looked. Some averted their eyes while others stammered incoherently. By the tremor of her lips and glimmer of her eye, she found their reactions equally amusing.

"Gentlemen," she said and took her seat.

Slowly, they lowered themselves into their chairs. All except one. Armen Ferrys, an elderly man who served as a council member since King Conall's rule, remained standing, a gentle smile on his face.

"Your Majesty," he said, his kind eyes glowing in the deep wrinkles of his face. "May I be the first to congratulate you." He bowed as deeply as his aged frame would allow, and carefully settled into his seat.

The queen smiled, as if the gentlemen were a relation, and thanked him. She scanned the faces of the other men and said, "Has anyone received word from the front lines?"

"Unfortunately, no, Your Grace," Lord Thomlyn Wyrwyk, a younger noble whom I'd known my entire life, spoke up sympathetically. "But the weather's been terrible. Snow storms have plagued Praed for weeks, so the roads are poor. And the northern regions along the borders of Torshul have experienced icy rain. It's impossible for messengers to travel safely."

"I see." The queen's face was impassive, but I could tell by her downturned lips and clenched hands she was disappointed.

"Our last reports were encouraging," another man said. I couldn't remember his name, but he was tall, and his long, elegant fingers were steepled before his pale face. "The Crif have avoided the Lochmal Gulf and Bluvert Bay since our forces are very strong there. King Karne hasn't been brave enough to show his face in Torshul. Our allied armies are no doubt too intimidating."

"No doubt," Laria said dryly. "We must continue to keep our men in our thoughts and hope for their safe return."

"Of course, Your Majesty," Armen Ferrys said. "We all look forward to the day when we can live in peace again."

The queen turned the conversation to local matters, which was my cue to excuse myself. I only wished to hear news from the front lines and had no interest in local politics. Laria understood, and graciously allowed me the freedom to come and go from the council chambers.

When I retreated to the library, eager to lose myself in the pages of a novel, Olim was pacing before the hearth. He stopped when I came in, and I almost turned around to leave, but I wasn't quick enough. He strode toward me purposefully and my heart sank.

"What's wrong?" I held out a hand to halt his progress.

"I just heard someone say they saw the queen go into council," he said in a rush. His eyes were feverishly bright.

"She often does." I swept past him to scan the shelves for a book.

"Is it true?"

"Is what true, Olim?"

"Is the queen with child?" He whispered, as if the entire castle wasn't already privy to this new information.

"She is."

"It must have been terrible for the king to have to leave her in such a state."

"Yes," I said evasively. I retrieved a novel and nestled into my favorite chair. Olim sat nearby—sans book, I noticed. I did my best to ignore him.

"Are you going to leave Praed?"

Olim spoke so quietly I nearly missed the question. I laid the book flat so I could look him in the face, noticing a touch of sadness and a hint of betrayal in his eyes.

"What makes you think that?"

His cheeks flushed pink, and he looked away to study his boots.

"Duveesa mentioned you might," he said.

"You and Duveesa were talking about me privately?" Anger rose within me at the thought of my friends gossiping behind my back, but then I studied Olim's awkward shifting, and my outrage faded, replaced by a flutter of amusement.

"Olim? Do you and Duveesa speak alone often?"

The prospect did not arouse any jealousy but made me rather pleased.

"No." He shifted in his seat. "Are you going to answer my question?"

"I haven't decided."

"Where would you go?"

"I don't know. We were talking hypothetically. I have no plans to leave, especially now."

His hand shot out and painfully gripped mine. I gasped at the intensity of his piercing blue eyes and tried to pry my hand away, but he took the other and stilled my movements.

"Ula," he said in a tone that ceased all arguments before the words could be formed. I swallowed, my throat dry, and listened. "You're not happy, and I know it's not just the war. If leaving Praed is what it takes for you to find happiness again, not only should you do it, but I'd even help you."

"You would?"

"You don't think I'd let you wander around the world by yourself, do you?" His mouth was curved in an indulgent smile, and I glimpsed the man I'd been missing since...well, since I made one of the biggest mistakes of my life.

"I would feel much safer with my ever-vigilant knight to protect me." I squeezed his hands affectionately and he released me. "Once I've made a decision, I'll let you know." My eyes traveled past his shoulder to the window. Delicate snowflakes fluttered in swirling gusts of wind. "It probably won't be any time soon."

He followed my gaze. "You wouldn't let a little thing like that stop you, would you?"

"You call a Praed winter little?"

"You've overcome worse." He was smiling, but his tone was mournful.

I nodded.

"Well, it may not be snowing *everywhere* on the continent."

"Precisely!"

I squinted suspiciously. "You're not just encouraging me to travel because you're bored, are you?"

"I swear I'm not." He placed his right hand over his heart.

"All right, then. Enough of this topic for now. Tell me, how long have you been courting Duveesa?"

The hue of his skin deepened to red. "I'm not!"

I raised an eyebrow, unconvinced.

"There's no need to become defensive. Duveesa is very sweet, beautiful, and intelligent. I think she suits you."

"Stop it." He turned away to hide his face, but not before I caught a hint of a smile. I suppressed a grin of my own and resisted embarrassing him further. We took our usual places, buried our noses in our books, and remained silent for the remainder of our time together.

The children were predictably ecstatic after learning they were soon to have a new sibling, and we spent most of the afternoon answering their myriad of questions. Alyx, as the oldest child, was an old pro at this stage and fielded many of the questions himself, much to his mother's amusement. The boys naturally hoped for another brother while Lilias asked politely for a sister.

Sulwen had no opinion either way as to the sex, most likely because the idea of a child growing in her mother's stomach was difficult to grasp in general. The toddler could put two to three words together now, and every day, seemingly out of nowhere, she would look up at one of us and ask, "Fa-fa home?" And every day we disappointed her. So, when she placed her tiny hand on the slight swell of her mother's abdomen and was told a baby was in there, we hoped this would be distraction enough to elicit a new string of words.

"Baby?" she asked her mother dubiously.

"Yes." Laria stroked the soft, ginger head of her daughter. "There's a baby in there. It's going to grow big and come out to meet you in a few months."

"Fa-fa come?" Sulwen asked hopefully.

Laria paused briefly, her eyes filling with tears, and gathered her daughter into her arms.

"I hope so," Laria said. "I miss him, too."

It had been an emotional day, but when I helped Laria into bed that night, instead of a wistful sadness, her countenance was serene. Our eyes met in the mirror, and she smiled beautifully, a glow illuminating her skin. The peace in my sister's heart filled me with a calm reverence, and for the first time in months, I wasn't worried about her.

When I lay in my own bed staring up at the ceiling, I gave my thoughts freedom to play. The children were well, my sister pulled herself out of her depression, and Olim was moving on after I cruelly disappointed him. There was no one left to worry about except myself. Duveesa and Olim encouraged me to find my way, even if it meant leaving. Even Laria expressed a wish to set me free. But if I were to leave, where would I go?

A jolt shuddered through me, and I sat upright in bed as if I'd been struck by lightning. For months, I'd been searching not only for answers, but for the question that would lead me in the right direction. At that moment, I felt with absolute certainty the question had been posed. If I were to leave, where would I go? The answer came to me in a brilliant flash, and I lay back down in astonishment. At long last, my truth was revealed, and I knew where I must go, where I would find happiness.

The front lines.

Chapter 27

When I awoke the next morning, I made the decision to leave Praed, travel to Torshul, and find my destiny. By the time I finished breakfast, I'd found a million reasons to stay. The journey was dangerous, I'd be gone too long, Laria would worry…By midday, I'd countered the cons with the pros. Olim would protect me, we'd be back in time for Laria to give birth, I needed to do this.

I *needed* to find him.

When all the arguments fell away, I was left with one indisputable fact. There was a man out here I needed to find. I needed to know how he felt, how *I* felt.

Before it was too late.

Olim stared in open-mouthed shock when I told him of my plans to travel to the front. He seemed so wholly incapable of speech that I picked up my book and began reading while waiting for him to recover.

"Have you gone mad?"

"Not at all," I said. "I know it seems unorthodox—"

"Not to mention dangerous!"

"But," I continued with a trace of annoyance. "I've made my decision. I've given it much thought, and I'm convinced that's where I must go to find the answers I seek."

"Is it because Finton Ekhane is there?"

"Perhaps."

He crossed his arms and glared down at me. "It could take four weeks to get to the front."

"Did you have plans?"

"I'm supposed to be here protecting the royal family!"

"Yesterday you said you'd come with me!"

"That's before you said you wanted to go to the front!"

"All the more reason you should accompany me."

A vein pulsed at his neck, and I could practically see steam coming out of his ears. I stared impassively, and he sighed irritably.

"I don't suppose there's anything I can say to change your mind?"

"Not a thing," I said, my chin raised in determination.

"Fine," he huffed.

"I'm sure we have much to do to prepare. I trust you to make sure we're ready to depart as soon as possible."

His eyebrows shot up and he glanced out the window. The snow stopped falling, but the ground was covered in a thick layer of ice after a particularly cold night.

"Do you think you can handle that?"

"Of *course* I can!"

I felt a little guilty antagonizing him, but I didn't want to waste time with a lengthy conversation.

"Do you think it would be better to take a carriage or go on horseback?"

He considered before replying, "Horseback would be faster given the snow. I'll go over the maps and plan the best route."

"Thank you." I smiled. "Now all that's left is to inform the queen."

"She doesn't know yet?" I sensed a lecture quivering at the tip of his tongue, but he was wise enough to hold it.

"I wanted to make sure I had your support first. I wouldn't be able to leave without you."

He gave a quick nod then quit the room to prepare for our departure.

I paced in front of the door to the council chamber waiting for the queen to emerge. I wrung my hands nervously, my fingers cold, and my knees shook. Excitement and dread mingled inside me, twisting my stomach in knots and sending my heart into a thunderous tempo. What a difference a year can make. It wasn't too long ago that the prospect of journeying away from Praed left me terrified, and now here I was, planning to travel hundreds of miles toward a war.

The door opened, making me jump, and I covered my mouth to stifle a scream. People filed out of the room, and I scanned their faces searching for the queen. When she didn't emerge, I pushed my way inside. She was deep in conversation with one of her trusted advisors, a short man with unsettling dark eyes and a crooked grin. He was often in the company of a tall lord. I called them Bean and Pole.

It's embarrassing how horrible I am at remembering the names of the councilmen.

I fidgeted as I waited, pleading silently with her to finish their conversation. She noticed my impatience, smiled at the lord, and asked they resume their discussion later. He smiled at me, showing all his teeth, and bowed low to the queen. She took my arm, and I practically dragged her from the room.

"What's the matter?" she asked as I pulled her down the hall.

Despite her heavy breathing, I didn't slow my pace until we were alone with the door locked.

"I need to talk to you and it cannot wait," I said breathlessly.

She sat down to catch her breath and gestured for me to go on.

"I've found the answer I've been seeking," I said.

She nodded in understanding. "Which is?"

"I have to leave."

She bowed her head. "I thought you would. Where will you go?"

"To the front."

Her eyes flew up to meet mine and she paled.

"What? You cannot! It isn't safe." The color rushed back into her cheeks and her green eyes flashed.

"Olim will protect me. He's already agreed."

"Has he?" She pushed off the settee and stomped to the window. "How noble of him."

"You yourself said the time would come for me to fly."

"That doesn't mean you should fly toward danger! If the war at the front doesn't kill you, the journey certainly could."

"I have to do this."

"Absolutely not! I forbid it."

A wave of sympathy washed over me, and I spoke to my sister in calming tones.

"Laria, you won't stop me and you know it."

"I know nothing of the sort. You can't–" She shuddered and turned away. "I've just sent my husband off to war. I can't send you, too."

I walked boldly up to my sister and wrapped my arms across her shoulders. She did not embrace me back, but she didn't pull away either.

"A messenger made it to the castle today," she said, so quietly I almost missed it.

I stilled and waited for her to continue.

"He had been traveling hard for many days. He changed horses several times because he rode them to exhaustion."

When she didn't speak again, I asked, "What did he have to say?"

"King Karne has arrived in Torshul."

The floor tilted and I clung to my sister to keep from falling.

"Oh, Laria."

"When he left, the messenger said the line was holding. But who knows what's happening now."

I couldn't formulate platitudes to comfort my sister. She turned from the window, and though pain marred her features, she did not weep.

"It's a long and treacherous journey, Ula. Especially for a woman."

"I won't be alone."

She stared at me for a moment, and I felt her intense scrutiny. Without another word, she pulled away and strode to her vanity, opened a drawer, and reached inside. I followed curiously, and she pulled herself to her full height, her eyes defiant.

"Is there any chance you'll reconsider?" she asked, a challenge in her voice.

"None at all."

She nodded shortly, grabbed my hand, and placed a dagger on my open palm.

"What's this?" I whispered.

"For protection."

"I don't know how to use it!"

"You stab the pointed end into your enemy," she said with a slight twitch of her mouth. My eyes widened, and she bit her lip to keep from laughing.

I turned the sheathed blade over in my hands. "Where did you get this?"

"Risteard gave it to me."

"Have you ever used it?"

Instead of answering she said, "Have Olim teach you how to wield it properly."

She moved back toward the window, and I hastily tucked the dagger into the folds of my gown and joined her. The clouds parted, and the sun turned the cold snow into a glittering landscape.

My heart trilled in my chest, and I could hardly breathe. It was really happening. I was leaving Praed.

"Don't tell me when you're leaving. I don't want to know how much time I have to try to talk you out of it. I'd rather wake up and find you gone." She turned to me with a wry grin, and I nodded. She returned her attention to the window, her mouth still curved in a reflective smile. I reached out and entwined my fingers with hers, and to my relief, she squeezed back.

I found Olim in the library that evening surrounded by maps and lists. He barely acknowledged me when I entered and scanned the vast array spread out before him. I recognized the map of Praed, but I'd never explored its southern border beyond the hills jutting from the earth to form the Kreeg Mountains. Beyond those hills was a barren landscape, the dwelling place of vagabonds, bandits, and the Kli'air Hine, itinerant nomads from the east famous for elaborate entertainments. It was several days' journey from there to the northern borders of Torshul. Among the maps were Olim's notes regarding the terrain, stops along the journey, and a list of supplies that would keep us and our horses fed and warm.

"Impressive," I said. It truly was an exceptional feat for an afternoon. "How long have you been planning this exactly?"

"It's prudent to be prepared," he said irritably.

"I agree. And you've done a splendid job." I picked up one of the lists, an inventory of clothing, and felt very overwhelmed.

"How will we possibly carry all of it?" I asked in a hushed tone.

"I think it would be wise to have a cart. Something small for provisions. It would mean having three horses to feed, but it would lessen the burden on our mounts."

I ran a finger along the main road running south to the last estates before the mountains. "Will we stop here?"

"I've already sent word to a couple of estates along our journey asking for permission."

"You're very efficient."

"I've been trained to be."

"So." I dropped onto a chair. "What's the plan then?"

His eyes flickered to mine, and he became very still.

"Have you obtained the queen's permission?" he asked.

"I have."

I locked eyes with him, and in my unwavering stare, he saw the truth of my words. He nodded, placed several maps in front of me, and began detailing our route to the front lines of Torshul.

"We have three hundred miles from the castle to the last estate just before the mountains. We'll have to ride through the snow, so it will take a fortnight at least. Once we're traveling along the eastern ridge of the Kreeg Mountains, it will be another hundred miles or so until we reach a place where the river is wide and deep enough to hire a boat to take us to the borders of Torshul. We'll have to walk from there."

"What about the horses?"

"They'll be used as payment to barter our way onto a boat."

"How far will we have to walk?"

His eyes were hard when they met mine, as if he was preparing to issue a challenge.

"A hundred and fifty miles."

"A hundred and fifty!" I croaked, the blood draining from my face.

"Give or take."

My eyes drifted to the map, and the images blurred.

"You can still change your mind."

"No." I rubbed my traitorous eyes. "How soon can we leave?"

"How soon can you pack your things?"

I perused the list and determined it would take me only a few hours. Olim stared off into the distance for several seconds, then said if I wished, we could leave the day after tomorrow.

"Pack as lightly as you can," he cautioned. "Bring sturdy frocks and extra coats and stockings. Remember, you'll eventually be carrying whatever you bring."

"Don't mention when we're leaving to the queen."

"Why not?"

"She doesn't want to know. Just trust me, all right?"

"Fine."

"Well." I rose from my chair. "As it appears there is much to be done tomorrow, I believe I'll retire early."

"See you in the morning," Olim said without looking up from his papers.

I pressed his shoulder affectionately to get his attention.

"Thank you, Olim. If there's anything I can do to repay you, please don't hesitate to ask."

He gave me a lop-sided smile. "I'll think of something."

Early the next morning, I sorted my gowns. Since becoming lady-in-waiting, my wardrobe mainly consisted of finely spun linens wholly unsuitable for traveling. There was no time to have any new frocks made, so I dug into my closet and found a few older, sturdy dresses to withstand the rigors of travel. I followed Olim's advice and resisted packing a gown for each day and hoped there would be opportunities to wash. I was so preoccupied with organizing my clothes I lost track of time and was a few minutes behind tending to the queen. When I entered her room, her eyes widened in shock, and she sighed in relief. She must have thought I'd left. I pulled her into a firm embrace.

"Not yet," I said around the tightness of my throat.

It was surreal to think this would be my last day in the castle for some time. Instead of dwelling in sadness or anxiety, I chose to spend my time quietly observing. Laria and the children were swathed in fur-lined coats and played in the snow of the inner courtyard. Their laughter echoed as they built ramparts and tossed snowballs at each other. At one point, the children decided it was them against their mother, and they chased her until her cheeks were flushed and she was laughing so hard she could barely breathe. A soft smile settled on my features, and though the upcoming journey left a nervous tingle in my belly, my heart was full of peace. We settled in front of a roaring fire in the library to warm up with hot drinking chocolate and listened to Laria tell stories. The smaller children dozed in our laps while Alyx poked at the flames to watch sparks fly into the chimney. The evening meal was a family affair away from the main hall. Though Laria didn't know when I was leaving, I'm certain she sensed it was soon. I hugged my nephews and nieces tightly that night and managed to contain my tears.

I acted naturally when I helped Laria prepare for bed. She cast me furtive glances while I brushed her hair, but I kept my eyes averted lest I break down and confess

I didn't plan on being there in the morning. When she settled into bed, I wished her goodnight without meeting her eye.

"Ula?"

Laria's voice was small, like that of a child. Her green eyes were wide and shimmering, and her knuckles were white from clutching the bedclothes.

"Yes?"

"You know how much I love you, right?"

No longer able to hold back the tears, they traced hotly down my cheeks, and I could do nothing but nod jerkily in affirmation.

"I love you, too." I clasped her hand. She held fast for a moment, then released me with a knowing smile.

Looking back, I'm certain Laria knew perfectly well she wouldn't see me in the morning, and she was saying goodbye in her own surreptitious way. It was easier than saying the actual word "goodbye," and meant so much more. She always believed she lived in my shadow, the shadow of a perfect daughter beloved by her parents for all the reasons Laria was ignored. But the truth was, it was I who wished to emulate her in some way. I could not be ambitious and witty like her, so I painted, played piano, and sang. Now, I'd summoned the courage to step out of *her* shadow, leave the nest, and fly.

Chapter 28

Snow crunched under my boots, echoing Olim's sure steps leading me to the stables before the sun barely crested the horizon. The canvas pack filled with my wardrobe weighed heavily on my shoulder. I shifted it and absently worried I wouldn't be able to handle carrying it later. I'd selected my sturdiest and plainest winter gowns. The one I currently wore was gray with a fur-lined hood and sleeves. I'd also donned an extra pair of stockings, a knit cap, and thick mittens. A scarf Mother made for my birthday protected my lower face and neck from the bitter cold.

Olim stopped and waited for our horses and cart to be produced, and I looked back at the castle one last time. The rising sun cast a golden hue against the stones, and wisps of smoke leisurely climbed into the sky. The servants would be the only ones awake at this hour, preparing the castle for the inhabitants' eventual awakening. Behind me, Olim cleared his throat, and I turned to see him staring at me expectantly, the reins of a sturdy, wooly-haired horse in his hand.

"Last chance to change your mind."

I could tell by his tone he was only saying this to satisfy himself that he had done everything he could to talk me out of it.

I handed him my bag and swiftly swung myself into the saddle. He secured the pack before mounting his own horse and reaching out for the lead rope secured to the stout draft horse pulling the cart. Without so much as a glance in my direction, he urged his horse into a steady walk and headed down the mountain. I followed, not looking back once.

The road through Market Town was heavily traveled and clear of snow—shopkeepers had diligently shoveled the front of their stalls for unimpeded perusal of their wares. Whenever I visited, people swarmed the city like bees, flitting from place to place and buzzing loudly. But this early in the morning, it was quiet, the closed shops frozen in time until the sun breathed life back into the world. Chimney smoke rose over the tops of buildings and lingered in a gray cloud over the city. People would emerge soon enough, and Market Town would thrum with activity.

The city sprawled out from the main road like points on a compass with the King's Road dividing the city in two from east to west. We left the main road and headed south into the tightly packed houses and businesses. During the siege almost nine years ago, most of the buildings were destroyed, leaving behind piles of rubble. There was little growth during King Conall's rule, but in the years since Laria took the throne, a bustling city rose from the ashes of despair. Praed and Ilano merchants mingled as neighbors, selling their wares in harmony.

When the sun lit the city with morning rays, people filtered onto the streets in a steady trickle bundled from head to toe, heads down as they passed. The wind funneled down the narrow alleys and whipped through the city in cold bursts. The sky was clear, and we stayed dry.

A group of children raced past, giggling and shouting over their shoulders. A young girl, dark hair unbound and billowing behind her, chased after them with a snowball in each hand. I slowed my horse to watch, but Olim yanked on my reins and I nearly pitched over the side.

I pushed myself back in the saddle and shot him a disapproving glare. "What are you doing?"

Behind me, liquid splashed on the ground, and the pungent odor of stale urine filled my nose.

"You were standing in the privy drain," Olim said.

I pinched my nostrils and trotted away from the ditch lining the street that drained out of the city.

"We're heading into the less savory part of the city," Olim said when he caught up to me. "No indoor garderobes or outhouses. Watch where you step and don't look up."

I wrinkled my nose and scowled, but followed his advice.

"I'm not staying here," I said.

Olim rolled his eyes, but I crossed my arms and staunchly refused to enter the three-story, peaked roofed building. Music and raucous voices drifted through the thin, dark paneled windows. A young woman in a simple frock with an unnecessarily low neckline swept the front stoop. My eyes darted to her then back to Olim. I raised an eyebrow, then pointed at the sign swinging above the door.

"They're known for their fruit pies, you ninny!"

I read the sign again, still unsure.

"And they distill their own brandy!" The annoyance in his voice was bordering on irritation.

"You're sure it's reputable?"

"Absolutely. Best inn this side of Market Town." He jabbed a thumb at his chest. "I'm going in. You sleep out here if you're so worried about it."

A gust of warm air and voices blew out when he opened the heavy, iron-slatted door and quickly vanished when it slammed shut behind him.

I blew into my hands, rubbed them together, and looked up and down the street. We hadn't passed another inn for hours, and I didn't know how far it was to the next one. I sighed, reread the name of the inn–Tarts & Spirits–and summoned my courage.

The ground floor was a vast space dominated by a bar in the middle and a large fireplace on the far wall. Long tables were packed with patrons, and barmaids darted between them with trays of ale and steaming plates of food. I inhaled the mouth-watering aroma of fresh bread, savory meats, stewed vegetables, and sweet pies. Musicians in the back of the room played a lively song about summer games, and couples twirled and stomped to the beat. Smiles abounded, from the people having a drink before heading home, to the smartly dressed bartender, to the round-faced barmaids.

There wasn't a woman of ill repute to be seen.

Olim was standing just inside the door as if he'd been waiting for me. I grinned sheepishly, and he shook his head.

"Told you," he said.

I rolled my eyes at his back as he led me to a vacant table. After we ordered food and had tankards of ale in front of us, Olim left to tend to the horses and secure rooms for the night. I took a few sips of ale and pushed it away.

"Problem, honey?"

I looked up into the blue eyes of a blonde girl no older than seventeen. Her full figure strained against her gray blouse and green corseted dress, and her pink cheeks dimpled in a wide smile.

"No problem," I said. "I'm a little cold, but the fire's helping."

"You poor thing! Your nose is red!" She reached out and grasped my hand. "And your fingers are frozen! Lemme get you somethin' to warm you up proper."

Before I could stop her, the girl disappeared behind a wall of people and headed toward the bar. She came back minutes later cradling a ceramic cup.

"There you go, honey. Drink it slow," the girl said.

Hesitantly, I sniffed the drink and was struck by a strong, biting odor that brought tears to my eyes. The girl nodded enthusiastically and motioned for me to drink. I took a tentative sip, and fire blazed down my throat. I coughed, but the girl encouraged me to drink more. The liquid warmed me from the inside, bringing feeling to my fingers and a flush to my cheeks. I smiled at the girl, and she nodded in satisfaction before returning to her duties.

Olim dropped into his chair shortly after our food arrived and conversation was non-existent while we ate. The room tipped and swayed, and my face felt fuzzy. I was completely aware of the effects of the alcohol, but I didn't care. My belly was full of a hot meal and my head with warm thoughts. I pushed the cup toward Olim. He eyed the light brown liquid, peered at me over the rim, and raised an eyebrow.

"It'll warm you up," I said, my words low and languid.

His brow crinkled disapprovingly, then he chewed at his lower lip. His eyes dropped to the cup. He shrugged and gulped down the remainder of the drink. He wiped his mouth and grinned. It was nice to be with this relaxed version of Olim. He deserved a break. He waved over the barmaid and ordered another round. The sweet girl blushed when Olim flashed an endearing smile and used his best manners, and I'm sure he didn't miss the suggestive wink and swaying of her hips when she walked away.

"Flirt," I said.

Olim's eyes widened and he pointed at himself as if to say, "Who? Me?"

"Careful," I said. "She'll fall in love with you and then you'll have two silly young women to deal with on this journey."

He rolled his eyes, but the pink sweeping across his cheeks belied his indifference.

Before I finished my second drink, my eyelids were heavy and I couldn't stop yawning. Olim announced it was time to retire, and I rose from my chair as if I were swimming toward the surface of the Rhyvor. I swayed, and Olim steadied me with an arm wrapped around my shoulders. He led me upstairs, dodging patrons and bracing me against the wall so I wouldn't fall. At the top of the stairs was a corridor that branched to the left and right. He took the left hallway and passed several doors before stopping. I leaned against the doorframe as he dug through his pockets and produced a key.

"I'm right next door if you need anything," he said.

My hand closed around the cool metal. It felt soothing on my warm skin, so I placed it against my cheek and sighed.

"There wasn't anyone available to help you prepare for bed," he continued. "But there should be fresh water."

"Thanks," I said drowsily. I fumbled the key into the lock and rattled it around far too long before a satisfying *click* filled the deserted corridor. I pushed the door open, and the enticing crackling of a fire drew me inside.

"Lock the door behind you," Olim said before the door closed.

"I thought you said it was safe?" I said.

"Do it anyway."

"All right, I will. Goodnight." He didn't move, so I closed the door in his face. I listened, but he didn't walk away until I slid the bolt, locking the door.

We stayed at inns the following two nights, but once we left the more populated areas, our progression was laborious. The snow came to the horses' knees, and we rode in silence as we trudged on, our horses stepping high to negotiate the terrain. Snow ceased to fall, but the wind bit against my bare cheeks. I wrapped a thick scarf across my nose and pulled the hood of my coat lower so only my eyes were visible. Though I wore two pairs of gloves, my fingers were stiff with cold after a few hours, and I wiggled my toes to keep the numbness at bay. Plumes of mist rose from the horses' noses as they huffed with exertion, and my mount's neck was dampening with sweat. Before I could suggest a rest, Olim pulled his horse to a stop and waited for me to catch up. He pointed to a stand of trees, and we sought shelter from the wind under its thick branches. The horses munched on a ration of oats while we filled our bellies with bread, hard cheese, and dried fruit. We didn't speak, and when Olim deemed the horses rested enough, we resumed our journey.

Through the layer of fabric wrapped around my face filtered in a hint of something acidic. I pulled down the scarf, leaned over my horse, and inhaled. It smelled of sweat, earth, and hay. I shrugged off the unusual odor, but soon the smell grew stronger and more pungent. It bit into my nose, watering my eyes. It smelled of rot, unclean bodies, and soiled stalls. I pinched my nose and looked at Olim.

"What's that awful smell?" I asked.

Olim raised his nose to the wind and took a deep breath.

"Our stop for the night," he said.

"What?" I sat up straighter and looked around.

"Be nice," he said before kicking his horse into a trot.

"Olim, where are we going?" We rode toward a line of black smoke rising from a peaked roof building surrounded by three smaller outbuildings. Poles were placed in even rows, and as we got closer I could see fabric stretched between them. The smell was stronger, but Olim didn't stop.

A man was crouched over a large structure draped with a reddish cloth he was scraping with a long knife. He looked up at our approach, and when we were close enough to make out his features, I couldn't help gagging. It wasn't fabric on the poles or laid out in front of him. They were skins.

"Good evening, Tandir," Olim said. He dismounted, and the man wiped his hands and extended one for Olim to shake.

"Good evening, Olim. Was worried you wouldn't make it before nightfall," Tandir said. He turned to me, the corners of his brown eyes crinkling as he smiled. "My lady."

Olim motioned for me to dismount, but I had serious reservations about staying. Not only was the odor overwhelming, but I found the mess of blood and flesh disturbing.

"Ula," Olim said as he tugged me off the saddle. "Let me introduce you to Tandir. He's been gracious enough to allow us to stay tonight."

I stumbled forward and tried not to look at anything but Tandir's friendly expression. He held out a hand, and I placed the tips of my fingers on his rough palms. He bowed over our clasped hands, his long, gray-streaked brown hair obscuring his face. My eyes were drawn to the block with the skin draped over it. Bits of flesh littered the ground, and a knife longer than my forearm gleamed wet and sharp in the evening gloom. Bile rose in my throat, and I swallowed several times to keep from being sick.

"Tandir is the best tanner in northern Praed," Olim said. "He makes leather softer than goose down."

Tandir dropped my hand and chuckled low in his chest. "Come in out of the cold. My wife's been cooking all day."

We followed Tandir toward the main house, and I peered closer at the skin. Grayish-tan fur was mixed with the discarded flesh. A deer. I winced at my idiocy. Tandir turned raw hides into leather, a smelly process.

A small boy no older than thirteen ran out of the house and took our horses without a word, his eyes on the ground and urgency in his movements.

"My boy," Tandir said. "In that sullen stage of life. Doesn't talk except to grunt and complain."

A bark of laughter thrust out of me, and with it went my tension. Tandir led us into a front room with shelves of rolled up leather along one wall. In the middle of the room was a dining table, and on the opposite wall a fireplace flanked by two chairs. At the back of the room was a staircase, and from the entryway next to it came a girl carrying servingware. The scene reminded me of the houses I'd visited in Ilano, and I moved to the fire to hide my melancholy. I blocked out the sounds, feeling guilty for not offering to help. The savory scent of stewed meat soon drew me to the table, and I wordlessly sat next to Olim. Tandir locked eyes with a lithe woman with light blonde hair, then the pair turned to me with matching smiles.

"My wife, Anna." Tandir gestured toward the woman with kind green eyes. She smiled warmly and placed a loaf of bread in front of me that'd been hollowed out and filled with chunks of meat and root vegetables.

"You must be so tired," Anna said, her voice soft and motherly. "I'll show you to your room after dinner."

"You'll be sleeping with me!" the girl said. "I'm Didi. I just turned eighteen yesterday." She flipped a lock of blonde hair over her shoulder and stuck her nose in the air. The boy who'd tended our horses snorted rudely, and she elbowed him. This triggered a heated back-and-forth exchange that ended with Tandir slamming a fist on the table.

"We have guests!" He jerked his head toward Olim and me, and the siblings slunk over their dinners with mumbled apologies.

"I remember being their ages," I said to fill the tense silence that followed. "It can be quite challenging."

"For everyone," Anna said with a smirk.

Olim and Tandir dissolved into a discussion about the best bark to finish off the tanning process while Didi and her brother poked each other under the table. Anna divided her attention between shooting glares at the children and asking me questions about our journey. When I told her we were headed to the front, the table fell silent and the family stared at me open mouthed.

"W-why would you go there?" Anna said.

I glanced at Olim, but he remained focused on eating, so I turned back to Anna.

"There's someone there I need to talk to," I said.

Anna narrowed her eyes. "Couldn't it wait? You could be killed."

"So could he." I didn't mean to sound so callous, but I was too tired for politeness. Before I could consider offering an apology, Anna covered her mouth to smother a sob and hurried away from the table. My chest tightened with guilt and regret, my face warm from embarrassment. I could barely look at Tandir, but I forced myself to rotate in my seat and meet his sorrowful gaze.

"I didn't mean to offend," I said, my voice straining through my painfully tight throat.

"Don't trouble yourself, my lady," Tandir said, his tone equally rough. He blinked, shook his head, and coughed. "Didi, show Miss Audrey upstairs."

"Yes, Papa," Didi said quietly.

I rose to follow and looked back at Olim. His shoulders were slumped and his blue eyes shimmered, but he quickly returned his attention to finishing his meal before I could ask questions.

Didi led me down a short hallway into a small room containing a dresser, a modest sized bed with a trunk at the foot, and a table and chairs tucked under a window. My things had been brought up and left in a heap on one of the chairs, and I shuffled over and dug out a nightgown. The rustle of fabric behind me indicated Didi was undressing for bed as well.

"I'm sorry about Mama," Didi said, her bright voice muffled. I turned around as her blonde head popped out the top of the simple white linen nightgown. She jumped onto the bed, wiggled under the covers, and patted the spot beside her.

The effort to smile took all my energy, and I gracelessly dropped onto the bed. Didi giggled and tucked a quilt around my shoulders. Idly, I stroked the fur of the deer pelt draped across our chests, the stiff guard hairs pricking my soft skin. Didi chattered on as lonely girls do, into the void without requiring a response. Laria and I used to talk late into the night during our childhood at Riverstone, conversations of carefree girls before the siege took away our innocence.

"Mama's worried about Ernan, but Papa says not to talk about it because that makes it worse."

"Who's Ernan?"

"My older brother. He's a soldier. Papa says he did it to disobey him, but Ernan always wanted to be a soldier. He said it's more exciting than soaking hides in piss all day."

I squeezed my eyes shut and groaned. Anna's son was fighting in the war. No wonder I'd upset her. I couldn't seem to control my stupid mouth.

"I hope he comes home," I said. I wanted all the sons, brothers, fathers, and friends to come home. But I wasn't the naive girl listening to stories and telling secrets under the blankets at Riverstone. After watching our stables burn and living in the bowels of the castle as a laundress for three years, I'd learned life was cruel and unfair. Not every story ends happily ever after.

But it was worth a try.

Our stay at a farmhouse the following evening was less dramatic, and we once again set out at sunrise. A fresh dusting of snow had fallen while we slept, and powder bloomed behind us as we continued south. In the afternoon, we stopped to rest next to a lake, its surface glittering with shards of ice. A breeze scattered snowflakes and rattled the frozen grass. I shivered as if I were a blade of crystalized prairie grass and tucked my hands under my knees. A bird rustled in the long grass, stuck its head out, and chirped at me. I smiled and held still, barely breathing. It hopped out and tilted its head, its tail feathers bobbing up and down and dotting the snow. The bird could fit in the palm of my hand, but it's breast fluttered mightily when it trilled a song that echoed across the frozen lake. Its body was brown with flecks of black, but when it bounced around pecking at the snow, its wings flapped, revealing a pop of yellow. In a flash, it flew away, and seconds later Olim's footsteps crunched beside me.

"Time to go," he said.

I stood and brushed the snow off my backside while gazing blankly in the direction we'd come. I could barely see the tip of the Center of the World, the highest peak in Praed, rising from the gray haze, Praed Castle merely a memory in its shadow.

"How far away are we now?" My voice was so quiet even the plume of white rising from my mouth was small.

"A hundred miles or so," Olim said as he mounted his horse.

I grabbed the pommel of my saddle and hauled myself up with a groan. It'd been a long time since I'd journeyed this far south, but it was always by carriage. Before I followed Olim, I looked back toward the mountain, then east toward Riverstone. I knew the area around my childhood home like an old friend. The Rhyvor, the

Sessyl Forest spreading like a vast, green blanket on the opposite bank, every rise of prairie, and every inch of rocky shore. Ahead me was the unknown, but I wasn't about to run home now.

The sun dipped below the horizon, and it was becoming more difficult to see. Lamplights from a house stretched across the snow like beacons, and as we neared the front entrance, the door opened wide, and a figure stepped forward holding a lantern aloft.

"Hello there!" a man called out. "Is that Olim?"

"It is," Olim said as we came into the light.

Two men appeared to take our reins, and we dismounted. My legs ached, limp with fatigue, and I gratefully allowed myself to be led into the warmth of the manor house.

"Peter?" Olim reached out a hand to the man in the doorway.

Before he could reply, a woman's voice called from within the house.

"Have they arrived?" The woman appeared, and in my weary state, I didn't immediately recognize her. She was tall, perhaps my mother's age, with golden hair interspersed with gray, and light brown eyes.

"They have, my lady," the man said before bowing and moving aside.

"Thank goodness!" She took my hands. "You look spent. Come. Let's get you out of those wet clothes. We have prepared a late supper for you."

The lady led me up the stairs, and I glanced over my shoulder and spied Olim place a few coins into the hands of the butler. A knot formed in the pit of my stomach. I would owe Olim more than gratitude after this.

"You must be half frozen to death." The lady drew me into a modest room warmed by a roaring fire.

I unwrapped my face, removed my gloves, and stood before the flames, fanning out my fingers to collect its glowing warmth. Behind me, the lady moved about the room directing a maid to pour a hot bath while I continued staring blankly into the hearth.

"Come, my dear," the lady said. "Let's get you out of these clothes and into that hot water."

They removed my clothing, but I lacked the energy to help after a long day of travel. My limbs hung limply by my side as I shuffled into the bath and lowered myself into the water with a sigh of relief. It wasn't until the maid started scrubbing my tired body that I remembered my manners.

"Apologies, ma'am," I said to the lady as she lay my wet clothes to dry by the fire. "But I have been remiss in introducing myself. I'm Ula Audrey, and I thank you for your hospitality."

"Oh, we've met before, though it's been many years," she said.

My face reddened in embarrassment.

She smiled, a full, gentle smile that crinkled the corners of her eyes. "Don't trouble yourself about it. You were much younger, as was I. I am Lady Iseult Tristram."

She'd aged considerably since I last saw her, but I recalled she was the wife of a knight who served with my father. I resisted the urge to ask after her husband. His absence at our arrival spoke of his fate.

"How are Berin and Branwin?" I asked. Berin was a year or two older than Laria, and even as a child had been intimidatingly large with ash brown hair and matching eyes. In contrast, his younger sister, Branwin, was petite and fair-haired like her mother.

"Branwin married three years ago," Lady Tristam said, smiling proudly. "She's just had her first child."

"Congratulations," I said. The maid held out a towel and I stepped out of the bath. After I was thoroughly dry, she helped me into a simple gown for dinner. "And Berin?"

Her happy expression plummeted. "Fighting with the king. He was knighted a few years back. It was a proud moment for him."

"I'm sure for you as well," I said.

"It's what his father always wished for him." She indicated the door. "Come now. You must be starving and in need of a good night's sleep."

Olim was waiting in the dining room, and the three of us took our seats as platters were placed in front of us. Olim hungrily piled his plate high with fish pies, bread with berry preserves, soft cheese, and stuffed tubers while I delicately assembled a plate of my own with small, ladylike portions despite my growling stomach.

"There's no need to be so modest," Lady Tristram laughed. "No one here will judge you for eating larger portions. You need your strength."

Without requiring further prompting, I filled my plate and stuffed mouthfuls into my cheeks to quell my ravenous hunger. For several minutes, the only sound in the room was the scraping of utensils as Olim and I ate until our bellies were distended. I drank glass after glass of weak wine to wash down the meal, and rested against my chair, too tired and full to bring another bite to my mouth.

"You poor souls," Lady Tristram said. "Is there anything else I can offer you?"

"You have done more than enough, my lady," Olim said, rising. I followed his example, swaying on my tired feet. "We should retire for the night since we'll be leaving at dawn."

"Of course," she said. "My maid will escort you back to your room, Miss Audrey. Goodnight and good rest to you both, and please accept my wishes for a safe journey."

"Thank you, Lady Tristram," I said, stifling a yawn. "We are most grateful."

She smiled at me then turned a wistful expression toward Olim.

"If you happen to see my son..."

"I shall pass along your affections," Olim said with a gentle smile.

Lady Tristram inclined her head in thanks, and we took our leave.

"Do you know Berin?" I whispered as we ascended the stairs to our rooms, the maid close behind as chaperone.

"Yes."

The maid once again was on her own when it came to pulling off my clothes and helping me into my nightgown. I mumbled a thanks and collapsed onto the soft bed. Within seconds, I fell into a deep, weary sleep. My legs and back were sore, and I worried if I had the fortitude to complete this long journey. Then a memory of dancing with Finton flashed in my mind, and I could practically feel his arm around my waist and the sensation of my hand in his. The recollection gave me renewed purpose, for I refused to accept that our final moments together were truly our last.

The following two days passed in much the same way as we traversed toward the southern boundary of Praed. Though I collapsed into bed every night, my stamina grew stronger. We emerged from a farmer's home to the silent wonder of an early morning bathed in the orange and pink glow of a sunrise. Snow fell so thickly I could barely see a few feet in front of my horse's hooves, yet Olim led us with a determination that gave me absolute confidence in his ability to find our route. I tucked my chin tightly against my chest to avoid the cold flakes and wrapped my fingers in the long mane of my horse to warm them. Our progress was slow due to the inclement weather, and I feared the delay would put us behind Olim's tight schedule.

During a momentary break in the storm, I glanced around at the bleak, white landscape. There was nothing but vast prairie, and in the distance, I could barely make out the tops of chimneys. Olim pointed us toward them, the snow swirling in thick ribbons up the dark spires. I called out to Olim to ask where we were going, but between the wind and the scarf wrapped around my face, he couldn't hear me.

The house emerged, its peaked roofs buried under several inches of white. Frost sparkled on the red and gray stones, and the last rays of the sun reflected off the rows of windows. I reined in my horse and pulled down my scarf to inhale deep breaths of cool air. A moat surrounded the house, a shield against invaders. We crossed a stone bridge and rode through the gatehouse, ice cracking under the horses' hooves. Torches flickered in the courtyard, sending tendrils of orange and yellow dancing over the snow covered hedgerows and vines climbing up the side of the house. Servants rushed forward to take our horses and escort us to the front entrance. The heavy doors creaked open and banged against the walls, announcing our arrival.

The butler ushered us down the corridor past the kitchens and pantry and into the little hall where private dinners were held. Covered dishes awaited us, and my hunger became so overwhelming I didn't notice the man at the head of the table. He shot out of his seat, sending his chair skittering across the polished floor. I jumped back in alarm and collided with Olim's chest.

"Finally!" the man said, adjusting his golden doublet. He brushed a delicate, pale hand down his chest and tucked a strand of hair behind his ear.

"Apologies, my lord," Olim said. "There's a storm."

"Yes, yes." The man waved a hand toward a chair to his right. "Please be seated, Miss Audrey. Sir Olim, you may dine in the kitchens."

Olim's eyes met mine. I raised an eyebrow, and he shrugged one shoulder. Whether in a dining room or kitchens like a common servant, Olim didn't care where he took his meals.

"Miss Audrey." The man frantically gestured toward the chair again.

I rushed to my seat before the poor man had an apoplexy. Servants appeared and uncovered the dishes, revealing poached fish, dried fruit, and warm bread with butter. Once they retreated into the shadows, my host meticulously cut his food into bite-sized pieces and carefully placed them in his mouth. Absently, I nibbled on a piece of bread and watched him dab his clean lips with a handkerchief. There was something familiar about him. His mousy brown hair was pulled back from his face and so thick with oil it didn't move. A faint tinge of pink colored his pale cheeks. Was he ill?

"Pardon, my lord," I said.

His dark eyes that were much too small for his face fixed on me like prey that's noticed a predator. He swallowed and straightened, laying his handkerchief on his lap. He inclined his head toward me, and I realized I'd been staring.

"Are you well, my lord?" I asked.

"Yes, thank you, Miss Audrey," he said. "And you?"

"I'm well. Tired." I half smiled, but he didn't return the sentiment. When he didn't reply, I said, "I'm sorry, my lord, but we haven't been properly introduced. You seem to know me, but I can't recall your name."

"Oh!" A sharp smile cut across his face, but it didn't reach his eyes. "Brock Gefroy, tenth generation Gefroy of Doraka Manor."

Oh. Oh my. I tried swallowing a morsel of bread and choked. He recoiled as I coughed until tears came to my eyes. His dark eyes were full of concern, but most likely because he worried I'd spit food on him. The last time I saw Brock Gefroy was almost nine years ago when he'd visited Riverstone to court Laria. It didn't end well.

"Thank you," I wheezed. "For your hospitality." I hunkered down and avoided his stare. "Is your father well?"

"No." He scraped a knife across his plate, making me wince at the sharp screech. "He's been confined to bed since my mother's death three years ago."

"I'm so sorry." I reached a comforting hand toward his shoulder but pulled back when he flinched.

"It's been trying," Brock said with a sigh. "The estate has been struggling. Father tried to secure an advantageous marriage, but…"

His attempt to make a favorable impression on Laria failed miserably.

"The king has been generous in allowing us to pay the bare minimum of taxes."

The king probably had nothing to do with it, but I didn't say as much.

The rest of dinner was awkward. Brock was worse at small talk than Laria. I suffered through the meal as long as possible before asking to be excused.

"Of course." Brock bowed. His arms hung limply at his sides, but his fingers wiggled anxiously. I curtseyed, but before I could retreat, he cleared his throat, making me pause.

"Miss Audrey," he said. "I accepted Sir Olim's request for lodging so I could speak with you."

"All right." I edged toward the door and locked eyes with a maid. Her blank expression wasn't exactly encouraging, but it didn't signal fear either.

"The queen. Does she…do you think…" He shifted and picked at the table, inspected his pristine clothing, and tucked imaginary loose strands of hair behind his ear. I was too tired to wait for him to collect himself.

"Speak plainly, my lord," I said. "What troubles you?"

"Does the queen remember me, do you think? We didn't part on good terms, you understand."

I sighed. "She probably does. But if she harbors ill will toward you, she's never spoken of it. That was a long time ago."

"If that's the case, can she secure a match for me? When things are…more settled?"

My instinct was to retort that the queen had more important matters to worry about, but the desperation on his face made me pause. The fine clothing he wore did nothing to hide his thin frame and drooping shoulders. His fingertips drummed out a rapid rhythm on the table. He didn't simply *want* a marriage. He *needed* one. Sympathy washed over me, softening my resolve.

"Of course, my lord. It must be a terrible burden trying to keep the estate running on your own."

His cheeks reddened, and he looked away before tears fell from his shining eyes.

"Yes." His voice was rough from scraping across emotions he struggled to repress.

Not wishing to distress him further by bearing witness to his misery, I curtseyed and excused myself to bed. There were hardships to be found all across Praed. Even though Laria made significant changes, there was still much to be done.

A thick blizzard swirled around us, and the frigid temperatures stabbed my skin like knives. I shivered from the depths of my soul and could no longer feel my fingertips. I puffed hot air against my hands and felt little relief from the cold, but I kept doing it anyway for lack of any other recourse.

"Are we nearing the mountains?" I called out to be heard above the howling wind.

"Soon," came Olim's muffled reply. "We need to rest the horses."

We found a copse of trees near the base of a rocky hillside to wait out the worst of the storm. Olim fed the horses, and I regarded their weary expressions.

"I wish we could rest them a little longer," I said. "They're very tired."

"They'll be all right," he said. "They're bred for endurance." We sat close together to keep warm while we ate our afternoon portions of bread, cheese, and jerked meat.

"I wish we could build a fire." I rubbed my hands together.

He wrapped an arm around my shoulder. "We won't be here for long and we can't afford to waste the supplies."

Another four days passed before we stayed at another estate. This one wasn't the house of another of Laria's former suitors and we enjoyed a pleasant evening. They sent us into a calm morning with saddlebags full of jerked venison and fresh rolls, and I'm not ashamed to admit I ate a hearty portion before the sun crested the horizon. Olim gave me a disparaging look, but I stared back defiantly, daring him to say anything. He didn't.

Progress.

Chapter 29

A storm delayed our leaving a quaint hunting cabin for several hours. Olim paced in front of the tiny window and peered out at the blanket of white buffeting the house. The walls shook with the battering of snow, the wind howling down the chimney and threatening to extinguish the fire I huddled up to for warmth.

"The trees are getting thicker," I said, hoping small talk would cease his endless pacing.

"Yeah," he spoke in a distracted tone. He looked out the window again, stalked to the fire to warm his hands for a few seconds, then went back to the window to check the snowfall.

"Are we heading into a forest?"

"Uh-huh. The Ridhal Forest."

"Is it near the Kreeg Mountains?" Once we reached the Kreeg Mountains, I knew it was only a matter of time before we left Praed.

"It borders the northernmost peaks." He barely glanced at me before leaning closer to the thin pane of glass covered in steadily thickening frost. "I think the snow's let up enough for us to leave."

Snow continued to fall, but as the light waned, the wind relented, and we climbed into our saddles and hurried through the gloom at a trot to make up for lost time. I could sense Olim's unease as the sun sunk below the skyline, casting shadows across the cool blue glow of the snow. As the sun disappeared and the moon rose in the black sky, its glow illuminated each snowflake drifting quietly to the ground. The only sounds were the crunching of the horses' hooves and the squeaking of the cart's wheels echoing in the stillness. A sharp, mournful cry pierced the cold night air, startling my horse and raising the hairs on the back of my neck. Olim froze beside me, then signaled for me to hurry. Though I could only see his eyes, they told me he was nervous.

"What is it?" I whispered hoarsely.

The sound came again, a chilling call that sent icicles through my veins more thoroughly than any blizzard. It was closer now, echoing strangely through the trees. I held my breath and listened, until I realized the cry did not fade in the distance as an echo does, but rather increased in volume. Olim glanced over his shoulder, then handed me the cart horse's lead rope.

"What's wrong?" I asked, panic making my voice tremble.

Olim drew his sword and placed himself between me and the trees. My horse shied nervously, and even the normally subdued cart horse was wide-eyed and snorting.

"Wolves!" Olim shouted.

Another cry, louder, closer, sent shivers down my spine, as if I'd plunged into the spring fed waters of the Rhyvor. My heart thudded against my chest, my breathing rapid and hoarse. Wolves rarely ventured into the interior of the country after mass exterminations hundreds of years ago. They were considered pests, a threat to the horse industry, and were killed on sight. It was widely speculated that there still existed a population of wolves in the Sessyl Forest, but these tales were meant to frighten us into being home by dark.

Olim and I cantered along the tree line, the cart rattling and the horses puffing out large plumes of air into the icy night. Snow fell in large flakes, but not as thickly as mere moments ago, and I summoned my courage and peered into the forest. The dark trees were eerily silent, the hush permeating the night more frightening than the calls, and my teeth chattered and knees trembled. Arising as if from the darkness itself came a long, low howl, and then dozens of glowing orbs glittered from between the branches. I screamed, and my horse reared, nearly sending me toppling backwards to the ground. There was a snarl close to my right foot, and Olim's sword flashed in the moonlight. A squeal followed, and I caught a glimpse of fur disappearing into the woods.

"Go!" Olim shouted. "I'll cover you! Head straight and don't stop."

I kicked my horse into a gallop, controlling our frantic dash from the scene so I wouldn't lose my grip on the cart horse. Our supplies crashed against the cart, and more growls and yelps arose behind me, but I didn't look back.

In the distance were lights, not from shining eyes or stars, but emanating from a house. I glanced behind my shoulder to tell Olim we were almost there, but just as I shifted my weight, something grasped my left foot and tugged hard. Pain radiated up my leg like flames on seasoned wood, rendering me incoherent. My horse bolted to the right, and I cried out as I was pitched to the ground. Vaguely, I heard Olim calling my name, but his voice was overshadowed by an ominous growl. My horse shrieked and retreating hoofbeats accompanied by the careening of the cart faded into the distance. I pushed off the ground and lifted my face, only to become paralyzed with fear.

It's strange the thoughts that race through your mind when you're afraid, the seemingly random and senseless chatter that springs to the forefront. When I locked eyes with the snarling beast before me, my first thought was that none of the stories described how massive they are. The wolf was enormous, its shoulder easily coming up to my horse's belly, with a thick body and dense black fur. It must have weighed a hundred pounds and stared at me with bright, yellow eyes. Its lip curled, revealing sharp, white teeth, and moonlight glinted off a trail of saliva dripping thickly from its mouth. The growl rumbling in its throat was so low my ears barely registered it over the rush of blood in my veins. I couldn't move, couldn't shout, could hardly breathe. My brain screamed for me to run, but the message wouldn't reach my numb limbs. Something tickled at the back of my mind, a sensation that seemed out of place on my body. Slowly, I pressed a hand against my side, and recognized the shape of the dagger Laria gave me. I didn't know how to use it, but it was better than nothing. The wolf watched me intently, its snarls intensifying, and just as I freed the blade, it lunged.

Fragments of sensations crowded into my brain—warmth spreading over my hand, screams hurting my ears, a pungent smell in my nose, and a heavy weight pressing me into the snow. I squeezed my eyes shut and waited for the pain. A heartbeat, then two passed, and the weight shifted, and something shook me hard. I flailed wildly and something grabbed my wrists tight enough to break bones. Muffled sounds reached my ears, then a voice, then shouting. Cautiously, I opened my eyes, and Olim's face swam before me. He was shaking me by the arms and calling my name. Slowly, I turned and looked down at the beast laying limp by my side, the snow stained red by its blood. Snapping out of my trance, I crawled backwards, kicking the animal in the head as I did.

"Ula, look at me."

My eyes met his, and my breathing quickened.

"Are you hurt?" he asked. He shook me and repeated himself when I didn't answer.

"My ankle," I said.

"Come on." He helped me to my feet. "My horse is over there."

He supported my weight as I hobbled to his horse, and he practically threw me into the saddle. He led the horse back to the dead wolf, leaned over and wrenched the dagger from its chest before climbing up behind me. We rode dangerously fast, following the tracks of the other horses, until we found them, tossing their heads and whinnying into the night, their leads clutched in the hands of shadowy figures.

Burning tears blurred the shapes crowded around the horses into ghouls, their spindly arms outstretched to end in curling fingers. Sharp sounds barked into the night, and I became convinced that after our narrow escape from the wolves, we were about to fall prey to a different sort of predator. Before I could open my mouth to warn Olim, a large shape stepped forward and spoke in a distinctly human voice.

"Ho there!" a man called out. "That wouldn't be Olim, would it?"

"Yes," Olim called back. "We've met with some trouble."

"I can see that."

Once he was close enough, the light of the moon revealed a middle-aged man with graying hair and deeply lined eyes. He was broad chested and thick legs bulged against his worn leather breeches. I could barely make out his face past a bushy beard, but his eyes sparkled kindly up at us.

"The house is just over there," he said, pointing behind him. Our horses calmed down and were being led by shapes I now recognized as people. "Is anyone injured?"

"The lady," Olim said, kicking the horse forward.

"I'll rouse the missus."

The man ran ahead, and the house shortly appeared nestled amid a grove of trees. The worn, moss-covered stones made the house look older than the castle. It was small yet sturdy, with one chimney billowing smoke into the star-studded sky. A young boy came forward and took our horse's reins, and Olim helped me dismount. He insisted on carrying me inside, and I was too tired and painful to argue.

The house twinkled with lit candles, and the flames of an enormous hearth reflected off expertly crafted polished furniture. Olim sat me on a chair by the fire and carefully placed my injured ankle on a footstool. A maid carrying a bowl of water came in followed by an older, voluptuous woman.

"Let's see the damage, hmm?" the woman said, grinning genially.

She reached for my leg, but I instinctively pulled away. A flash of irritation crossed her face, but she relaxed. "You're right, young miss. We haven't been properly introduced. Mac!" She called over her shoulder in the direction of the hallway, and the large man lumbered into the room. He was bigger up close, even devested of his heavy woolen coat.

"What's the matter then, Ellie?" he asked.

"We haven't been introduced. I assume that's Olim," she said, indicating my companion.

"Right. Olim, this here's my wife, Ellie. And you, young lady, I assume must be Miss Ula Audrey?"

I nodded, still trembling with cold.

"I'm Mac. Pleasure to meet you."

"If we're quite finished introducing ourselves," Olim said tersely. "Miss Audrey is injured."

Ellie thrust her fists against her generous hips and fixed Olim with a stern glare that spoke of years of practice disciplining children. "I can't treat the girl if she's too nervous to let me."

Olim crossed his arms and turned his back while Ellie removed my boots and started peeling away the three layers of stockings.

"Come on, lad." Mac patted Olim on the back. "I have a spread laid out for you. I'm sure you're starved."

Olim reluctantly allowed himself to be led away amid Ellie's chuckles.

"That's a fine knight you have there," she said. "Lucky, too. Maybe luckier you wore so many layers."

"Yes," I said. "It's been very cold." My voice was small, barely audible, and quivering.

Ellie carefully removed the last stocking and inspected my leg. "Luckier it was just playing with you," she murmured.

"What?" I breathed.

"Was it wolves that attacked you?" she asked, her eyes darkly serious.

I nodded shakily.

"To be honest, miss, it wouldn't matter if you wore armor. A wolf could bite straight through to your bones if he wanted to."

"It pulled me off the horse."

She nodded knowingly. "Trying for a better grip I'd say."

I shivered and looked down.

Blood coated my foot and lower leg, originating from a few small punctures and two larger gashes. Heat flushed my cheeks then dropped to my toes as a wave of nausea overtook me. I took several deep breaths to steady my nerves, but the scent of blood left me dizzy. Ellie poured water over the wounds, the blood diluting to a rosy pink.

I used to like pink. Now, every time I see the color I'll struggle not to vomit.

She probed the bruised area with her fingers, making me wince. She twisted my foot and I cried out, tears spilling from my eyes.

"I know it hurts like nothing else," she said. "But it doesn't feel like any bones are broken. Lucky girl."

She cleaned and dressed the wound, and I wished Finton was in her place, tending to my injuries as he had done almost a year ago. A whole year. Tears of remorse fell from my eyes as I considered how much time we lost.

"I can still ride," I said.

She looked at me, and I stared back in grim determination. She considered commenting, thought the better of it, and finished wrapping my ankle.

"I'll pack you some fresh dressing. And wash your stockings."

She lifted the blood-soaked garments from the floor, and my stomach flipped at the sight of the heap of red fabric twisted together like intestines. She balled them up in her fists and regarded me as if I were a puzzle she couldn't solve.

"Thank you," I said. "You have been very kind."

"I'll have some food brought in." She smiled and left without expressing whatever she struggled to contain.

Moments later, Olim and Mac came in, and a maid set a tray beside me containing food and drink.

"We didn't want you to eat alone," Mac said.

For the next several minutes, I shoveled food in my mouth while Olim and Mac spoke companionably.

"Not many people can boast of killing a wolf," Mac said. "Most will go their whole lives without even seeing one."

"Those people are lucky," Olim said.

Mac chuckled and slapped Olim's shoulder. "You have my people to thank for that. My family have been keeping the packs in check ever since they were driven out of the city."

"Why haven't you bothered to wipe them out completely?"

Mac shrugged. "Not hurting anybody way out here, and there's plenty of game to go around."

"An interesting perspective, but your willingness to live in harmony with those monsters nearly cost us our lives."

Mac shrugged again, as if this was a fact of life. Out here in the desolate places where no one ventured, survival was a day-to-day trial.

"Are our horses safe?" Olim asked, his brow furrowed suspiciously.

"Oh, yeah." Mac bit off a chunk of bread. "Wolves don't come near the house. And they only come out at night, so you can travel easy in the morning."

Olim didn't seem entirely convinced, but he held his tongue.

"Will you be able to travel?" Olim asked me when I finished eating.

I moved my leg from side to side to assess the pain. It was bordering on unbearable, but I hid my discomfort behind my raised goblet.

"I'll be fine," I said. "It's not broken." Even if it was, I would have continued. Olim eyed me speculatively, but between my glare and knowing I was too stubborn to quit, he said nothing.

He was growing as a person.

Ellie announced that we, particularly me, needed rest, and Olim insisted on carrying me to my room to prevent further injury. Once I was settled onto a chaise in a modest bedroom, Olim was shooed away and sent to his own room. The lady of the house herself helped me undress and tucked me into bed like a child.

"Such a long journey for a young miss," Ellie said, more to herself than to me. "And without a chaperone."

"Olim *is* my chaperone," I said. "The king himself assigned him to protect and watch over me."

"I don't mean to insinuate anything," she said. "I hope the rest of your travels are free from misfortune."

It was on the tip of my tongue to apologize for my tone, but my resentment prevented me. It occurred to me that an unmarried woman traveling alone with a man would raise questions, but I was prepared to either ignore or defend myself against any disparaging comments. Olim was one the most honorable men I knew, and I felt completely safe with him. To me, that mattered more than the talk people would whisper behind our backs.

"Thank you again for your hospitality, Ellie," I said. "Goodnight."

"Goodnight, Miss Audrey," she said. "May your sleep be restful and free of nightmares."

The dear sentiment Ellie left me with unfortunately did not take. My dreams were filled with fangs and glowing yellow eyes, and I spent most of the night tossing in bed and waking with fright. When I awoke at first light, I was certain I only managed to sleep a few hours. My appearance most likely confirmed this as Olim studied me with a raised brow. I dared him to say anything with a dark glare, but he was wise enough not to comment. Most of the household was still abed, but Mac met us at the stables and sat with me in companionable silence while Olim saddled our horses. At one point, Olim ducked inside to ensure all our things were intact after the hasty trip the cart took, and Mac used the opportunity to speak privately.

"Olim wasn't very free with the details as to why you're taking this risky journey," Mac said quietly. "There's a lot more danger than wolves waiting for you once you leave Praed. I only hope it's worth it in the end."

I swallowed the lump in my throat. "I do, too."

Olim re-emerged and helped me into my saddle. My left foot dangled out of the stirrups to avoid making the throbbing pain in my ankle worse by putting weight on it. Olim shook Mac's hand briefly, then without further ceremony, we departed the last dwelling before crossing the Praed border.

It stopped snowing by the time we broke through the trees, and very little remained on the ground except for a dusting on the peaks of the Kreeg Mountains. We rode along a trickling creek that soon met the Dehan River, which Olim explained would widen into a travelable waterway.

It was much easier to negotiate the terrain once we left Praed and the snow behind, but it still required concentration to avoid rockslides and loose stones. With every movement of the horse, the pulse in my ankle throbbed, and my boot seemed tighter. I could tell by Olim's relaxed posture we were making good time, so I broached the idea of taking a break. Not only was I hungry, but the pain in my ankle was becoming unbearable, and I would need to change the dressing.

I gritted my teeth and carefully pulled off my boot while Olim tended to the horses and unloaded some food for our afternoon repast. Each inch of boot that brushed over my ankle brought tears to my eyes, but I squeezed them tightly and recited passages from books to keep my mind off the pain. I paused to catch my breath and noticed Olim heading toward me. The last thing I wanted was for him to see the difficulty I was experiencing, so I rolled up my scarf, jammed it in my mouth, and bit down hard while I wrenched the boot off in one hard pull. My head swam and I nearly passed out, but I didn't scream.

"Do you need any help with that?" Olim asked, indicating the soiled dressing.

"No," I gasped.

I took a minute to compose myself, then unwound the bandage. The wounds had opened, and blood oozed during the ride, but not very much. Olim handed me a flask of watered-down wine, and I poured a little over the bite marks. I hissed.

"Talk to me, Olim," I said through gritted teeth.

"We'll have to set up a camp tonight," he said. "No one respectable lives out here, so we'll be missing out on a soft bed."

"I can manage," I said through gritted teeth. The wounds were cleaned of blood, and I was patting them dry, careful to avoid opening them further.

"So far, we've been lucky to avoid bandits. I've been told they roam these forests near the mountains."

"Luck seems to be our theme on this trip."

"Perhaps it's just too cold and wet this time of year. Poor riding conditions don't bode well for vagrants looking to rob travelers."

"No."

I carefully re-wrapped my injured ankle and laid back to rest before pulling on my boot. Olim handed me a piece of buttered bread, and I took a bite and chewed lazily as the throbbing subsided in my ankle. Above me, droplets of water trickled through the branches of trees, but we remained dry beneath the shelter of the leaves. A few rocks tumbled down the mountainside followed by the skitter of clawed feet. I sat up, the hairs on the back of my neck raised, and I nervously scanned my surroundings. I heard the sound again, and my eyes darted to a twisted tree projecting out of the stone. Relief flooded me when a tiny, furred face peered at us from behind the weathered trunk and then quickly scampered higher, its bushy tail flicking indignantly.

"Where did you get this dagger?" Olim brandished the weapon in front of me.

I focused on the blade, still red with the wolf's blood, and shuddered at the memory of having to use it to defend my life.

"The queen gave it to me," I said. "She told me I should have you teach me to use it."

He turned it over in his hands, studying it reverently. Carefully, he wiped the blade clean and asked for the scabbard. I hastily pulled on my boot with only the barest whimper and shuffled over to my saddle bag. Once I produced the sheath, Olim slid the dagger home with gentle purpose.

"I thought I recognized it," Olim said.

"You do? How?"

"I've seen it wielded before. I held it in my hands after disarming the person who threatened a life with it."

"Who was that?"

He met my eyes and said with deliberate care, "The queen."

The blood drained from my face. "What? Who was she threatening?"

He ran his fingers over the worn leather and shrugged. "The former princess."

"Princess Caelyn? Why?" Laria notoriously kept her past a secret to spare me from worrying about things I couldn't change. This was a shocking revelation, more shocking than learning about the cruel Lady Sharp or that she planned a revolution for two years.

Olim sighed. He knew more than I did about the events of her past, and he always respected her privacy. In the end, he relented, I imagine because our distance from Praed made it easier for him to loosen his tongue.

"She was protecting herself. I was standing outside Princess Caelyn's rooms when she screamed for help. When we entered, there was the mute lady-in-waiting pointing a dagger at her mistress. It was confusing. Despite how awful Caelyn was to her, the queen did everything she said and never fought back. She was a loyal servant, but for some reason, she turned on the princess. I managed to convince her to relinquish the dagger, but the princess wasn't satisfied." He paused to eat a few bites of jerked venison.

"What prompted Laria to act so violently?"

"We soon found out. The princess ordered me to...divest the queen of her clothing."

"She *what*?"

Disturbed at my cry, a flock of birds burst from the trees in a cacophony of flapping wings and trilling calls. Olim's eyes darted around, looking for potential danger, and I sheepishly clapped a hand over my mouth. Once he was satisfied no bandits heard my outburst, he shot me an admonishing look and proceeded.

"I refused, but another knight was not so bound to decorum. When her frock was removed, it became obvious why the princess was so angry. She said some choice words then ordered her lady-in-waiting thrown in the dungeon."

"Why? What did the princess see?"

"The queen's swollen belly."

"Oh."

"The princess had been adamant about the behavior expected of her lady-in-waiting. She even forbade her to dance, except when it suited her own ends. The princess said as her lady-in-waiting represented her, she must be pure. Obviously, pregnancy was evidence of disobedience.”

“How awful for Laria. Did she try to explain she was married?”

“No. She made no move to defend herself. The king had been sent away a few months prior and couldn’t defend her either.”

“What did the princess do with her?” Part of me wanted to know more, but another part was loath to hear another word.

“Had her imprisoned, as I said. She spent the night in a cell and was placed on trial the next morning. I believe the charges were indecency and assaulting the princess.”

“That was the morning she liberated Praed.”

“Yes. After it was over, the king approached me and asked after the dagger. I still had it and gladly handed it over. He said no more about it, and I set aside my curiosity in lieu of more important matters.”

“I asked her if she’d ever used it, but she wouldn’t say. She doesn’t like to talk about the past.”

“I would think not. It wasn’t easy for her back then.”

“Apparently it was so dangerous the king felt it necessary to arm her.”

Olim narrowed his eyes inquisitively at this statement.

“It belonged to Risteard?”

“Yes. I’m sure he’s the one who taught her how to use it.”

This new information swept over Olim, and he studied the dagger more thoroughly. He inspected the pommel, placed his finger on it, then leaned forward so I could see. Etched into the metal were the very small letters: R.E.

“The king’s initials,” I said. “As I said, *he* gave it to Laria.”

“It must have some sentimental value for him to have carved his initials into it.” He handed the dagger back to me.

I considered the weapon in my hands. It had belonged to a powerful knight, a lowly servant, and now a queen. Laria used it to protect the life of her child, and I’d killed a wolf. I trembled to think what horrors it witnessed, how many lives it took, and what future atrocities awaited. Did I want to be responsible for more blood on its hilt? My sister felt I was ready for the responsibility of wielding such a precious item, but did I want to?

“Killing a wolf is one thing,” I said, more to myself than to Olim. “But I don’t know if I could use this against a person.”

“It’s amazing what one can do to protect themselves,” he said. “When faced with danger, even someone as sweet-tempered as you can become a warrior.”

“I wouldn’t go that far,” I said with a wry smile.

He prepared for us to move on, and I struggled to my feet. I hobbled over and watched him organize the cart and check the tack as I contemplated bandits, marauders, and villains on a mission to steal virtuous women. If I were to learn how to properly use the dagger, at least Olim wouldn't have to fight alone were we to be attacked.

"If you're willing," I said after Olim helped me into the saddle. "I would like to learn how to use this." I indicated the dagger before tucking it into my coat.

"If the queen desires me to do so, then I will of course do as she bids."

"What about what *I* bid?"

"I obviously have no problem doing that," he said dryly before kicking his horse into a trot.

Chapter 30

The temperature dropped, and rain fell by the gallon as we furthered our way south along the small fork of the Dehan River, an unimpressive body of water Olim assured me would become a torrent dwarfing the Rhyvor. While we traveled, Olim began my lessons in combat by lecturing me on the first places I should aim for when under attack. When he described how slicing the back of a heel would render the assailant crippled, I wanted to vomit. And when he told me a sliced throat would cause a man to pass out within seconds and bleed to death in a matter of minutes, I spit out bile over the side of my saddle. Olim eyed me dubiously and asked if I was sure I wanted him to continue.

I ran a trembling hand across my mouth and nodded feebly.

Olim didn't spare any gory details when he explained the techniques involved in knifework, which I suspected was an attempt to either convince me I didn't have the stomach for it or to test my resilience. I didn't appreciate his methods, but when I didn't experience any nausea after listening to a particularly vivid story where a knight accidentally lodged his sword in an enemy's rib, I knew I'd become desensitized enough to try some of the moves once we stopped for the night.

Olim set up our shelters while I cleared a space for a fire and gathered wood. The rain moistened the ground considerably, but we found a place protected from the worst of the elements, and I managed to find a few dry sticks and branches. Olim showed me how to arrange them and struck a flint to create the sparks necessary to light the tufts of horsehair he used as fuel for the kindling. While he set out to hunt for our evening meal, I laid out our bedding under the flaps of heavy fabric spread under the trees and falling to the ground like a temporary house, one sheet falling in the middle to create two rooms for privacy. Pain pulsated in my ankle by the time I finished, and I eased myself onto the ground in front of the fire to tend to the bandage.

When the light faded and still Olim hadn't returned, I started panicking and picturing all manner of scenarios from his falling and breaking a leg to an encounter with thieves. I pulled the dagger from the inside of my coat, laid it across my lap, and listened. The trees were thick and changed from short, broad-leaved varieties to tall behemoths with thin, needle-like leaves carpeting the rocky ground. The mountains loomed overhead to the west, and a meandering creek bubbled amid the occasional chirp of a bird or chatter of a small rodent. I added another few pieces of wood to the fire and shifted them around with a stick, when I realized something was wrong. I unsheathed the dagger and stood in the middle of camp. My ears strained to pick up on whatever unsettled me. The sounds of animals ceased, leaving behind an eerie hush. I crept behind a tree close to the horses in case I needed to hastily retreat and squinted in the low light to see into the increasingly dark forest. I gripped the dagger in my shaking hand, my knuckles bright white against the hilt, and held it out in front of me as if it was a talisman against evil. Laria would laugh at the thought, but I was willing to entertain superstitious nonsense if it meant protecting my life.

A twig snapped a few feet away and I clapped a hand over my mouth to keep from screaming. Out of the twilight emerged a shadowy form. I shrank against the tree, raising the dagger high above my head to strike if the figure moved closer. My body shivered from head to toe, and I gripped the weapon tighter to keep from dropping it.

"Ula?"

I nearly fainted when Olim's voice whispered my name. I rushed out in relief and he raised a finger to silence me. I clamped my mouth shut, and he ushered me further into camp. To my astonishment, he kicked some dirt onto the fire to diminish the flames, leaving only a flicker of light and heat to sustain us.

"Why did you do that?" I whispered.

"I came across a small band of suspicious looking vagrants while out hunting," he said.

"Where are they?" I squeaked and looked back into the trees.

"Far enough away they shouldn't stumble upon us by accident, but I don't want to draw any attention with a large fire."

"Are you sure we're safe?" Panic had firmly taken hold and I was ready to leap onto my horse and find another place to camp. "Shouldn't we move camp?"

"It's too dangerous in the dark without at least moonlight to guide us," he said.

I craned my neck to look up at the sky, but between the dense trees and a blanket of gray clouds, there was no light to speak of.

"Besides," he continued, "they were already deep in their cups when I found them. As long as we keep quiet, they won't notice us. We'll leave at dawn."

"Are you sure we'll be all right?"

"Well, once I teach you to use that, we'll be better," he said, nodding toward the weapon held awkwardly in my hand.

I sighed, relaxing my grip, and slid the dagger into its scabbard. Olim produced two rabbits and a squirrel and proceeded to skin and clean the carcasses in preparation for dinner. Together, we arranged a meal of roasted meat, bread, cheese, and wine that was surprisingly tasty considering the rustic circumstances.

A light misting of rain swept into camp, dampening the already meager flames while we cleaned up. My arms puckered into gooseflesh and my teeth chattered. Instead of building up the fire, Olim erred on the side of caution and allowed the flames to sputter into embers. To keep warm, I crawled into the tent and burrowed under my blankets while Olim tended to the horses. Despite the layers I wore, my appendages numbed, the tips of my fingers bloodless. By the time Olim retired to his side of the tent, I was shivering so violently the sides of the fabric were quivering.

"Are you having a fit?" Olim asked as he drew the privacy sheet aside.

"C-c-c-cold."

He pulled the sheet down and wrapped it around me. "Better?"

I curled into myself. "A li-li-little."

"Are you wearing layers like I told you?"

I nodded. He stared down at me, chewing at his lower lip, a deep furrow between his brows. His shoulders slumped, and he scooted closer, so our bodies were almost touching. My eyes widened, but I didn't object to the proximity of his warmth.

"Don't tell anyone," he muttered. "Especially if we end up lying next to each other."

"I w-won't."

Sleep dragged my eyelids shut, but Olim remained fully awake, listening to the forest, ever alert to the possibility of danger. Were he any other man, I might not be so comfortable falling asleep in the middle of the woods with only a few layers of blankets and clothing between us, but I slept beside him feeling completely safe. Not only was he my staunch protector, but also my friend, who knew my heart lay hundreds of miles to the south. Ever a devoted knight, he would deliver me unscathed. Even if it meant shielding me with his own body.

Olim rustled my shoulder to wake me the next morning, but before I could groan my complaint, he covered my mouth and motioned me to silence. I held my breath and listened. Rain pounding against the canvas above my head echoed the beating of my heart, and the distant burble of water flowing over rocks and fallen logs drowned out the rushing of blood in my ears. I shook my head, then froze when I discerned voices echoing through the trees. Olim motioned for me to stand, and we quickly and quietly dismantled the tent and tossed our belongings into the cart. The voices were closer now, and Olim paused to ascertain the direction they were coming from while I hastily saddled the horses.

"How many?" I mouthed.

He held up six fingers.

The voices receded into the distance, and Olim grabbed the horses' leads and ushered me forward.

We carefully maneuvered the horses under the low-hanging branches of the dense trees. My heart thudded as the voices became no more than a whisper on the wind. I leaned into the horse and tried to walk tiptoed, but with each step, a surge of pain shot up my leg. My face flushed, and beads of sweat trickled down my back, but I held my tongue.

My breathing harshened, occluding outside noise, so when Olim stopped and raised a hand, I couldn't immediately discern what alarmed him. I inhaled deeply through my nose and slowly exhaled past barely parted lips. To my right, something large crashed through the trees, snapping branches and crushing vegetation. A male voice drew closer, cursing as he stumbled toward us. Olim waved me back and silently drew his sword.

The pain in my ankle was forgotten as I quickly led the horses a few paces away. There was no hope in hiding them despite the thick foliage, but perhaps the man wouldn't bother to notice in his distracted state. Olim backed against the trunk of a massive tree and peered around it, his sword and stance ready for an attack. Though fear trilled through every muscle, I couldn't stop myself from trying to catch a glimpse of the stranger. For several minutes, we could only hear his grumblings, then a loud curse reverberated through the trees and the man tumbled into view. Olim tensed, and I clamped my teeth shut. The man was large, but not with muscular shoulders and a strong physique like Risteard or my father. He was thick in the middle, and his face was wide and red as he struggled to his feet. By the looks of him, he was either recovering from the evening before or still intoxicated. He wore thick leather breeches and a stained undershirt untucked and haphazardly buttoned. His greatcoat was gray and torn, his boots scuffed and dull. His unkempt appearance didn't look very menacing, and my fear subsided when he fumbled toward the flowing creek and dropped to his knees to wash his face.

I waited patiently for him to finish his ministrations, and by the grace of fortune, the horses were quiet. With luck, he would go back the way he came without glancing in my direction. I looked toward Olim, but he was no longer positioned behind the tree. I stepped out from behind the horse and scanned the area in search of him. The man rose from his knees and shook his ruddy face free of water droplets and residual drunkenness, stretched his arms wide, and bellowed. The sudden cry startled the three horses, and the man turned toward the sound of their shifting and snorting. I pressed my back against a horse's flank and held rigidly still and hoped he wouldn't investigate.

"What's that? Who's there?" the man called out gruffly, squinting into the trees.

His heavy footsteps approached, and I squeezed my eyes shut and covered my mouth to keep from crying. Closer and closer he came until I could smell the musky odor of stale alcohol and moldy cheese. He muttered incoherently about stray horses ripe for the taking. Without realizing it, I removed the dagger from the scabbard at my hip and held it tightly against my chest, ready to swing my arm outward to stab wherever I could reach.

"Anyone here lose some horses?" The man was unexpectedly close, and I jumped before I could stop myself.

The horse concealing my presence shied away, and I stumbled forward and nearly fell. The back of my coat was grabbed and pulled, throwing me off balance so roughly it knocked the wind from my chest. Without thinking, I swung my arm wildly and the blade in my hand connected with fabric and flesh. The man swore and grabbed my wrist, then twisted it hard. I cried out and dropped the dagger.

"What do we have here?"

The man slurred in my ear, and at the hot foulness of his breath, I had to swallow hard to keep from vomiting.

I desperately wondered what happened to Olim, but those thoughts were eclipsed by the terror coursing through my veins. At any moment, this man could throw me to the ground and perform all manner of vile deeds or take me as a prisoner to his cronies and pass me around from man to man. But in the blink of an eye, his grip loosened, and I slipped out of his grasp. I spun around. The hatred and fear in the murky brown depths of the man's eyes rattled up my spine. Beyond his shoulder was Olim, his blue eyes fixated on the back of the man's head and the tip of his sword pressed between his shoulder blades.

"Where have you been?" I hissed furiously before I could stop myself.

Olim's gaze flickered to me, and I was further angered by the annoyance in his eyes.

He twisted the blade and the man winced. "Making sure he was alone. And he is."

"Now, let's be reasonable," the man said. "We can both go about our business. No harm done."

My gaze swept over the man, and I was satisfied to see a plume of red on his left arm where I'd struck him. Though it was a weak blow, at least I drew blood.

"You expect me to let you go so you can run off and tell your friends where we are?" Olim said.

The man swayed to the right, shifting Olim's sword, then quickly sidestepped left and swung his thick bulk to deflect the weapon and punch Olim in the face. A valiant effort, but his debilitated state made the motion awkward. Olim took a step back and effortlessly dodged the attack while simultaneously plunging his sword in the rogue's chest.

The man collapsed to his knees, clutching the wound, blood pouring in red torrents over his fingers. He cried out, begging for his life. A single word, echoing through the trees, bouncing off each droplet of rain falling from the sky.

"Kit!"

Olim slashed the man's throat so deeply his head was nearly severed. He slumped forward, his eyes unblinking as the ground became saturated with his blood. The sounds of the forest were muted, as if I were sinking under the cool water of the Rhyvor in spring. Olim was shouting in my face, but his voice was a mere mumbling of muffled noise. He pulled me toward the horses, and I reached down numbly to retrieve the dagger. The next moment, Olim threw me onto the saddle of my horse, and I twisted my fingers into its mane to keep myself from falling as we raced along the edge of the water as fast as the terrain allowed. The horses slipped on the wet rocks, almost pitching me over the saddle. We managed to put several miles between us and the dead man before Olim slowed our pace. My injured ankle throbbed dully, but I gritted my teeth and didn't complain.

We paused briefly to rest the horses and hurriedly cram food in our mouths before setting out again. Neither of us mentioned what happened, and I was content to never think of it again. I'd never watched anyone die before, and I couldn't close my eyes without seeing the life drain from his face. Olim acted completely normal, as if killing a man was as routine as eating breakfast. But I felt permanently altered, and that night as we prepared to camp again in the open wilderness, I knew I had a choice. I could either allow myself to become desensitized to death like Olim or regard it as precious and risk losing myself in grief when it crossed my path.

When my mind was made up, I strode over to Olim sitting in the firelight watching over camp. He looked up into my determined face and raised a questioning brow. Without a word, I took the dagger from my hip and placed it in his hands.

"I don't want to know how to use this," I said.

"You might need it for protection."

"I thought I'd be alright with that. But I'm not. I don't think I could live with myself if someone died by my hands."

"You don't necessarily have to kill someone to protect yourself."

"Perhaps not. But I would always wonder if I wounded a man if he survived. I don't want to live with the guilt."

"You get over it," he said, not unkindly.

"I don't want to 'get over it.' I don't ever want to be as blasé about human life as you are. I know you have to be, but I don't. I won't."

Olim nodded in understanding and didn't seem offended. I left him to his nightly vigil for the comfort of the tent, burrowed into the blankets, and closed my weary eyes. Before drifting off to sleep, I silently sent my condolences into the ether for the man whose life was lost today. Though he was a blackguard with evil intentions, at one time he was someone's son, perhaps brother, and a comrade. Even if he didn't deserve our mercy, those he left behind deserved our sympathy.

Chapter 31

Thunder rumbled overhead as we slogged through deep mud on the last twenty-mile stretch to the small village laying at the major fork of the Dehan River. The horses shifted nervously when lightning etched across the sky, illuminating the murky woods. Little light penetrated the trees and storm clouds, and rain fell in a deluge despite the dense foliage. Water dripped off the tip of my nose and hood to pool in front of the saddle and under my legs and seat, leaving me uncomfortably cold and damp. I rode hunched over the neck of my horse to withstand the worst of the wind and rain, but by the time we stopped for a rest, I was soaked to the skin.

"Can we please have a fire?" I unwrapped my injured ankle. The bite marks were healed over with thin, reddish tissue and no longer bled, but the bruise was a deep purple and blue and ached dreadfully. My ankle wasn't the only discolored part of my body. My toes and fingers had a bluish hue, which I'm sure matched my shivering lips.

Olim opened his mouth to deny my request, but when he looked at my face, his lips snapped shut and he obediently cleared a space and built a small fire. I wiggled my numb toes close to the flames to dry my foot before re-wrapping my ankle, then stretched my hands out and the bliss of warmth returned to my frigid appendages.

Regardless of his concession in making a fire, he was not willing to grant any more. Within minutes of having the feeling return to my body, Olim extinguished the flames and gestured for me to mount up. I trudged to my horse, my boots squelching in the mud, and pulled myself into the saddle. My horse grunted and shook off sheets of water and caked dirt. Sweat clung to the long hairs along its neck, and from the knee down, it was completely black from miles of filthy travel. I patted the animal reassuringly and promised his journey would soon be over.

The closer we ventured to the front, the more anxious I became, but I didn't feel the topic of meeting Finton was one which Olim cared to discuss. I settled with talking to the horse, rehearsing the speech I intended to deliver when I saw Finton again. Aside from the occasional snort and puff of exasperated air, the tired animal had little to offer in the way of constructive advice.

The forest thinned and the sun was setting when I was able to make out the thatched roofs of houses. The roar of the wind and rain had diminished to a drizzle, only to be replaced by the rushing of water. The tiny trickle of a creek dropped into a waterfall and met a fork coming off the mountains to form a swath of river. In the deepening dusk, the water looked like a black, writhing mass cutting through the land. It was indeed impressive, dwarfing both the width and depth of the Rhyvor.

"We're here," Olim said. We rode past a port where several long, narrow boats were moored. "We'll spend the night at the boarding house and arrange passage in the morning."

The inn turned out to be a modest, two-story building with a crumbling roof I hoped didn't leak, weathered wood exterior, a sconce with a meager flame above the door, and a small paddock with stalls outside. The moment our feet touched the ground, a thin, balding man emerged holding aloft a lantern asking us to state our business.

"I am a knight of Praed escorting the lady south," Olim said authoritatively.

The man wasn't impressed. He narrowed his eyes and held the light high to inspect us closely. I raised my eyes boldly and tried to control my shivering as I met his gaze. Olim stood rigid, a hand on the hilt of his sword, but still the man didn't invite us inside. I was about to despair when a voice sounded in the doorway.

"For the love of Volturnus, Nev! Why's this door wide open!"

A woman's face appeared in the doorway. She was thin with silver hair and light brown eyes set deep in her wrinkled face. Her hardened features softened when she saw us, and when she smiled, I tried not to stare at the gaps where teeth should be.

"We wish to secure two rooms for the night if you're able to accommodate us," Olim said.

"Customers!" the woman exclaimed. She turned a vitriolic stare at the back of the man's head and whacked him with a dirty dish towel. "What's wrong with you, Nev?"

The man waved off her attack. "Watch it, woman! You want me to open our doors to every stranger who shows up in the middle of the night?"

"If it means coin in our pockets, yes! Go help with the horses while I tend to the lady." She turned her punctuated smile upon me again and welcomed me inside.

I glanced at Olim, but he was already busy with the horses, so I followed the old woman willingly.

"Come on, now, dearie," she said.

She placed a hand against my back to lead me into the main room. The space took up most of the ground floor and contained a few long tables with empty benches, a stone hearth with a fire warming the entirety of the room, and a bar with an array of bottles and barrels behind it. Next to the bar was a doorway with a sheet draped across the entrance, followed by a staircase to the upper floor. Candles sputtered in sconces and candelabras dotted around the room, bathing the dark space in an inviting glow.

"You're soaked to the bone! I'll have a hot bath prepared right away." She called sharply toward the door beyond the bar and a waifish girl fluttered into the room.

"Yes, ma'am?" The girl couldn't take her curious eyes off me.

"Go ready our best room and prepare a bath for the lady," the woman snapped. "Quick as you can." She shooed the girl away with her towel and linked her thin arm with mine.

"You've caught us in our off season, so to speak. We don't get many travelers at this time of year. What brings you and your husband to these parts?"

"He's not my husband!" I spoke a little too loudly.

The woman stared open-mouthed, and I apologized for my raised voice.

"Olim is my protector," I said. "He's a knight escorting me on business to Torshul."

"I suppose the business is none of mine." The woman grinned, revealing a gap between her two front teeth.

I smiled back and allowed my lack of response to answer for me.

"I trust you have two rooms available?"

"Oh, yes," she said with a wave of her hand. She settled me near the fire, and I gratefully extended my hands toward the flames. "I'll go prepare a meal for you. The name is Val if you need anything."

"Thank you, Val. My name is Ula."

She curtseyed and disappeared behind the bar. After several minutes, she reemerged carrying a pot, placed it on a hook, and swung it over the fire. A medium-sized carcass of an unrecognizable animal was skewered and placed on a spit. I chose not to ask questions.

Olim and the old man, Nev, entered the inn just as Val prepared to serve the evening meal. She laid a place for five people, then pounded the ceiling with a broomstick. Within seconds, footsteps thudded on the stairs, and the young girl dashed into the room and took her place at the table. Val set before me a plate of stewed vegetables, a sizable piece of greasy meat, a chunk of hard bread, and a mug of ale. I waited patiently for everyone else to be served, all the while wringing my hands in anticipation of the hot meal about to fill my growling belly. Val waved her hands toward our plates and entreated us to eat. I tried to show restraint in front of the strangers and took small, polite bites. Olim had no such qualms, and I watched him enviously as he unabashedly crammed food into his mouth.

"No need to be shy," Val soothed. "The sooner you finish, the sooner you can have a soak."

I cleaned my plate faster than Olim.

With a satisfied smile, I followed the lady of the house upstairs. She led me to a small room containing only a bed, a chest of drawers, and one chair with stuffing coming out of the seams. I retrieved my nightdress and she brought me to another small room with a modest fireplace and an old slatted wooden bathtub lined with a yellowed sheet. Steam plumed from the hot water inside, and a pleasant smell originated from the bath that belied its humble appearance. I breathed deeply of the earthy aroma, and Val commented the scent originated from a mixture of the needle-like leaves from the local trees and oil manufactured from their bark. She helped me out of my frock, and I sank into the hot water with a sigh. Parts of my body I never knew existed were sore, and with each passing minute, the strain ebbed from my aching muscles.

"Did you really come all the way from Praed?" Val asked.

"Yesss…" I said, the words falling lazily from my lips.

"What a journey to take at this time of year."

I ignored the tinge of disapproval in her voice.

"I'm not alone," I said.

"Just worried and not a little curious. We don't see many high fashioned ladies around these parts."

I shifted uneasily and busily washed with a threadbare washcloth.

"I wouldn't call myself *high fashioned*. I'm just...me."

"That's all any woman should be," she said, more to herself than to me.

I didn't want to pry, but her distant look made me just as curious about *her* as she was of *me*.

A hesitant smile formed on my lips. "I'll tell you my story if you tell me yours."

Her eyes glittered as if gossip were the food she truly craved. With a mischievous grin she scooted a chair close to the bathtub and leaned forward eagerly.

"You first," she said. She smoothed her weathered hands over her worn dress then folded them in her lap.

"I do have orders from the Queen of Praed," I said. "But that's not the primary reason I'm venturing to the front." Heat crept into my cheeks that had nothing to do with the hot water.

"A young man?" She gave a knowing smile.

"Yes." The word came out as a rush of air pulled from my aching chest.

She shook her head and tsked. "Ah, that's an old story, dear. I hope he's worth all this trouble and danger you're putting yourself through."

"He is. He's the best man I've ever known. He's kind, intelligent, witty, and he truly cares about people."

"And handsome I hope." She winked.

My blush deepened. "Yes." I finished washing and sank further in the water to submerge my hair. The warmth soothed my tired scalp and relaxed the tension in my face.

"Does the young man know you're coming?"

"No. He doesn't even know how I feel."

"So, you're traveling hundreds of miles to tell him? Don't you think such a thing could wait?" She looked at me as I'm sure Mother would if she knew what I was doing, as if I was not only being foolish but disappointing at the same time.

"Not if he doesn't come home."

I rinsed my hair to cover the sadness enveloping me like a blanket and twisted the extra moisture from my dark locks, the pain as the hairs pulled at the base of my roots a distraction from the pain in my heart. I stepped out of the tub and Val wrapped me in a thin towel.

"I don't mean to judge," she said.

"I don't blame you. It is a crazy scheme if you think about it rationally, but I suppose rational thinking doesn't enter into it when you're acting out of...love."

"No. It doesn't."

Once I was dressed in my nightgown she escorted me back to my room. I waited for her to share her story, but she remained silent. She turned down the bed, watched me climb under the covers, and laid a candle on the tiny bedside table. I looked at her expectantly, but I was too shy to prompt her to talk. She sat beside the bed, the chair creaking painfully with the strain of supporting even her slight weight, and leaned back with a sigh.

"A woman needs to be careful," she said.

My heart sank, but instead of a grave expression, a small smile played at her lips.

"I told my daughter that at least five times a day. 'These are dark times,' I would say. I guess every mother tells her daughter that."

I nodded, just barely, unwilling to break the magic of her words.

"My daughter wasn't like the other girls. She didn't spend hours fussin' over her hair or losin' her mind over boys. She was pretty but didn't pay herself any mind. She spent most of the time watchin' people hire the boats and bothering them with all her questions. The dock master chased her away many times." She laughed at the memory, but the smile didn't reach her glistening eyes. "She was curious, you see, about faraway places. Her pa would tell her to stop dreaming, do her chores, and concentrate on findin' a husband. Other girls were married or betrothed before they turned eighteen. But not her. Not my Bess. One day, a stranger came into town wanting a place to stay and a boat to rent. She looked at him, and he looked at her, and that was that. She ran off with him the next day. Her pa was the maddest I'd ever seen him, and I was heartbroken, but how can a person stop the river from flowin' or the wind from blowin'?"

"What happened to her?"

She lowered her gaze. "She had that girl downstairs. Showed up on our doorstep one night with a note asking us to take care of her until her Ma came back. That was more than ten years ago now."

"Have you had any word from her at all?"

"Not a one."

She didn't seem angry despite the hardship of having to raise her grandchild without knowing what happened to the girl's mother.

"She always did go her own way. She never thought to send any letters, the flighty thing."

I smiled, remembering Laria as a young woman with wild ginger hair flying behind her as she rode bareback across the valley and her staunch refusal to be the proper lady Mother wished she would be.

"I know someone a little like that."

"Her pa's still holdin' onto his anger, but I couldn't blame Bess. We always knew she was different. Being different is hard when you're a woman. Everyone looks at you like you've gone mad. We had a lot of sympathy after she left, but I know there was gossip, too. Still is, I think."

"Well, I hope she's happy, wherever she is."

"Me, too, dear." She rose and tucked the covers in around me. "Sleep now. The boats start early in the morning."

The moment my eyes closed, I instantly fell asleep, and the night was filled with dreams of tangled-hair girls following their own paths, no matter the consequences.

Chapter 32

We stood shivering beside the swollen Dehan River, and I clutched my collar tightly to ward off the rain. Moored at the docks built from ancient timbers were boats made to withstand rapids and rocks. Oars were raised along the rear of the vessel, and men were scurrying along the deck preparing to depart. The sails along the single mast rising high in the air whipped furiously in the wind. Olim presented our meticulously groomed horses to the ship owner as payment for the two-day trip downriver. The man inspected the animals with a wary eye. Olim took this as a personal offense and stated they were three of the strongest horses in the King of Praed's stables. The man narrowed his eyes suspiciously and asked if the king himself might come looking for the animals.

"No, he will not," Olim said with a menacing glare, his face red.

The man wasn't moved by Olim's fury, but he appeared more inclined to entertain the offer.

"All three horses?"

"Yes. Three horses in exchange for passage for myself and the lady."

The man locked eyes with me, and I stared back impassively. Olim warned me not to try and sway the shipowner with sweet smiles and batting eyelashes. He would consider it an insult to his shrewd business sense.

"He would never live it down if he allowed a lady to sweet-talk him out of a seat on his boat," Olim had said. "Don't speak, don't move, don't smile. Just act like this is something we do all the time."

My expression was blank, but my stomach fluttered, and my heart pounded. What if he wouldn't accept our offer? The horses were worth at least twice as much as our passage, but the man obviously didn't want Olim to know how keen he was on the trade. He shrugged, shook Olim's hand, and swept his hands together as if he was dusting them off. The deal was sealed.

Relief coursed through me, and I hefted the canvas bag containing my belongings over my shoulder. Olim did the same, and together we followed a ragged looking deckhand across the gangplank and on board our transportation for the next hundred miles.

The river was deep from the heavy rains and mountain runoff. It flowed south in a dangerously unsafe torrent. But the captain guided the vessel expertly around boulders and fallen logs, and I soon became accustomed to the tilt and sway. Olim, however, was not so lucky. He stayed below deck in a cabin he shared with three other men, embarrassed that such a strong knight couldn't keep his stomach on the water. I spent as much time in the open air as possible, except when the weather was so poor my teeth chattered and my clothes soaked through. There were only a few women aboard besides me, but no one bothered making friends.

The crew lowered the sails when the wind picked up, and our speed increased until my hair was loosened from its pins and my cheeks were numb from the cold wind buffeting against my skin. Several hours into the journey, the rain lightened to a mist, and I watched the landscape roll by in a whirl. Dense forests gave way to sparse, rocky terrain devoid of life save the rare deer or furry rodent. Olim emerged in the evening while I dined on a meal of mashed greens, hard biscuits, and fish some men caught earlier in the day. One whiff of the pungent meal sent Olim running back to his room. Poor fellow.

The sky cleared as night fell, and I gazed up at the stars littered across the inky blackness. The boat was moored in a calm part of the river for the night, and it rocked in the current, the soft lapping of waves breaking against the sides. It was relatively quiet on deck as most of the workers were asleep under a makeshift shelter erected using the mast and sides of the vessel as tie points. As I traced the patterns of the stars with my fingers, a shooting star blazed a trail across the sky, and its brilliance reminded me of the light display I watched on a visit to the Derville estate. With the memory came a rush of feeling, for sitting next to me that night was Finton. My eyes brimmed with tears when I recalled the lights reflecting on his spectacles and the warmth of his body pressed against my side. Could he be looking up at the sky now? Could he have seen the shooting star and thought of me, too?

"I'm coming," I whispered into the sky in the hopes the star would fall to earth and bring my message to Finton.

The sky remained clear the next morning and even a shaft of sunlight warmed my upturned face. Hairpins kept blowing loose in the wind, so my dark locks hung in two plaits to my waist. Olim now felt well enough to join me, but he still refused to eat.

"You'll need your strength," I said.

"I won't be of any use if I'm weak from vomiting," he said, his voice rough as if scraped over stones.

We watched the landscape change from crumbling wasteland to rolling green hills dotted with twisted, leafless black trees and winding dirt roads. There were no buildings, no villages, and no people. Olim gripped the railing until his knuckles were white, his green-tinged face glowing from a sheen of sweat.

"We're very close," he said. "We'll reach the border of Torshul in the morning. There's a port at a fork in the river where we'll disembark."

"How many days to the front after that?"

"Several."

I didn't press him to elaborate. Truthfully, I found the walking portion of our journey daunting.

My heart trilled in anticipation as I lay in bed listening to the soft snoring of the woman who shared my cabin. With every passing mile, we were nearing closer and closer to the front lines. I still wasn't certain what I would say to Finton when we arrived, but I had a feeling the words would come to me once I saw his face.

The rain remained blessedly absent when I awoke, and before the woman sleeping in the bed next to me could even lift her head, I was dressed and carrying my belongings onto the deck. Olim was waiting, and I clenched my hands together as the boat maneuvered next to a dock. A man on land caught a rope tossed by a deckhand, and he tied it securely to a piling while another deckhand lowered the gangplank.

"Everybody off!" the captain barked. "We don't take passengers any further south than this. There's a war going on."

As if he needed to remind us.

Everyone shifted uncomfortably, some averting their gazes to hide unshed tears. In silence, we all disembarked at the northern border town consisting of a smattering of houses occupied by the dock workers. There wasn't an inn because they didn't want visitors to stay overnight, but there was a public house, which many men chose to patronize once they touched dry land. Olim and I had no time to waste, so we found the road leading out of town and began trekking into unknown territory.

I've never been much of a walker. Aside from the occasional stroll around Riverstone and Praed Castle, most of my expeditions involved traveling on horseback. For the first few hours, I marveled at the rain-drenched rolling green hills punctuated with twisted trees and gold leaf brambles bordering stone walls. But after several miles without a change in the scenery, I ended up staring blankly at Olim's back. We stopped only briefly to eat and drink, and by the time Olim deemed our day of walking finished, I was searching for a word meaning five times past exhaustion. My feet hurt more than the dull ache in my injured ankle. The bruising yellowed at the edges, and the bite wounds were no longer in danger of opening and bleeding. I valiantly tried to help Olim prepare camp, but in the end, he ushered me away.

"How much further," I murmured when I drifted toward sleep.

"Far," Olim said.

My muscles were so stiff the next morning I could barely move, but Olim showed no mercy. Just as the sun crested the horizon, camp was packed and we were walking again at his grueling pace. My shoulders ached within minutes from the heavy burden of my canvas pack. No rain fell since we left the river, and the trail we trod was dusty with golden-brown earth. Though my legs throbbed, I concentrated on putting one foot in front of the other, and I ignored the sharp pain in my shoulders and lower back. The monotony of the journey was almost as painful as my muscles, and I almost wished a bandit or wolf would threaten us to stimulate my imagination. Almost.

Seconds after the thought passed through my mind, Olim grabbed my shoulder and wrenched me off the road into the thick bracken. Branches scraped against my skin, and Olim covered my mouth to keep me quiet. I looked to the road, and a caravan of brightly colored wagons pulled by shaggy-haired stout horses rumbled by. I held my breath, clutching Olim's sleeve for support. He tensed, then whirled around, pulling me with him. I stumbled backwards and looked up into the faces of dagger wielding men. Olim drew his sword and yelled for them to drop their weapons, but they yelled back in a foreign, yet not unfamiliar language. I scrambled to my feet and swore I recognized the two men with long, dark, wavy hair. They were dressed simply in billowing shirts, brass-buttoned vests, and faded breeches. They continued to face off with Olim, and there was no sign of either party backing down. Exasperated, I placed myself between the three men, my hands outstretched.

"Stop!" I yelled.

At the same time, I heard another voice call out, "*Chava*!" and a young woman crashed through the bushes with her arms raised.

The woman had eyes only for the young men, and she spoke to them hurriedly in their native tongue. Based on their annoyed expressions, they were probably being served a stern lecture. I looked closer at the woman, and my heart soared when I recognized her.

"Elasha!"

She spun around and met my eye suspiciously, but in the next instant, she smiled.

"Oo-la!" she exclaimed before drawing me into a tight embrace.

I hugged her back just as fiercely, relieved at finding a friendly face. She pulled away and spoke frantically in her language, but I shook my head, reminding her I couldn't understand. She gestured toward the wagons, and I picked up my bag to follow.

"Wait." Olim gave a sideways glance at the two men, Elasha's brothers.

"She's the King of Torshul's daughter, remember?"

He hesitated a moment longer, but the two men lowered their weapons at their sister's insistence, so he relented. Elasha led us to the stopped wagons, which were unlike any I'd ever seen. Where our carriages were square-shaped and polished wood with little adornments, these were large, domed structures elaborately painted in bold colors and designs. Faces watched us with a mixture of suspicion and curiosity, but with a few words from Elasha, their expressions transformed into openly friendly smiles.

Elasha screwed up her face as if she was trying to formulate a question. She gestured to the north, east, south, and west, ending with a raise of her brow. I pointed south. She dropped her hands and her jaw fell open. I nodded in affirmation, and she stared at me uneasily. She looked up at an older woman sitting at the reigns of an extravagantly decorated wagon and hurriedly filled her in on the silent conversation. If I didn't know any better, I was certain she inserted a few choice words into the discussion. She turned back to me, her eyes moving up and down my body with an unmistakable expression indicating she thought I was crazy.

"We're going south," I said firmly, pointing in that direction again. "It's important." I ignored Olim's snort and put a hand over my heart, hoping she would understand.

Her eyes softened, and she nodded knowingly. She gestured toward us, then the wagons, then herself with a smile.

"They'll take us," I said to Olim.

"I gathered that," he said.

Elasha's brother motioned for Olim to follow while the older woman assisted me onto the footboard of the wagon. Elasha climbed up beside me, then opened a small door and beckoned me inside, where I was met with an amazing sight.

Praed carriages were simply built for travel with bench seats and storage for trunks, but these wagons were moveable homes. To my left was a pantry with shelves stocked with provisions next to a washbasin and a plush bench seat. All along the ceiling were books and precious keepsakes stacked on shelves built to enclose items to prevent them from falling during travel. To my right was a vanity, another bench seat, and more storage. To the back of the wagon were two beds tucked into an archway, one on top of the other. Every inch of space was expertly used to maximize comfort and utility. But what was most impressive were the colors. The beds were draped brilliantly in pink, yellow, and blue coverings, the seat cushions a bright red, and each inch of paneling was painted in elaborate floral designs. After marveling for some time in open wonder, I smiled at Elasha, and she raised her chin proudly. She took my bag, opened a panel under one of the benches, and tucked it inside She pointed to the upper bed, then me, then herself.

"We'll sleep there?" I mimed laying my head on a pillow.

She nodded, then led me back outside. We sat next to the older woman, who promptly flicked the reins and directed the caravan south.

Elasha introduced me to the woman, then pointed to her and said, "Britvu." She indicated the woman's stomach, then placed a hand over her own chest, and made a motion as if rocking a baby.

"Your mother?" I asked.

She smiled, and I inclined my head respectfully in the Queen of Torshul's direction.

"I'm honored, and I thank you," I said. Even if she couldn't understand me, I hoped my tone and gestures conveyed how grateful I was for their help.

"No thank," Queen Britvu said. "Elasha's friend."

"You speak my language!"

"A little."

"Is King Qoyahdii at the front?"

"Yes. He send us away."

"I'm sure he wanted you to be safe."

"Maybe so. Maybe he saw you coming."

"Well, no matter the reason, I'm grateful you're here."

Queen Britvu said no more. For the rest of the day, I became Elasha's student, repeating the words of objects as she pointed to them to learn a little of their language. By the time we stopped for the night, I learned several useful words and could almost form a coherent sentence. Olim came up to me with a proud smile on his face and said a full sentence in Torshul without messing up one syllable. But instead of praise, the queen narrowed her eyes, then both she and Elasha smacked a brother each soundly across his head.

"It was bad, wasn't it?" Olim said sheepishly.

I laughed. "It certainly wasn't an appropriate greeting for the Queen of Torshul"

He flushed an endearing shade of red, then his eyes darkened, and I guessed a simple cuff on the head was only the start for Elasha's brothers.

Chapter 33

At the end of the day, the wagons encircled a clearing bordering a stand of gnarled trees. While the men tended to the horses, the women gathered wood and built an enormous fire at the center of the circle for the evening meal. The savory aroma of thin, cured meat frying in large pans next to heavily seasoned sausages permeated the air, making my mouth instantly water. The older women rolled out dough into flattened sheets and cooked them over the open flames, while others stirred vegetables into a large pot. I chopped onions until my eyes stung and discovered the sweet, tangy flavor of a soft, red fruit Elasha said were *tomats*. The meat was eventually added to the pot, and my stomach growled hungrily at the melding of pungent smells. The taste did not disappoint, though my mouth burned from the overabundance of black pepper.

While we reclined with full bellies, several men played stringed instruments and sang while the ladies danced. I clapped along, enjoying the familial atmosphere. Even Olim relaxed and learned how to play a card game from Elasha's brothers.

In exchange for Elasha's help, I started teaching her my language. She was a dedicated student with a good ear, probably because she heard her parents speak it on occasion. An easy friendship blossomed between us, and we laughed and teased each other throughout the evening.

Elasha fell silent. The smile disappeared from her face, her lips forming a grim line as she glared over my shoulder. Confused, I glanced around, and spotted a young man. He removed a short-brimmed, black hat, brushed back his shoulder-length curly hair, and inclined his head toward me before speaking to Elasha in earnest. Her expression remained hard as he spoke, and she didn't add any comments of her own. When she continued to stare at him impassively, he huffed in exasperation, nodded at me politely, and stalked away, cramming the hat back on his head and kicking the dirt as he left.

I gestured toward the young man's retreating form. "Who is that?"

"Laanfeyn," she said tersely.

"A friend? Umm…*mora?*"

She shook her head vehemently.

"What did he want?"

She made the face I called her 'thinking scowl,' and I waited patiently for her to find the words to explain. She made a motion as if to put coins in my hands, and when I said, "Money," she nodded.

"He wanted money from you?"

She shook her head and pointed to herself.

"He wanted to give you some money?"

"Money for me," she said.

I was visibly confused, so she made as if to take money from her pocket and give it to me, then she clasped her hands together.

Realization struck me like a hot poker. "Oh! Money to trade for you. For marriage, I assume."

She shook her head, not understanding my words, and I did my best to pantomime a marriage ceremony. In the end, I used her parents' names as an example, and she finally understood.

"Yes," she said. "Mare-age. *Abniché.*"

"You don't want to?"

She shook her head.

"Why? Is he mean...um, *benlau*?"

"No."

I wondered if she was being forced into the situation, but I had no way of asking such a complex question, so I merely draped an arm across her shoulders and hugged her reassuringly. We tried to resume our easy comradery, but Elasha had an air of moroseness until we excused ourselves to bed. As I drifted off to sleep in the warmth of the wagon listening to the muted conversations and music outside, Elasha spoke into the darkness.

"You *kabiré*...er..." she felt around until her hand rested on my heart.

"Love?" I asked.

"Love...*un gadom*?"

"Yes," I whispered. I swallowed the lump in my throat and blinked back tears. "I love a man."

"*Lungo misli*?"

"Yes. I've traveled hundreds of miles just to see his face."

"Me," she said sadly. "No for Laanfeyn."

I squeezed her hand. "I understand." He was not a scoundrel or considered unworthy because of his wealth. She did not find him unattractive or dull. She couldn't marry the young man with the desperate eyes because she didn't love him. She would never brave the unknown or risk death by wolves just for a chance to tell him how she felt. I couldn't fault her for that.

The gentle sway and creaking of the wagon was as comforting as a lullaby after two days of traveling through a rainstorm. Heavy drops battered the roof, drowning out the clopping of hooves and low murmur of voices. To stay occupied, Elasha and I taught each other words and phrases from our languages while drinking black tea and eating sticky pastries. I sucked remnants of the dessert off the tips of my fingers and narrowed my eyes at Elasha as she tried to hide a smile.

"What?" I asked.

She gestured toward my face and turned away to stifle a giggle. I turned to look across the wagon at the mirror over a vanity. I peered at my reflection, leaning close while gripping the chair to maintain my balance as the wagon shifted and rocked. A swath of sugar swept over one cheek, glittering in the lamplight. I scrubbed at the mess with my sleeve and shot Elasha a glare when she snorted.

"Like a child," she said, nearly falling out of her chair laughing.

"It's very sticky!" I protested but couldn't help laughing. We were in the midst of war, surrounded by uncertainty, mothers missing their sons, and wives wondering if their husbands would return. We were strong women doing what we must to survive, leading countries, raising children, harvesting crops, and ensuring a steady stream of supplies made it to the front. We were a continent bound by a common purpose, chewing our nails in anticipation. We were allowed a moment of reprieve now and then.

When the rain petered out to a light drizzle, Elasha coaxed me out of the wagon. I hesitated, not willing to brave the cold. She waved me forward, and I reluctantly reached a hand out. Droplets splattered onto my palm, warm and fragrant like spring dew. I looked up in surprise, and Elasha eagerly nodded and pulled me outside.

Rays of sunlight filtered through the twisted branches of dark trees. Silence reigned save for water dripping from leaf to leaf. I spread my arms wide and lifted my face to the sky, opening my mouth to catch raindrops like Laria and I used to catch snowflakes. Elasha mimicked me, and together we danced in the rain. Strings were plucked, soon to be joined by another, then a drum. Someone sang, and soon dozens of people were dancing around the wagons.

"What's happening?" I asked breathlessly.

"Rain. It is a gift. From Zema."

"Who's Zema?"

She raised her hands to the sky, smiling with a love so pure and reverent my heart swelled with awe.

"She is the Mother of All Things," Elasha said. "She made the rain, the earth, the sky." She lowered her gaze and cupped my chin. "She made *you*."

In Praed, we don't worship gods, practice magic, or subscribe to 'superstitious nonsense' as Laria was fond of calling it. We believed in men making their own fates, being the lords of the land, and if something good or bad happened, it was a result of our actions, not 'divine providence.' But unlike Laria, people who believed in a force outside their own will fascinated me. They trusted in something they couldn't see and put their lives in its hands. The music, dancing, art, and songs arising from such faith were beautiful indeed.

The blanket of content that had settled over the caravan was ripped away the next day when riders spotted a wisp of black smoke snaking through the cloudy sky. The wagons were huddled into a protective circle and the horses unharnessed. One of Elasha's brothers, Nosuslov, rode over while we were saddling a horse and let loose a string of frantic words so quickly I couldn't translate. Elasha responded tartly, and he huffed and fidgeted until she mounted the horse.

"You come, too," Elasha said, reaching for me.

"Is it safe?" I asked.

She raised an eyebrow, and I almost cried at how like Laria she looked.

"You not here for safe," she said.

Fair point.

I took her arm and barely situated myself behind her before Nosuslov kicked his horse into a gallop and Elasha's took off after him. I gripped the back of Elasha's coat so tightly my hands cramped, and the stout horse thundered across the muddy grass. Elasha's dark curls whipped across my face, so I looked up at the trail of smoke. The wisp had grown to a torrent, covering the sky in shadows.

"Elasha! What if it's Crif?" I yelled.

She didn't answer, but I felt her shoulders tense and she leaned over the horse's neck. We came to a stand of trees at the crest of a hill and slowed. Besides me and Elasha and her two brothers, Olim and two other men had come to find the source of the smoke. We dismounted, secured the horses, and quietly edged through the trees, dropping to our stomachs before easing over to peer into the valley.

A dozen or more wagons were swarming with people. For a heart-wrenching instant, I thought the wagons were on fire and the cause of all the smoke. But a second look and a relieved sigh later, I saw the ground was black with charred grass, and flames flickered among the ashes. The people shouted and flung their belongings into the wagons, and horses nervously twitched their ears. A man holding a torch strode toward the burning swath of ground and placed it on a fresh patch. Once the flames ignited the plants, he moved to a row of trees. It looked like…an orchard?

"What is he doing?" I whispered.

The men spoke amongst themselves while Elasha stared down at the scene, jaw clenched and chin jutted forward. I looked back as the man set the trees ablaze, sending more waves of black smoke and embers in the air. I shuddered and buried my face in the crook of my arm. My lungs burned with the memory of inhaled ash, the remnants of a nightmare that'd only begun. I gulped lungfuls of earth scented air and tried not to panic. It'd been more than eight years since King Conall burned the Riverstone stables to the ground, and yet the sight of embers swirling in a cloud of smoke still paralyzed me with fear.

I yelped in surprise when Elasha shook my shoulder. She blinked curiously, then jerked her head back toward the trees. The men were already disappearing into the twisted branches, though Olim hung back to wait. Slowly, I rose to my knees and shakily stood to follow. Elasha took my arm. I nodded at Olim to indicate I was alright, and we returned to the horses.

I didn't look back.

We met up with the strangers' caravan as they left the valley. The men raised their arms in greeting, and the head wagon stopped. A thin, elderly woman leaned over to speak to Nosuslov, and a lock of white hair came loose from a red scarf wrapped around her head. They spoke in heavily serious tones punctuated by the bracelets tinkling on the old woman's wrists.

"What's going on?" I whispered to Elasha.

The old woman's eyes flashed upwards and held my gaze. I swallowed my unease as she stared at me with striking golden-brown eyes. She turned her nose up and tucked the loose strand of white hair into her scarf with a gnarled, leathery hand. She gestured toward me and made a bold declaration. I understood what it meant and narrowed my eyes.

"Little girls who wander too far from home get lost."

"I'm not lost," I said in her language.

Her eyebrows lifted in surprise, then the corner of her mouth quirked. She spoke, too fast for me to understand, which I'm sure was her intent. Elasha answered, and the old woman nodded knowingly.

"*Con dah*," she said with a flick of her wrist.

Nosuslov nodded, and our group led the caravan to our wagons.

"What just happened?" I asked Elasha. "Why were they burning the trees?"

"Food," Elasha said. "They burn food. Crops. Fruit. Nuts."

Once the newcomers were settled, the old woman and Queen Britvu disappeared into one of the wagons. Fires were lit to prepare an afternoon meal while Elasha and I tended to the horses. She explained the crops were part of a communal farming system. Her people were nomadic, but as they traveled, they tended to the crops and harvested what they needed before moving on. Though a caravan may go months without seeing another, the practice linked the people together and ensured

Torshul's survival. Burning them was a defensive 'scorched earth' practice to deny food to pursuing enemies. An army could not continue forward movement without food.

"Seems risky. Aren't you afraid of starving?" I asked.

"If Crif comes, they will, too."

"Who's the old woman?"

"Mother of her caravan. Ziseva. She sees."

"Sees what?"

She stilled and slowly turned.

"Everything."

Ziseva stared at me for the entire meal, her unnerving gaze never wavering even when bringing food to her mouth. I tried to ignore her, but she scooted closer, put her plate aside and grabbed my hand. I pulled away, but her grip was surprisingly strong. I dropped my plate, spilling food in the dirt, but she didn't relent. I dug my nails into her skin to pry her off me, but Elasha stopped me with a firm reprimand.

"No danger," she said, removing my offending hand and holding it firmly in hers. She nodded toward Ziseva, and the old woman turned my hand palm up. She traced the lines with a long finger, her skin weatherworn and deeply tanned.

Carefully, she released my hand with a look that told me not to move. My palm was frozen in place as she reached into a bag tied at her waist. Whatever she clutched in her hands rattled as she held them up, closed her eyes, and mumbled. Then she shook the objects in her hands and dropped them onto my palm. I inhaled sharply through my teeth and would have recoiled if Elasha hadn't reached out and held my wrist. Though some had clattered to the ground, in my open hand were small bones with symbols painted on them. My throat tightened. Ziseva studied the bones intently, my palms growing slicker and my face heating with each passing second. She sat back and met my panicked eyes.

"Girl, you are brave." She spoke slowly so I could understand. I leaned in to hear. "Still lost."

"I know where I'm going," I said. Hopefully correctly.

She shook her head. "Not wrong road." She put a finger to my chest. "Here."

I frowned. "I know my heart. He's where I'm going."

She shook her head again and clicked her tongue. "Love is one part. Find the rest. Find you."

I looked down at the bones, stark white and shining against my skin once so creamy it rivaled milk. After weeks of travel, even in the snow and rain, my palms were rough, my skin sun-browned. My straight, shining black hair was in two braids with tendrils flying free instead of styled atop my head. I'd changed inside, too. I left Praed Castle, without Laria, on a daring mission that may end in heartbreak. But I was still afraid in many ways. I feared failure, and I feared for my family. I feared small rooms and stone steps, embers in a dark sky, and large men I didn't know.

I closed my hand around the bones and squeezed until the sharp edges dug into my skin. Then I opened my hand and watched them tumble to the grass. I met Ziseva's unwavering stare.

"I'll find it," I said.

She nodded.

Elasha graciously allowed me to sleep late the next morning, and I awoke to the pleasing aroma of breakfast cooking outside. I jumped out of bed, splashed water on my face, and pulled on a frayed frock before dashing out of the wagon. Children raced around my feet laughing behind their hands, and I swear I heard one of them say the word *"lenesh"* under their breaths.

That means *lazy*. Little imps.

We stopped to water the horses and have a simple meal, when Olim came up to me with a disconcertingly wide smile.

I shifted nervously. "What is it?"

"Nosuslov said we're half a day from the front."

I shivered so violently I almost dropped my food.

"So close?"

"Uh-huh. I hope you have your speech prepared." I shot Olim a glare, and he gave me a gentle shove. "It's not like it's a secret."

"Did you hear me talking to the horses?"

"Only a little. If I were you, I would open with the number of miles you traveled to be here. It's what *I* would want to hear."

"Thanks for the advice."

"I hope it'll be worth it." His tone was not cruel, but rather sympathetic, and his eyes were filled with compassion.

"Me, too," I whispered.

I was an absolute mess by the time we stopped for the evening. I tried to help the women prepare the meal but was subsequently dismissed after cutting myself several times and almost slicing off a finger. The horses had already been fed and watered, but Elasha set me to grooming them, teasing that I couldn't possibly hurt myself with a brush. I shrugged off her jests and disentangled the long manes, tails, and feathers and cleaned off the dirt. The animals munched contentedly while I worked to groom their coats to a glossy shine, and I reveled in the cathartic act that brought me back to my childhood, to Praed. I glanced toward camp. We were alone, so I nuzzled into a mane and took a deep breath. The earthy aroma of hay, dirt, manure, and horse sweat was a comfort I needed desperately.

"I've come hundreds of miles," I murmured. "Crossing rivers and forests, rocks and snow, on horseback, by boat, by foot, and by wagon to see you. To tell you..."

I sighed. It seemed well and good to plan a grand speech, but in the end, all I could think of was his face and how I wanted to see his smile, and my words failed me. I would feel like a fool if I prepared something to say and then faltered at the sight of him. I twisted my fingers in the long, thick mane and tried not to cry. I failed.

"Oo-la," Elasha said, her hand on my shoulder. "*Caben.*"

The evening meal was being served, and I was blubbering like a child. I took several deep breaths to collect myself, but when I turned around and saw the concern in her eyes, I broke down again. She gathered me into her arms and held fast, stroking my hair and waiting patiently for me to exhaust my tears.

"Elasha, I'm so scared," I said.

She may not have understood my words, but she couldn't mistake my chattering teeth and trembling body. She pulled away and smoothed her hands over my face, closed her eyes, and mumbled something. I closed my eyes, too, though I wasn't sure why. When she stopped talking, I opened them again, and she drew symbols on my forehead with her finger.

"What was that?"

She placed her palms together and bowed. I didn't understand what that meant, but I smiled and thanked her anyway. Though the words were foreign, the intent was to ease my discomfort. To be honest, it worked a little.

Olim sat next to me while I numbly ate stuffed greens and stared into the fire. I could feel him watching me, but I wasn't in the mood to field questions about my fragile state of mind.

"This is the end of the line for them," he said quietly. "Nosuslov said they won't journey any closer to the front. It's only another few miles. We walk from here."

I nodded.

"We wait," Elasha said. She squeezed my shoulder then turned away to eat her meal and give us some privacy.

"Meet me outside your wagon early," Olim said. "We should try and make it to the encampment before..." He hesitated, picked at his meal, and wouldn't look me in the eye.

"Before any fighting starts?" I prompted.

His head bobbed in a short nod. "I'd be remiss in my duty if I didn't offer you this last chance to change your mind. I'm not sure what we'll find when we get there."

"We've come this far. It would be foolish to stop now."

"Not to mention a waste of time and money." He smiled and winked, and I shoved him playfully.

"I don't know how I'll ever repay you," I said. My throat tightened at the thought, for I knew there was no amount of money I could give that would adequately express my gratitude.

"You'll think of something," he smirked. "Name your first kid after me." I blushed and turned away, but he didn't miss the tiny smile playing at my lips. He nudged me with his shoulder, and a short laugh escaped my mouth.

"There you go," he said. "You needed to relax a little. You're making *me* edgy."

I didn't stay up to partake in the revelries for I wanted to be as well rested as possible. As it was, I was certain I would sleep very little, and I needed all the help I could get. I flailed wildly when Elasha came to bed, crying out in the darkness, and I'm certain she thought I was a lunatic.

She was probably right.

I tossed and turned, my stomach in knots so tight I worried I might vomit. My plan to get a decent night of sleep was going horribly awry. I snatched snippets here and there, until I glanced out a window and saw the first light of dawn. I sighed in resignation and climbed out of bed, dressed for walking, and quietly left the wagon.

A light mist clung to the grass, bathing the morning in an eerie calm. I jumped when Olim stepped out of the gloom, and without a word, we headed out of camp toward the front lines. I crossed my arms across my chest to keep from shaking. The walk was easy enough, but I breathed as if we were traveling through treacherous terrain. The sun was high overhead when Olim reached out to stop me.

"They'll be just over this ridge, right outside the Orkyef Forest. You can see the knights patrolling the perimeter. They'll see us coming," he said. "Are you ready?"

In truth I was terrified and worried that I was making a terrible mistake. I didn't know whether to cry or run. What would Laria do if she were here instead of me?

"Yes," I said. "Let them see us come. We'll be taken into camp faster that way."

Olim nodded and extended his hand, inviting me to lead. I took a deep breath, held my head high, and strode confidently toward the encampment, just as I imagined Laria would.

Chapter 34

We were only two steps toward the camp when a knight ordered us to stop.

"State your business," he ordered gruffly.

"My business is my own," I said. "Stand aside."

"Explain yourself or answer to the king." His hand hovered over the hilt of his sword. Olim shifted behind me, and I pictured his own hand resting on his weapon.

"Take us to the sentry," Olim demanded.

The knight looked over my shoulder, but whether he recognized Olim or not, I couldn't tell. He jerked his head for us to follow, and he led us over the hill. One glimpse down into the shallow valley left me breathless.

Spread out as far as I could see were the white shapes of tents rising out of the earth in a cluster resembling the ruins of an ancient foundation. Surrounding the perimeter of the tents were earthen and stone ramparts edged with trenches and long wooden spears. Wisps of smoke trailed into the air, punctuated with the soft whinnying of horses and the pounding of metal on metal. Olim pressed his hand to my back to get me moving again, but though my feet carried me forward, I couldn't turn away from the encampment as we came closer and closer. I could make out the square structures of stables and mews and smell cooking meat and straw. The gruff knight led us to an opening in the ramparts where two men stood guard.

"They're your problem now," the knight said without preamble and strode away.

"I need to see the king," I told the sentry in my best authoritative tone.

He looked behind me at Olim, but he wore a stony expression that gave nothing away.

"On what business?"

"Royal business," I replied in the commanding voice I'd often used on the children when they were up to mischief. "I'm the lady-in-waiting to Queen Laria."

The sentry's eyes widened, and he glanced behind me again to look to Olim for confirmation. He paled at Olim's silent assent, and without wasting another minute, the sentry motioned us inside and led us through the labyrinth of tents.

The sound of banging metal grew louder as we walked past a tent where a blacksmith repaired weapons and armor. He paused briefly in his work, his hammer raised overhead and a puzzled expression on his face. We must have been an interesting sight indeed—a pair of scraggly looking vagabonds.

Word of our arrival traveled throughout camp, and soon battle-weary knights and soldiers were emerging from their tents to gawk and whistle. The closer we came to the center of camp, the thicker the mood became, as if the occupants were tensely waiting for something to happen. The sentry stopped, and I looked over his head at a large tent adorned with flags rippling in the wind.

"Wait here." The sentry went inside.

I shot Olim a satisfied smile and he shook his head.

"You've only made it this far. Don't start celebrating yet," he said.

The tent flap burst open and Risteard stepped out looking just as formidable and intense as ever. The scars, one above his left eye and the other below his right, were white against his windburned skin. His hair was shorn close to his scalp, but his beard was full. His face was clean, but his clothes were in dire need of washing. And if the purple hollows of his eyes were any indication, he was in dire need of sleep. I was so overwhelmed at seeing him I almost burst into tears right there.

Before I could open my mouth, he asked, "Is it Laria? Is she all right?" His eyes roved my face worriedly, as if I had the answer written in my expression.

"Yes, she's well," I said. Before I could explain why I was there, he interrupted.

"The children?"

"Are all well, I assure you. I'm not here because of Laria."

He stared at me expectantly, and I nearly lost my nerve under the scrutiny of his severe cerulean gaze.

"I've come to speak with Finton, the surgeon."

"Are you injured?"

"No. Please. It's important."

His eyes narrowed suspiciously.

"Is it...personal?" His voice held a dangerous undertone.

"It is."

Risteard looked behind me at Olim and jerked his head toward the tent. We followed him inside, and a crowd of men surrounding a table covered with maps straightened.

"A minute, gentlemen." Risteard gestured toward the open tent flap.

The men exchanged puzzled glances but left without a word. I fidgeted with the hem of my cloak, my pulse pounding as I glanced toward the closing entryway. We didn't have time for this. I felt it in my bones. We didn't have time for lectures.

"You put her life in danger for a triviality?" Risteard's voice was low and threatening, his eyes dark, staring at Olim.

Olim paled at the accusation.

"No." I held out my hands to form a barrier between them. "You mustn't be angry with him. He has done his duty in protecting me. If he hadn't accompanied me, I would've come alone. You know how determined we Audrey women can be."

Risteard's mouth twitched, but he did not yield.

"Go back to Praed." He turned toward the tent flap.

"Wait! Please. There may never be another opportunity. What if he doesn't return?" My throat tightened and my vision blurred at the thought, but I managed to contain my tears. "This may be my only chance, and we're running out of time."

Risteard turned to face me, and I was relieved to see his features had softened.

"I'll deliver a message to Laria in exchange."

"An exchange?" he asked incredulously. "You wouldn't do that anyway?"

"Perhaps not." I pressed my lips together to keep from smirking.

"Are you giving your king an ultimatum?"

Olim took a step back and swallowed audibly.

"If it'll work." It was the bravest thing I'd ever said. I only hoped it was worth angering my brother-in-law.

He searched my upturned face, his eyes glowing with…pride?

"You have five minutes," he said. "Tell Laria she's constantly in my thoughts. She knows the rest."

"Can I tell her when you believe you'll return?"

"I cannot promise that I will. I'm sure she knows that."

"You can't die here," I said. "She needs you."

"I know, but I can't make such a promise. Realistically, I may not survive, and it would be unfair of me to raise any hopes. Even those of my wife and children."

"The queen's pregnant!"

Our heads snapped to Olim. My eyes widened and my mouth dropped open. Olim flushed from forehead to collar bone.

Risteard stepped around me and loomed over Olim. "Excuse me?"

Olim's throat bobbed, and he tried to speak, but only a choked sound emerged. He looked to me for help.

"Laria carries your sixth child," I said. "She didn't want you to know. She was afraid it would distract you."

Risteard slowly turned toward me, and Olim sagged in relief.

"You once promised to give her half a dozen children, and you kept that promise. I'm begging you to make another."

I wasn't proud of myself for manipulating my brother-in-law, but I was desperate. His carefully composed features crumbled, though barely—just enough for me to see the longing struggling just below the surface.

"I promise," he said. "Tell Laria I will come home to her before the child is born." His eyes shone, but his features remained stoic. "The medical tent is that way." He pointed to his right. "Five minutes."

I stepped forward and kissed him on the cheek before his stoic countenance returned, then moved away.

Risteard turned to Olim and spoke in a voice that brooked no refusal. "You. Let's discuss the repercussions of your inability to say 'no' to an Audrey woman."

If Olim was worried before, he was now terrified. I mouthed, "Good luck," as he disappeared behind the tent flap, his eyes wide and face bloodless.

With growing trepidation, I walked down the line of tents, averting my gaze from leering soldiers and ignoring their entreaties to...well, do things I don't care to imagine. A sickly-sweet smell drifted into my nostrils, becoming stronger as I approached a large tent with its front flaps open to the air. Around the outside were scraps of clothing being thrown into a roaring fire. I covered my nose as the smoke carried into the sky remnants of blood, tattered cloth, and unidentifiable waste. A voice called out for help and a man bellowed in pain, and I rushed inside.

Finton placed a thick piece of leather into a man's mouth and told him to bite down. The man writhed on a table, blood dripping down the sides of a cloth and pooling on the dirt floor. For a heartbeat all I could do was stare, first at the carnage, then at the man whom I'd traveled over an incredible distance for the mere chance to see. His hair was longer and disheveled, his cheekbones more prominent, and there was a crack in one of his lenses. The collar of his linen shirt hung open, revealing a familiar swath of muscled, dark-haired chest. There wasn't time to blush over the warm feeling the sight gave me for I was instantly distracted by the stains of blood, sweat, and dirt soiling his clothes.

Didn't these men know how to wash?

"Donal!" Finton yelled, startling me out of my observations. "Where are you? I need your help! And more opium!"

Without hesitation, I threw off my cloak, rolled up my sleeves, and hurried forward.

"What can I do?" I asked.

Finton's wide eyes met mine in shocked surprise, and I would have laughed at the way his mouth opened and closed without making a sound, but the situation was dire. A groan from the patient brought him back to his senses and he shook his head.

"Hold these clamps," he said.

I reached into a gaping leg wound to hold the proffered instruments. The metal was cool to the touch, but the warm blood seeping under my hands made my stomach roil, and I clenched my fingers.

"Carefully," he added, "while I suture the vessel."

He meticulously stitched the tissues together with a tiny needle and thread, and I lost myself in the intricate dance of his working fingers. The patient groaned again, then spit the mouth gag out.

"I must be the luckiest man here to have such a pretty nurse holding my leg," the injured man said.

I blushed but smiled good naturedly at him.

"That's only the blood loss talking," I said.

He tried to laugh, but the motion was painful.

"Keep him talking," Finton said quietly.

"What would your wife think if she heard you flirt with another woman?" I asked the man. Blood coated my fingers, and I looked at Finton worriedly, but his focus was solely on his task.

"No wife," the man said.

"A sweetheart then?" I asked.

"Not me. Was never lucky enough to catch a woman's eye."

"Perhaps there's a young woman waiting for you to declare yourself. She could have feelings for you she cannot express. An admirer from afar."

Finton shifted his gaze briefly to me before he resumed his intense concentration. I watched him expertly join broken flesh and vessels until I could bear to look no more and turned away before I became ill.

"A wonderful thought," the injured man said. "If it were true, it would be enough to convince me to stay in this realm."

"Don't talk like that," I commanded as if he were one of the children. "You're going to live."

"What do you say, Doc?" the man asked. "Is the lady right?"

Finton looked at me gravely. A heartbeat passed. Two.

"For the time being," he said.

"Dr. Ekhane is an excellent surgeon. If there is hope of making it home, you couldn't find yourself in more capable hands."

"I hope you're right about the woman waiting for me."

His eyes drifted shut, and I frantically looked at Finton as he pressed his fingers against the pulse at his neck.

"He's passed out. Almost finished. You're doing a fantastic job."

I blushed and looked away to watch the slow rise and fall of the man's chest. After what seemed like forever, Finton said it was time to let go.

"What?"

"Let go of the clamps. Gently."

I shook away the fog and carefully released my hold. Finton removed them from the man's body, then watched for several seconds.

"What are you waiting for?"

"Making sure the bleeding stopped before I close," he said. He began stitching the wound closed, and without meeting my eyes asked, "What are you doing here?"

In all the drama, I'd lost sight of my purpose in coming. There was no time for long, rehearsed speeches or dancing around the issue.

"I came to see you," I said. "To tell you something."

He froze in mid-stitch, his needle poised in the air.

"Is it Father?"

"No, nothing like that. Everyone is in good health."

"What is it then?" He resumed his task, and I glanced around at all the people who would surely hear what I had to say.

I leaned across the unconscious man between us and whispered, "I don't suppose we could talk in private?"

He paused again and slowly peered up at me over the rim of his spectacles. His hazel eyes darkened, and I worried I'd offended him, though he didn't appear angry.

"Of course," he said in a low voice, then he called again for his assistant, who appeared sweating and out of breath.

"Sorry, doctor," the man said between gasps. "Was running all over delivering supplies. I have the opium." He held up a satchel and Finton smiled tightly.

"It's a little late for that now but thank you. Could you finish up here, please?"

The man nodded, narrowing his eyes curiously at me. Wordlessly, he took the needle and resumed sewing up the wound. Finton cleaned his hands then handed me a wet cloth for my own while gently guiding me to a secluded corner occupied by a sleeping patient.

"Go on," he prompted when we were alone.

"There isn't much time," I said, glancing at the opening of the tent. "So, forgive me if this sounds rather strange and unforgivably forward."

He smiled, the sight of it sending my heart into a frenzy.

"I'm intrigued. Continue."

There was no time to explain how I felt, what I'd been going through the last several months. There was only time for one gesture. It led me to trouble before, but I hoped this instance would be different.

"May I please kiss you?"

The smile vanished and his expression became unreadable.

"You don't have to say—"

"Yes," he breathed huskily. "You may."

Before losing my last ounce of courage, I grasped the front of his shirt for balance and lifted myself toward his face on the tips of my toes. Tentatively, I touched my lips to his and breathed in the scent of his skin. He smelled of campfire, wet grass, and a strange sweetness coupled with a distinctly masculine aroma. He cradled the back of my head and pressed his lips more fully against mine, and a pleasing, heavy warmth spread from my mouth throughout my body. I settled back on my feet and gazed up into his hooded eyes. A pang rushed through me at the loss of his touch, and I was acutely aware of every tingling nerve and pulsing vein in my body.

My mind flashed to the memory of Olim's kiss. It'd left me feeling uncomfortable and filled with regret. But the moment Finton's lips left mine, I wanted nothing more than to reach for him and never let go.

"I knew it," I whispered.

"Knew what?" he whispered back as he cupped my face in his hands.

"It was you." A tear trailed down my face. "I have feelings for you."

"Feelings?" He brushed the tear away with his thumb.

"I believe I am in love with you."

"You came all this way to tell me that?"

"Yes." I hadn't expected that response and it planted a growing disappointment inside me.

"You brave woman. I'm so happy you did."

"You are?" My heart pounded so fast I could barely breathe.

His face lit up. "Yes. I am in love with you as well."

"Really?" My joy was so palpable, I could float away upon it.

"Most definitely."

"Then you'll marry me?" I asked before I could stop myself. I clamped my hands over my mouth and blushed furiously as he laughed.

"That's a bona fide offer if I've ever heard one, Doc," the patient, no longer asleep, spoke up from the bed.

If lightning would just strike me down at that moment it wouldn't be soon enough.

"Go back to sleep," Finton ordered the man good naturedly.

My voice was muffled behind my hands. "I shouldn't have said that."

Finton's eyes glimmered mischievously. "But you did. Did you mean it or were you wanting to take it back?"

I lowered my hands and said, "Well, I suppose since the words have already been spoken there's no sense wishing them unsaid."

"So, you're asking?"

"Yes, I am."

He smiled broadly, showing all his perfect white teeth. "Then I accept."

I threw myself into his arms. The man in the bed clapped and cheered as Finton kissed me between our smiles, laughter, and tight embraces.

"Ula," a very recognizable voice said from a few feet away.

I buried my head in Finton's shoulder to steady my breathing and waited for my wild heartbeat to settle.

"Your Majesty," Finton addressed my brother-in-law.

"Ula, it's time," Risteard said.

I nodded and extricated myself from my betrothed.

"Come home soon," I whispered before turning away, walking past Risteard, and out into the sudden downpour of driving rain.

"I suppose it's to you whom I must apply for permission to marry her?" I heard Finton say.

"Granted," Risteard said.

"That was easy," Finton said with a sigh of relief.

"It wouldn't have been if I didn't approve of you."

My heart swelled with affection for my brother-in-law at that moment. He hid behind a mask of intimidating strength, but sometimes he allowed a glimpse of the man beneath. That man was honorable, loyal, and more of a romantic than he would ever admit. I looked forward to laughing with Laria about it when I returned home.

Chapter 35

My hair was heavy with rain and water ran in rivulets down my cheeks and nose as Olim as I were led out of the encampment. No longer regarding us as objects of scrutiny, knights and soldiers scurried around donning armor and taking up their weapons. They were obviously preparing for battle, and my heart twisted at the thought of these brave men fighting for their lives. How many would lose?

Olim kept a hand on my back to propel me forward, knowing full well if I paused to consider the activity around me, I would falter. The ground was saturated, and I sloshed through the water in soaked-through boots. I trudged on, keeping my focus solely on the opening in the ramparts.

When I passed a lavishly adorned tent, a voice called, "My lady, Ula!"

I turned in time to be enveloped into the embrace of King Qoyahdii. The stout man smelled of incense and delicious food. I disentangled myself to look into his face, and when my eyes met his broad smile, I nearly wept with joy.

"Your Majesty!" I grasped the king's hands. "It's so good to see you!"

"You are cold." He removed his heavy cloak and wrapped it around my shoulders. "You have come a long way to be so."

"It's a long story," I said. "But I want you to know your family helped me, and I'm very grateful for them."

"Have they? Then I am proud, though I did tell them to stay away." He waggled his finger and quirked an eyebrow, but he didn't seem very angry.

"I will tell them I saw you in good health."

"For now." The happy expression became forlorn. "King Karne has challenged the borders and will not listen to talk, so our armies will be attacking him today."

The blood drained from my face and my limbs went limp. I swayed and both Olim and King Qoyahdii reached out to steady me. I gripped the king's arms, but the desperation on my face was the only form of communication I could muster. He smiled kindly and tweaked my nose.

"Do not worry, child. We fight on the side of right. It is a blessed cause."

I didn't share his confidence, but I managed a small smile and nodded appreciatively.

"Take care of yourself, Your Majesty." I hugged him again, then turned away before he could see me cry.

I strode hurriedly out of camp, the heavy coat of the King of Torshul keeping the rain and wind at bay. We climbed the hill and stopped to look back down at the increasing activity. Olim shifted uncomfortably, probably drenched through with rain, but I didn't move. He kindly allowed me a moment to observe the scene below for another few minutes in silence, but alas, it was not to last.

"Are you all right?" Olim asked.

"How many of them do you think will make it home?" He winced at the emptiness in my voice.

"You can't think like that. You'll drive yourself to misery."

"At least we made it in time."

He tugged my sleeve to lead me away, and I didn't resist. We didn't speak as we trudged through the increasingly heavy rain toward Elasha's caravan, not once stopping to rest until it was visible in the distance. Then Olim hesitated.

"Was it worth it?" he asked. "Was the five minutes the king allowed worth traveling hundreds of miles, getting attacked by wolves, and the life of that bandit?"

"I don't know if it was worth a man's life," I said with a tremor of remorse. "But it was worth everything else."

He jerked his head toward the caravan, and we continued walking.

"Then I suppose congratulations are in order?"

"Yes." A pleasant warmth spread over my face.

Elasha had evidently seen us coming and was running toward us, calling out and waving toward the wagons.

"So wet," she said breathlessly. "Come warm." She took my arm, then froze, staring at my coat. She met my eyes with a silent question in her worried face.

"I saw the king," I said. "He's well."

She closed her eyes in relief and her lips moved in a silent conversation I wasn't a part of. When I turned back to Olim, he'd disappeared.

Despite the unrelenting rain, I rode on the back of the wagon until the ridge hiding our armies disappeared behind a veil of mist. Elasha poked her head out and entreated me to come inside, and I reluctantly agreed. She peeled off my outer layer of clothing and tutted over my chilled skin.

"Too cold," she said. "You'll be sick."

"I hope Finton will be safe," I said. "How can the soldiers see in the rain? Do you think he's warm enough? Is he thinking about me?"

A grin fluttered over Elasha's face but quickly disappeared.

"We used to rain. Crif is not."

She made a good point. The rain gave us an advantage against people raised in the desert.

I rubbed my hands together while Elasha draped a heavy blanket around my shoulders. We huddled together on the bed, and she undid my braids and used her fingers to untangle the wild strands.

"He loves you?" she asked.

Warmth spread through my body and I beamed. "Yes. When he comes home, we're going to get married."

"We bless your marriage tonight."

I leaned against her and she wrapped her arms around me.

"Thank you, Elasha. I wouldn't have made it without you."

That night, an enormous fire was built in the middle of the circle made from the wagons, and the air soon grew thick with the smells of fresh bread and spices. Elasha explained when a Torshul couple became engaged, three days of celebrations followed to symbolize the past, present, and future. On this first night, the eldest women would cook traditional dishes and offer slices of bread to the spirits. Elasha instructed me to taste every dish and listen to the stories of the recipes passed down for hundreds of years. She also told me to pick out a piece of clothing I didn't mind losing.

"Why?" I asked.

"To burn. Burn the old, ready for the new," Elasha said.

Music brightened the night and young women danced in their finest clothing. One by one, the elderly women presented me with stews, meats, vegetables, and pieces of bread. Even when my belly was full, I couldn't say no to the delicious morsels. After a cue from Elasha, I approached the fire with an old dress worn through from the journey. The music ceased, and Queen Britvu bestowed a blessing on mine and Finton's ancestors. Then she nodded at me, and I tossed the dress into the flames.

"The past is gone," Elasha said. "Tomorrow, we honor *you*."

I didn't think it was possible, but it rained harder the next day. When thunder rumbled across the sky, the caravan took to the shelter of the trees. Elasha spent the day sewing a dress, but I quickly grew bored. Braving the weather, I left the wagon and searched out Olim.

"Get in here before you get struck by lightning!" he said. He grabbed my sleeve and pulled me inside.

I nodded at Elasha's brothers and they jerked their heads in my direction before going back to sharpening knives.

"I hope we're not stuck here long." I shook droplets of water off my coat and avoided the men's dark glares.

Olim handed me a steaming cup of tea. "It's another five or six days to the northern border of Torshul." He drew back a curtain and scowled at the gray clouds. "If we get going as soon as the rain lets up, we'll make good time."

The weather broke a few hours later, and golden rays of sunshine warmed the sogging ground. Elasha and I walked alongside the wagon through layers of eerie vapor. We giggled about my new fiance, and shared stories of her childhood. I looked over my shoulder toward the front lines several times, and she scolded my anxiety.

"It does no good," she said, shaking her finger the same way her father did.

In the evening when the fire roared and music played, I relaxed. A bottle was produced, and each family poured a little of their own wine inside. When the bottle was full, an elder said a blessing and offered it to me. I took a sip expecting the mixture to be foul, but it was surprisingly flavorful. I drank deeper and passed the bottle. Around it went, each person taking a sip. Then one by one, the head of each household laid a coin at my feet. Elasha warned me it would be insulting to refuse, so I folded my hands in my lap and accepted each offering with gratitude.

On the final night of my engagement celebration, I danced around the fire with the other ladies. They taught me how to move with swaying hips and sweeping arms. I tried to show them a traditional Praed dance, but when I tried to mimic both the man's and woman's parts, the ladies laughed so hard they couldn't see past their tears.

"Why do the man and woman dance differently?" one lady asked, enunciating each word so I could understand.

"They compliment each other," I said, hoping I was getting the words right. "Like…well…a dance."

"Do they trade?"

"No. They men always dance the man's part and the woman hers."

The ladies looked at each other, their faces contorted in confusion. Then they shrugged and fluttered away in a swish of skirts and tinkling bells.

"In Torshul," Elasha said, "men and women dance the same."

"Who leads?"

She tilted her head, and I explained that a man will lead the steps and a woman follows.

"In Torshul, there's no lead. We're equal."

I looked toward the dancers and saw several young men join in, and I watched, entranced, as men and women moved as one, like blades of grass rolling along the prairie or birds suddenly changing direction. A truly beautiful partnership.

At a signal from Queen Britvu, the music stopped, and she gestured for everyone to gather around me. I was grateful for the darkness so no one could see my self-conscious blush and fidgeting. The queen raised a glass and began chanting. Everyone lowered their heads, so I did, too. She spoke too fast for me to understand, but I caught the words 'lifetime,' 'happiness,' and 'prosperity.' This was the blessing for the future of mine and Finton's marriage.

Queen Britvu placed a hand on my head, and everyone raised their hands toward me and repeated her words. Elasha leaned over and translated.

"Zema, bless this woman's mind. Let her be wise, let her forgive, let her know she is loved. Give her pleasant dreams. Keep her free from fear."

Everyone answered, "Zema, bless her."

The queen's hand moved to my chest. "Zema, bless this woman's heart. Help it guide her. Let it be filled with happiness and love. Let the beat make music with her beloved's."

"Zema, bless her."

Her hand drifted further and settled on my belly. "Zema, bless this woman's womb. Let it give life to children if she so chooses. Let it nourish her future. Let it continue her story."

"Zema, bless her."

Everyone lowered their hands, and one by one, they presented me with gifts. A pouch of seasonings, a bracelet, scissors…simple things for a new couple. With each gift, I found it more and more difficult not to cry.

Elasha came forward with a wrapped bundle and eagerly put it in my hands. I recognized the shimmering, sky blue fabric. It was the sewing project she'd been working on. I unfolded it and held up a tiny dress.

"If the future brings a daughter," she said. "To teach her of Torshul."

I pulled her into my arms, and the tears I'd tried to suppress slipped down my cheeks.

"I'll tell her about my friend, Elasha," I said. "And how she saved me."

Four days later, Elasha's caravan graciously supplied us with two sturdy horses for the ride back to Praed. Olim and Elasha's brothers parted with all the comradery of lifelong friends, laughing and patting each other on the backs until even *I* was rolling my eyes. Both of us were outfitted in new clothes and given slick coats that repelled water like goose feathers as well as enough rations to last until we reached Praed. I was sorry to part from Elasha, but I was eager to be on my way home again. I missed the children dearly, and I had an important message to deliver to Laria.

"Good travel," Elasha said.

"*Benecu de mancar buné si musika vensula.*" This phrase basically wished her good luck and health.

She smiled and indicated I'd correctly pronounced all the words. We embraced once more before I mounted my horse, and I waved goodbye until she and her family receded into the distance.

"I hope we see them again," I said.

"If everything goes well, we'll have many new allies," Olim said, his voice muffled behind a thick scarf. "I'm sure the King of Torshul will be invited to Praed Castle in the future."

The rain relented, but the wind blew cold as we traveled along the Dehan River. The only time we saw other people was when a riverboat passed. The trees offered little shelter from the weather when we stopped to rest, and I blew warm air into my hands to return feeling to my frigid fingers.

"I don't think I've ever looked forward to spring more than at this moment," I grumbled, rubbing my arms.

When we made camp a day and a half later, the weather hadn't yet improved. The sky remained a dark gray, threatening snow. The horses bore the falling evening temperatures well, but we had to wrap ourselves in every stitch of clothing to keep from shivering. Olim built up a sizable fire despite his reservations that it would draw attention, for he reasoned it wouldn't make a difference if it meant we froze to death.

Thoughts of Finton warmed my heart more than any flames, and even though it was so cold my breath came out in a white plume, a giddy euphoria lay over me like a down comforter. Alone in the tent, I traced my fingertips along my lips imagining the warmth of his mouth on mine, and a shudder passed through me, pooling in my belly. Heat blossomed from neck to scalp. Olim busied himself with settling in the horses for the night and wasn't near enough to see my scarlet cheeks. Laria would laugh at my foolishness. Finton would soon be my husband after all, and wasn't it perfectly natural to think of him this way?

Olim ducked into the tent and I hastily rubbed my face, desperate for the heat and hoping to cover my embarrassing thoughts.

"Olim?" I ventured after he made himself comfortable. "Can I ask you something personal?"

A bark of laughter escaped his lips before his teeth clacked shut. He cleared his throat and asked, "Do I have a choice?"

I scowled. "Yes."

"Go on."

"Do you think of Duveesa?"

He didn't answer for several seconds, and I thought he was ignoring the question. Olim was very private about his feelings. Well, except when he was angry. And considering our past, it wouldn't surprise me if he chose to keep quiet regarding his courtship of my friend.

"Sometimes," he said. "I try not to."

"Why?"

"What would be the point? She's far away."

"And it would be too distracting?"

"Exactly."

"Because it would make you sad?"

"The thought of her doesn't make me sad. But I also can't afford to let my mind wander when we have to be on our guard."

"I guess that makes sense. I've been avoiding thinking of home, the children, and Laria until now. I feel a weight has been lifted and I'm finally free to think of them."

"You've been understandably preoccupied."

"Does it annoy you? That we came all this way for only five minutes?"

"It would have been more annoying if you'd come all this way only to have him call you daft and send you home crying."

We shared a chuckle at the jest, though the idea sent a pang through my heart.

"And to be honest with you," he said. "I've enjoyed the adventure. The castle had been getting a little too mundane."

"Well, you're welcome." I nudged him playfully and he shot me a wry grin.

Within moments of our conversation disappearing into the stillness of the night, I heard a soft snore from beside me, and seconds later, I fell into a deep, dreamless sleep.

⁂

The barest of touches fluttered against my skin, tracing from the top of my forehead to the tip of my nose. In my sleepy haze, my mind attributed the sensation to the fingertips of my betrothed. I smiled dreamily, picturing his hands trailing down my cheek, my neck, and across my shoulders. The sound of laughter drifted through my mind, but it wasn't Finton's. And it didn't belong to one man.

My eyes flew open and focused on an object dangling above my face, tickling my nose. A feather. A man I didn't recognize loomed over me, and I scrambled backward. I opened my mouth to scream, but he placed a finger to my lips to shush me, shaking his head reprovingly. A quick glance around revealed several bearded men, all dressed in plain tunics and dirty breeches, baring their yellowed teeth. They appeared in stark contrast to the man in front of me.

He wore a high-collared blue doublet with gold brocade accents and leather leggings hugging tightly to his lean frame. Tall black boots were shined to perfection, and a scarf was wrapped around his wide-brimmed hat. He tucked the striped feather into it and grinned. The black outline around his eyes contrasted starkly with his amber skin as did the thin black stripe of hair stretching from his bottom lip to chin.

A scuffle prompted me to jerk to the left, and my heart sank when I saw Olim struggling against bindings being held by three men, a gag wrapped around his mouth.

"We've been looking for you for a long time," the man before me said.

I took in his amused expression and my ire rose. I dug my fingers into the ground to keep from shaking and jutted out my chin defiantly.

"I'm afraid you've made a mistake, sir."

Everyone laughed, making me more irritated and confused.

"Did you hear that, lads? She called me 'sir.'"

The men laughed again, louder this time, and he allowed it for another few seconds before raising his hand, instantly silencing them.

"No mistake, madam," he said, the amusement gone from his expression. "Did you happen to encounter a rather large and foul-smelling man in your travels? Before the river village?"

My eyes darted toward Olim.

"Maybe," I said, and cringed at my inability to keep the quiver from my voice.

"That's unfortunate. You see, he was one of us, and when he didn't return after wandering off to take a piss, we went looking for him. Someone nearly lopped his head off, it turns out."

He made a gesture to demonstrate, but I said nothing and tried to remain as stoic as possible.

"You have any idea who may have done that?" He raised an eyebrow.

I shook my head.

He leaned closer. "Are you sure?"

Again, I shook my head, pursing my lips to keep from trembling.

"Then tell me, madam, who does this belong to?" He produced a necklace, and my hand flew to my chest. I hadn't even known it was lost, but it must have happened during the struggle. It was all the confirmation the man required. His eyes sharpened, and I frantically formulated a defense.

"We had no choice! He attacked me!"

"That's his job," the man said darkly.

"Is it his job to attack innocent young women?" My voice was just as challenging, fueled by fear and anger.

"It's his job to rob women, yes."

"Then if you can reasonably grant that a person doing their job is innocent of wrongdoing, then you can concede that since *he*," I pointed at Olim, "was doing his job in protecting me, you have no reason to hold us."

He chuckled lightly. "Clever little thing, aren't you? Normally, I might let you go with such a speech, but the thing is, though that man was disgusting and frightfully dressed, he was, regrettably, my brother. And as such, I'm duty bound to avenge him." He reached for his sword.

"Wait!" I held out my hands imploringly. "You can't."

"And why is that?"

"Because if you do, you'll be the one hunted."

He raised an eyebrow. "You've piqued my curiosity. Why is that?"

"I'm..." I looked at Olim, but he shook his head, urging me to be quiet. "I work in the royal household at Praed Castle."

Olim rolled his eyes in exasperation.

"Do you? And what are you doing so far from home?"

"I'm traveling on royal business. If you allow us to go free, I promise no harm shall come to you."

"But you see that leaves us with this small matter of avenging my brother, madam. I cannot in good conscience let you go without feeling that I have somehow dishonored his memory."

The men snickered, but a swift look from their leader wiped the grins from their faces.

"I know no amount of money could replace your loss, but if you release us, you will be compensated."

"You have that much influence?"

"Yes." Olim protested through his gag, and I gave him a sharp glare. One of the men punched him in the stomach, and I winced as he doubled over. "Anything you want."

"Anything? Well, in that case, I want my own castle." He grinned flippantly at me while his men seconded the request.

I narrowed my eyes. "Within reason. Why don't you try asking for something a grown man would want—not a child's fantasy?"

His smile vanished, and his men coughed into fists and jeered.

"Something for a grown man?" he repeated, his voice low. "And what would you suggest, madam?" He ran a hand up my leg, and I sprang to my feet, slapping him away as if he were a snake.

"How dare you! Keep your hands off me. I am engaged!"

He rose as gracefully as a swan and jerked a thumb over his shoulder at Olim. "To him?"

"No. He's my friend."

"Then your fiancé isn't here to object, is he?"

"If you touch me, you'll get nothing. But I promise, if you allow us to return safely and with my virtue intact, the Queen of Praed herself will give you whatever you ask. Again, within reason."

He drummed his fingers on the hilt of his sword and glanced at Olim.

"How can we be sure she's tellin' the truth?" asked a gap-toothed brute.

"Because she's been trembling this whole time. Until now. She's telling the truth, or she believes she is. Either way, it appears we'll be going to Praed. It's been a long time. Eh, lads?"

They clapped and cheered and Olim was pulled to his feet.

"The name is Kit Renard," the leader said. He removed his hat with a flourish and bowed. I inhaled sharply through my teeth at the sight of his bald head, the only hair a stripe of sun-lightened brown across the top of his scalp. "And you are…?"

"Ula," I said quietly. "And that's Olim."

"A pleasure," Kit said with a bow toward Olim. "I'm sure my men would agree. You can learn their names as we go. It's a long way to Praed."

A long way indeed. And now it seemed we were to make the rest of the journey with a band of outlaws.

Chapter 36

Olim remained bound and tethered to his horse as we were led through the forest away from the river. I looked back until I could no longer see it, the sound of the rushing water fading in the distance, then sighed and stared blankly ahead. The trees were growing denser on the journey northward. Olim wore a defeated expression, as if all of this was somehow his fault, but there was no way to comfort him. Kit forced me to ride behind him, making any conversation between Olim and I impossible. Our things were ransacked for valuables, our clothes and food taken as well as Olim's sword and Laria's dagger. Kit wore it on his person, but I could not devise a way to steal it back. Our luck, it seemed, had run out.

When we stopped for the night, I slid off my horse in an exhausted heap. Before I could slump to the ground, tent supplies were shoved into my arms and I was pointed toward a spot to pitch it. Behind me, the men were already singing songs and toasting themselves on being expert thieves and masters of their domain.

If there is any justice in the world, a tree will fall on Kit's tent tonight.

As I hammered in the last tent stake, I shook my head to clear the dark thoughts, not wishing for the situation to turn my heart cold.

"You appear to be quite useful."

I whirled around and met Kit Renard's wild eyes, the color of grass at the end of summer and as full of glittering sunlight. Where Finton's eyes held humor and warmth, Kit's held the promise of mischief, and not the childish kind.

"Shouldn't you be busy drinking with your friends?" I flinched at the comment, knowing it was something Laria would say and might lead to trouble. Astonishingly, instead of being angry, Kit laughed.

"I've been remiss, I confess, but I gallantly thought you might need assistance and thought to offer myself."

"I want nothing from you." A thought occurred to me, and I studied him for a moment. Beyond the ostentatious ensemble, Kit wasn't what I expected from an outlaw. He was clean shaven and a strong odor didn't waft off him like it did his brother. He bore himself as a gentleman would—shoulders back, chin up, and smugly grinning.

"You speak very well for a... well, for a..."

"Highwayman? Thief? Criminal?"

"Vagrant."

He tsked and waved a hand. "I wasn't always."

"What made you choose this life?" I asked, genuinely curious despite my reservations.

He smiled, his teeth blindingly clean for a man who lived in the woods. "Come on. Food is ready and drink is flowing."

"I'm not inclined to eat just now."

"Well, if you don't, you might find it all gone when you are 'inclined.'"

I stalked over to the fire without another word and dropped heavily next to Olim. Channeling my sister, I pierced the nearest man with my harshest glare and ordered him to untie my friend. The man was taken aback and looked to his leader.

"Go on, Mik. You heard the royal lady," Kit said with a bow.

Olim was unbound, so I held my tongue. The man called Mik was skinny and missing a front tooth, had shaggy brown hair, a short beard, and a scar above his right eye. If we made it to Praed in one piece, I would turn over as many names as possible.

"I hope you have a great plan," Olim whispered. "Because making friends with the criminals doesn't seem like a good idea."

"At what point did it look like I was making friends?" I hissed.

"You practically invited them to the castle."

"To save us! What do you think will happen to them once Laria finds out what they've done?"

"Good point. I wouldn't turn your back on any of them if I were you. Especially after they've been drinking. These aren't exactly what you would call honorable men."

"I would feel much better if you still had the dagger."

"Me, too. Let's just keep our heads down and make it to Praed in one piece."

Olim and I refrained from speaking for the rest of the evening to prevent anyone from getting suspicious. However, once the men reached an epically intoxicated level, we could have been openly discussing rebellion and no one would have paid attention. The men sang so raucously I covered my ears, and even the horses whinnied in protest. One by one, the drunkards passed out, and the silence that followed was a relief. The only man who retained his senses was Kit. When the only people still awake were me, Olim, and the leader of thieves, the latter rose and extended his hand toward me. I stared at his open palm in a mixture of confusion and disgust, and when I didn't take it, he wiggled his fingers in front of me.

"Come, come, madam. You must be exhausted," he said.

"Where do you intend for me to go?" I hoped my trepidation wasn't evident in my voice.

"To the shelter of the tent, of course. What sort of gentleman would I be if I allowed a lady to sleep in the open?"

"You're no gentleman," Olim said in a dangerously low voice.

"Don't make me tie you up again," Kit said. "I suspect if the lady sleeps under my guard, you'll stay close. But if not, I'll gladly bind your feet and hands to keep you from escaping."

"I will not share a tent with you," I said.

"You don't have a choice," he snapped. "Now, you either come with me willingly, or you can risk sparking my temper, in which case I may no longer be able to control my...impulses." His eyes roved over my body, and I crossed my arms over my chest protectively.

"Fine," I said.

Kit smiled graciously and extended an arm for me to precede him. I stalked away and practically threw myself into the tent and burrowed under the covers. I tensed when Kit entered, but he kept his distance. Every movement had me sitting bolt upright. And every time I awoke, Kit was staring at me, a smug smile on his face. I scooted over as far as possible, but I felt his eyes on me, pulling me into an abyss I could not escape.

I made it through the night with my virtue intact, and aside from lecherous stares, no one put their hands on me. It seems there's honor among thieves after all.

Olim and I were allowed very little time to converse before he was gagged again, and he suffered the humiliation of being bound to his horse and having the men toss remnants of their meals at him. He bore the torment humbly, but after several miles without the amusement running thin, I'd had enough. I trotted up beside Kit, squeezing my knees together to keep them from shaking, and fixed a stern expression on my face.

"Can you please ask them to stop?" I said. "It's humiliating enough to be rendered helpless without being treated worse than an animal."

His attire was equally as extravagant as the day before—a thick, ivory-colored wool doublet with a frilled collar and red breeches. Strange that he dressed in such finery while his men were slovenly. He turned casually in my direction, the feather in his hat lilting in the wind, slowly looked behind us, then lazily met my furious gaze.

"I suppose," he said. "But if I tell them to stop, they may turn their attention to you."

My cheeks burned. "Don't you have control over your own men?"

His eyes darkened and his jaw clenched, but just when I thought he would explode with anger, he burst out laughing.

"I do enjoy your spirit. I don't know what I'll do for amusement once you're gone."

Angrily, I reined my horse away and spent the rest of the day riding beside Olim. I estimated we were near the village where we boarded the riverboat, but our path was so far away, I couldn't even see chimney smoke. Eventually, we came to a small stream, and though the sun was long from setting, Kit announced we were finished traveling for the day. At this rate, we wouldn't reach Praed for weeks.

To avoid direct contact with anyone, I made myself useful and observed the band from a distance. So far, I placed names with most of the faces and felt confident I could give accurate descriptions of all of them should the need arise. I distracted myself from our dismal situation by imagining what Laria would do once she discovered what happened, and I couldn't suppress a smile when my thoughts jumped from her reaction to the king's. These blackguards would regret their actions, indeed, if they lived to tell the tale.

"When a pretty girl smiles to herself, it usually means she has secrets."

Kit's voice mere inches away almost made me drop my brush, but I didn't turn around. I busied myself with grooming and feeding the horses and pretended not to hear him in the hopes he would leave me alone. I wasn't so lucky.

"Praed people are close to horses, I hear," he said.

When I didn't answer, he grabbed my arm and spun me around to face him.

"I don't abide rudeness." The words came out in a growl, and he bared his teeth. He squeezed my arm painfully tight, and I struggled to free myself, but he wouldn't relent.

"Yes," I gasped. "We are."

He let go of me, and I nearly toppled to the ground.

"That's better. When I speak to you, I expect an answer."

My arm would surely bruise, and I rubbed away the pain before returning to my task.

"Where are you from?" I asked, cursing my manners. Mother instilled the notion that a lady matches a gentleman's questions with inquiries of her own, and it seemed that even a scoundrel elicited such a deeply ingrained habit.

"The fringes of society."

He looked down his straight nose at me, his hands clasped behind his perfectly-postured back. It was a decidedly proper posture for one who came from such lowly circumstances. Though I was curious, I didn't care to converse with him more than necessary, so I didn't press.

"You're a mystery to me. You appear to be a delicate, well-born lady. And yet you travel with only one escort hundreds of miles toward danger. In the winter. It must have been something of great importance for you to risk your life." His eyes searched mine, and I turned away to avoid his reading how acutely I missed Finton and wished he were here now.

"It was."

"Secrets perhaps?"

"It's not really any of your business, is it?"

He chuckled at my obstinance, and anger spread from my toes to my scalp.

"I will figure you out before we reach Praed, Ula. I promise you that." I couldn't help the fear that flooded my face or hide the paleness of my skin at those words. But he shook his head and said, "Don't worry. I don't mean to defile you before your new husband has a chance. I'm not a monster."

"Time will tell," I whispered at his retreating back.

Kit insisted I ride close to him in addition to sharing his tent at night. Thankfully, he continued to keep his hands to himself, but that didn't stop the shame from creeping into my soul. Olim saw I had no choice, but what would Finton think when he found out? I owed him a lot of explaining once we were together again.

I was afforded little privacy, not even to bathe in the cool water of the stream running along a series of jagged peaks. It was not the Kreeg Mountains, for these were much smaller, but I didn't ask about them because the last thing I wanted was to draw anyone into conversation. I sat on the banks in my shift trying not to think about Kit keeping watch and managed to clean myself. He at least allowed me to dress with his back turned, but I did catch him peeking once or twice. The rake. Strangely, he no longer stared at me with a lascivious gleam, but rather with unrestrained curiosity, as if I were a puzzle he couldn't work out. He'll be disappointed when he discovers I'm not that interesting, but I decided to let him fret about it because the alternative was worse.

The men eventually grew tired of throwing things at Olim, but they still jeered and prodded him to get a response. For his part, Olim remained the stoic, well-ordered knight, and I was proud of him for maintaining his temper. He was still bound when we rode, but he no longer wore the gag. No one could hear us if we screamed anyway.

"How much longer do you think until we reach Praed?" I whispered to Olim while the men drank themselves into a cacophony of noise.

"A few days," he whispered back. "I think we're traveling near the Little Lavee River. It runs along the Gris Hills, the northern border of which isn't too far from one of the outlying Praed estates. If we can make it there, we can try to escape and find help."

"How? Your hands are always tied, and they hold your horse's lead."

"If we earn their trust, they'll let their guard down. Or if nothing else, convince them we mean to stay with them the whole way and they'll grow complacent."

"I think their trust is the last thing we should try and earn."

"It's our only chance. Do you really think they'll march us right up to Praed Castle and let us go? Most of these guys are fools, but that one isn't." He jerked his head at Kit sitting apart from his men surveying the scene and periodically watching us. "He'll use you as a bargaining piece to get what he wants. After that, who knows what he'll do."

I shivered and looked away.

"What should I do?"

"Practice those socializing skills that secured you a husband."

"I can't!"

"I'm not saying you should flirt with him. Just...be friendly."

"I couldn't." Bile crept up my throat. Vomiting on the man certainly wouldn't be considered a friendly gesture.

"Ula," Olim urged. "Think of it as a play. You're just acting."

"I'm terrible at acting."

He knew I couldn't hide my true feelings. He said it was because I was too honest. In truth, I was a terrible liar. I also had horrible stage fright.

"Pretend he's simply another traveler we met on our journey. It's not too far from the truth."

"I thought you said making friends with them was a bad idea?"

"That was before. It bought us our lives. It could buy us our freedom."

"Why don't *you* befriend them?"

"I'm not charming enough," he said dryly. "And most importantly, I lack something very important which you possess."

"What's that?"

"Femininity."

"Stop it," I muttered. I glanced toward the raucous group and saw Kit had left his seat, taken several steps forward, and was staring at us suspiciously.

"Please," Olim whispered. His eyes flickered toward the crunching of boots, and we lowered our heads to hide our mouths. "Please, try."

Kit's footsteps grew closer, and it took every ounce of restraint to stop myself from looking.

"All right," I said just as Kit loomed over us.

"You two have had too much time together. I think it would be best if you sat with me from now on." Kit extended a hand toward me. I glanced at Olim, and he inclined his head, urging me to comply. Sighing, I took Kit's proffered hand, but I couldn't bring myself to return his smile. He tucked my hand under his elbow and led me to the other side of the fire, drawing snickers from the other men.

"Look at me, lads," Kit said. "Escorting a real lady."

They burst into rolling laughter, clutching their sides and falling over. I dropped to the ground crossly and did my best to ignore their pleas to be 'next.'

Kit sat down beside me. "Have you had enough to eat?"

"Yes." My tone was sharp, then I remembered the agreement with Olim and plastered on a thin smile. "Thank you."

Kit narrowed his eyes at my sudden politeness but made no comment. I kept a small smile on my face for the rest of the evening, and by the time everyone started passing out, my face hurt. When Kit deemed I could retire to bed, I allowed him to help me to my feet and open the tent flap for me.

Once I was tucked under several layers of blankets he said, "You've been rather compliant and agreeable this evening."

"I'm just trying to make the best of the situation. Don't get used to it. You might start to like me."

He studied me closely, murmuring, "I wouldn't dream of it."

"Well, goodnight then," I said lightly.

"Goodnight, enigmatic Lady Ula."

My insides twisted with an overwhelming sense of disgust. The last thing I wanted was to ruin my integrity by acting in such a diametric manner than what I felt. I reminded myself I was doing this for survival, but I still had to repress the urge to vomit.

Chapter 37

Kit wouldn't allow Olim and me to sit together to avoid conspiracies after he caught us in deep conversation. He was no fool, in several and unexpected ways. He knew exactly where my cloak and dress came from, and not just Torshul, but specifically from the king's own caravan. He identified the jeweler in Praed who crafted my necklace and the cobbler who made my boots. If he wasn't such a blackguard, I might've been impressed. His wardrobe consisted of an impressive array of colorful doublets and form-fitting breeches, all of which exhibited his lean frame. His attire and his swagger pointed to a confidence bordering on arrogance.

I pushed past my general distaste of the man and tried to appear friendly, but it wasn't easy. I started small, making comments on the weather and complimenting his choice of clothing. But he was distrustful of my sudden cordiality, giving me hostile glances and either ignoring my questions or giving perfunctory answers. In despair, I retreated into myself, and for the rest of the day, I kept quiet.

The evening was dry and crisp, and the fire crackled and popped. Embers fluttered upwards, flaring briefly before snuffing out. For the first time in years, I watched the tiny sparks dance without trepidation. There was more to fear than bad memories. I picked at my food despondently, wondering what I could do to endear Kit, when a fight broke out between two of the men.

A burly man named Bret yelled, "Stop digging at it, Mik!"

"Don't tell me what to do! You're not my pa!"

They shoved and wrestled each other around the campfire. This didn't seem to upset anyone else unless the pair came close to spilling a goblet. Kit ate impassively as they continued to tussle, lifting his plate out of the way when they came too close. I wasn't so quick. Bret landed a solid blow to Mik's jaw, sending him toppling into my side and pitching us both to the ground.

Kit sprang to his feet, yelling, "For the love of Solamun!"

I didn't know who Solamun was, but I'd never heard Kit declare love for anyone. While I lay awkwardly on the ground, Mik hauled himself to his feet and apologized profusely. Not to me. To his leader.

"Sorry, Kit, but Bret started it," Mik said, pointing a stubby finger at the other man.

"Stop acting like children, you clumsy fools," Kit said before striding over and pulling me unceremoniously back onto the boulder I'd been sitting on.

"Tell him to stop acting like my pa," Mik grumbled.

"You're going to make it worse," Bret said.

"It's *my* leg!" Mik said, raising a fist.

Without a second thought, I jumped up and held my hands out to stop the inevitable fight and exclaimed, "Gentlemen! Please, what's this all about?"

The two men eyed me without answering, but Mik couldn't help but place the blame where he felt it was due.

"I cut my leg and Bret won't stop nagging about it. A regular mother hen," he said, glaring at the other man.

"Say that again when it goes rotten," Bret said.

"He's obviously concerned," I told Mik. "It would surely be tragic if the wound became infected. It could kill you."

Mik curled his lip and tilted his head in confusion.

"Could it?" he asked. He looked to Kit for confirmation, and in response, his leader raised his eyebrows and hands.

"If the lady says so," Kit said.

"Would you allow me to see the wound? Perhaps I can be of assistance?"

Mik jerked back as if I'd struck him and looked again at Kit.

"Whatcho think, boss?" Mik asked.

"That's entirely up to you. But if it were me, I'd leap at the chance to have the lady's hands on my leg."

Mik laughed and started unlacing his breeches. I turned away, blushing violently. He stripped down to his drawers and stuck his leg out for me to inspect. I pursed my lips when I saw the location of the wound was his lower calf. He could've simply rolled up a pant leg. Scoundrel.

The wound was indeed angry, most likely due to his poor hygiene. The odor of infection eclipsed his general stench. Bret raised a flask to his lips, but I snatched it and poured a generous amount on the jagged cut. Mik cried out and let loose a string of curses. I paid no attention to his protestations and cleaned the wound of dirt and debris with my last clean handkerchief.

"Do you have any honey?" I asked Kit.

"What for?"

"I need it for the wound. Trust me."

He stared at me unmoving while my heart pounded against my chest. It was a bold thing to say. We both knew there was no trust between us and to ask for it was outright galling.

"Jon," Kit addressed one of the men watching my ministrations in slack-jawed wonder.

Jon shook out of his trance and said, "Yes, boss?"

"Was there any honey in the bag we snatched from that old couple?" Kit asked.

"Maybe. There was a lot of tea."

"Go check."

Jon scurried off to do as he was told, and Kit's eyes met mine once more. We waited, the silence between us tense, but I didn't break eye contact. Jon returned triumphantly holding a small jar, which he placed into my outstretched hands. It contained a small amount of honey beginning to crystallize. I spread a liberal amount into the wound, then ripped a long strip off the hem of my frock to wrap around it in a bandage. Once finished, I felt immensely satisfied with myself and wished Finton was there to see my work.

"Impressive," Kit said. "Where did you learn how to do that?"

"My fiancé," I said, trying to contain the sadness creeping into my voice. "He's a physician and a brilliant surgeon."

"We're duly honored to host the fiancé of such an exalted man, aren't we lads?"

Their mocking laughter echoed throughout camp, but I tried not to let it affect me.

"Feels better already, boss!" Mik said, pulling his breeches back on. "I'd entrust my leg to the lady any day."

I offered the man a small smile, then returned to my seat to stare blankly into the flames. The men soon thereafter lost interest in me and commenced drinking themselves into a stupor.

Kit resumed his place beside me, sitting close enough for me to smell the curious mixture of powder, sunshine, campfire, and fine linen I'd come to recognize.

"What's his name?"

"Leave me alone." I spoke before I remembered I was supposed to befriend the man.

He casually leaned back, stretching his legs toward the fire. "I've never liked the idea of being beholden to one woman. Afraid I'd get bored."

"I think that's more *your* failing than the ladies'."

"Perhaps. But at least I know myself well enough not to raise anyone's hopes."

"I doubt you factor in any woman's hopes."

"That's very cruel of you to say, Lady Ula."

I looked up worriedly, afraid I'd angered him. But he wore a half smile and his eyes glittered mischievously.

"I'm sorry," I said.

"I ask again: what's his name? And don't forget how I feel about unanswered questions."

"How could I." I pictured the bruise on my forearm. "His name is Finton." My voice broke upon saying his name, and I hoped Kit didn't notice.

He did.

"You're fond of him then?"

"Of course, I am! Why else would I marry him?"

"The usual reasons. Wealth, convenience, to escape from ruination..."

I thought of Olim and our plan for escape. If I was to lure Kit into a false sense of security, I had to engage him in conversation. My throat was parched, and I swallowed several times before I could speak again.

"I'm not a Lady," I blurted out. "I mean, I'm a lady...a woman...but I'm not a titled Lady."

"So?"

"So, you don't have to keep calling me 'Lady' Ula. I'm just Ula."

"From what I've seen, you're not 'just' anything."

I shifted uneasily, but he made no move to avert his penetrating gaze. I pulled my knees up to my chest and wrapped my arms around them.

"You're mistaken. I'm not worth this study you've made of me."

"Time will tell."

My face reddened upon hearing the words I'd spoken two days prior, words I thought he hadn't heard.

"Go to bed, Just Ula."

I bolted from my seat like a green horse seeing a snake and ducked into the tent without further prompting.

Several hours later, I awoke to hear Kit stumbling into bed, which was quite out of character considering he usually didn't overindulge. I pretended to be asleep as he tossed off his clothing, but I cracked open one eye when I heard a metallic clatter. Kit's discarded doublet, an emerald-green piece with black stripes, lay open on the floor. And inside glimmered the pommel of Risteard's dagger. My attention flickered to Kit. He already appeared asleep. I returned my focus to the weapon. If I moved very slowly, perhaps I could retrieve it...

Unfortunately, the moment I made the slightest movement, Kit's eyes flew open and locked on me. I'd extended a hand toward the doublet, but when he awoke, I pretended I was simply stretching my arms and rolled over. I held my breath for several seconds, waiting for him to say something, but he remained silent. I let the air out of my lungs in a *whoosh* and didn't move a muscle for the rest of the night.

In a few days we reached the southernmost borders of Praed, which Olim conveyed with his uneasy stare. I chewed at my lower lip, aware he was counting on me to aid our escape, but Kit made me so nervous I found it difficult to fall into conversation with him. I asked myself again what Laria would do. I hid a smile when I pictured her exchanging witty banter followed by a few choice snarky comments and engaging smiles that would have the entire gang eating out of her hand. She would have been fast enough to snatch the dagger from Kit's doublet and have it at his throat before he could blink.

"More secrets?" Kit asked from where he rode beside me. He caught me wandering around in my own thoughts again, and I mentally kicked myself for losing focus.

"No secrets. Just thinking about my sister." I chose to be honest because I wouldn't remember a lie, nor be creative enough to weave a believable one.

"Does she live in Praed Castle, too?"

"Yes."

"And does she also believe in love and monogamy?"

"Yes. She's happily married."

"How dull." He rolled his eyes.

It wouldn't be in my best interest to antagonize him, so I counted to ten to keep from screaming about all the reasons her life was anything but dull.

Hoping to change the subject from Laria, I asked, "Who's Solamun?"

He whirled in his saddle, blinking rapidly at my question.

"You mentioned you loved her yesterday."

"*Him*," he clarified.

"Oh." I shifted in my saddle, unsure of what to say to that confession.

He clicked his tongue in exasperation. "Where I come from, my people pray to him."

"What does 'pray' mean?"

His features twisted into utter disbelief. "You don't have gods in Praed?"

"No."

"They're higher beings," he said. "Praying is another term for talking, except when a person talks to gods, they don't get an answer. At least not visibly. Sometimes the answer comes in a sign or something as simple as a plentiful crop. It's difficult to explain..." He placed a finger to his lips as he thought how to make such a confusing subject easier to grasp. "Who do you go to for comfort during hard times?"

"My family."

"What if they're not around?"

"Friends?"

"If you're unpopular?"

I considered his question seriously, but without friends or family, whom else would I talk to?

"It comforts some people to have someone to talk to, even if they can't see them. Even if the only evidence of their existence is their belief that they do," he explained.

"Like ancestors?"

"In a sense. Except there's some debate as to whether gods ever existed at all. Regardless, it makes people feel better in times of need and lessens their responsibility if things go poorly."

"And it must help when people feel lonely to think someone's listening."

"I suppose." He wouldn't meet my gaze and ignored any further inquiries. Apparently, his rule of answering questions only applied if it was him doing the asking.

By the time we set up camp for the night, I was fully panicking. I was no closer to securing their trust and we were close to Praed. Olim was counting on me, and I was failing. I couldn't ask for his advice because we weren't allowed to talk to each other. The thought of flirting made me want to vomit, so that was out of the question. I enthusiastically groomed the horses while I debated what to do, removing every inch of dirt from their shaggy coats, muttering to myself that if I didn't use my brain, we were in trouble.

I brushed the last of the grime from my horse and gave it a firm pat, then turned toward camp. In my haste, I didn't pay attention to my surroundings and collided straight into Kit's chest.

"Sorry," I breathed, pushing away from him.

"You seem...unhinged."

I couldn't help the hostility in my tone. "Can you blame me? My friend and I are hostages subject to your whim. You may not understand our circumstances, but surely you can sympathize with our lack of freedom."

"I can."

His nostrils flared and his chest rose and fell much too quickly. A trill of fear coursed up my spine, and I took a step back. I had to turn this conversation around before I ended up bound and gagged myself.

"What happened to you?" I asked.

"I don't go around spilling my secrets to every woman who asks," he snarled.

"No, I suspect you wouldn't. I'm sorry."

His jaw clenched and his eyes briefly fluttered closed.

"Come and eat," he said hoarsely before stalking away. His hands were clenched in fists behind his back, the muscles of his lithe arms flexed.

Unless I was mistaken, he was upset and barely in control. It pained me to use someone when they were vulnerable, but mine and Olim's lives were at stake. I followed closely behind, studying his stern expression. He didn't look at me, and he didn't allow me to catch up. I remained by his side for the rest of the evening, preventing him from gaining distance and reestablishing control over his emotions. This annoyed him, but I was relentless. He even positioned himself at an angle when I sat next to him at the fire, and I met Olim's gaze across the flames with a satisfied smirk.

Kit excused himself to bed early, and I rose to follow. He raised an eyebrow and made a salacious comment, but the sentiment didn't reach his eyes, so I knew he was putting on a front to frighten me away. I declined his invitation, to do what I won't say, and nonchalantly readied myself to sleep. He watched me, and I could feel his annoyance filling the tent.

"Was there something you wanted to talk about?" I feigned innocence.

He blew a puff of air out of his nose, and I shrugged my shoulders and pulled the covers around myself. The blankets were ripped off, and as I reached to grab them, Kit pulled me out of bed. He loomed over me, his nose nearly touching mine, and my skin ran cold at the dark intensity of his stare.

"You're playing a dangerous game, Ula," he whispered through clenched teeth.

"I'm not," I squeaked.

"Aren't you?"

"No. I swear I don't know what you mean."

"Don't you?"

I shook my head, too afraid to speak. He searched my face, his expression unreadable. Alarmingly, he inched closer, and I suddenly feared he would try to kiss me. He must have sensed my apprehension, for his face twisted into a sneer and he roughly pushed me away.

"I'll be glad to be rid of you once we reach Praed," he said.

You and me both.

Chapter 38

I failed. I failed Olim, and I failed myself. I succeeded not in drawing Kit closer, but in pushing him away. When I awoke the next morning, he'd already left the tent, and one of his cronies ordered me to pack everything up and be ready to leave in five minutes. I did as I was told, throwing blankets and clothes into the canvas bags and bringing down the tent without any help. When finished, I was sweating and out of breath. Kit practically ripped the tent from my hands to tie it to a pack mule and waved me away when I hadn't moved. When I tried to speak, he held up a hand and stopped me with a harsh look. My heart sank, and I shuffled over to my horse dejectedly. I searched out Olim but couldn't signal that all was lost. I didn't try to ride beside Kit, and he didn't force me to remain close as he had previously. It appeared we would be heading to Praed Castle together.

Unexpectedly, Kit called for a rest after only a few miles. His men seemed just as confused, but they followed their leader's orders without question. Olim and I shared a look before he was tied to a tree, and the men settled into the rations after clearing a space of wet leaves and snow. The closer we traveled to Praed, the colder the temperature. But even though there was a dusting of snow on the ground, the sun was making more of an appearance, melting the residual evidence of winter. The trees were changing, and I recognized the tall monoliths with sharp, needle-like leaves. I estimated we would cross the border into Praed the next morning if we continued.

After several minutes and more than a few pints of ale, no one seemed very interested in leaving anytime soon. In frustration, I looked around for Kit to argue that the sooner we reached the castle, the sooner he would be paid, but he was nowhere in sight. I checked the horses, but he wasn't there either. The men gathered around the clearing were raising their glasses to one another and singing loudly, oblivious to my movements. So I followed the sound of the Little Levee River, intending to wash. If Kit wasn't there, it might be my chance to run for help. It couldn't be far to the nearest estate. If I ran as hard as I could, I would have a decent head start. It was our best chance, though I would be leaving Olim behind.

The rushing of water over stones grew louder when I pushed aside a low-hanging branch. There, a man was kneeling on the bank, his naked back toward me. I heard Laria's voice in my head pointing out this wasn't the first time I'd seen a man's bare torso. But this instance did not fill me with the embarrassment and excitement as when I saw Finton. I felt surprised and inquisitive. The back was darkly tanned, lean but not muscular, and had a series of drawings extending from the right shoulder to waist. Water ran down his skin, but the marks somehow remained. I stepped forward for a closer look and a twig snapped, the sound echoing off the rocky hills and sending a flock of birds flying wildly into the air. The man rose quickly and spun toward me. *Kit.*

"What are you doing lurking back there?"

"I was coming to the river to wash." I walked forward and managed to restrain myself from teasing that his observational skills were sorely lacking. I wasn't exactly being stealthy.

He relaxed his shoulders and sighed in exasperation, then stooped back down to the water.

"Can't a man have a little moment to himself?"

"Now you know how I feel."

He shot me a glare, then shrugged as if agreeing I'd made a fair point. I inched closer to the river, keeping my eye on him, and splashed cool water on my face and neck. His attention darted to me briefly, but he mostly ignored me. I sighed, feeling defeated, and racked my brain for something to talk about that might ease the tension between us. Being perpetually shy made it difficult to talk to people I didn't know very well, even to discuss something as mundane as the weather. When he wasn't looking, I studied his prone form, and I struggled for something to say. Then my gaze alighted on his back.

"What do those marks mean?" I asked, hoping the subject wouldn't somehow annoy him further.

He paused, clutching the shirt he scrubbed against the rocks. I held my breath in anticipation of his reaction. Shoulders relaxed, he resumed his task.

"They were placed there by my family. They're symbols of my people," he said, his tone bored and disinterested.

"How were they placed there?"

"By very sharp instruments. They cut into my skin and left ink inside permanently."

"Did it hurt?"

He sneered. "What do you think?"

I turned away, my cheeks burning. He certainly knew how to make me feel foolish.

"And they won't go away?"

"That's what permanent means."

I rolled my eyes but refused to be discouraged. He was talking to me again, and I didn't want to waste this opportunity.

"What do they signify?"

He sighed dramatically, wrung out his clothes, and carried them back to camp. I followed, struggling to keep up. The men straightened when he came into view, as if they didn't want him to see how intoxicated they'd become. Kit strode over to the fire and hung his clothes over a tree branch to dry while his men eyed each other nervously.

"You idiots have ten minutes to sober up," Kit barked.

Like birds scattering from a tree, the men scrambled to their feet and rushed to ready themselves. Instead of gathering his own things, Kit dropped to the ground before the fire and stared into the flames. Hesitantly, I lowered myself and tucked my knees to my chest. He didn't acknowledge me, even to say something disparaging, nor did he cast a glance my way. I wrapped my arms around my legs, rested my chin on my knees, and waited.

"I don't know what it is you hope to hear," Kit said. "If you're wanting me to reveal some history explaining my current situation, you'll be waiting a long time I'm afraid."

"I have no expectations."

He looked at me then, and I was relieved he didn't appear angry. His yellow-green eyes reflected the flickering flames, and I watched in amazement as they darkened, imperceptibly at first. I blinked, and they were black. I shrank away, afraid and uncertain.

"Such a pity," he said, "to have no expectations. On the other hand, a person without expectations is one who is never disappointed."

"Have you been disappointed?"

"Many times."

"Is that why you left? Your family I mean." I cast a glance toward the tree where Olim was tied and stared meaningfully.

I won't let you down.

"What is it you want me to say?" He tossed a rock into the fire, sending a plume of sparks crackling into the air. "Are you hoping to hear a romantic story? That I loved a woman, had my heart broken, and couldn't bear to live in the same country as her? That's a fairy tale for children, and I know how you feel about those."

He sounded resentful, but somehow, it didn't feel entirely directed toward me.

"I think the idea of you loving anyone but yourself is the true fairy tale." I couldn't stop myself. I tensed, anticipating a stern response, but then relaxed when he laughed heartily.

"You know me well enough already to suspect that no such woman exists. And you're right. I have no romantic stories, and I never will. A man who falls in love is a fool on the brink of ruin."

"Who was he?" I asked. "The fool."

He looked at me sharply, and I summoned all my courage to not look away. I set my jaw and stared back boldly, waiting for him to wave me away or answer.

"My father," he said through gritted teeth. "A classic fool who fell in love with a woman for the worst possible reason."

"What reason is that?" I tried to control the rapid beating of my heart by squeezing my legs tighter against my chest, afraid he could hear how loudly it pounded.

"Beauty." His lip curled as he looked me up and down. "A beautiful woman who knows how intoxicating she can be is more dangerous than a band of roving bandits."

An explosion of laughter escaped my lips. What a mad comparison to make. "Arguable."

Kit grasped the neckline of my dress and wrenched me close. I swallowed hard as he drew me inches from his face and glared at me contemptuously.

"My father fell in love with my mother," he said, spitting out the word 'love' like it tasted foul in his mouth. "Married her, had children with her, then was betrayed by her. She made a fool of him. Several times. And when he had enough, when he'd practically begged her to stop and remain faithful to him like a whining dog. She laughed in his face."

"I'm sorry," I choked out. I tried to pull away, but he twisted his hand and tightened the dress painfully across my skin.

"He beat her until she lost consciousness then beat her some more. I watched as my father nearly killed my mother."

"Nearly?" I squeaked.

"My brother and I screamed for him to stop, but when a man is in such a rage, even the sounds of his sons crying in his ear are muffled behind his anger. I reached for the dagger he kept sheathed at his side, and before he knew it was in my hands, I stabbed him with it at least a dozen times."

I sucked in a breath but couldn't speak.

"My father bled to death before my eyes, and my mother moaned on the floor, but before I could go to her, my brother dragged me from the house, and together we fled the country and never returned."

"You saved her life," I whispered, tears now crawling down my cheeks from the pain of his grip and the sadness of the story.

He pushed me away, and I rubbed the raw area of skin at my neck.

"I'm not a good man, Ula. Stop trying to make me one."

"I never said that," I snapped. "And I certainly don't think it. Yes, you defended your mother, but look how you've lived since. You steal from innocent people, you terrorize the forest, you kidnap a young woman and tie a man to a tree." I indicated Olim, who was currently struggling against said binds. "You're a monster."

"A fact you would do well to remember," he growled, his face a breath away from mine.

I bit the inside of my lip to keep from trembling at the dark expression in his eyes. His gaze flickered over my face and down my body, and my stomach twisted sickly. He drew away and stood over me. I slowly released the breath I'd been holding and looked up at his impassive features. Wordlessly, he extended a hand, and I inspected it warily.

"Come now. We may never be friends, but we can at least be civil. I don't mean any harm."

"I don't believe you," I said, cringing at my unsteady voice.

"I've had plenty of opportunities to take what I want from you. And I haven't. Is that not reason enough to trust me?"

Slowly, I reached out and took his proffered hand, and he pulled me to my feet so forcefully I was propelled against his bare chest. Before I could push myself away, he gripped the back of my head and whispered in my ear.

"And trust me, Just Ula. I want you."

I braced my hands against his chest and pushed as hard as I could. He released me. I fixed him with my most intimidating glare, and it took all my self-restraint to not slap the smug smile off his face. I couldn't bear it any longer. Tonight, somehow, Olim and I would make our escape.

We traveled several more miles before stopping for the night, and I felt certain we were very close to Praed. The clouds had broken, the trees became sparse, and in the distance, I could see a mountain looming out of the fog. I locked eyes with Olim from across the camp, and he inclined his head, just barely, so I would know he agreed it was time. I still didn't have a solid plan for slipping by Kit, untying Olim, and escaping unnoticed, but I couldn't spend another night dreading Kit would break his word and touch me. I wasn't so naïve to think he would let me go if I asked nicely, nor was I willing to play the seductress. The thought alone made me sick, and I drank several deep gulps of water to wash the bile from my mouth. Once the tent was erected—by myself—and everything was unpacked inside— again, by myself—I wandered into the trees to gather wood with a strict warning that if I took too long, one of Olim's fingers would be broken for each minute I remained missing.

With each piece of firewood I picked up, I felt loaded with the heavy weight of helplessness. Olim and I had run out of time.

I became so discouraged I didn't pay attention to where I was going and slipped on a patch of wet vegetation. I tumbled forward, sticks and branches flying. My hands scraped against the rough earth. I rolled onto my side and rubbed my hip where it struck a fallen tree. That's when I spied the answer I'd been searching for.

Growing in a bunch on the rotting log was a cluster of brownish-gold pods I recognized from the medicines in Finton's bag. Once, I'd asked him to name the contents of the vials he kept, and he eagerly pointed to each and explained their properties and uses. I didn't understand most of what he said, but I recalled seeing the strange, squat-shaped plants growing before me and remembered Finton saying they were used to treat insomnia.

"What's that?" I asked.

"It's when you can't fall asleep," Finton said. "Some people will stay awake all night trying. A small amount of this fungus will render a person unconscious, but too much might kill them."

With a shaky hand, I reached out and harvested several pieces of the strange plant. It was soft and spongy and smelled of old dirt. I tucked them into the folds of my frock and wiped my hand clean on the hem. My heart thudded as I gathered up the scattered firewood and hurried back toward camp. If my plan for Kit worked, Olim and I would be safe. And Kit would either sleep soundly through the night or die by my hand. It wasn't what I wanted, but Olim was right. A person sometimes had to go to great lengths to survive.

None of the men paid attention as I prepared a stew of jerked meat and a random assortment of whatever vegetables we had left. They reveled in the firelight, singing of loose women and fast horses, their cups raised to toast one another's conquests. Olim stared morosely into the flames, his hands bound. Once I determined each man was satisfactorily occupied, I took the plant I'd found from my frock, tore it into pieces, and stirred it into the pot. I didn't know how much to use, but there was no time to consider the consequences.

I allowed the stew to steep for several minutes, then spooned it onto plates and passed them out, hoping no one would notice the shaking of my nervous hands. I passed one to Olim, but when he reached for it, I didn't immediately let go. I held the plate firmly and met his gaze. His brow furrowed, and I glanced down, then shook my head once. I let go and hoped he understood the message.

Once everyone was served, I sat down with my own plate and pretended to eat, but when no one was looking, I would reach toward the fire, ostensibly to stoke it, and drop pieces into the flames. I worried the odor of burning food would draw attention, but if the men smelled it, they didn't comment. I glanced at Kit several times to see if he noticed, but he seemed to be avoiding me. I saw Olim reach for a morsel, glance at the man beside him, and drop it onto the man's plate when he wasn't paying attention. I hid a smile and returned my focus to my own plate.

It didn't take long for the men's eyes to become drowsy and heavy-lidded. One by one, they shuffled off to bed or fell over where they sat and snored. Kit seemed puzzled and his eyes darted to me suspiciously. Casually, I stretched my arms overhead and yawned loudly, then rose to shuffle off to bed myself. Behind me Olim asked lazily to be untied so he could sleep. My heart sank at Kit's harsh reply.

"If you can piss with your hands tied, you can sleep with your hands tied."

But I detected a slight slur to his voice. He rose clumsily to his feet and stumbled toward the tent. Inside, he collapsed in a heap and struggled to push himself into a sitting position. I watched impassively, still as a rabbit avoiding a hunter. He raised his glassy and unfocused eyes to meet mine.

"What'd you do…?" His voice reminded me of mine when I'd drunk too much ice wine.

I shook my head. "You left me no choice." Even now, I pitied him. He'd seen horrible things as a child, and it left him so scarred he lived the rest of his life trying to escape the trauma by inflicting pain on others.

Unable to hold himself upright, he slumped onto his back, breathing heavily, fighting the effects of the sleeping draught. I crawled toward him and ran a hand along the sides of his doublet. I found what I was looking for and began undoing the silk buttons.

"I knew it." A lazy smile spread across his face. "You couldn't…" He breathed deeply several times before continuing. "Resist my charms."

"Don't flatter yourself."

I pulled Laria's dagger from inside his doublet. His eyes widened, and I glimpsed the first trace of fear I'd seen in him.

"Don't." His eyes opened and closed painfully slow as he fought to remain conscious.

"You're the monster, not me, remember? This belongs to my sister, and I intend to return it to her."

His eyes opened again and he smiled in relief.

"I'll…"

His voice faded, and when his eyes closed, they didn't open again. I watched the steady rise and fall of his chest for a few seconds to assure myself he was asleep before moving toward the open flap of the tent. Kit groaned behind me, and I froze when he spoke again.

"…find…you."

I didn't move, didn't breathe for ages, until I heard Kit snoring. I crawled out of the tent and gazed around the camp. Men were laid out asleep all around me, except for one. Olim sat patiently at the fire, and I dashed over to sever his binds. Without a word, we raced to our horses. We set the others loose before jumping onto their bare backs and rode blindly in the direction we'd seen the mountain.

Chapter 39

We rode for hours, stopping only to water the horses at the measly puddles left from the melting snow. We had no food for ourselves and had to satisfy our thirst by holding clumps of snow in our hands and drinking as it thawed and dripped into our mouths. The land around us changed from rocky hills and tall stone behemoths to short scrubs and wispy-branched trees. Shoots of grass poked out of the snow blanketing the rolling prairie that would soon be covered in wildflowers and grazing horses. We saw the first sign of civilization in days. My heart soared as Olim and I kicked our horses into a gallop and crossed the border into Praed.

The chimney of a manor house rose above the white landscape, followed by another, and the gray façade of Alluvale, the seat of Lord and Lady Grissen, followed. Lord Grissen had been close friends with my father, so I knew he would offer us shelter. I dug my heels into my horse's sides and surged forward, Olim close behind, and we sped onto the estate grounds, passing puzzled servants as we thundered up to the front entrance. A few men rushed forward to take our horses as we leapt to the ground and stumbled on weary legs toward the opening door of the estate. An aged man regarded our ragged clothing, wild hair, and dirty faces disdainfully and asked us to state our business.

"Please, sir," I breathed. "Are Lord and Lady Grissen at home?"

"Who may I ask is inquiring?"

"Ula Audrey."

His eyes narrowed and he looked at me doubtfully.

"If you spend the afternoon gawking at Miss Audrey without offering her shelter," Olim said. "You'll have to defend your position to your master."

The man paled and decided to risk allowing us to enter. He led us into the drawing room, where Olim and I gravitated to the roaring blaze in the hearth. We stood there, our hands extended toward the fire, our eyes glazed with exhaustion, when we heard footsteps rapidly approaching. The door burst open, and Lady

Alluvale rushed forward, her husband close behind. She hesitated, taking in our haggard appearance.

"Miss Ula?" he asked. "Is that really you?"

"Yes, my lady," I said.

My eyes brimmed with tears as I silently begged her to recognize me. I had known her my entire life. Where her husband was boisterous, she was reserved. And where she had no patience for Laria's animated personality, she always seemed to favor my meekness. She took another step forward and reached to wipe my face with a stark white handkerchief. She gasped when the dirt was cleaned away, and turned toward the servants milling in the doorway.

"Don't just stand there," she commanded. "Prepare Miss Audrey a bath and fetch her some dry clothes. Now!"

The frantic footfalls of the servants echoed down the hallway as they retreated, and Lady Grissen turned her attention to the knight waiting stoically behind me.

"And you are?" she demanded.

"Olim Lemichs," he said with a bow. "A knight in His Majesty King Risteard's army. I am sworn to watch over and protect Miss Audrey."

"Well, Sir Lemichs." Lord Grissen strode forward. "It would seem you're in need of a drink." He clapped Olim on the back and led him away, no doubt to indulge in the aforementioned drink—several most likely.

When we were alone, Lady Grissen took me by the shoulders and guided me upstairs. I could barely lift my legs to climb the immense staircase and gripped the handrail tightly to keep from tumbling.

"You look positively spent, my dear," Lady Grissen said. "What happened?"

"It's a long story." I gasped and spun to face her. She gripped me tighter to stop me from falling.

"What's the matter, Miss Audrey?"

"We escaped bandits. They may be coming after us."

Her lips formed a grim line and the color rose in her cheeks. "I'll alert the watchmen. If bandits are about, they'll not reach this house."

I nodded and slowly made my way upstairs.

"We'll take you the rest of the way to Praed Castle ourselves in the morning," Lady Grissen said. "Tonight, you must put yourself to rights and rest well."

"Thank you, my lady."

"Anything for a daughter of Riverstone."

Though the journey took more than a week, Lord and Lady Grissen insisted on escorting Olim and me to Praed Castle in their personal carriage. At every stopover, we were inundated by questions, but one question in particular was asked more than others:

When will the war be over?

It broke my heart to answer. "I don't know. But the king and our army are strong."

Their hopeful eyes would widen and glisten with unshed tears, and I'd smile confidently to prove my point. War was not unusual to the people of Praed, but living in peace for so long lulled them into a blissful dream. They had to remember how to live in fear again, to worry about their loved ones, to watch for another to usurp the crown.

For the first time in two months, I glimpsed the impressive view of the white mountain. I opened a window and breathed in the smell of the trees flanking the King's Road as we ascended into the clouds, and tears stung my eyes when the castle itself came into view.

When the carriage stopped at the front steps, I didn't wait for the groom to open the door before I climbed out and hurried into the castle. I squeezed through the doorway before it was fully opened. Olim followed close behind, and I stopped in the entryway to take in the familiar sight. A few people stared curiously, and once they recognized me, came forward to welcome me home. I waved away their questions about where we'd gone and staunchly ignored the sly glances showing their suspicions of what Olim and I had been doing.

I raced through the castle, poking my head through doorways looking for Laria. Considering what was happening at the front, I suspected she was in council, so I ran in that direction, Olim's footsteps echoing behind me. People jumped out of our way, and Olim issued apologies in our wake. I grabbed the door handles of the council chambers, but just as I was about to wrench the doors open, they were pushed forward, and I stumbled backward into Olim's arms.

"Ula?" It was Laria's voice.

We threw our arms around each other, locked in a fierce embrace, crying and laughing. Olim was led into the council chambers to give his report, and we were left alone in a joyous reunion. Laria stroked my hair, tangling her fingers in the thick strands, and I saturated her shoulder with my happy tears. Reluctantly, we separated, but we did not let go of each other's arms.

"You look awful," Laria teased.

"And you look enormous."

She laid a hand against her abdomen and nodded knowingly.

"Did you see Risteard?" Her voice was calm, but the desperation in her green eyes betrayed her worry.

"Yes, and he's well."

She sighed in relief and rubbed her sides. "This one has been giving me a lot of trouble. I look like I'm about to go into labor."

I covered her hand with mine. "It must be very strong and healthy."

"Come," she said, and wove her arm around my waist. "Tell me about your journey."

Laria and I lay in my bed, our hands entwined, filling the room with our laughter and stories. I told her everything—about the wolves, the kindness of strangers, the riverboat, and about the man Olim killed to defend my honor. She listened attentively, gasping when warranted, admonishing me when I spoke of my injuries, and beaming appreciatively when I told her about my friendship with Elasha and how it saved us. She tensed when I described what it looked like at the front lines, and I paused while I waited for her to stop trembling.

"It's all right," she said when I remained silent. "Go on. Tell me what happened."

"We spoke," I said.

"You and Finton?"

"Me and Risteard."

A painful sound emanated from her. She muffled her cries behind a hand and squeezed her eyes shut. I turned her to face me. She opened her eyes and tears spilled down her cheeks. I smiled warmly.

"He told me to tell you that you're constantly in his thoughts, and that you would know the rest."

She closed her eyes and smiled. She clung to my sleeve, her breath hitching in her throat.

"And…" I continued.

She opened her eyes.

"He promises he will return when…soon."

"He said that?" she asked, her eyes green pools of hope.

"Yes."

It was the best news she could have heard. Peace settled over her, and all the tension eased from her body. I hugged her, my brave sister, brave in a way I only pretended to be.

"And did you see Finton?"

I turned away to hide my blush. "Yes."

"And?"

"I kissed him, Laria."

"And?" She was smiling widely now.

"And I liked it."

"I knew you would! You just needed to find the right man. What else happened?"

"I told him I love him."

"My darling sister." Her hand was cool on my warm face.

"And he said he loves me, too."

"He would be a fool not to."

"Then I sort of blurted out a proposal of marriage."

"You did *what?*"

"It popped out before I could stop myself! I was so humiliated, but I couldn't very well take it back."

"How did he answer?"

It was my turn to beam with happiness. "He accepted."

"Oh, gem!" Laria wrapped her arms around me. "All I ever wanted was for you to be happy." Her voice broke on the sentiment, and I held her tightly. It was true. Laria always looked out for me, ever since we were children. It was her duty to make me laugh, to comfort me, and to protect me. Now, she could relinquish that role to my future husband.

"I haven't told you all." I pulled away from her. "When we were leaving the encampment, I saw the King of Torshul, Qoyahdii. He said the men were preparing to meet King Karne on the battlefield."

Her features fell and her body trembled before she blinked back tears and set her jaw.

"I hope they send him back to the desert as a pile of ashes," she said darkly.

"Me, too," I said, though with less conviction.

"How was your return journey?" Her change in subject was jarring, but I suspect it was to avoid the thought of her husband charging into battle.

"It was...eventful." I held nothing back when I told her about Kit Renard and his miscreants. I told her, without shame, how I tried to befriend him to save our lives, how I poisoned him, and the awful things he said to me. I hesitated, then confessed he made me sleep in the same tent, hurriedly adding he didn't touch me.

"You acted very bravely."

"You think so?"

"You did what you needed to survive."

"Do you think Finton would agree?"

"Of course he would!" she insisted as if it was the most obvious answer in the world. "You did nothing which warrants regret or shame. I'm sure he would agree, more so because everything you did not only saved your own life, but Olim's as well. He would be proud if he knew."

"I hope you're right, because I do intend to tell him everything."

"As you should. Honesty is always best, especially between a husband and wife."

My cheeks flushed, and we giggled like children. We spoke of more pleasant things after that, of weddings and dresses and the future. Later, she brought me to see the children, and the tears flowed once more to have my beloved nieces and nephews in my arms again. I regaled them with tales from my journey, and Laria allowed them to stay up well past their bedtime so we could catch up on everything I'd missed. Sulwen proudly displayed a new tooth while Tyrnan pointed out the resulting bite. Alyx had grown almost half an inch since I saw him last. Rian carved a sword out of wood and Lilias painted a picture of Praed Castle. For a three-year-old, it was quite good.

That night, I collapsed into bed exhausted but filled with gratitude. My heart was full of family, of friends, and of love. I pictured Finton's face and dreamed of the life we would have together. Once the war was over. Once he came home.

My life returned to the same routine I established before I left, but I didn't regard this as a bad thing. There was something to be said for normalcy, for idleness, and for performing the same tasks repeatedly. At least I didn't have to worry about wolves and scoundrels. I was filled with a newfound appreciation for what I had and would never take it for granted.

After preparing Laria for the day and spending the morning with the children, I sat with my sister in the library and read. This past month, Laria spent less and less time on her feet at the behest of her midwife, Seline. She told me she resisted at first, but when Seline expressed concern about the child's size and effects of too much exertion, Laria relented. No doubt, the events of last summer flashed through her mind, and she would do anything she was told to prevent another miscarriage.

The only sound in the warm library was the turning of pages and the crackling of flames, when the door opened, and the familiar footsteps of the king's steward followed. We set aside our books and sat up straight as he entered, bowed, and addressed the queen.

"Forgive me, Your Majesty, but there is a... a gentleman here wishing to speak with you. He says it's a matter of business."

I tilted my head in confusion at his stumble over the word 'gentleman.' What sort of man was it that disconcerted the normally unflappable steward so?

"What sort of business?" Laria asked as she rose.

"He wouldn't say specifically. Just that he required an audience with Your Grace."

"Required?" She arched an eyebrow at me. "Well, we mustn't keep him waiting then."

The steward bowed and Laria took his arm. We were led to the throne room and the steward opened the door. Under the watchful eyes of the queen's guards, a man dressed in yellow satin stood in the center of the floor marveling at the splendor before him. No one could have missed my surprised gasp or the blood draining from my face.

"Who is it?" she whispered.

"It's *him*," I managed to say. I swallowed, my throat unbearably dry. "It's Kit Renard."

Laria's eyes hardened and she waved away the steward. With magnificent poise, she entered the room with me trailing behind trying to remain hidden. Kit whirled at the sound of our footsteps, smiled ingratiatingly, and bowed.

"Your Majesty and…" he paused when Laria lowered herself onto her throne, revealing me standing beside her. "Just Ula," he finished with a devilish smile that turned my stomach.

"Mr. Renard," Laria said coldly. "To what do we owe this unexpected and unwelcome visit?"

He placed a hand over his heart. "You wound me, Your Majesty."

"I doubt it."

"I've come to settle a debt with *that* woman." He pointed at me.

"Really? And what debt is that?"

"She killed my brother and promised me monetary compensation for it." He spoke without the remorse one might expect in a man who'd lost his brother.

"I told you," I interjected. "It was self-defense. He threatened to…" I hesitated, then with a surge of courage said, "defile my virtue."

"What do you say to that, Mr. Renard?" Laria asked coolly.

He shrugged. "I can't blame him."

I huffed in exasperation and Laria's eyes darkened menacingly.

"Be careful, Mr. Renard," Laria said. "Rape isn't something I regard as lightly as you do."

A glimmer of fear momentarily shadowed Kit's features, but it was quickly gone.

"Where I come from, Your Majesty, we have a saying: a life pays for a life. If someone has a life taken from them, that person is owed a life in return."

"Is that so?" Laria asked, an eyebrow raised.

"Yes. In this case, I was willing to forgive the life for an appropriate sum of money. I magnanimously agreed to bring the lady safely back to Praed Castle, where I was promised to be rewarded. Then I was betrayed." He cast a dark glare toward me. "Poisoned, it would seem. Surely you can appreciate my distress."

"Your distress?" Laria rose with deliberate care from her throne. I took a step back, and Kit's brow furrowed. I stared at him boldly, thinking how thoroughly he would regret coming here.

"You slink around in the trees preying on unsuspecting travelers, stealing their money and who knows what else," Laria said. "You claim an honorable code from wherever you're from as an excuse to stalk a woman who was defending herself against your pig of a brother. You kidnap her and a knight of this castle under duress. And when she has the courage to escape, you blithely try to use it to evoke pity from me?"

Kit stepped back, wary of my sister's anger.

"You have made a grave mistake in coming here, Mr. Renard, thinking you would be given a single coin from my treasury." She stepped down off the dais, and he took another step back. "You wish for a life in exchange for the death of your brother? Then I shall grant you one. Your own. If you leave Praed this instant and never show your face here again, I shall not have you hanged for putting your filthy, thieving hands on my sister."

His eyebrows shot up and his eyes widened in shock.

"Sister?" He looked up at me. The side of his mouth curved. "No secrets indeed. Very clever. I should have kept a closer eye on you."

"Mr. Renard," Laria said firmly to bring his attention back to her. "Do we have an agreement?"

"My life for hers? A fair trade, Your Majesty. I accept." He bowed elaborately. "Please, give my regards to His Majesty when he returns."

"You should consider yourself lucky he isn't here. He would not be as merciful as I."

A slow smile spread across Kit's face, and unless I was mistaken, respect filled his eyes as he regarded my sister.

"What a fierce queen you are," he said. "I would be happy to call you mine."

Her fists clenched.

Kit was quick to add, "My queen, that is." He bowed again, and his eyes looked past her shoulder to where I stood on the dais.

"Might I have permission to address the royal sister?" he asked.

"Such permission is not mine to grant," Laria said. She glanced over her shoulder, and I stepped down, my legs unsteady. I nodded to Laria, and she resumed her place on the throne.

"Go on," I said to Kit. "But don't expect an apology."

"I was about to say the same thing."

I bristled at his impertinence, but I didn't give him the satisfaction of arguing.

"It seems this shall be the last time we see each other."

"Thank Solamun," I snapped.

His grin widened. Before I could react, he grasped my hand and placed a firm kiss against my fingers. I wrenched my hand away and held up the other to keep Laria from flying at him in a fury. Reluctantly, she lowered herself back into her throne, and waved the guards back.

"Try something like that again, and she'll revoke her deal. You'll find yourself hanging from a rope before you can protest."

"An intriguing challenge. How far can I go before I'm seized and in chains?" His eyes roamed over my body, and I crossed my arms over my chest.

"Enough," I said. "This talk is wearing thin. Do you have anything else to say to me?"

"Only that I wish you great felicity in your upcoming marriage."

I said nothing, but my hard features softened. He bowed, that same enthusiastic and elaborate bow, and clasped his hands behind his back.

"Goodbye, Just Ula," he said. Almost sadly.

"Good riddance," I said, though not with the vehemence I intended.

He winked and backed out of the room, and when the door closed behind him, I released a *whoosh* of air and nearly collapsed. Laria rushed to my side.

"Are you all right?"

"Yes," I said.

"I'm very proud of the way you stood up to that awful man."

"Thank you. I hope that's the last we'll see of him."

"If he values his life, it will be."

I was the last person to speak well of Kit, but he never struck me as stupid. It wasn't courageous of him to come to Praed to demand money from Laria–it was suicide. What did he expect would happen? Even if I were a simple servingmaid, surely he didn't think Laria would overlook his villainy and compensate him for his troubles?

Driven by an impulse I couldn't name, I ran after him. By the time I reached the foyer, the doors were closing. I shouted for the guards to wait, and I slid through the gap to stand at the top of the stairs. Kit was mounting his horse. I blinked in astonishment when I saw he was alone. He rode away, and it was at the tip of my tongue to shout. I didn't like unanswered questions, and Kit's entire personality was a mystery.

Instead, I remained silent, and watched Kit gallop down the mountain until he disappeared. I suppose some questions weren't meant to be answered.

Though we waited with breathless anticipation, we received no word from the front over the next month. Laria bore the stress with her usual grace, and the children bravely offered each other words of comfort to keep from missing their father too much. Alyx was especially impressive, acting as a pillar of strength for his mother and younger siblings. They looked to his example, and when the snow stopped falling and the first rays of spring sunshine illuminated the valley, he led his brothers and sisters into town so the people could see the unwavering hope in their faces. They whispered as we passed, commenting that surely if the children believed the king and their loved ones would come home, then they should, too. One man said to his wife, "One day Prince Alyx will make a fine king." When I watched the young prince take the hand of an elderly woman and give her a sweet treat, his dark hair ruffling in the wind and his startling blue eyes shining, I had no doubt he was right.

Tyrnan became obsessed with boats after I told him about mine and Olim's trip down the Dehan River, so Rian enlisted the help of the blacksmith to carve a rudimentary craft for his brother to float down the Rhyvor when we visited Riverstone. Tyrnan beamed proudly and held the boat out for me to see. Lilias painted it his favorite color, blue, and he was anxious to see it on the water with its new decoration.

"But it might wash off," I said.

"Please, Aunt Ula?"

I smiled wistfully, remembering this time last year he could barely say my name.

"All right, then," I said. "Let's go set off!"

"Cast off," Tyrnan corrected with evident annoyance.

"Sorry."

I mussed his hair and was about to leave the room when hoofbeats thundered outside. I glanced out the window and saw a messenger ride his frothed horse up the front steps, throw himself to the ground, and race inside.

"Tyrnan." My voice wavered and my hands shook as I seized the boy's shoulders. He looked up at me with his deep blue eyes, and I could tell he heard the tremor of worry in my voice. "Go find Duveesa."

He took off without argument, and I clasped my hands together and hurried to find Laria without drawing attention to myself.

The messenger was being led away from the council chambers with promises of food and drink. I peered into the eerie stillness of the room and spied the council members silently watching Laria read the delivered missive. I edged forward, my limbs as heavy as the tension in the room. Laria looked up, her eyes wide and shimmering, her mouth moving without making a sound.

"What news?" I whispered.

"The king." Her voice was thick with emotion. "He's coming home."

A collective sigh of relief swept the room, followed by cheers of celebration. The only two people not caught up in the exultant moment were Laria and me. She buried her face in her hands, her shoulders shaking with the effort to restrain her tears. The council members left to spread the good news, and I pushed past them to kneel at Laria's feet. I placed a hand on her shoulder, and she turned and favored me with the most radiant smile.

I gathered her in my arms and rocked her as if she were a babe. She released a torrent of tears, and with each sob the tension and worry drained from her body, to be filled with the joy of having her husband once again by her side.

All of us gathered on the steps of Praed Castle to welcome home the king and his surviving knights and soldiers. And by *all of us*, I mean *all* of Praed. Lines of people stretched from the topmost step down the mountain, all eagerly waiting for the first glimpse of the king. Laria wrung her hands impatiently beside me, and I held her arm tightly to keep her from tipping over as she bounced on the balls of her feet. The children and their nurses stood behind us fidgeting just as much as their mother.

Laria gasped, and I craned my neck to see past the bend in the road. A plume of dust stirred by thundering hoofbeats gathered into a dark cloud, but the trees obscured my view. A figure rounded the corner, clad in clothing matching his black horse, a shining ring of gold around his head. Laria lurched forward, and I helped her navigate her heavily pregnant form down the steps. I held up a hand to keep the children back so she could have a moment alone to welcome the king.

Risteard dismounted before the horse came to a full stop and bounded up the steps. I released Laria, and she surged forward so quickly I feared she would fall. She was in his arms in an instant, and he was holding her as tightly as her figure would allow. The echo of applause and cheers reverberated around the mountain, but for Laria and Risteard, there was no one else alive at that moment.

Risteard set her feet firmly on the ground. "Don't you ever leave me again," Laria said.

They shared a lengthy and passionate kiss, and I waved the children forward before things got too carried away. They swarmed their father in a rush of excitement, jumping around his legs and talking over each other. Risteard dropped to one knee and hugged Tyrnan and Rian together, squeezing them so tightly they pretended to be choking.

Alyx was next. "I kept Mama and the baby safe," he told Risteard.

"Good man." Risteard kissed the top of his son's head, and even from my position a few feet away, I saw the tears welling in his eyes.

Lilias waited patiently for her turn to hug and kiss her father. Behind me, Sulwen struggled impatiently out of Duveesa's arms and toddled down the steps. Lilias had barely stepped aside when the girl shoved her way past. Risteard scooped her up, and his eyes closed contentedly as he hugged his precious daughter. Laria linked her arm in his, took Lilias' hand, and urged the family into the castle. The boys continued to clamor around Risteard's feet, and I smiled when he made noncommittal responses in their direction. There would be time to listen to his children's stories of what happened when he was gone, but for now, he had eyes only for Laria.

The royal family was complete once more. I watched them climb the steps with an overwhelming sense of relief. Olim stood nearby, but he wasn't looking toward the king. His eyes were focused behind me, and when they met mine, he gestured for me to turn around. I did, and there at the bottom of the steps, hands in his pockets and a half-smile on his face, was Finton.

My breath rushed from my lungs, and I pulled up my hem to dash down the steps. He opened his arms, and I propelled myself into his embrace, knocking him off balance. He chuckled, and I tightened my arms around his neck and buried my face in his chest, breathing in his scent and willing myself not to cry.

"I hope this means you've missed me." He pulled back to look at me.

"More than you know."

He lowered his face, his lips hovering over mine as if asking permission. I smiled and breached the distance, kissing him without restraint or care as to whoever might be watching. His hands pressed against my back, and I worried if someone didn't summon children to distract us, we might be in danger ourselves. Finton ended the kiss, but his lips stayed close enough to graze mine as he spoke.

"We should probably go inside."

"Yes," I whispered against his mouth and rubbed his nose with mine.

He smiled and brought his hands up to cradle my face.

"Do you still want to marry me?" he asked.

"More than anything."

"Good."

He tucked my hand into his elbow and led me into the castle. I lay my head on his shoulder and simply enjoyed being near him again. There was much to be said before we married, but right now, I contented myself with the euphoria of our reunion.

A feast was held in the king's honor. The great hall was full of people mingling with knights and soldiers, dancing and drinking in celebration of the end of the war. The only people who weren't indulging in the festivities were Finton, myself, Laria, and Risteard. The latter two were only a few feet away, speaking quietly to each other while everyone around them ate and made merry. Risteard's hand rested on Laria's swollen belly while she spoke animatedly, her hands waving wildly as she described something that happened while he was gone. He listened quietly, laughed occasionally, and gazed at her lovingly.

"Wolves?" Finton said.

I'd been telling him about my journey to the front. Obviously, it wasn't long before Finton had something to say on the subject.

"Yes," I said with mock impatience. "*Wolves*. May I continue?"

"Were you injured?" His voice rose to a ridiculously high pitch when he was worried.

"A little."

"I want to see."

"It's healed!"

"I want to see anyway."

"Not here," I whispered and looked around at the other guests.

"Why not?" Finton asked. "I am a physician after all."

"Because," I huffed, "it would require me lifting my hem above my ankle in front of all these people."

Finton turned away to hide the smile playing at his lips.

"Later then?" he suggested, his voice low.

"If you insist. From a purely medical standpoint."

"I have purely clinical intentions," he said, but when our eyes met, we couldn't contain our laughter. There was more to tell him about my journey, but I allowed our merriment to hang in the air. I doubted there would be little to laugh about when Finton discovered everything. Especially regarding Kit Renard.

"Ula."

Laria stood over us. Finton and I rose, and she inclined her head toward my fiancé.

"Is everything all right?" I asked.

"Yes," she said. "I'm ready for bed, that's all."

I was taken aback. I glanced at the party around us. It was quite early to turn in for bed, though it'd been a long day. "Of course. Shall we?"

Laria gave a curt nod and spun on her heel to leave. I promised Finton I would be back and hurried after her.

For a woman who was due to give birth, Laria was surprisingly quick on her feet. I was more out of breath than she was by the time we reached her chambers.

"You must be quite tired," I said between breaths. "To leave the party this early."

"Can you hurry up and unpin my hair?"

"I'm sorry," I muttered and hastily pulled pins from her ginger locks.

"No." Laria sighed. "*I'm* sorry. That was rude of me."

"What's the matter?"

The last strands of hair fell untamed from her perfectly arranged coiffure.

"I haven't seen my husband in months." She stared at me meaningfully, and I understood the reason for her haste.

"Then let's get you out of this dress," I said.

She smiled, and I loosened her stays and had her donned in her nightgown without a moment to spare. The door to her bedroom flew open and the king strode in, his eyes trained on Laria. I curtseyed in his direction as I left, but I'm certain he didn't see me.

A small smile curved my lips as I closed the door behind me and returned to the party. Finton was engaged in conversation with a noble, so I leaned against the wall to observe the room. The castle was filled with unbridled joy, and I contented myself with just sitting back and enjoying the moment of blissful happiness.

Olim reclined beside me. "Everything turned out for the best, it seems."

He looked more relaxed than I'd seen in months—shoulders low, arms casually crossed over his chest, a lock of hair grazing his forehead, and an easy smile on his face. Instead of his usual knight's tunic, he wore a forest green jerkin over a cleanly pressed undershirt and soft brown breeches.

"You look very handsome tonight," I said.

"You clean up pretty well yourself." He nudged my shoulder. "How does it feel to have your fiancé here?"

"Good," I blushed.

"Some of the knights have been talking about him. Apparently, he saved many lives after the campaign against King Karne."

I puffed out my chest with pride. "He's a very good surgeon. Were there many casualties?"

"Some, which is to be expected."

"How awful for their families."

"They fought for a true cause. That should be comfort enough."

"What happened to King Karne?"

Olim looked down, his expression twisted in thought as he considered whether to tell me the truth.

"According to a knight who was near when it happened, King Risteard met King Karne on the battlefield. When they came to blows, it was clear they were well matched. My friend was worried, and he made his way toward the king to help. But before he reached them, King Risteard overpowered Karne, and was giving him a chance to surrender. Instead of laying down his weapon, Karne made one last attempt on our king, but the move was anticipated, deflected, and met with a sword to the throat."

I gasped. "How awful!"

"You asked."

"What happened after that?"

"The remaining Crif soldiers fled. Without their leader, they were simply a scattered mob of men who couldn't plan on their own. Our army cut down as many stragglers as they could and left the rest to spread the word of Crif's defeat."

"War is a messy business."

"Look at it this way—now we can live in peace."

"But at such a high cost."

I could practically hear Olim roll his eyes at my sentimentality.

"I think we've had enough dramatics to last a lifetime, don't you?"

"Yes." I grinned wryly. "And now it's time to enjoy ourselves. How's Duveesa?"

"Go dance with your fiancé," Olim grumbled and pushed away from the wall.

I stifled a laugh at his discomfort and watched him weave his way into the crowd of people. Olim had indeed been a true friend. He was my confidant, my protector, and a shoulder to lean on. He accompanied me on a dangerous errand even after I broke his heart. I could travel thousands of miles and never find a knight as loyal. No one deserved happiness more.

Finton emerged from the crowd and distracted me from my musings. What would he think when I told him about Olim? Would he be angry? There was no other choice but to tell him because I could never be easy with secrets between us. But that could wait. He reached for my hand, and I took it. We danced and laughed into the night, and for the first time, there was only hope for the coming morrow.

Chapter 41

The carriage ambled toward Riverstone, and I breathed in the scents of moist earth and sun-warmed stone. Piles of melting snow dotted the rolling prairie, shoots of spring grass breaking up the monotony in flashes of green. Winter runoffs fed the starving Rhyvor, turning the sleeping giant into a torrent whose echoing roar led us to my family estate. Riverstone's tower appeared bathed in afternoon sunlight, turning the gray stone golden. It eased my rattled nerves, though the blood pounded deafeningly in my ears. I glanced across the carriage at Laria, whose blissful smile hadn't faded since her husband's return. She met my eye and her smile broadened.

"There's no need to be nervous," she said.

"I know," I said, though the tremor in my voice would suggest otherwise.

Beside me, Finton shifted, and a comforting hand closed around mine. The corners of Finton's eyes crinkled when he smiled encouragingly, and though a trace of apprehension flickered behind his spectacles, his quiet confidence helped me relax.

He'd been understanding when I confessed to kissing Olim so many months ago.

"You were going through a horrible ordeal," he said. "We all were. It's only natural for you to try and find comfort in your friend."

"I thought I had…I was confused."

"And now?" he asked. "Is there any confusion?"

"No. I know exactly what I want."

He was less sympathetic when I told him about Kit Renard. I'd seen Finton angry before, but the quiet fury darkening his features was more unsettling than if he'd exploded in a tirade of yelling and broke furniture. He didn't blame nor direct his anger toward me, and I didn't feel he thought less of me for what I'd done to survive. But woe be to Kit if he ever broke his word and wandered into Praed.

"I'll kill him," Finton said.

"No, you won't."

"He forced you to share a tent with him and put his hands on you."

"He was being an ass."

"He must have known you'd put up with almost anything to save yourself."

"He is indeed a manipulative and cruel man. But he kept his word and didn't...well, I'm unharmed."

He hugged me fiercely, as if he needed to convince himself I was unscathed. There was nothing more looming between us. All that remained was this one visit and our wedding preparations could begin.

"Everything's going to be fine," Finton said. His optimism me laugh despite my nervousness.

"You've never met Mother."

Once at Riverstone, we were barely in the foyer when Mother appeared in a perfect dither. Though the only people who would notice were Laria and I. Outwardly, she was composed, poised, and without a hair out of place. But she stepped much too quickly, her fingers fidgeted, and one perfectly groomed eyebrow was raised. She was annoyed.

"Your Majesty." Mother's voice rose a bit. "You shouldn't be traveling in your condition."

"It's not as if I'm going to Torshul," Laria said, sending a conspiratorial wink my way.

"Nevertheless." Mother gestured for us to follow her to the drawing room. "Come rest yourself."

Once Laria was seated on a cushioned sofa, Mother acknowledged my presence with a kiss on my cheek. Then she noticed Finton.

"I don't believe we've met," Mother said.

"Mother," I said brightly. "This is Finton Ekhane."

"Don't I know that name, Ekhane? Where have I heard it?"

"It's the name of the Lord Protector of Ilano, Mother," Laria said irritably. She knew perfectly well who it was.

"To what do we owe the honor of your visit?" Mother fanned out her skirts and perched gracefully on the edge of a plush chair intricately embroidered with a herd of horses running through wildflowers. She had made it after returning triumphantly as Lady of Riverstone when Laria was crowned queen. She folded her hands and stared patiently, her chin raised.

Finton came straight to the point. "I've come to ask for permission to marry Ula."

Mother's eyes widened imperceptibly, and she turned to me.

"Ula, explain yourself."

"Finton and I are engaged to be married, and we would like your blessing. He comes from a very good family, as we've explained, and is very accomplished in his own right."

"Is that so?"

"Yes. He's a brilliant physician and is studying to be a surgeon. He served on the front lines with the king and saved many lives."

Mother sneered. "A surgeon? Don't surgeons cut people up?"

"We generally try to piece them back together," Finton said.

Mother wasn't impressed with his cheerfulness. I winced at the cold glare she fixed upon him.

"And you expect to be able to support my daughter with that profession?"

"Absolutely. Your daughter will be quite comfortable. What's more, I will spend the rest of my life ensuring she's happy. She will want for nothing."

"Can you give her a house such as this?" Mother raised a hand, indicating Riverstone. Finton's eyes briefly traced the room, but before he could respond, Mother continued. "She was born in this house and lived here *very* comfortably until she was twelve. And for the past five years, her home has been Praed Castle. Can you match that level of security?"

"I perhaps cannot afford quite so many rooms, but—"

Mother cut him off with a wave of her well-manicured hand.

"Ula comes from a long and well-bred line. Her father's ancestors built this house, and ever since Riverstone has symbolized prosperity, dignity, and honor. We are one of the greatest houses in Praed, which comes with great responsibility. I don't expect you to understand coming from Ilano."

Laria stood abruptly. "Mother, may I speak to you in private?"

Mother eyed her warily. "If you wish, Your Majesty."

Laria turned to me. "Why don't you show Finton the library."

I took the invitation and led Finton from the room.

"Your mother is terrifying," Finton said when we were alone.

"I'm so sorry about that. She still harbors resentment toward people from Ilano. Please don't take it personally."

"I won't." He caressed my face, his hand settling against my warm cheek. "As long as she doesn't take offense to me marrying her daughter even if we have to elope."

I'll never know what Laria said to Mother, but it had the desired effect. Mother was much more willing to entertain the idea of her precious daughter marrying a man from Ilano, though her manner toward him didn't thaw. It was the best outcome we could have hoped for.

"Where do you plan to marry?" Mother asked before bringing a teacup to her lips.

"Riverstone. With your permission," I said.

She froze, the teacup poised at her mouth. She took a long sip and set it delicately on its saucer before answering.

"In the gallery?"

By the slight shine in her eyes, I knew she was pleased with my request.

"Along the Rhyvor," I said.

"When were you planning to wed?"

"After the queen's baby is born."

"You don't have to wait that long," Laria interjected.

"It isn't too long," I said.

"Indeed," Mother said. "And it's better to have more time than not enough." She set her teacup down. "We'll need time to send invitations and prepare wedding clothes."

My eyes widened and I looked at Laria. She shrugged and shook her head resignedly. She was right. I suppose I should indulge Mother. After all, the more involved she felt, the less resistant she would be to the idea of her daughter marrying a foreign upstart from Ilano.

Everything was falling into place, and the feeling was strange. A part of me waited for something to upset our peace, and the other was breathing a sigh of relief. We absorbed ourselves in wedding preparations, even the children. Tyrnan wanted us to leave Riverstone via a boat on the Rhyvor, but I pointed out that it leads out to sea where we'd surely get lost. Rian wanted to wear a sword for the occasion, and once I granted him permission, both Alyx and Tyrnan wanted one, too. The poor blacksmith had quite a bit of work on his hands. Lilias happily helped with the floral arrangements while Sulwen was all too willing to taste-test confectioneries.

I insisted on making my own wedding gown. Laria argued against it, saying I shouldn't have to work so hard, but when I reminded her how well her own dress turned out, she softened and agreed no one could rival my talent. There was only one thing left to sort out, and it made me so nervous my stomach flipped just thinking about it.

Laria, Risteard, and I relaxed in the library after the children went to bed. Risteard was still catching up on correspondence he'd missed in the months he was gone, and Laria read contently, a hand resting on her belly. I tried to read, but the words blurred, and the pages shook when I turned them. I spent the whole day looking for my courage, and I still hadn't found it. I peered at Risteard from the corner of my eye. Despite everything I'd been through, I still found speaking to him intimidating. I closed my eyes, took a deep breath, and told myself that if I could escape a group of bandits and kill a wolf, I could ask my brother-in-law a simple question.

"Risteard, may I ask you something?" I spoke in a rush without taking a breath.

"Yes," he said, his eyes never leaving the letter in his hand.

Laria set her book aside and listened curiously.

"We almost have everything coordinated for the wedding," I said.

"Good."

"There's just one thing that needs to be settled: who to perform the ceremony."

He still didn't look up. "I see."

"Your Majesty—Risteard…Finton and I would be honored if you would consider officiating."

Risteard met my hopeful gaze, and Laria inhaled sharply. I looked nervously to my sister to get her take on my request. She clutched a hand to her chest, her gaze fixed expectantly on Risteard.

The crackling flames echoed in the still room. I jumped when a log shifted and sent jittery sparks up the chimney. I held my breath to calm my nerves. A heartbeat. Two…three. I feared he wouldn't answer, I feared he would. I hoped I didn't lose consciousness before he spoke.

"I'll do it," he said.

My heart soared. I would've hugged him if he'd allow it.

"Thank you."

Laria squeezed my hand tightly, and I beamed at her like an idiot.

"Go on to bed," Laria said. "You look quite tired."

"What about you?"

"I'll manage." She glanced at her husband. "Go on."

Now that I would soon be a wife, I understood my sister completely.

"You look awful, Laria," I said to my sister a few days later.

Her skin was pale, and a sheen of sweat covered her brow. And every so often, she would wince as if she were in pain or trying to keep from vomiting.

"Good," she said dryly. "I *feel* awful."

Seconds later, she cried out and doubled over, clutching her abdomen.

I signaled an attendant. "You there! Have the midwife brought to the castle and send a message to Lady Audrey at Riverstone telling her the queen's labor pains have begun."

Once the attendant ran off to do as she was ordered, I escorted Laria back to her chambers.

"I don't think I'm ready for this," Laria said.

I stripped off her gown. "I think the child is big enough."

"That's not what I mean."

"What then?"

Before she could answer, Laria was struck by another pain, and we began the ritual of walking around the room and breathing through the contractions. It wasn't new for us. I'd assisted Laria's previous births, and we fell into a comfortable rhythm practiced time and again. It wasn't long before we were joined by Seline, who'd brought Laria's other children into the world.

"How are we?" Seline asked brightly.

"How do *we* look?" Laria responded bitterly.

Laria was a delight when in labor.

"I informed the king," Seline said. She went on as she rolled up her sleeves. "He's waiting close by with, er, *Finton* I believe he said his name was?"

"Yes," I said. "He's my fiancé."

"Congratulations!"

"He's a physician. In case we need any help."

"So he said. I'll keep that in mind," Seline said.

"Yes, we're all very proud of my future brother-in-law," Laria grumbled. "Can we return the focus to me, please?"

Seline and I shared a hidden smile, and together we commenced the arduous task of assisting Laria's labor.

Mother arrived several hours later, and I could tell she was surprised we were still walking Laria about the room and had made little progress.

"Not moving fast enough for you, Mother?" Laria hissed through a painful spasm.

Mother directed her attention to Seline. "Usually, the children come faster after having so many."

"This child seems to have its own ideas," Seline said good-naturedly.

When more time elapsed with no sign of the child, even *I* became nervous.

"I think I should break your waters myself," Seline said. "It will help the labor progress."

Laria nodded, her features marred with worry. It seemed to work. Once her waters were broken, the pain grew worse and the contractions came closer together. Seline ordered Laria onto the bed to start pushing. This part always went quickly, and I could see the relief I felt reflected in Mother's eyes.

The relief was short lived.

Chapter 42

Some moments in life are fleeting and we cannot remember a single detail. Then there are those that are so etched in our minds we can't forget even if we tried. That day in early spring, I could recall the pattern of stitching on my mother's dress, the curl of Laria's fingers as she gripped the stained bedclothes, the sound of my heart thudding in my chest, and the tiny bead of sweat on Seline's temple when she looked up at said:

"Something's wrong."

"What?" Laria croaked.

"The baby's stuck and won't move." An undercurrent of panic colored Seline's voice. "I'm trying, but I can't get it out."

Without a second to announce where I was going, I raced from the room, throwing open the door with such force it careened against the wall with an echoing *bang!* I wasn't five steps down the hall when Risteard blocked my path. His exhausted eyes looked at me with expectation, followed by confusion when my gaze slid from him to Finton.

"We need your help," I said to my fiancé.

He nodded and reached for his bag that he'd kept close by. He placed a comforting hand on Risteard's shoulder, and the king was so dazed he didn't even notice, a testament to how stunned he must be. He never allowed anyone but Laria and the children to touch him.

"What seems to be the holdup?" Finton asked genially when we entered the room.

Mother raised an eyebrow at his easy manner, but Laria relaxed when she saw him.

"She's started to push, but the baby's stuck," Seline said.

"Maybe she's shy?" Finton said. He sat on the bed and examined Laria.

"Shy?" Laria laughed. "This is *my* child after all."

Finton's brow furrowed. He felt Laria's abdomen. The intensity of his concentration frightened me, but I couldn't bring myself to ask questions.

"Has this pregnancy given you more trouble than usual?" Finton asked.

"Yes," Laria said breathlessly and squeezed her eyes in pain. "But I thought that was to be expected."

"Seline, was it?" Finton asked the midwife while he removed his jerkin and rolled up his sleeves.

"Yes, doctor?"

"You know the names of the instruments?"

"I do."

"Good. Assist me, will you, please?"

Seline positioned herself near Finton and began laying out instruments.

I clutched Laria's hand and watched, the feeling of dread increasing as each shining tool was laid out. The light was fading, and candlelight flickered against the cool silver like swords in firelight, making me shiver.

Finton and Seline worked diligently, ignoring Mother's entreaties to explain what was happening. I pointed out the doctor could hardly concentrate with her asking so many questions. For her part, Laria remained silent, saving her strength.

"All right," Finton said to Seline. "I'm going to push the child back a bit and then you're going to turn it."

"Doesn't that defeat the purpose?" Mother asked archly.

"Unless you want it to remain lodged in the birth canal forever, it must be done," Finton snapped.

Mother glowered but remained silent.

Together, Finton and Seline pushed, shoved, and twisted Laria's poor stomach. She cried out and clung tightly to my hand, agony etched in her features. My eyes burned with tears threatening to fall, but I held them back.

Finton wiped an arm across his brow. "She'll need help. When you're ready, Your Majesty."

Seline braced herself against Laria's stomach, and with the next contraction, Laria pushed. The room filled with a cacophony of encouragement mixed with her cries of exertion, each second dragging on interminably. When Finton announced he could see the head, I nearly fainted. Laria gritted her teeth and doubled her efforts. Time ceased all together, until I blinked, and a tiny cry filled the room, silencing everything else.

"It's over." Laria fell against the bed. A tear trickled down her cheek, though I could barely see it through my own blurred eyes.

"What is it?" Mother asked.

"It's a boy," Finton said. He handed the precious bundle to Mother instead of Laria. "And you're not finished yet, Your Majesty."

"What?" Laria lifted her head to look at him. "But I thought—"

"There's one more child waiting to be born," he said, a hand on her swollen belly. "Right now."

I don't know who was more shocked: Laria, me, or Mother.

"Twins?" Mother had to sit down with the baby to keep from fainting herself.

"Come on." Finton urged Laria back up. "You can rest after."

I resumed my place at Laria's side, and with the last ounce of strength she possessed, she pushed through the pain and exhaustion. I chanced a glance down the bed. A swath of red spread across the sheets. I tried to catch Finton's eye, but he was focused solely on delivering Laria's baby. By the time a raspy wail joined the first, I worried Laria had no more strength nor blood to give.

Finton quickly wrapped the babe, passed it to me, then called out instruments to Seline. Laria's eyes opened and closed languidly, but her breathing was steady and her color rosy. I clutched the second child to my chest and rocked it, its tiny fist opening and closing in time to its mother's eyes. I peeked under the blanket to determine the sex of the child.

"A girl," I said to Laria. I wrapped the blanket snuggly around the little girl and smiled. "One of each. What shall you call them?"

"Something..." Laria's voice was small, far away.

"Finton?" I couldn't help the fear in my voice.

"It's all right." Finton adjusted Laria's legs to a more comfortable position. "She'll be all right."

"Thank you, Dr. Ekhane," Laria said tiredly. "For allowing me this one last time."

"What do you mean by that?" I asked.

"You're welcome, Your Majesty," Finton said.

"What do you mean 'last'? Laria?"

"I can't have any more children." Laria shrugged. "Not anymore."

"But Finton said—"

"That I could have more children. But there was a chance the next time would be my last, wasn't there?"

"You're very astute, Your Majesty," Finton said while he finished cleaning up.

"Oh, Laria."

"It's all right, Ula," Laria said, looking up at me with the most magnificent smile, her features peaceful. She reached for her new daughter and I placed the child in her arms. Mother brought the boy over and laid him next to his sister.

"I asked Risteard for half a dozen children," Laria said. "And I got my wish. Plus one."

Laria thought it would be hilarious if we surprised the king with his newborn twins instead of telling him outright. Mother wanted no part in the joke, so she left the room with Finton when he went to tell Risteard Laria was well and ready for visitors. I hid behind the door with the little girl while Laria lay on the bed with the boy, so when Risteard strode through the door toward her, he didn't even notice me.

"Risteard." Laria smiled dreamily. "We have another son." She passed the babe into his arms, and he gazed lovingly at his newborn son.

Laria sighed. "My arms feel so empty without him."

"You want him back?" Risteard asked.

"No need. I have another."

She beckoned to me, and if I could have, I would have painted a picture of Risteard's face to keep forever. His mouth fell open in shock and his wide eyes followed me as I placed the girl in Laria's arms.

"Wh-what?" Risteard's inability to form words was almost as comical as his expression.

"It seems we made two this time around. Not a bad way to end my career as a broodmare."

Risteard shot her a narrowed glare.

"Have you thought of any names?" I asked.

"I have. With your approval." Laria met Risteard's eye. His features softened, and he nodded for her to continue. "I would like to name the boy Khyr and the girl Kyra."

Kyra was the name of our great aunt. Mother said she'd had auburn locks and emerald eyes and was impulsive and wild. She preferred horses to men, and Khyr was the name of her prized stallion.

"Those are lovely names," I said.

"Yes," Risteard said. He leaned forward and kissed Laria on the forehead, the cheek, then the lips. "Whatever you wish, Your Majesty."

I left them to their privacy and slumped exhausted against the closed door. Finton was waiting, and he took my hand to lead me away.

I leaned against him. "I could sleep for days."

"Imagine how she feels."

"Right now? Blissfully happy. Thank you, Finton." I wrapped my arms around him, and he kissed the top of my head.

"Can we get married now?" he asked in a low voice.

"Yes," I said, holding him tighter. "As soon as my dress is finished."

"And when will that be?"

I pulled back and looked up at him with a raised eyebrow.

"Not that I'm in a hurry, but I'm rather in a hurry."

I laughed and lay my head against his chest.

"Then I'll work day and night and see my fiancé married within the fortnight."

I was true to my word. After all, it wouldn't be a good start to a marriage to disappoint your future husband so cruelly. Between helping Laria with the new twins and entertaining the other children so she could rest, I worked on my wedding gown. It was made of crushed velvet the color of a summer sky with a neckline lower than I'd ever worn and sheer sleeves showing every inch of skin from my shoulder to my wrist. Glass beads lined the collar and splashed across the bodice like stars tossed carelessly in the night sky. When I moved, light reflected off the clear beads, making me shimmer like sunlight on the water.

I twisted the soft fabric of my sleeve and observed the multitude of guests Mother deemed necessary to invite. The entirety of Praed must be here milling about and taking their seats in preparation for a royal wedding. Laria joined me at the window and watched silently as Mother directed everyone to their proper places, even Risteard, who regarded her with his characteristic silent stoicism. The sun reflected off the crown on his head, and I blinked rapidly to clear my vision. Laria also looked down at the king. And there was no mistaking the gleam in her eyes.

"He looks very handsome today," I said.

"He does," she said without taking her eyes off him.

"Can you refrain from looking at your husband so lustily?"

"Never." She broke away to look at me. "You'll understand soon."

I blushed and looked away.

"Ula, I know Mother must have spoken to you about tonight, and I cannot imagine how awkward it must have been."

I shuddered at the memory.

"I want you to know if you have any questions, I'm happy to answer them."

"I understand the basics." I twisted a piece of fabric between my fingers. "But...Laria, I don't know what to do. What if I disappoint him?"

"Let me tell you something Morgan told me on my wedding night. Lovemaking is in your blood. Your body will help you. And you could never disappoint Finton. He adores you. As he should." She wrapped an arm around my shoulders and pulled me close. "You have plenty of time to learn one another. That's half the fun."

She winked and I relaxed into my sister's embrace. Mother entered shortly thereafter and asked if I was ready.

"Yes." I gave Laria a meaningful look. "I'm ready."

The air was crisp with the promise of spring, the Rhyvor high with runoffs from the mountains. It wasn't as swollen as it would be in a month, but the soothing sound of the water pushing past stones eased my embarrassment at being stared at by hundreds of people. They rose when I appeared on Mother's arm, and I was grateful for her steadfast presence. She strode forward, chin high, setting a leisurely pace. Hushed conversations followed in our wake. Appreciative nods and pointing fingers distracted me and I nearly tripped, but Mother held fast. Heat spread from my cheeks to my ears, and I looked down at my dress and regretted how much skin it revealed. I glanced at the dense crowd of people. How many more would I have to pass by? How much further?

I looked down the path to gauge the distance and all thoughts ceased. There he was, the reason I was here. Finton was smiling with such warmth it rivaled the sun. I couldn't help but smile back, so wide my face hurt. My focus on him alone, the distance between us shortened, and in the blink of an eye, I was standing before him.

Mother presented me to Finton, and once my hands were in his, all the guests melted away with my shyness and reserve. My heart swelled with the love and affection in his eyes, and I barely heard my brother-in-law speak.

Risteard said, "I admit, I remember very little from my own wedding ceremony." This elicited a general ripple of laughter from the guests and an indulgent shake of the head from the Lord Protector. "Because I was so focused on the woman before me, on my love for her, that nothing else mattered. It's the same look I see on Finton Ekhane now. Affection and devotion are essential to a lasting marriage. In the end, it really doesn't matter what I say regarding the institution of marriage or boring anecdotes on why people choose to form lasting bonds. All that matters are the promises these two people make to one another, not only publicly before everyone gathered, but in private to each other. And that they keep those promises, no matter what."

I met Risteard's eye and smiled knowingly.

"Finton Ekhane of Dullorga, do you take Ula Audrey of Riverstone to be your wife? Do you promise to support her in her endeavors and learn when to say no?"

I narrowed my eyes, and Risteard's mouth quirked in a half smile.

"I do," Finton said.

"Ula Audrey of Riverstone, do you take Finton Ekhane of Dullorga as your husband? Do you promise to stand by his side as he pursues his ambitions and grant him patience when he describes his work in painfully explicit detail?"

Finton shot the king a look over the top of his glasses.

"I do." I struggled to suppress my laughter.

Risteard nodded to Finton, and he produced a delicate silver ring.

"Ula," Finton said. "I give you this ring as a symbol of my unending devotion to you. It will connect me to your heart and show the world we belong together." Finton slid the ring on the third finger of my left hand.

Laria warned me this was a part of Ilano weddings, and she said she gave Risteard a bracelet in place of a ring. I didn't have a bracelet, but I had something infinitely more dear.

"Finton," I began. "I don't have any fancy baubles to offer you as a symbol of my love. All I have is my heart. And I give it to you freely, to protect and nurture for the rest of our lives."

His eyes filled with adoration, and Risteard's next words couldn't come soon enough.

"With the exchange of vows and tokens of affection, there is nothing left but to seal your marriage with your first kiss as husband and wife."

Without further prompting, Finton took my face in his hands and kissed me while our guests celebrated.

I have flashes of memory from the remainder of the evening, but I couldn't describe the intricacies of any particular moment. I remember the children laughing and running about our feet, and the delicious food served alongside lively music. I remember commenting to Laria her husband had more humor than I supposed, and her saying I had no idea how often he made her laugh. But mostly I remember Finton, the feel of his hands as we danced, his laughter when Laria toasted to our health with her characteristic sarcasm, and the feel of his warm breath as he nuzzled my neck. Our life together stretched before us, and I couldn't wait to see what fate had planned for us.

Epilogue

A shaft of sunlight and trilling birdsong pierced my dreams and drew me into reluctant wakefulness. With a groan, I flopped onto my stomach and burrowed into the blankets. The dawning of this new day meant I must leave Praed. Finton could no longer delay his studies in Hrgun because the new term was about to begin. His studies would span at least three years. For my part, I decided to study painting and music. The time to concentrate on my own interests was long overdue. We would be very busy, a welcome distraction so I wouldn't think about how much I missed my nieces and nephews. Though I was excited to start our new lives together, the thought of saying goodbye to my family spoiled the sentiment. So, I squeezed my eyes and buried my face deeper into the pillow, because I wasn't ready. Beside me, I felt the warmth of Finton's body still in the bed, and I thought perhaps he wasn't ready either. Then I heard the turning of pages, and I cracked open one eye to see what he was reading.

I sat bolt upright and snatched the book out of his hands. "What are you doing?"

"Reading," he said, his hands folded innocently in his lap.

"Where did you get this?" I looked down at the book. A book I hadn't read in months. A certain book that landed me in trouble. *The* book.

"It was in the nightstand." He was trying not to laugh.

I scowled. "You shouldn't go through other people's things."

"I'm sorry." He bit his lip.

"I haven't been reading it."

"That's a shame."

"What? Why?"

"It's entertaining. And…" He reached over and flipped to the middle of the book. "There's something in here I thought we might try."

"Finton!" I gasped and turned red from my scalp to my toes.

He scooted closer "Read it."

Reluctantly, I looked down at the pages and started reading.

"Out loud," he said huskily, his breath warm on the skin just below my ear. He placed a light kiss there then trailed more down my neck to my shoulder.

I granted his request and read the particularly salacious passage. After all, I'm not a monster.

"I don't want to let go," I said through the emotions stifling my breath. Laria and I were holding one another in a tight embrace, neither of us willing to release the other.

"We'll see each other soon," Laria said. She pulled away and wiped the tears from my cheeks. "I'm so proud of you."

"I'm proud to be your sister."

She smiled and stepped back so I could say goodbye to the children. Alyx bore the separation bravely, but the others were openly weeping. I promised to write them stories from the magical far-off place they were convinced I was traveling to.

"Are you taking a boat?" Tyrnan asked.

I laughed. "Not this time, little man."

He looked more disappointed by this fact than by my actual leaving.

I kissed the soft skin of the twins' heads and hugged Duveesa.

"I know you'll take good care of them. I'm so grateful for you," I said.

Duveesa hugged me tighter, choking back a sob, and whispered, "I'll miss you."

"I'll write. I promise." I stepped back and she smiled through the urge to cry. I squeezed her arm reassuringly and turned to her companion.

Olim and I regarded each other for a few seconds in silence, then he pulled me firmly into his arms.

"Who am I going to keep out of trouble when you're gone?" he asked.

"There are plenty of troublemakers here," I said, indicating the children.

Olim regarded the children with horror. "Erm…you sure you don't want to stay?"

I turned to Duveesa. "Take care of him, too." I gave a nod toward Olim.

Her skin turned an adorable shade of pink.

I stood before the king and thought how strange it was that merely six years ago he terrified me. His imposing form still intimidated me, but he'd become as dear to me as a brother. He looked down at me impassively, and I smiled.

"May I hug you?" I asked.

His eyes flickered to Laria, who responded with a raised eyebrow. He patted my shoulder perfunctorily, and my smile fell.

"Oh, well, goodbye," I mumbled, lowering my eyes. I shouldn't have been hopeful. He was as immovable as the White Mountain and just as affectionate.

The unfamiliar sound of a low chuckle rumbled in my ears.

"You're a brute," Laria said.

I looked up into Risteard's face, his cerulean eyes sparkling with mischief.

"Apologies," he said before opening his arms.

Afraid he would change his mind, I didn't hesitate to throw myself against his chest and wrap my arms around his back in a firm hug.

"Thank you," I said. "For everything." I extricated myself before he became uncomfortable, and then he did the most astonishing thing.

He extended his hand for Finton to shake.

"I expect great things from you," Risteard said.

Finton smiled and shook Risteard's hand enthusiastically. "Thank you."

We climbed into the carriage and Laria linked her arm with Risteard's. I nearly stumbled when she asked if he needed to lie down after so much physical exertion.

"Only if you're offering," he said.

A whip cracked and the carriage jerked forward. I leaned out the window and waved until my family disappeared behind a bend in the road. Even as the carriage ambled and bobbed down the mountain, I couldn't bring myself to turn away until the turrets of Praed Castle dipped from view. At the base of the mountain, we headed west along the outskirts of Market Town. After a few hours, we passed the cemetery at the base of the mountain, the final resting place of kings, nobles, and prominent citizens in the middle with common folk radiating like sunbeams outwards. It was crowded today with families struggling to let go of loved ones lost in the war. Even when faced with such heartbreak, I couldn't look away. Years may pass before I step foot in Praed again, and I want to remember everything.

"Any regrets?" Finton asked.

"None," I said.

"I know it's going to be difficult to move about in a place where you don't know anyone."

"Yes, but I've had some experience with that." I turned and gave him a mysterious smile.

"Yes, you have."

We regarded each other companionably, then Finton patted the seat beside him, and with one last glance outside, I moved to sit next to him.

"Did you bring it?" he asked.

"Yes."

"Excellent. There's something on page one hundred and three I'm hoping you'd consider for tonight."

I laughed. "You're incorrigible."

"I simply understand the importance of thorough study."

"I know this to be true." I entwined my fingers with his, and he raised my hand to his lips and kissed it, then looked into my eyes with a mischievous grin.

"No," I said. "We can't."

"The carriage is already moving! They won't notice."

"No."

"It appears you're right." He sighed. "I am incorrigible."

"It's all right." I lay my head on his shoulder. "I like it."

We lapsed into a comfortable silence and watched the landscape gradually change from rocky prairie to grassland as we circled around the Center of the World on the North Road toward Hrgun. I recalled the last time I watched the world roll by in this manner. So much had changed in a year. Last time, I traveled with nerves twisting in my belly, afraid of anyone I didn't know. Now, I looked forward to new experiences with pleasure, and it wasn't fear but tenacity stirring my soul.

Finton's fingers curled around mine and I glanced up. He was watching the trees go from tall with sparse needle-thin leaves to stout and densely packed broad-leaved varieties. A reddish-tan deer with a black tail raised its head, then darted into the thick brush when we passed, and a flock of bright blue birds exploded out of a tree in a flurry of chatter and frantically flapping wings. There was wonder and excitement in his eager gaze as his eyes flickered from one new discovery to the next. He sighed, a blissfully content sigh.

"It's amazing, isn't it? To see so many new things?" I said.

He dangled a hand out the window and his fingers danced in the warm wind.

"There's so much world to experience. Are you nervous?"

I rested my head on his shoulder and said, "Not anymore."

My life's adventures had only begun, and for the first time I felt no fear as I faced the unknown.

Acknowledgments

Whenever I write a character, they inevitably reflect me in some way. In The Rise of Riverstone, Laria had my sense of humor and Risteard was introverted. But Ula is the opposite of me in many ways. From her optimism to her musical abilities to having multiple admirers, Ula represents everything I'm not. Writing her was a fun exploration into a person I could never be but sometimes wished I was.

A lot of research went into this book. I learned more about medieval medicine and the different travel times of horses, riverboats, and carriages than a normal person should. Remember folks, an expert might read your book someday. Do your homework.

Thank you to those who read *The Rise of Riverstone* and asked every day when this book was coming out. Your support and enthusiasm mean the world to me. Knowing people love my stories as much as me fills me with joy.

Thank you once again to my editor, Ron, who thinks I should write the fictional book Ula reads. Maybe someday.

It was amazing to work with Rena on another cover. She's so talented and I can't wait for book 3!

Of course, if it wasn't for the love and support of my husband, this series would never be in print. From beta reading, to edits, to being my man-spective, your help was instrumental in bringing book 2 to life less than two years after book 1. I know you're excited about book 3, so let's get to work!

Thank you to the wonderful author community on Twitter! You are all an inspiration and I've enjoyed getting to know you!

You can find me on the following social media platforms:
Facebook - @RiverstoneSaga
Twitter - @RiverstoneSaga
Instagram - @riverstonesaga
YouTube - Riverstone Saga
Goodreads Author Profile

Please consider leaving a review! It helps readers find their next exciting book!

About the Author

Mandy is a Certified Veterinary Technician specializing in small animals on the Oregon Coast. When she's not saving lives, she's weaving tales of strong women using their intelligence to pursue incandescent happy endings. Her previous title, *The Rise of Riverstone,* was the debut novel in her *Daughters of Riverstone* series. She lives on the Washington coast with her husband and their four children. Besides leaning uncomfortably over a computer screen, Mandy enjoys camping and hiking with her family, reading, and drawing maps of her world.

Mandy Schimelpfenig

THE SERIES CONTINUES:

VOYAGER OF RIVERSTONE

Daughters of Riverstone - Book 3

9/30/24